Praise for _The Daisy Ring_:

'Elizabeth Gibson has the gift of giving detail of such vitality
that people and places described come off the page as
genuine... The momentum of this book, moving between
countries and people, is kept going like a sea swell.'

Christian Herald

Praise for _Old Photographs_:

'I much enjoyed Old Photographs; that the characters in it
behave like real human beings does not detract from it as a
romantic story. The end is very moving and, like the title, the
whole story stays in the memory a long time.'

Jilly Cooper

Elizabeth Gibson is the author of four previous novels,
including the award-winning _Old Photographs_. Born in
Norfolk, she studied both in Ireland and in Philadelphia,
then spent many years teaching and writing in the United
States, where she travelled widely. Her two children were
born in New York State. She returned to England in the same
year that her first novel, _The Water Is Wide_, was published.
She now lives in Kent. _Parallel Lives_ and _Sons and Brothers_
are her other novels.

Also by Elizabeth Gibson:

The Water Is Wide
Sons and Brothers
Old Photographs
Parallel Lives

THE
DAISY RING

Elizabeth Gibson

A LION BOOK

Published by
Lion Publishing plc
Sandy Lane West, Oxford, England
ISBN 0 7459 3308 4
Albatross Books Pty Ltd
PO Box 320, Sutherland, NSW 2232, Australia
ISBN 0 7324 1260 9

First hardback edition 1995
This paperback edition 1996
10 9 8 7 6 5 4 3 2 1 0

The author gratefully acknowledges the help and encouragement of many
friends and relations: on the farming side James Alexander of Eysnford, Kent;
Paul and Carolyne Warren of Stawell, Somerset; Ted and Judy Hopkins, Sam
and Lucia Beer of Allegany County, New York; on the medical side Julian and
Vanessa Dussek of Guy's and Bryony Beaumont of Maidstone; and on the
editorial side Pat Alexander and Maurice Lyon. Any howlers left in the story
after all the useful advice are the author's, not theirs!

A catalogue record for this book is available
from the British Library

Printed and bound in Great Britain
by Cox & Wyman Ltd, Reading

For my mother Joyce
and for John
With love

Contents

The characters shown on these family trees appear in four different novels: *The Water is Wide*, *Old Photographs*, *Parallel Lives* and *The Daisy Ring*.

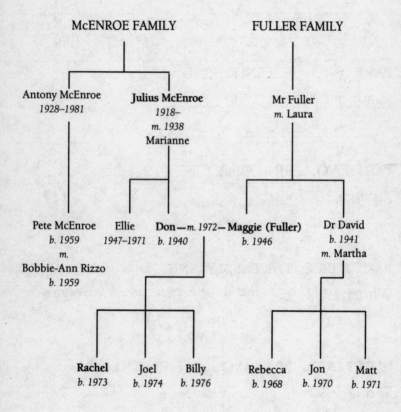

McENROE FAMILY

Antony McEnroe
1928–1981

Julius McEnroe
1918–
m. 1938
Marianne

FULLER FAMILY

Mr Fuller
m. Laura

Pete McEnroe
b. 1959
m.
Bobbie-Ann Rizzo
b. 1959

Ellie
1947–1971

Don — *m.* 1972 — **Maggie (Fuller)**
b. 1940   *b. 1946*

Dr David
b. 1941
m. Martha

Rachel
b. 1973

Joel
b. 1974

Billy
b. 1976

Rebecca
b. 1968

Jon
b. 1970

Matt
b. 1971

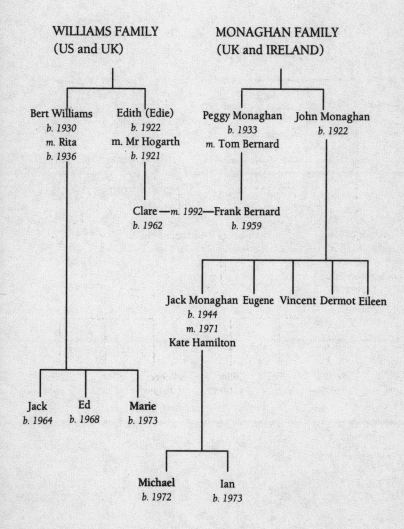

WILLIAMS FAMILY
(US and UK)

MONAGHAN FAMILY
(UK and IRELAND)

Bert Williams
b. 1930
m. Rita
b. 1936

Edith (Edie)
b. 1922
m. Mr Hogarth
b. 1921

Peggy Monaghan
b. 1933
m. Tom Bernard

John Monaghan
b. 1922

Clare —m. 1992— Frank Bernard
b. 1962   b. 1959

Jack Monaghan Eugene Vincent Dermot Eileen
b. 1944
m. 1971
Kate Hamilton

Jack   Ed   Marie
b. 1964   b. 1968   b. 1973

Michael   Ian
b. 1972   b. 1973

Part One

Eternity Ring

SUMMER 1992

1

Rachel McEnroe's quick eyes darted from her mother's to her father's face. She read the resignation on Don's face, because she had seen it so often before when anything went wrong on the farm. And she read the disappointment on Maggie's face, because she felt it herself.

'It's no use, Maggie,' Don had said. 'It's all very well for you to forget the poultry and the house for a few days, but I can't leave the cows. Not now, anyhow. Or the hay, for that matter.'

Don sounded abrupt, not his usual self; Rachel knew how frustrated he was, but she knew she could say nothing—not yet, at least. She watched her mother stiffen in response, draw back with that familiar little quirk at the corner of her mouth which always betrayed hurt.

Don reached out his arms. 'Sorry, honey. Truly I am.'

'I wonder if you really *wanted* to go.'

'Maggie, sweetheart! You sound so bitter.'

'And you sound patronizing.'

Don sighed and ran his hand through his hair. 'I'm sorry, I didn't mean to.'

'She's *your* mother, after all.' Maggie went on as if he'd said nothing. 'She'll miss you so much on her birthday.' Her face took on an unfamiliar and, to Rachel, haunted expression. 'And it's not as if Ellie will be there, is it?'

Don straightened and threw out his hands in exasperation. 'Hey! That's a bit below the belt. Don't you think I'm not aware . . .? But what am I supposed to do, for goodness sake? Larry's in hospital, and even with Tony and the boys around, I'll be hard put to manage.'

Maggie shrugged. Slowly, she said, 'OK. You're right. There's nothing else for it. Rachel and I will go alone.'

Rachel could stay silent no longer. 'If you're sure you can't go, Dad, couldn't Joel or Billy come in your place? There'll be an extra air ticket—' Her voice faltered, seeing his grim face. '—now you're not going.'

He shook his head. 'Can't spare either of your brothers. Especially not now.' He waved vaguely at the window. 'Just walk out past the barn—never mind the cattle for a moment—and you'll see the problem. We can't afford to let the first hay-cut rot while I go gallivanting off to a birthday... even if it is your grandmother's. And without Larry to work the baler, the rest of us'll be fortunate to get the hay in before the weather turns.' His lips pursed. 'There's just no way. Oh, if this were a big deal—like her seventieth was—I'd see if I could work out some contingency plans, even if only for twenty-four hours. But I can't this time. Not for GraMar turning seventy-three. Let's keep things in perspective, can we?'

In a change of mood that was typical of her, Maggie suddenly smiled at both of them. 'All right. Rachel, we might as well give in graciously.' She turned and put her arms round Don's neck. 'But, Don, I'll not forgive you in a hurry if you end up getting the hay in early because someone else comes along to help after all, and you *still* miss the trip.'

Don gave her an ironic grin. 'Unlikely, I fear.'

Rachel understood how they both felt, but it was her mother's disappointment that most affected her. For weeks now, since she had come home from college for the summer vacation, they had all been talking of their holiday in Boston. It was rare for her father to leave the farm at all, but they had planned for it, allowed for it, this time. They had all looked forward to it—even her brothers, who would have had charge of the farm under the supervision of the two farmhands, Larry and Tony.

But that morning everything had changed.

Doing a repair to the silo on the corner of the yard, Larry Harper had fallen twenty feet off the silo's outside ladder. Rachel herself had found him in the yard, both his legs broken, his mind clouded with concussion and confused about what day it was and why he was lying there.

In the emergency wing of the hospital, where she had gone with Larry and her father, she had tried to take in the fascinating details of what went on around her. But for the whole hour while they awaited the surgeon's verdict, she couldn't switch on the objective, clinical vision that she hoped she'd one day have, as a doctor, herself. Instead, all she could think of was that her father would now certainly want to remain in Western New York. It was typical of the unpredictable life that the farm dealt them.

Farmers, Don always said with a quick gesture of helplessness, *gee, they never get a vacation.*

Farmers, Rachel thought now, *everyone thinks they live life to a neat pattern of the seasons: the drilling, fertilizing, harvesting, and storing; the feeding, culling, milking, and breeding—but it's never that straightforward.*

She left her parents in the kitchen and went upstairs alone. Perhaps, she comforted herself, it didn't matter whether her father went with them, after all. There would be the rest of the summer to be with him at home—helping (or getting underfoot, he might have said)—and even his absence wouldn't lessen the joy she'd feel in seeing her grandparents again. She smiled, picturing them.

In her room she wound open the screen window. How was it possible, she wondered, that a man as shambling and untidy as her father, as *rural* as her father, could be the son of urbane Julius and still beautiful Marianne McEnroe? Already her father was more lined than Julius: his face and neck grained and sanded by years in fields and barns. And while GraMar was fine-boned, with chiselled features and a body slender as a bird's, her father looked coarse and roughened. His hair needed to be cut as badly as the fields of alfalfa hay outside, and his shoulders bulged hugely beneath everything he wore.

What a strange mixture my family is! Rachel thought. *My mother so small and self-contained, my father so big and raw, my grandparents*

14

as glamorous as an advert for a senior citizens' condominium or an ocean cruise.

In the end she was happy to travel just with her mother. It was rare, now that she was away studying, for her to have so much of Maggie's undivided attention.

In the seat beside her, Maggie was chattering like an excited girl, pulling forward in her seat against the lap belt, leaning towards the window to watch the harbour, the trees and houses come into focus. All the heartaches at the farm were set to one side.

Rachel laughed. 'Boston's home for you still, I guess.'

'Yes. No. Oh—I don't know.'

'You always act like this when we come over here for a vacation.'

Her mother smiled. 'Do I? Well, maybe I do, though it's a short vacation, this.'

'But needed.' Rachel ran her eyes more critically, now, over Maggie's face. 'You look pretty tired, Mom.'

'Probably do.'

'Do you think—after the lunch party, I mean—could we get out somewhere? Just the two of us?'

Her mother smiled—a shy sort of smile, Rachel thought—then patted Rachel's hand. 'Nice idea, but since your father couldn't come, I'll stick pretty close to home. Your grandparents'll want to talk. So much to catch up with. I can't think when we last—'

'It was when Grandpa McEnroe came out to go hunting with Dad.'

'No, that was before Christmas. We came here at Christmas, remember?'

Rachel did remember. Years of Christmases, all important to her, paraded and merged in her mind's eye. 'But Dad couldn't come *then*, either.'

Her mother nodded. 'Ironic, really. GraMar's not crazy about making the trek to Western New York, can't stand to leave the city; and Dad never liked Boston the way I did—can't stand to leave the country. Total opposites.'

'Can't stand to leave his cows, you mean.'

Maggie grinned ruefully. 'Right, but I knew that when I married him. It doesn't make a scrap of difference. McEnroes always made me feel I belonged with them, anyway. All of them. I think I feel more at home in "McEnroevia East"—'she pulled a wry face, using Don's ironic name for the house '—than your father does.'

McEnroe himself was waiting for them. Rachel guessed he had taken time from his office in the State House to meet them, and that he would pay for it later, sitting up late poring over briefs and policy documents, scratching notes in the margin, as she had seen him do in the past.

She fell into his big arms, Maggie hovering behind. They were all laughing.

'Well, how's my favourite granddaughter?' he was saying, nuzzling her ear and then letting her go.

She smelled about him the mixture of aromas she always associated with him: fresh air, a tang of aftershave, cigars, and his own particular warmth. So different from her father, but just as dear to her. She noticed, also, though, that in the few months since Christmas the skin of his face had become more seamed than ever—laughter lines growing at the corners of his eyes, but sadder folds appearing under his eyes and around his mouth, as if he had been pressed with worry.

'Seems a long time since I got to kiss such a cute little gal.'

'Oh, I reckon GraMar's cute enough.'

'So she is, Rachel. Oh, Maggie, it's so good to see this girl. And you, sweetheart.' Now McEnroe folded her mother into his arms, squeezing her against his chest.

'Don called you, I hope?'

'Yes, honey.' He released her, and his face became serious. 'Not having an easy time of it, I guess.'

They collected the luggage from the carousel and made their way to where the car was parked, below the terminal. 'It's just like that sometimes,' Maggie said.

'Same as in politics.'

'Same as in politics. You've said so a thousand times, and it's true.'

'But don't let's gab all day, Maggie. Rachel, GraMar's doing some last-minute shopping. I said we'd swing through town on the way home and pick her up.'

Rachel found herself in the front of her grandfather's car, the June light bursting in on them as they emerged from the underground parking lot. 'I'll just rest my eyes a little on the way,' her mother had said, and promptly slept, her head nodding with the motion of the car.

Leaving the airport sweltering behind them, they stopped and started their way past the ranks of traffic lights into the city. On Copley Square the fountains' spray flew drifting in the afternoon breeze, shoppers strolling over the flagstones. This was the opulence Rachel associated with Boston—so different from the small, drab confines of Arcade, where she had grown up. Here the early afternoon shadows fell short on the bleached concrete, and every building and bench seemed honed to a sharp definition in the white-hot light.

'There she is!'

Marianne was waiting for them outside the main doors of Lord and Taylor. Rachel smiled at her, waving. GraMar was radiant in a broad-brimmed white hat, her platinum hair escaping in curls around her face. She looked cool, classically beautiful, and scarcely more than sixty.

'I'll get in the back with Mom.' As McEnroe drew the car into the kerb, Rachel scrambled out and held the door for Marianne.

GraMar smelled of a fresh, lemon perfume, and the soft stuff of her silk blouse slid away under Rachel's hands. The brim of her hat came close to her forehead as she kissed her.

'Happy birthday. Happy birthday, GraMar! Here, let me get those for you.' Rachel took the parcels out of Marianne's hands and pushed them into the back seat next to her mother. Maggie slept on, scarcely stirring.

'You look pretty as a picture, Rachel. Oh, and there's poor Margaret—'

McEnroe leaned out. 'She's OK, honey. Get in. I'll have a traffic cop on my tail.'

As he drove, Rachel watched the way her grandfather's head turned to look from the passers by to the rising tower of a colonial church, then back again to the down-at-heel men gathered on the street corners, cigarettes dangling from slack mouths, hands empty of work. She saw his mouth flatten into a line, and she knew without hearing him say it what he was thinking: *I must get those men off the streets and back in jobs.*

They left the centre of Boston behind, and she noticed other things, too, that she would never have seen on the street corners of Arcade. Unkempt teenagers in oversized boots, their hair matted and their clothes streaked with dust and filth, clustered outside bars and on the stoops of battered brownstone apartment houses. While the traffic stopped and started through the city, she saw more than she wanted to see. A boy of no more than twelve passing a syringe to his friend. Another stretched prostrate on the sidewalk, his feet splayed dangerously near the kerb, utterly oblivious to all passers.

The weight of her grandfather's responsibility as a state senator fell heavily on her, suddenly, and she wondered how he could stand it. What made him fight to stay in office, year in, year out, when other, younger, men waited in the political wings to take on his load?

But McEnroe's face was solemn, and she hadn't the courage to ask anything, afraid of where the question would lead. Wanted only to enjoy the moment with the family, to think of nothing but the immediate joy of arriving in what had once been her parents' home town to celebrate GraMar's birthday.

He swept them away through the suburbs to Bedford, on the very edge of the city, and to the tree-lined peace of the place Rachel thought of as her second home; loved as much as she knew her mother loved it. Even now, in the heat of June, it was green and lovely, still lush with the brightness of early summer. Her worries for McEnroe retreated, and she began to relax.

Once in the hush of the big house, Rachel left her mother to talk with McEnroe and sat quietly with her grandmother on the patio. Below the sun-warmed flagstones lay neat gardens and a swimming pool, just recently uncovered for the season, with its filter gurgling softly as they talked. 'How do you feel, GraMar?' Rachel asked her.

'Fine and dandy. Happy as I could be that you're here. Sorry your daddy couldn't make it, but not surprised.'

'He told you why.'

'Sure. Harper was a fool for climbing up like that without proper safety precautions . . . no fool like an old fool!' Marianne frowned. 'And no doubt your father's going to have to answer to the insurance company for letting him do it.' She shuddered. 'But it's not my problem, and it shouldn't be yours. Forget it.'

'I'll try.' Rachel wondered if she would, but didn't say so. 'It's great to be here again.' She stretched out on the lounge chair and felt the heat cut through the thin cotton of her tee-shirt and shorts. 'I'm glad you have a *summer* birthday.'

'Me too.'

'What's Grandpa giving you?'

Marianne flicked an invisible piece of dust or leaf off her dress. 'Ah—that. Well, he's already given me something.'

Rachel sat up. 'What? Tell me.'

In answer Marianne held out her left hand. As well as the familiar bands of gold and diamonds her grandmother had always worn, there was a new ring.

'That's pretty,' Rachel breathed. 'Silver, is it?'

'No. Platinum. It's an eternity ring.' She eased it off her finger. 'He was going to give it to me on our golden anniversary, but somehow, he says, he never got around to it. He said this week was as good a time as any.' She laid the ring gently on Rachel's outstretched hand. 'If you look carefully, you'll see it's engraved.'

Rachel held the circlet in her palm and peered at the minute daisies on the outside of the ring and at the words on the inside. *For ever my love*, with the next day's date. She felt her face colouring. 'Oh, that's romantic, GraMar.'

Marianne was glowing with pleasure. 'Grandpa McEnroe may look tough, but you know what he's really like.'

Rachel nodded.

'One day, sweetheart, that ring'll be yours . . . if you want it.'

Rachel out let her breath in a little gasp. Then her eyes filled with tears. The day's perfection was marred now. 'Oh, don't say that.'

Marianne held out her hand for the ring, still smiling. 'In good time, dear. But for now I intend to enjoy myself.'

Rachel laughed unsteadily. 'OK. Let's do that. Especially tomorrow on your day. And, GraMar, you do look gorgeous.'

Now she reached across and squeezed Rachel's shoulders. 'Bless you. And so do you. You're like spring to my winter.'

'Winter? Baloney! Autumn, at the latest.'

'Let's not waste time on a dumb argument like that. Tell me about your father, and Joel, and Billy. Tell me about Ohio Medical School. Tell me *all* your news.'

'On condition that you tell me what's happening tomorrow, first.'

'Oh, that's easy. Just McEnroes for lunch, and Williams. No big deal this time. It's been a hectic year.'

'Williams?'

'You don't remember Mrs Williams—Rita?'

Rachel scanned through her memories of parties, weddings, and other family gatherings over the lifetime of her visits to Boston. 'Not right away, I can't place her.'

'She has a marina down in Lynn Harbor. She and her husband—though Bert's been dead three years—knew our family from way back. And then there's the church, of course. We see Rita and Marie there, usually, as well.'

'No relation, then?'

'No. Just friends—for years. Bert Williams came over from England as a young guy. Bought the marina from a friend of your great-grandfather's—the one who had a marina himself, if you recall hearing Grandpa talk of it.'

Something stirred at the back of Rachel's memory. 'Oh, dimly. Just remember ... and they have sons. About my age, right?'

'And a daughter. The boys are long grown and gone. Rita's by herself now, except for Marie.'

'I don't recall anyone named Marie.'

'You might when you see her tomorrow. Vivacious girl.'

'So it's McEnroes and Williams. Anyone else?'

Marianne's lips curved slightly at the corners. 'We did invite your other grandmother—just to keep the peace, of course. But she said she'd hope to see your mother another time. Couldn't make it.'

Rachel laughed. 'You two!'

'Never been a lot of love lost between us, I admit.' Marianne sniffed. 'But McEnroe thought it a good idea to ask her, at least.'

'The political thing to do.'

'Naturally. But never mind tomorrow. That'll take care of itself. I want to hear *your* news.'

Rachel leaned back again and began a recitation of all that had happened since Christmas. Her success in her studies, but her niggling conviction that she should not necessarily remain in Ohio for the full term of medical school; her application to a London hospital for medical studies, a chance to break away from home— even from the country as a whole—to find out for sure where she wanted to be, who she was, perhaps; to find a sense of perspective she never felt she'd had, growing up in smalltown middle America. This she knew her grandmother—lover of city life—would understand.

'But why *England*?'

'Because it's there.' Rachel began to laugh. 'Like the man said about climbing Mount Everest. It's somewhere I always wanted to go, that's all. Sort of a pipe dream. I'm competing with a bunch of other medical students, but I thought—'

'Ah, you're just like your mother. A trier. A dreamer who doesn't stop at dreaming, but goes after it.' Her grandmother smiled again, twisting the daisy ring back onto her finger. And soon began to doze in the sun.

Rachel lay with her eyes shut. She thought of what her grandmother had just said to her, took the words out and held them up to the light of her mind, turning them over as she had turned the daisy ring in her palm under the glinting light. Then she pushed the thoughts away, not wanting to think any more about herself. She tried instead to picture Rita and Marie Williams—and could not.

When she saw Marie the next day, however, the girl's oval face, clear skin, and brown eyes were faintly familiar. *I must have seen her at mass,* she thought, still piqued that she couldn't remember.

Marie flashed her a vivid smile as the two Williams women came across the lobby at the front of the house, ushered in by the McEnroes' elderly housekeeper. It came to Rachel that the lunch party was really for older people; that Marie had been invited merely to keep her company. But for whatever reason, she was glad to see her.

All the same, when they were left by themselves for half an hour before the lunch was served, she felt suddenly shy. It was one thing to smile across a church or lobby at a perfect stranger; quite another to look each other closely in the face, to size each other up as allies for the day. Marie spoke first. 'I'm Marie Williams. And you? Don't I—haven't I—?'

'Rachel McEnroe. I think we might have seen each other once or twice.'

'Daughter, or granddaughter?' Marie's eyes were twinkling. 'Mrs McEnroe looks so young, I was thinking...'

Rachel laughed. 'GraMar might like to hear that, but not my mother. Granddaughter. The one and only. Such a pain, sometimes. I've got two brothers.'

'They here?'

'No, thank goodness.' She swallowed, still wishing Don had come. 'Nor's my father. Just Mom and I.'

'And just Ma and I.'

'Poor McEnroe. Totally outnumbered. Though I guess he won't object too loudly!'

'McEnroe?'

'My grandfather. Sorry. I forget. Most everyone calls him "McEnroe". Just that—don't you, too? Sometimes GraMar calls him "Julius", but not often. Listen, I think we're meant to entertain each other while the elders chat a little. D'you want to see round the place?'

Marie's eyebrows rose in surprise.

'Oh—' Rachel stammered awkwardly. 'You must've been here a thousand times. Sorry, but I—'

22

Marie pushed her hands into some invisible pockets at the side of her print dress. 'No, no. Sure I've been here a few times, but not quite like this. Not as often as Ma. I've never seen upstairs. And this is such a dream house, I'd love to.'

Rachel led the way. 'We don't get here as often as I'd like. Dad's got a farm in Western New York.'

'Miles from the city, right?'

'Right! Around four hundred, in fact.'

'That's cold country up there.'

'Sure is. But Dad chose it. I know my grandparents would've liked him to take a farm in Massachusetts somewhere; but Mom says he was dead set on Western New York. So there we are—miles and miles away. Coming here's a real treat for Mom.'

They turned into one room after another. Rachel tried to see the house through Marie's eyes, struggling to remember her own first impressions; but it was far too long ago; her parents had brought her to 'McEnroevia' at least once a year since she was a baby; she felt now as she had always felt—much like her mother—that she belonged in the house in some ways more even than her father did. Especially as he needed no excuse not to come at all.

Marie was gratifyingly impressed, and Rachel felt more and more proprietorial as they went around. 'This is the room Mom and Dad always have when we're here ... This is where my brothers Joel and Billy sleep, if they come.' Her voice was sing-song, full of pride. She looked at the lush furnishings and thick curtains with almost greedy possessiveness. Everything was ordered, tidy, and peaceful. Her grandparents' home echoed part of her personality. It was the house where her mother had first dreamed of loving her father, dreamed of a daughter like herself. It was precious to her, and she knew she was loved in it.

Marie sighed as they went back downstairs again. 'You're right. It's all beautiful. If you came to our home, you'd think it was very small, and full of junk. Jack and Ed've been gone since just after Dad died.' Her voice did not waver, Rachel noticed, as she spoke of her father. 'My brothers—they both left for jobs in Springfield. But the house is never tidy, even with only two of us.'

Rachel stopped so suddenly that Marie bumped into her. 'Oh—sorry.' She laughed, seeing Marie's embarrassment and feeling silly herself. 'You mustn't think *we* live like this. No siree!'

Marie came and stood beside her, turning her head in surprise. 'You don't? I thought anyone with the name of McEnroe was a millionaire.' She waved her arm. 'Like this, for example.'

Rachel snorted, thinking of the kitchen at home, of her father's cluttered office at the back of the house, and of the untidy corner of the barn where he tried to keep up the farm records. 'Oh, if only you could see my house. Chaos and more chaos. The boys can never find their clothes. There're dairy Co-operative printouts everywhere—even in the bathroom. Mom says one day she'll paper the bedroom with them; they occupy so much of Dad's time. Dad just laughs and reminds Mom of how organized she used to be—when she was a schoolteacher here in Boston. But not any more. The house looks mostly like a parish rummage sale. Worse, some days. That's one reason I went away to college—I'd had enough.'

They stepped down into the lobby, moving more slowly now, reflecting. Marie said, 'But don't you miss it, now you've been away?'

'There isn't much time to miss it, the way life goes for me.'

'I know what you mean. Only I'm at community college. I stayed home, instead.' Marie's bright eyes clouded for a moment. 'I thought Ma might be glad of the company.'

'Yes.' Rachel suddenly didn't know what to say. She felt slightly selfish after what Marie had said. It was a novel and strange feeling, a piece of grit in her mind, grating and worrying at her.

Perhaps Marie noticed some of her discomfort, because she abruptly changed tack. 'Anyway, Ma won't be seeing a lot of me this vacation—except when I'm at the marina. I've decided to work two jobs this year.'

'You'll be exhausted.'

'I want to do it.' Marie shrugged. 'And I need the cash. There's a wedding ... my cousin in England's getting married in August. I want to be there.'

Rachel thought about mentioning her own faint hopes of going to England, but decided against it. 'You're flying over for the wedding?'

'Ma and I are going. Clare was supposed to be married a couple years ago, but her fiance was very sick—in and out of hospital with pneumonia. The wedding got postponed once, then again. I haven't seen Clare in a while.' Her face lit up. 'I can't wait. Frank's OK now—no reason to think they'll call it off again. I felt sorry for Clare these last couple years, but things look good for them now.'

McEnroe came and found them, then. 'Making friends, you gals? That's what I like to see. But come on, now. Mrs Watowski's putting our luncheon in the dining room, and your grandmother's ready for her little party. Let's get in there, shall we?'

They followed him into the book-lined dining room, Marianne's favourite room, where she kept her collection of fiction in teasing defiance of McEnroe's penchant for legal books. Here south-facing windows opened onto banks of June roses, and midday brilliance flooded everything. Lunch passed with the tinkle of crystal glasses, the rustle of white linens, and the nods and smiles of comfortable conversation. Covertly, Rachel watched Marie, chatting and at ease with her family. *I like her,* she decided. She also watched Marie's mother Rita, observing the bruised shadows around her eyes, the lines of tiredness that made her look so much older than her own mother. And she looked at McEnroe.

He was, she thought, even more in his element than GraMar; he positively expanded under the attention of five women. She seemed to see the lines of his face iron themselves out as they ate and drank together, toasted Marianne, and talked about their hopes for the future. Strange, she said to herself, how although it was Marianne's day, McEnroe's presence commanded as always the most attention. Without putting on any show, he starred. (It was from him, Maggie had told her once, that Aunt Ellie had got her flair for drama, her presence as a model, and her charisma.) Watching him now, she could see exactly what her mother had meant... though she would never meet Ellie... And she realized that however much she cared for GraMar, it was McEnroe she loved the most.

When the meal was over, a birthday cake cut and eaten, and everyone was leaning back replete, Marianne beckoned Rachel and Marie to join her. 'I want to take a stroll around outside,' she said. 'You coming? All the roses are in full bloom.'

Marie jumped up immediately. She smiled at Rachel, her eyes widening in enquiry.

Rachel caught a look between her grandparents as if something had been pre-arranged. A conversation between McEnroe, Rita Williams, and Maggie—but about what? For once she did not feel inclined to go along with other people's plans. She was too curious about the expression on McEnroe's face, and wanted to stay at the table with him. She felt uncomfortable about Marie's eagerness, but determined. 'Er—well, I'd like to sit here, I think.'

Marie flashed her that big smile again. 'That's OK . . . Mrs McEnroe, I'd be happy to walk around the garden with you for a while.' And they went through to the family room, out of the french doors, and vanished down the steps that led from the patio to the lower lawns and gardens.

McEnroe looked round the table at the three women, his eyes finally resting on Rachel. He touched her forearm where it lay on the white cloth. 'Well, that's handy. There was something I wanted to speak to your mother and Mrs Williams about. Are you sure you won't go with—?'

'It's fine, McEnroe.' Maggie had leant forward to gain his attention. 'If it's what I think you want to talk about, Rachel can handle it. She's not a little kid any more.'

Rachel frowned. *What do they want to talk about?* The conversation seemed somehow to have shifted gears. Bewildered, she looked from one to the other for an explanation, telling herself, *But this is GraMar's birthday! Why the sudden seriousness?* Then she recalled her grandfather's face in the car the day before, remembering too the weight of responsibility which she'd briefly guessed at. He couldn't compartmentalize his life into politics here, social responsibility there, church in one place, family in another. To him, she suddenly understood, it was all of a piece.

26

Some instinct told her that he was going to discuss something important. And that it was something he might not have another opportunity to discuss with them, if Marianne were in the room.

So she waited.

He took out a hand-painted wooden box that Rachel recognized from time out of mind, opened it, and produced a cigar. He unwrapped it, rolling it between his fingers and muttering appreciatively about the aroma. 'Rita, Maggie—ladies—you won't object?'

'Not at all.' Rita Williams and Maggie shook their heads, and Rachel copied them, unthinking, her eyes filling because she loved him so much, and because she felt a chill of apprehension.

Deliberately, McEnroe snapped the lighter open, puffing and drawing until the cigar was lit, then fixed his eyes on Rachel's mother first. 'Maggie. Rita has an interest in what I'm going to say. It's not just for family ears any more. The Williams' marina—I'm sure Rita here will explain—lost a lot of money these past years because of the drug traffic around here.'

'Fine. Go on.' Rachel noticed her mother's knuckles whiten on the edge of the table.

'And, Rita—Maggie and her husband have known for years, at first hand, what some of the sick subcultures in this city can do to people. So what I'm going to say is for you both. And I can't think of many times when I can get the two of you in one room to talk about what we're going to do.'

Rachel sat frozen. *Drug traffic... sick subcultures... what we're going to do.* What was McEnroe talking about? An iceberg of dread was crushing the tranquility she had felt the day before.

'Rachel—' He was looking right at her, now, his blue eyes troubled. 'You won't know any of this, I suspect. Except maybe bits about your Aunt Eleanor. So just listen, would you, honey?'

She nodded, swallowing, wishing now that she had gone outside after all. The atmosphere in the dining room was taut.

'First, then, Maggie—I guess you know I never in all these years stopped looking for Garcia—Garshowitz... whatever the heck he calls himself these days.'

Her mother's face was white, her chin trembling with an emotion Rachel had never seen before. 'I thought you would do that, yes. But—'

'But you didn't ask. Wisely, I think, Maggie. It was better that you didn't know too much. The DEA would take care of it, I thought at first. They'd nail him. I couldn't afford to get too involved—that's what my advisors said. "You're a prosecutor, a politician—not a damn detective." That's what the guys all said to me, you know.'

'I'm sure they did.'

'But they weren't Ellie's father. They didn't know how I felt when she died. They don't know how I walked the floor upstairs some nights and tried to work out how to bring that man to justice after he'd taken our girl. Oh, it's been in my confession every time I go for the sacrament of reconciliation—that battle I've had with myself about going after Garcia, or letting be, letting the *professionals* catch him. Then perhaps confronting him in court.'

Rita shuffled in her seat. 'The "professionals"?' she echoed. 'And what a fine job they made of it, McEnroe, three years ago!' She turned to Rachel. 'Drugs were going around in some wild parties at the yacht club next to our marina a few years ago. Loud, vulgar parties. No one in his right mind would have wanted in there. But celebrities and political people were dropping in and out. I witnessed some things I wish I hadn't. It was a *mess*. I was angry at the DEA—the "professionals".'

McEnroe held up his hand. 'No Rita, it's no use thinking in that bitter way, my dear. Don't forget they got some of your charming neighbours locked up. You mustn't forget that. It was a job well done. There's no telling where the marina would be by now, if after all that scandal on the waterfront the DEA hadn't done such a good job.' He shook his head. 'No, let's give credit where it's due. But of course I wanted to go one further. I wanted to nail the man I've always thought was the kingpin—myself. And, Maggie, I've never stopped looking.'

Suddenly McEnroe turned his eyes on Rachel again. 'There was a man once, here in Boston, who should have answered for your Aunt Ellie's death. *Your father's sister*, Rachel. And your mother's best friend.

Oh, he wasn't the murderer. Not directly. Much too smart for that. But he killed her, all the same. A drug pusher of the most ruthless kind. A stop-at-nothing guy who used Ellie, and when he'd had enough, abandoned her in Miami. Say what you will about Ellie—that she was wild and irresponsible, and that she ran with the wrong crowd... except your mother, I mean... but Garcia should have stood trial for her death. You know the rest, I think.'

Rachel sat stiffly. She knew only that her aunt had died under mysterious circumstances twenty years before. No one had told her much more, and something had stopped her from asking. Feeling out of her depth, she murmured and gestured, still waiting.

'Garcia went underground for a while after Eleanor died. The press were on his tail, as well, but he was too clever to surface up in the North again—for a while. He had contacts everywhere on the East Coast. We knew that much at least. The DEA caught some of his henchmen, but they never managed to corner *him*.' McEnroe nodded gruffly at Rita. 'Hence the raves they had in the compound next to Rita's place a few years ago. Sure, I still don't know for certain if Garcia was behind them; but, in the end, they were just his style. Always went after the "beautiful people"—the rich upper and middle classes. The yacht club crowd would have brought rich pickings. He was bound to be behind the network somehow, I thought.' He rubbed his scalp wearily as he spoke. 'OK, so I'm a prosecuting lawyer. I have no business pre-judging someone before he goes to trial. But I know what he did to Ellie, and there's plenty of evidence of what he did to others. It doesn't take much to convince *me* he should be locked up.' He grinned sheepishly. 'All we gotta do is get the evidence, and get the guy. Sounds simple? Well, it ain't.'

Rita blinked. 'Excuse me, McEnroe. I guess I'm a few steps behind, here. You're saying seriously that there's some weird connection between what happened to your daughter twenty years back, and what happened in Lynn Harbor three years ago? Honest to God, you've never said... I hardly think—'

'The DEA didn't think so, either, or if they did, they couldn't follow it up. But I thought so, I still think so. I still believe Garcia's behind it all, and I want to do something about it, before my time's up. But the story doesn't end there.' He blew cigar smoke in a blue ring towards the ceiling. 'Garcia's obviously a man with an eye for the main chance. And he's no fool. He was into crack when that was the in thing, and now it's speed. He's worked out that, after cannabis, amphetamines are the most popular drug right now. He's a businessman, right? So he looks at the market, jumps ahead of it, and tells the market what it wants. Then produces and sells what it's persuaded it wants.'

He spoke more softly for a moment as Marianne and Marie passed below the windows, their voices melodious and sweet in comparison with the harshness of his.

'We've got definite evidence that he's not operating out of South America any more. In fact we're fairly sure he's holed up in Amsterdam or London, where it's easier to make the stuff, and not that hard to ship it back in.'

Rachel rested her elbows on the table, glanced at her mother, then back at McEnroe, replaying what he had just said. 'Did you say *London*?'

'I've got reason to think so. Listen, if there's any way to do something a little faster, you can trust an American to think of it— and fast! The Europeans are getting the same. Everyone wants everything instantly, and they want it yesterday, not today. Speed feeds right into that stupid mentality. And Garcia hasn't been slow, either, to pick up on it. OK, so it's crack that's in the headlines all the time. But there's still a hideous death rate from speed; it's easy to produce, and even more available than crack. Not just available... respectable, almost.' He gritted his teeth. 'But not as far as I'm concerned. And I've decided—against everything your grandmother wishes, Rachel, or my advisors wish... that I'm not waiting any more on the DEA and the so-called professionals. I can be a professional in my own way, I figure. I'm sick of seeing the kids in this city and other cities in this state sell their souls to men like Garcia. Like I said, I want to stop him once and for all, and I'm working on it.'

Rachel watched McEnroe's face as he spoke. His cheeks, neck, and ears were suffused with blood, and a small vein throbbed by the corner of his eye. His breathing was laboured, and his voice had begun to shake with passion. She saw him in a new way—as a vulnerable old man—and felt afraid for him.

'Listen, I'm 74. I promised myself I'd find that guy before I turned 75. Time's running. I've got to get going on it, whether the DEA shares my agenda or not. So there you have it.'

He leaned back in his chair and shut his eyes. His posture reminded Rachel of one of her chemistry lecturers at the university: once he had delivered his thesis for the day, he seemed almost comatose afterwards: exhausted, hardly able to communicate further. She left her seat and went to put her arms around his shoulders. His wide hands knotted around her own, and she rested her cheek on the thick silver of his hair, the cigar smoke wreathing around them both.

'Do you understand,' she heard him say, after a moment's quiet, 'that I can't wait on the professionals? Not now. I'm too old to wait. Maggie—Rita—do you understand that I want this guy, and I'm going to get him?'

The other two women had remained motionless for most of the time he had spoken.

'I understand, of course I do,' Rita murmured.

'Me too. But, McEnroe . . .' Maggie's face was anguished. 'Oh, I hope you'll be careful.'

He laughed then, a great guffaw that knocked Rachel away as his head went back with it. 'Oh, you can bet your bottom dollar I'll do that, all right.' He reached backwards and pulled her around to the side of the chair so that she could face him. 'And you, honey? You're very quiet, Rachel. Come on—you're gonna be a physician some day. D'you understand what I want to try to do?'

Her mind and heart were full. She wanted to tell him how she had watched him in the car the day before, seen his concern. She wanted to say that she, too, empathized with the people she had seen the day before—and on other days. She wanted to tell him how much she loved him. But anything she might say, she decided, would sound melodramatic and immature. Rather than that, she would remain silent.

In answer, she hugged him again, fiercely, wordlessly.

'Right, then. I'll keep you all informed. No heroics, and nothing that will endanger anyone—except Garcia.' He extricated himself from her arms and stood up suddenly, shaking off his mood like a dog shaking off water. 'But let's forget all this now, and see what Marianne's doing. Rachel, why don't you go find Marie? You're going to be here another day or two. You could go sailing with her—tomorrow. How about it?'

2

Rachel could not sleep, that night, after the Williams had left and she had lain for endless minutes in the slow-ticking dark. All the joy of the June daylight that surrounded their arrival two days before had been eclipsed. She lay stiff, as if somehow any movement she made would endanger her grandfather; as if her breathing would (impossibly) wake a man who needed sleep before he did what he had to do. She knew it was all fanciful nonsense, superstitious, even; but her meandering mind still followed that dark path in the small hours of the morning.

Why is nothing simple any more?

She tried to breathe quietly, steadily, to fend off the fear. She could not remember ever being afraid for herself. But it was even worse to be afraid for someone else; for someone she loved.

Why is nothing simple any more?

Had life ever been simple? *Yes,* an inner voice screamed silently at her. And she remembered the farm as she had known it fifteen years before, as she had first really known it, in the way anyone can know anything.

There were roses by the back porch. She could see herself playing by them, watchful of the thorns after one blood-streaked encounter with them. She smelled their perfume. She was cross-legged on the bottom step of the verandah, her feet in the dust of the yard, and her mother's cats—kittens—miaouling and hissing somewhere behind her, feinting and hunting under the shadow of the wooden verandah floor.

There were calves in the barn, generations of them. Lowing, butting her with their curiously hard heads, licking her with their velvet mouths.

There were hay mountains, sweetsmelling and hopping with crickets in the late summer. Larry and Tony laughing and tossing her onto the hay waggon along with the bales. Larry and Tony who, though old, never seemed to get any older.

There were rides in the yellow schoolbus with children she had known since they had been christened together at the little church in the town, and teachers she used to see in the stores on a Saturday afternoon.

Yes, things were simple then.

She sighed and turned over, throwing the sheet onto the floor and hearing the cedars on her grandparents' back lawn seethe in the nightwind.

And they could be simple now, if I saw them simply, she told herself. And then wasn't sure if that were true.

It came to her, suddenly, that she could no longer live others' lives for them, trying to take their worries and pain onto herself the way she had unconsciously been doing all this week with her father, Larry, McEnroe...

'Life will throw you enough curved balls, as it is,' her father had sometimes said to her. 'No need to catch anyone else's.'

'But I'm going to be a *doctor*,' she had always argued.

'A good physician is like a good farmer,' he would answer. 'There has to be a measure of detachment.'

'But that's a lack of compassion.'

'You'll find it's not, and that you can't do anything effectively—' (simply, he might have said) '—if you mire yourself emotionally in everything that touches your life.'

This then is what I have to learn, she said to herself, *from today, from this week.*

And I will sail tomorrow, and feel the water under the boat, and that will be simple.

She turned over again, and slept.

After breakfast, she found McEnroe hefting his clubs out of his study. He looked reassuringly solid, present, and cheerful. 'We'll go to mass tonight,' he said. 'This morning I'm off to my golf. It's not often I get a Sunday like this, and one of my partners on the other side of town wants a game.'

She hesitated outside his door and watched him go through the rituals she had seen before, checking the clubs, looking out of the front door at the sky (cloudless, today), rushing back inside for a change of clothes.

'I'll leave you off at the marina. I'd already decided to go on over to the club at Lynn today, anyhow.'

'A bit off the beaten track for you, isn't it?'

'Yes, but, my gosh, willya look at this perfect day. Couldn't ask for a better to be up by the coast. Come on. Stuart and I are teeing off at ten. Go get your things together, and I'll give you a ride.'

They came to where Maggie was sitting in the family room with Marianne. All the doors and windows of the house were open. Marianne kissed Rachel warmly. 'Your mother and I are taking our ease today. You enjoy yourselves, too.'

'See you later, honey,' Maggie said. 'You've got the most heavenly day to sail.'

Rachel glanced outside. 'Will there be enough of a breeze?'

'On the water, yes,' McEnroe assured her. 'Just you wait.'

Soon they were driving Route 95 towards the North Shore. The concrete clicked steadily under the smooth wheels of the Oldsmobile, and the car's air-conditioning hummed against the wall of heat that rose already from the highway and from the shimmering cars around them. Others, Rachel saw, seemed to share their idea of a Sunday outside.

'You sure you won't come sailing with us?'

McEnroe gave her an amused look. 'Not this time. Marie grew up with a tiller in her hands. Her mother takes the tourists out onto the water all summer long, as well as providing berthing for sailboats year round. So in the summer when Marie's off college she works the boats with her mother. She's a good little sailor. You're in good hands, I reckon. Thanks for asking, but I need the slow peace of the golfcourse today.'

She nodded, watching him signal for the Peabody and Lynn exit.

'How long d'you want to be gone?'

He moved his shoulders. 'Oh—up to you. I'll be finished by two or three. We're playing eighteen; that's enough for an old guy. I'll want lunch, then. I can come by for you whenever you want.'

'If you're not in a hurry, how about four-thirty or five?'

'Fine. I've got some business I can do at the club while I'm there.' He gave her a quizzical look. 'You're such a landlubber. Think you can stand the nautical pace?'

'And not disgrace myself going green and hanging over the side of the boat?' she laughed.

'Right.'

'I think I'll be OK.'

He snorted. 'We'll see. All it takes is for a little swell coming broadside under the boat. I've seen it a thousand times. Green as grass, they go.'

'And you wouldn't.'

'Not me.'

'I'll stay upright and pink in the face if it kills me.'

The gates of the marina stood open. They nosed down the abrupt slope towards the marina office. Boxes of petunias and marigolds spilled and shined from the office windows, and the paint on all the boats moored by the jetty below shone brilliantly. Rachel glanced around happily; it was a picturebook marina—no matter what everyone had said the day before about the difficulties Rita Williams had faced.

For a moment, however, a shadow fell over her as she recalled again what they had said about the drugs, scandals, and the threat to the marina. Now, in the radiant light of a perfect June morning, it all seemed unlikely, impossible, that any harm could come to a place so tranquil, so set apart from the hurly-burly of Route 95, from the frenetic commercialism or, at the other end of the scale, dismal poverty, of Boston's city centre.

Little of the yacht club was visible from where she stood, though she could hear a few good-natured shouts as the morning's sailors and fishermen passed each other in a kind of relay.

Marie suddenly hailed her from the open front door of the office. 'Hey, Rachel! You gonna stand there all day dreaming, or are you going sailing with me?'

As she turned, a breath of salty air off the water twisted her hair into her eyes. She pushed it away, smiling. 'I'm coming.'

In the office, Rita was lifting life jackets out of a storage closet. 'Hi, Rachel. Nice to see you. What a day, huh? Marie, you can take the sloop you had out last week. It's not booked today.'

Marie grinned and winked at Rachel. 'What, that old thing? "Harrier"— the one with the paint peeling off?'

Rita rose to the bait. 'Paint peeling off? It most certainly isn't! She's a lovely little boat.' She turned to Rachel. 'Only three years old ... Here, you'll need this lifejacket. Yes, that's right ... tie those loops there. We don't want you drowning first time out.'

McEnroe stood with his hands in his pockets and his face creased with amusement. 'I want a full report, Marie, of how this girl does today.'

Marie grinned back and gave him a mock salute. 'Yes, Mr Senator, sir.'

Holding her jacket in one hand and a large picnic cooler in the other, she led the way down to the jetty. Rachel followed, and Rita came behind them both, her sandals clopping on the wood.

Balancing uncertainly on the edge of the jetty, Rachel smiled at Rita, who now came to stand quietly beside her. 'Don't you wish—?'

'I sure do. But there's a lot to do here, Rachel, even on a Sunday. You'll have yourselves a grand time.'

'I've sailed this sloop quite a few times,' Marie confided. Her face was alive with pleasure. 'I can't wait to show you what she can do.' She bent to check the gas gauge on the outboard. 'Just a minute, and we'll get you on board. I just want to check ... yes, they're OK.'

'What?'

'The inflatable dinghy and the oars.'

'You mean we'll have to *row*?'

'I doubt it,' Rita said drily.

With one hand in Rita's and the other stretched out to Marie,

Rachel climbed gingerly aboard. She laughed in delight as the boat shifted and settled under their weight.

'You sit right there,' Marie said, pointing. 'You can relax for the first bit.' She started the engine; it sputtered to life, and they waved at Rita.

'Have a great day, girls!'

'We will. Rachel's going to be as good a crew as I am by the time we get back.' Over the steady puttering of the motor and the ripple of the water, she shouted forward to Rachel, 'It's not nearly as hard as it looks.'

Thinking of what McEnroe had said, Rachel smiled again. 'I'll bet you were born on a boat. I can see you, cute as anything, lying in a Moses basket while your mother ferried the tourists round the harbour.' She paused as Marie smiled back at her. 'But I won't learn in a day what you've learned in a lifetime.'

'I know it. But you'll do all right. See, we're almost ready to hoist the sails.'

Rachel groaned. 'As long as you tell me what to do—I hope I can work out what you're talking about.'

Behind them Rita's waving figure diminished. Now Rachel had an open view from where she sat, both to the marina and to the yacht club. In the cockpit, Marie cut the outboard, and the boat drifted, rocking gently. The quiet resounded after the noise of the engine— only the swish of the water around them, the distant buzz of a powerboat racing up the coast, and the occasional broken shriek of a seagull. The world was blue, limpid, and full of light. Rachel felt again as if they would be sailing into a painting.

'You're very lucky,' she said. 'This is all so beautiful. Your mother's life must be pretty peaceful with just boats and water and a few tourists to watch out for every summer.' Then, hearing the words re-echo as she said them, she thought of her father at the farm. *Everyone thinks farmers live life to a neat pattern of the seasons ... but it's never that straightforward.* She looked hard at Marie, feeling again the flash of intuition and understanding she had felt for others, before. *No,* she thought, *I bet it's not simple here, either.*

Marie's face was more shuttered than usual. 'Oh, it's beautiful, all right. But it hasn't been peaceful the last few years. We had a couple bad storms and lost some of the boats then—some of our own, and some belonging to Ma's regulars who leave their sailboats here year round. Last winter a big storm took one of the boat houses clean away—they didn't even find the wreckage. Ma was covered by insurance, of course, but I guess something else was going on as well.' Marie stopped, frowning.

Rachel pulled a strand of hair out of her mouth. How much did Marie know of what McEnroe had told the women yesterday? *My comment about the beauty of the marina was insensitive,* she decided. Yet again, too, came the shiver of fear for her grandfather. 'I didn't mean to drag any of that out of you,' she said softly. 'In fact I was thinking last night that nothing's ever—'

Marie waved her hands impatiently. 'Come on,' she interrupted. 'Let's forget all that and enjoy the day. We could sail a bit, then anchor in one of the coves just there and see if we can catch something. Would you like that?'

Rachel nodded gratefully. 'I'd love to.'

'Then here's what we do,' Marie began. 'You come astern—take your time—and hold the tiller for me.'

Unsteadily, but determined, Rachel climbed back to sit beside her. 'Like this?'

'Right. Now all you have to do is aim for that buoy over there. Easier than driving an auto, any time! When the mainsail's up, I'll tell you how to turn the boat into the wind so we don't fly over, OK? Just don't do anything suddenly—steady and easy, that's all, like the water.' She was confident, enjoying herself.

'You sure about this, Marie?'

'Sure I'm sure. This is easy as rolling off a log. All you have to do is sit there in the sunshine and steer.'

Marie unfurled the mainsail and secured the halyards.

'Great. Now—' she ran up the jib, climbed back to the cockpit, and recovered the tiller from Rachel.

At last they were scudding over the wavelets, a light breeze filling the sails. Rachel felt exhilarated. Her cheeks burned from salt and sun.

Keeping the shoreline clearly in sight, they sailed south-south-westerly with the breeze. The water foamed round the prow, occasionally sending spray into their hair and making them laugh.

Rachel looked at her watch, then at the cloudless sky. *Still perfect, and it's still quite early.* She caught Marie's eye.

'I could do this forever.'

'Me too! Pity the wind can't change and take us back the other way later on—it'll be a bit more work to bring her round. Then you'll see what real sailing's all about . . . but why don't we stop over there for a while?'

'And see what we could catch? This'll be good!' Looking along the scalloped rim of the shoreline, Rachel felt happiness enclose her, enclose them both, in a bubble.

They tacked back towards the shore until they found a secluded cove where Marie said she had fished before. Not a single person was walking over the pebble-strewn beach, and the rocky cliffs rose high over the water, dotted with scrub and reflecting back the fierce heat of the morning sun.

Marie talked Rachel through the furling of the sails and the dropping of the anchor. It was a plough anchor, quite heavy, and Rachel felt sweat bead her face. All the same, she was laughing by the time she'd released the winch and heaved it over the prow and into the water.

'I told you!' Marie crowed. 'You'll soon be as good at this as I am.'

Rachel beamed. 'I know that's not true, but I sure can taste the addiction!' The boat rocked and drifted on the gentle swells. In the Williams' bait tub, the night crawlers wiggled and writhed. Marie grinned conspiratorially at Rachel and lifted one of them, dangling it and grimacing before she attached it to her line. 'Now your turn,' she said, passing Rachel the tub.

Rachel said, 'Oh, you were good with that. If I'm going to be any kind of a physician, I can't afford to be squeamish. And you're one of the first women I've met who isn't.' She dipped her hand into the tub, laughing, and felt the ooze of the worms around her fingers. Then they dropped both lines over the side of the boat.

Marie laughed back, crinkling up her face. 'It's my brother's influence. He always loved fishing—Ed, that is. I never thought a thing about it.' She snapped the lid back on the bait tub and pushed it into the locker.

Rachel reflected for a moment. Joel and Billy had never fished, as far as she knew, and her father's hobby—whenever he had the time, in the fall—was deerhunting. 'I guess I didn't, either. My Uncle David lives on Nantucket. He's a doctor, himself. Used to take me fishing sometimes when we were on vacation there. But always from the shoreline, not off a boat.'

They lay back on the sun-soaked boards of the boat. A couple of seagulls had picked up the tang of the bait and wheeled lazily overhead; Rachel watched alternately the lines and the gulls inscribing rings against the eggshell blue above them. 'This is the life. But I hope we don't catch a whale.'

'Moby Dick, maybe.'

'No thanks.'

One of the lines stirred, grew taut, then hung loose again.

'They're just testing,' Marie laughed. 'The fish out here are cunning critters. They know better than to mess with my lines, I'll bet. We'll be lucky if we get three minnows before the end of the day!'

A shadow fell over the water near the boat. 'There's your whale,' Rachel teased. 'And you'd be lucky catching minnows here. They're freshwater fish, silly.'

Marie grinned at her. 'Trust you to know your zoology better than I do!' She narrowed her eyes to the sky. 'Uh-oh, here comes our first cloud. Great! Oh, well! We won't let a little thing like a cloud worry us.' She looked at her watch. 'How about something to eat?'

When Marie opened the cooler, Rachel saw that Rita had packed them enough food for four people. 'All we need is caviar, a corkscrew and a bottle of wine,' she commented appreciatively. 'Your mom's a genius.'

Marie nodded and bit into a tomato, the juice spurting over her tee-shirt. She wiped it away, and one of the seagulls dipped right overhead, air rushing through its wingfeathers as it beat past. 'Here,' she called, 'have some bread, compliments of Rita's Restaurant.'

Seemimgly out of nowhere, three more seagulls screamed and dived for the bread she tossed into the air. Her mouth full of sandwich, Rachel laughed with delight and broke her own bread, scattering it over the water and into the air. 'Poor starving babies, come and get your lunch,' she called.

They emptied the cooler and drained the flasks. More and more gulls circled the boat, but then drifted off landwards when the bread was gone.

Under the water, the fishing lines did not so much as stir. Rachel sat forward eagerly and twitched at one of them. She felt a giddy, childish excitement come over her. 'Our fishing's no good. So why don't we sail? That's what I came out here to do.'

'Right—let's.'

Together they reeled in the lines—both empty. 'It doesn't matter,' Rachel said, seeing Marie's disappointment. 'Just an optional extra while we were eating.'

'Right. Now we're going after Moby Dick, like I said.' Marie winched up the anchor. 'Grab the tiller again, will you? This is the bit I love, when the sails pick up that breeze and we go scudding out.' The boat yawed as she then went to the mast to unfurl the mainsail. Over her shoulder, she called back to Rachel, 'When I was little, I used to pretend I was sailing off to find the New World. There... that's right. You're getting the hang of it. I have a feeling you're one of those people who do well at whatever you turn your hand to.'

Rachel dipped her head and felt her cheeks flame. 'Stop flattering, or I might let go by mistake. It's not true, anyway, what you just said.'

Marie came back to her. 'No—you're doing well.'

'And you're not a bad teacher.'

Marie's face turned serious again, and Rachel wondered what she was thinking. One minute Marie could be lit up with laughter, and the next moment she would be pensive, reflective. *Ah, but perhaps I'm like that myself, sometimes,* she thought. She breathed deeply and looked away from Marie to the horizon again. The sailboat was picking up speed. 'That's a nice breeze coming up. It feels good to me.'

Marie was frowning. 'Hmm. It's still out of the north-east, but stronger. I'll take the tiller again.'

'Of course.' Rachel heard a hint of anxiety in Marie's voice.

Catching her eye, Marie said, 'The water may turn a little choppy, that's all.'

A gust of warm air worried at the sailcloth. Part of it flapped against the mast.

Rachel still felt exhilarated by the bursting air and the beloved smell of salt. She pointed out to sea at a mass of ridged clouds low on the blue skyline, but boiling up out of nowhere. 'You're right. The weather is changing.'

Marie's eyes sparkled. 'You worried?'

Rachel shook her head. 'Not in the least. Curious, maybe. I've never been out sailing in anything, and certainly not a storm.'

'Oh—nor have I. But don't worry, this won't be a real storm, or I'd turn around double-quick, let me tell you. We might end up in Florida otherwise! Or worse. It looks like a little squall, that's all. The weather report was fine. Nothing in the least to fret about.'

Rachel felt again the high, giddy excitement. 'Could be fun. Something to tell my brothers about when I get home.'

'Right. It'll be a bit bumpy, anyhow. Here—take this again, would you? Just hold her steady.' Marie handed the tiller back to Rachel and climbed across to reef in the sails a little.

Rachel felt the difference in the pull of the water against her hands. The boat was moving more and more swiftly now. Grey clouds massed and churned on the horizon, and the waves came faster and with breaking crests. 'Should we turn around... after all?' Gratefully, she surrendered the tiller to Marie again.

'I don't really want to.' Marie hesitated. 'All the same, I guess we'd better head back. This is one of Ma's better boats, and we shouldn't be out on a sea like this by ourselves—just in case it does get worse.'

The sky was changing steadily, the bright blue softening, even where there was no cloud, to a grey haze. The wind continued to freshen, turning now into a stiff breeze that made it a struggle for Marie to hold the boat against it.

Rachel watched her mark and remark their place on the smudged shoreline, which suddenly seemed frighteningly far away, and saw that they had drifted farther south than she'd realized; farther south than Marie must have wanted. 'Will we have to tack back into that?' she asked.

If Marie had made an error of judgment, she wasn't admitting it. 'Yup. But nothing to worry about. We can always turn on the outboard and skip straight in there again. Depends how much fun you want to have first. Just do as I say when I tell you to. You'd better stay close to me. I'll have to haul in the jib. And don't forget to watch the boom doesn't take a swipe at you and chuck you in, that's—'

A great swell heaved the boat up and dropped it down again. Rachel's stomach lurched. She clung to the side of the boat. Her head felt light, no longer attached to her body. The water surged around the sloop, noisy now. She made a lame attempt at a laugh. 'Here comes the fun I asked for.'

'That's right. But you're doing great, Rachel. There'll be more of that.'

Another wave took them up again, and from the top of the swell Rachel saw on the landward side the concave of Revere Beach, from this distance grey and uninviting. On the seaward side Bass Point looked unpleasantly near, and beyond it the mouth of the bay into the great Atlantic. She lost courage for a moment, but regained it again when she saw Marie watching her.

'Like I said,' Marie shouted over the wind, 'there'll be more of that.' She gritted her teeth. 'Sorry, but you'll have to take the tiller again.'

For the first time, Rachel felt the clutch of fear. 'Are you sure—?'

'You *have* to. Come on. I've got to get the jib hauled in.' Marie sounded annoyed.

Her hands turning white and her insides rising into her throat, Rachel took the tiller again. She felt dazed by the speed of the weather's change, then relieved again as Marie came back, almost pushing her away.

'Listen, this is nothing I can't handle. Here we go. I'm going to ease her round a bit.' She moved the tiller slightly, watching the boom. 'Here she comes!'

Rachel followed her gaze, but a few waves later, she could see Marie wasn't as confident. With a swift glance over her shoulder, the other woman reached to start the motor, shouting as she did so that Rachel must take the tiller yet again.

Rachel edged towards her, shouting back, wanting to encourage her. The boat was rolling hard, and for a few moments she caught the feel of how to ride the waves without letting queasiness engulf her, without letting the water take control of the boat. Some of her exhilaration returned. She held hard onto the tiller, nevertheless, relieved as she watched Marie yanking at the cord.

The motor hiccoughed, splattered water and the smell of petrol, oil and old exhaust fumes into the wind, but did not start. Marie tried again, then a third time.

Dread seeped back to Rachel. 'Is this what usually happens?'

Marie looked panic-stricken now. 'No, of course it's not.'

Rachel suddenly wanted to leave the tiller entirely to Marie. She would have tried anything rather than sit there holding it. 'Please, let me have a try.'

'But I thought—'

'I've never used an outboard, but I sure know how to start that kind of motor. It's the same as the powermower we've got for the grass at home.'

Marie's teeth were still gritted, her dark hair matted by the salt and spray and glued to her cheeks. 'OK, you do it. I'll get the dinghy.'

Rachel feigned a smile she did not feel. *Dinghy!* Rowing would be impossible in this kind of sea. 'But you said...'

Marie looked irritated again. 'Of course not! Joke, silly!' She jerked at the outboard cord hopelessly, but the motor wouldn't even oblige her with a hiccough this time.

Rachel changed places with her. She had no more success than Marie had. She hauled at it, jerked at it, pulled it with all her strength. She looked at Marie miserably, had no idea what to say. Rain began to fall: first a spindrift of drizzle that beaded their eyelashes and hair, then an increasing downpour that slanted through the wind and sliced into the angry foam of the waves so that sky and water seemed barely distinguishable. She shivered.

Marie released the tiller long enough to check that her lifejacket was securely tied and to throw on one of the slickers her mother always kept stowed in the boat. She bundled another into Rachel's lap, and Rachel abandoned the motor and pulled it on gratefully. Her clothes were plastered to her skin now.

They floundered on through mounting waves, tacking and reefing back the sails but seemingly without making any progress towards the shore. Then there was another sound over the slap and wash of the waves, the flap and rush of the wind. Simultaneously they looked seaward.

A launch was ploughing a straight furrow across the bay and back towards the harbour. 'Will they give us a tow?' Rachel shouted.

Marie was watching the well-appointed boat sceptically. 'Too much of a hurry to get out of this before it turns any worse. Look: they haven't even sent a glance our way.'

The vessel throbbed steadily through the waves, dipping and rising gracefully, a scarlet pennant flapping on the mast. Its owners seemed untroubled by the weather, but intent on getting to land before the sea grew any rougher. A white wake boiled behind it but was soon swallowed by the breaking waves as water streaked backwards in the wind.

Rachel felt powerless, and at the same time angry with herself for giving in to that feeling, and to fear. 'Could we radio them?' she begged.

Marie gave her a twisted smile. 'This is only a tourist boat. No radio on here.' She brought the boat around for another tack, shouting directions to Rachel all the while. The wind dropped for a few moments, and in the reprieve she called, 'She'll call the coastguard. Mom, I mean. Don't worry.'

Rachel tried to smile. 'Who's worrying?'

Marie lurched as another wave took the boat broadside. 'We both are, let's face it.'

Rachel laughed unsteadily. The spray stung her face, and waves were beginning to break now over the side of the boat. 'There's one consolation, at least—' She was afraid she would sound trite, but decided to blunder on anyway. 'I've heard it said that you can't do much with a sailboat in a flat calm, but you can certainly sail it in a wind. Here's our big chance to see what we're made of.'

Marie's eyes sparkled again. 'OK—good way to see it. That's how we'll play it.'

The tide was running fast against the boat, and the launch had already diminished to a faint blob among the whitecaps. Rachel kept looking landwards, and she knew suddenly that they were farther from the harbour now than they had been five minutes before. The exhilaration was gone, replaced by gut-wrenching fright. The horizon was drunk.

Marie could see her fear, she knew. 'Time to send up a flare, when the boat's going backwards and water's starting to come in,' she shouted. 'I need you to go forward and pull the flares out of the locker. Listen Rachel, I'm not leaving the tiller now. You'll have to get them ... and keep them dry!'

Rachel inched forward. A great gust hit them. It swung the boom viciously.

'Look out!' The tiller was wrenched from Marie's hands. She gave an involuntary shout that sent Rachel sprawling to the bottom of the boat just before the boom slammed across.

Winded for a moment, Rachel lay still, wondering if there was any point in holding the boat against the surging water. In a fog, knowing her own ignorance, she thought, *Wouldn't it just be better to let go and see where we drift to?* But then the enormity of that thought gripped her, and she scooted to her knees in time to see Marie grab for the tiller again.

'Are you OK?' Marie's face was as white as her own must be. Rachel wasn't sure if she could be heard above the waves, but she answered, all the same. 'Thanks to you.' Then she scrambled unsteadily forwards.

Marie's voice was faint behind her. 'Go for it!'

She reached the bow and jerked at the locker door, her heart pounding in her ears.

'I can't get it open!' She felt her face redden with exertion. She tried again and signalled hopelessly.

Marie beckoned her back to the cockpit, waiting until she was near enough to hear over the roar of the breaking sea. 'How can you be so stupid?' she accused. 'Here, take this after all. And don't let it go.'

Rachel took the tiller, bracing her whole weight behind her hands to hold it. Ridiculously in this violent sea, she found she was more upset by Marie's anger than by the rage of the water.

She watched Marie stumble forward and open the locker on the first attempt, light the flare and hold it. Rachel's eyes were rivetted to her as the flare streaked skywards, then the glare of the red star and the puff of orange smoke. *See it, please see it!* she prayed.

The last of the smoke died away in the wind. 'Coming aft!' Marie shouted.

A sudden wave tipped the boat violently to one side. Marie was darting towards the back of the boat. 'I'm going to reef the mainsail completely,' she called.

Then with a sickening moment of anticipation, and knowing she could do nothing about it, Rachel cried out, felt the tiller wrenched out of her hands, and saw the boom lash across like a scorpion's tail.

Marie ducked, but too late. The boom caught her hard on the side of the face and flattened her.

Rachel stared in horror, her teeth chattering. For an instant she told herself to get the tiller back; then decided to let it go. She flung herself onto the floor of the boat beside Marie. Uncertain if it would make any difference in the heavy seas which way Marie lay, she checked her breathing and looked for blood, then struggled to arrange her into the recovery position.

She lay still beside her, thinking. She remembered the flares. Marie had let only one go. There must be more.

With another look at Marie to reassure herself that it was safe to leave her, she dragged herself forward again. The locker door was open, and she knew the flares might very well be wet now. Her hand found them in the twilight of the locker. Cautiously, she sat up, sheltering the flare with her body, against the wind. She let first one, then the other, streak into the sky. The sea roared, but she heard only mocking silence: no answering offer of help. Bleak hopelessness settled on her.

After that she crawled back and lay next to Marie, wedged her against one of the seats and put an arm around her shoulders. She began to pray, her lips moving stiffly. The spray lashed at them, and the boat yawed, one way, then the other, and the wind roared. She lost track of time.

Something began to throb in her temples, and she tried to grasp at what had happened. Everything seemed to have slid away from her, except that she knew she wasn't in the water; that Marie wasn't in the water, either. It came back to her slowly that she should be at the tiller, and that the boat must be drifting now completely out of control.

Marie coughed. She raised her head an inch, then let it drop. 'What—?'

'The boom,' Rachel said. 'You'll be all right. Listen, I don't want you to choke. I'm going to tilt your head again. Please—don't fight me. Lie still.' She held her breath a moment, straining to hear. 'I think—maybe—I hear the coastguard coming. They must have seen the flares.'

Marie shut her eyes. 'Thank God!'

Rachel eased her back into position, adjusting her arms and legs for her, as if she were a rag doll. 'There. You'll be safer that way.' While Marie lay obediently still—or unconscious again—Rachel was shivering one moment, feeling oddly warm the next. The sea lifted and dropped them, rocked and rolled them, and she, too, went out on the ebb and flow of the water.

A droning sound filled her head, and she felt again the frenzied rocking of the sea, but something was different now.

'She's coming round,' a voice was saying. 'Come on, woman.'

She did not want to open her eyes, and groaned.

'Good!' That shuddering laugh, breaking almost into tears of relief, was Marie's.

She opened her eyes slowly, and light seemed to stab her pupils. It was not the soft grey light of rain, sea, and saturated cloud, but the wall light of a cabin she did not recognize.

'Easy, sweetheart.'

A young man in uniform was standing over her, Marie clutching his arm. She sported a bandage round her head, one side of her face purpled and swollen with bruises. She was swathed in blankets, and shaking—but more or less upright.

'Can you talk to us?' the man said to Rachel.

Confused, she blinked at them and moved a hand to shield her eyes. *Wasn't it Marie who was only half-conscious, not me?* 'Sure,' she said, but her voice sounded strangled, hardly recognizable.

The others smiled, and Marie took her hand. 'They came and got us, Rachel,' she said. 'Like you told me they would. The coastguard got us.'

'You were doing just fine without us,' the man laughed. 'But we managed to persuade you that we'd get you into harbour faster with a little help from your friends. Happy to oblige two such gorgeous chicks.'

Rachel searched for a memory of what had happened. Her mind had gone blank. She remembered Marie lying on the bottom of the boat, but she remembered no rescue by the coastguard.

Marie screwed up her face, flirting with the man. 'Black eyes and all.'

Rachel smiled at them, and she knew the smile was crooked. She felt drugged with exhaustion, her head cloudy.

'Never mind the black eye, sweetheart,' the coastguard was saying to Marie. 'You're safe now. We'll be into the marina any minute.'

'I had to send up another couple flares,' Rachel mumbled. It was coming back to her now.

The man fixed her with a sober stare. 'It must have been the last one we saw. For cripesake, we only saw one.' He glanced at Marie. 'And we got your boat in tow, as well, so you won't be in too much trouble from your mother. The mast snapped. No big deal compared to life and limb.' He pulled a droll face and drew her closer, supporting her. 'You're lucky, you know that, Miss Williams? Your friend here probably saved your life.'

Rachel looked foggily at them both, dismissing his words with a wave of one hand and a feeble smile. 'That's what friends are for.' She held Marie's eyes for a second, remembering the other woman's flash of temper, forgiving her. Then not able to form any clear thoughts beyond that. 'Shouldn't you— shouldn't she—?' Her eyes veered back to the coastguard's face.

Marie seemed to understand what she was trying to say. 'It's OK. I'm going to crash out again in a minute. I feel better now you're awake, but... sorry, Rachel, I was such a lousy instructor. Floored by a boom and rescued by the coastguard. What a day!' She rested a hand on Rachel's shoulder. 'I owe you one,' she said. 'I'll have to think what I can do for you one of these days.'

The coastguard was brusque, suddenly. 'Come on, ladies. You've no business going on like this. Shut your eyes, at least—both of you— for a few minutes.'

When Rachel next came to awareness, she was being helped off the bunk, and she knew by the gentler rocking of the ship and subdued sound of the coastguards' engine that they were in the harbour again.

Wrapped in a slicker, Rita was waiting for them at the top of the jetty. The wind still raged around them, but it was a surprisingly warm wind, and full of rain. Quietly, she gathered Rachel and Marie into her arms.

'The "Harrier"—' Marie cried wretchedly.

'Never mind the boat, you foolish girl.'

The coastguard stood awkwardly beside them. 'We'll be in tomorrow to speak with you again,' he said. 'Your girls are fine, Mrs Williams, apart from shock and a few knocks on the head. Keep 'em warm, and keep an eye on them. The guys'll unhitch your sailboat and bring it around wherever you tell them. It's—well, there'll be some report forms to fill out.'

Rachel saw a tremor of new anxiety cross Rita's face.

'No! Nothing to concern yourself about. Listen, *the girls are OK!* All routine stuff tomorrow. The weather office didn't predict this little squall. We've been bailing out a host of other sailors today. I'll have to go—'

Rita thanked him effusively, and Rachel stared dumbly after his retreating back. She felt numb, not quite able to make sense of what had happened. *It's mild shock, that's all,* the reasonable part of her said. She glanced at Marie, now clinging to Rita's other arm. She too looked shellshocked.

The marina office was deserted. Rita had turned on an electric fire, in spite of the warmth outside. She made them tea, fussing over them; but no word was said about the wrecked sailboat.

McEnroe arrived from the golfcourse in a shower of dripping waterproofs and with a face as grey as the sky outside. 'I came right off the course. I never dreamed...'

'McEnroe, I'm sorry. It's been disastrous.'

'Rita, don't talk crap. They're here. They're safe.' He smiled at Marie and took Rachel in his arms. 'The least said the better.'

'I'm feeling OK, Grandpa McEnroe,' she said into his wet coat.

'Like I said, then, the least said, the better.' McEnroe gently pushed her back into the chair that Rita had drawn up in front of the heater. He accepted a mug of tea from Rita and sat on her desk. Then he twinkled at Rachel. 'Well, I sure had a nice game until that little doozy blew up. I was headed for par—for a change.' He winked at her, then looked back at Marie's mother. 'So what about you, Rita? Been busy?'

How typical, Rachel thought, watching him, *that he should want to set everyone at ease.*

Rita stared as if he were mad. 'No, yes, well until—'

'I mean before you called the coastguard, or whatever.'

Rita shook herself. 'After what—I can't quite—' Her face suddenly cleared. 'Oh, yes! There was some great news today. One of the best Sunday mornings I can remember in a long time.'

Marie also brightened. 'What, Ma?'

'I sold berthing space to some new people. The Galloways—just arrived in town from somewhere in the south. Lovely white launch they've got. Big, with a gorgeous red flag hoisted. They've been out in her already for a little time—I guess she's been in dry dock for a while, just till they got situated. Gee, I was so pleased. They said they have other friends on the North Shore, as well, who might want to do the same. I could hardly contain myself when they signed, I can tell you.'

McEnroe was nodding. 'An encouraging day, then, Rita, after all.'

Rachel sipped her tea and let the talk wash over her. Her mind drifted as the boat had drifted, and she turned her aching head to look out of the window at the churning sky. A patch of blue heaven appeared, widening as she watched it. Watery sunlight penetrated the rain.

'Thank you,' she murmured.

3

All the way from Kent to the west of London: scarcely two hours in the car, but Michael Monaghan was uneasy about it. Not the journey—that wasn't the difficulty; it lifted his spirits at any time of the year to see the quilted spread of English countryside on either side of a motorway or country lane. And especially in August, when the fields were drying to burnished gold, the windy blue sky tilting towards early autumn, and larks trilling and tumbling over the chalk faces of the Downs.

And it wasn't that he minded, in spite of what the others might have thought, about spending a day in London or attending the wedding of Frank Bernard—a relative he hardly knew.

What disturbed him was having to spend so long in the company of his brother Ian and his girlfriend, Stacey; it would be even worse than he had expected, because his own girlfriend had dropped him the week before.

'Dumped you, did she?' Stacey had said in that nasal voice he disliked so much. 'I'm not surprised!'

He smarted, but bit his tongue because he had seen it coming, himself. Mortifyingly, Ian had seen it coming, as well. And now he would have to put up with two hours of their peculiar brand of hurtful teasing, all the way to the wedding, without any relief. No one else to soften things by making a mockery of Stacey, as he would have liked but somehow lacked the talent to do himself, though he could see her faults as clearly as his own. So there would be harsh words from Ian, who never bridled, but spat them all out; who now had an ally in Stacey to redouble the discomfort.

Well, you like directness, you always say. Thus Ian would shrug and dismiss the latest round of point-scoring.

And Michael would hate himself for not growing a skin thick enough to ignore whatever his brother dished out, for not being able to dismiss Stacey.

He took a slow bite of his toast, then stared across the breakfast table at his brother. Blithely crackling his way through the Saturday morning paper, Ian was unaware of Michael's dismay.

For a few moments, pouring a mug of coffee and staring into middle distance, Michael retreated within himself and tried to analyze the old rivalry between them.

There never seemed any tension between them, he reflected, when his father was around. Jack Monaghan had a way of defusing confrontations which went, Michael knew, far beyond the bounds of his sometimes shattering battles in the social services. It was a gift his father had, something natural to him, that he could listen and accept, that he could sharpen someone's wit, someone's faith, even, by a few quiet, simple words. He was *judicious*; that was the word. He turned things over before he answered. He saw into the heart of problems and refused to get stuck on the surface—as Michael recognized he himself did, all too often. Jack was a *good* father; but he was also the kind of good man that people liked to know. His wasn't the kind of starched, thin-lipped goodness that he knew himself guilty of, sometimes, that drove others away, or that gave people an impression of lofty idealism, even snobbishness.

Why am I like this with Ian, then, when Dad's not around? He had asked the question many times without finding an answer.

Ian's lazy voice cut across his meanderings. 'What's got you this morning, Mike?' Ian knew he hated to be called Mike. 'You look as if you've lost your queen and found a pawn instead.'

Michael leaned back in his chair. 'Oh, very good, Ian.' Something inside him shrivelled again, felt crushed both by Ian's sarcasm and by his own abrupt retort.

'Can you get through this day without her?'

He thought only for a few seconds of the girl who had written him a curt goodbye note, announcing that she was leaving the university for good and marrying a man she had known since childhood. He remembered her laughing eyes and sweet mouth, and his own feeling that he was the luckiest man in the biology faculty to have found her, that he was at last escaping from the shadows of his mother, his brother. *Wrong again.*

'I'll have to, won't I?' Consciously, Michael tried to answer the way his father would have done, then frowned, thinking fiercely that he must do things in his own way, not in relation to others any more.

Ian looked at his watch and flashed an irreverent smile. 'I ought to fetch Stacey if we're going to get there in time for the Bernards' bash.'

'I'll be ready in a few moments.' *Perhaps,* he thought, *there can be a little peace between us today.*

'I could just pop out and get her now—while you're finishing.' Ian abandoned the newspapers on the floor and moved to the door. His tone was too casual.

Michael hated having to put on the older brother act again. He hated it as much as he hated being a victim of his brother's scorn, in other circumstances. Cautiously, he said, 'I don't think that's a great idea—until you pass your test, I mean.'

Ian had failed his driving test three times so far, and during the long university holidays Michael had often been called on to accompany him and Stacey to one place or another in his mother's car. It would happen today, going to the wedding; their parents had left the night before, to spend time with the Monaghan relatives, most of whom had flown from Ireland for the wedding. So the brothers were stuck now with an interdependency they both disliked.

'Can't resist another cheap shot at my hard time with those impossible testers, I guess,' Ian jibed, saying it as if he were speaking of the testers' failure, not his own.

Michael looked at him as levelly as he could. 'That's not it, not at all. Just don't want you banned for several years for driving without a licence—or another person with you in the car. It would be inconvenient for us both, and I bet Stacey wouldn't like it much, either.'

Obviously bristling, Ian turned in the doorway and looked Michael right in the eye, a bitter twist to his mouth. 'Then get yourself in gear, will you? I'll drive to Stacey's, and you'll have to come with me.'

'Thanks.' He swallowed some bitterness of his own, then added in the most measured voice he could muster, 'Like I said, I'll be ready in a few moments.'

He sipped the coffee, cold now, then let his eyes slide to the open window. Clumps of his mother's favourite dahlias and tobacco plants lifted their heads in the breeze outside: vivid colours, resplendent petals, but all carefully staked by his mother so that they wouldn't snap when the autumn winds came.

My mother. Kate Monaghan was quite different from his father. Even Michael, knowing them from the beginning of his life with the kind of supposed familiarity that so often breeds ignorance far more than contempt—even Michael had known this clearly for as long as he could remember. Oh, his mother, too, was *good*, but not with his father's kind of unassuming straightforwardness. Instead, his mother was ambitious for herself and for her sons. She had guarded them carefully, arguing for them when the teachers at school had asked too much, in her view—but then demanding far more at home. Michael was to be a brilliant scientist, Ian a professional musician—no less.

At the age of twenty he knew already that he had disappointed her.

He also knew, however, that he wasn't stupid, though that was a label Ian had often tried to make him wear. *Why?* Michael considered the puzzle yet again. Perhaps his brother had absorbed some of their mother's disappointment in her elder son. At any rate, Ian did a fine job of projecting it in scorn for Michael's more practical bent. Ian had derided him from the lofty heights of a year behind him at school, knowing that he was (so they said) twenty points ahead of Michael on the IQ scale... whatever that signified.

But Michael had never wanted to be a musician... or a scientist. All he wanted was to earn enough and travel until he had found a small piece of land he could make his own, where he could farm. Nothing enormous or showy. No spectacular breakthroughs in a pharmaceutical or genetics laboratory deep in the subterranean mines of some university or other. He wanted none of that. Since the first days he could remember, hiking with his father across the

Weald or picking blackberries with his mother on Pilgrims' Way, he had wanted to work outside.

It wasn't an unfixed, vague ideal of crops and animals, land and weather—a rural daydream. He wanted to know the hard graft of the muck in the barn when the cows had lumbered out, but also the small triumph of a winning calf at the county showgrounds; he wanted to understand the heartbreak of oilseed rape fields flattened in the wet, but also to see the frothing delight of white milk foaming down clean, transparent vacuum lines into the tanks.

He wanted to experience farm life for himself, hold responsibility for it himself, work in the very ways he had learned this summer as he had worked on another man's farm. Why couldn't his mother accept his hopes and plans? Surely it wasn't too much to ask?

Come to that, why couldn't Ian accept him as he was, as well, and leave him to get on with his own life without the interfering, sneering, jeering commentary?

Why, he wondered, *do we so often define ourselves in terms of others, instead of finding out who we are for our own sakes? Here I am thinking of myself the way my mother sees me, or Ian sees me, as if all the problems I have came from them, and were not partly of my own making. Time to stop saying to myself, 'You're not as clever as Ian, not as good-looking as Ian, not as compassionate as your father, not as ambitious as your mother...' Time to be myself. Time to find out where I belong, and who I am.*

He smiled to himself. *The beginning is now—here, today.* Then he got up, cleared away the breakfast things, and went to put on a tie.

He spoke little on the way to the wedding, preferring to concentrate on the long, hectic reaches of motorway that stretched from central Kent all the way around the sprawling southern arc of London. *Only two hours,* he told himself wearily, giving himself up to be chauffeur because Ian had in the end preferred to sit in the back with Stacey.

Negotiating the traffic, he shifted to rambling speculations about Frank Bernard, whose wedding it was, and of whom he had only faint recollections from years before. Frank was at least ten years older than he was—he knew that much.

Today the dimly remembered Frank would be married to a woman from London who—so the letters from Frank's family ran—had the look of an Irish fairy queen about her, but who was in fact English, a journalist.

He glanced in the rearview mirror at Ian and Stacey, then quickly away again. Ian had 'acquired' Stacey during his first year at Cambridge, almost as he had acquired more music for his repertoire. She had clung to him for the entire year, in spite of the glittering whirl of university romances that beckoned in every other direction. Now she was inseparable, wrapped around him as much as the small car would allow. Her bright, painted lips mouthed clever little sentences that alternately mocked and chided, her dark eyes glittering at Michael in the driving mirror, sometimes, in spite of his determination to look away. He wondered vaguely what sort of a woman Clare was—Frank's bride—and whether she clung to Frank in the same way.

He shivered.

The wedding was packed. On the Bernard side Michael sat with his parents, his brother, and—a little apart—Stacey. There had been a minor scuffle as they went into the row of chairs, Stacey pressing herself forward to stay close to Ian, but Kate frowning fiercely from behind her gold-rimmed glasses to warn her back. Now he actually felt sorry for Stacey, who sat hunched at the end of the row with her kohled eyes huge and resentful, and her bleached hair flopped forward to cover her cheeks.

He glanced away, towards the chancel steps. He could see the back of Frank's head, the cleancut line of dark hair above the white collar and morning suit, and the way his second cousin turned his head, waiting for the bride. He watched, fascinated, trying to imagine what Frank must feel as Clare Hogarth floated in on a foam of white satin and lace, willowy and radiant. He caught a gleam of her copper-coloured hair under the mist of the veil, saw a hesitant, anxious smile, and remembered Frank's long fight with pneumonia. *Lord, they've waited long enough for this day!*

Behind the bridal party were the Bernard relatives from Bristol.

Because of where they sat in the front row, it wasn't hard to pinpoint Frank's parents, Tom and Peggy Bernard. *My great aunt and uncle,* Michael reminded himself. He knew none of the other Bernards. Then there were his father's people, from Belfast: the other Monaghans. He recognized one or two of his father's numerous brothers and sisters, the younger generation of Monaghan aunts and uncles. Then he gave up trying to sort them all out, and surrendered himself instead to the singing. Ian was mouthing some sort of criticism of the music at Stacey, but Michael, enjoying the exultant voices around him, disregarded them both. He watched dust motes dance in the cool green light shed by the church's narrow windows from the grassed banks outside, and he sang and sang.

When the ceremony ended, the small organ burst into a rippling peal of music that filled every crevice of the building and spilled down the steps outside. The newlyweds had turned to face the congregation. Frank leaned over and took Clare's shoulders in his hands, drawing her to him for a long kiss that somehow made Michael want to cheer and laugh. Now the bride's face was pink, her eyes bright.

Frank and Clare Bernard came down the aisle first, Frank beaming from behind his dark beard, and Clare smiling as if she couldn't believe it all. They were followed by the best man and a petite blonde bridesmaid who seemed almost lost behind the brilliant bouquet of chrysanthemums, asters, and dahlias. Then came a stout, elderly woman who must be the bride's mother. Tears were running down the woman's cheeks, and she made no effort to wipe them away—nor to wipe away the huge grin that also illuminated her wide face.

The Bernard family went down next: Uncle Tom Bernard, a big-boned man who wore a hearing aid; Michael searched his face, glancing also at the bustling, small Irishwoman beside him, Great Aunt Peggy. Frank's sisters and their families followed: a good-looking, cheerful-faced mob. He had forgotten how surprisingly small Aunt Peggy was for so tall a son, but her eyes were that same luminous blue, and she was smiling as happily as the bride's mother had been. A wedding everyone was happy about.

A groomsman was motioning Michael and his family to join the procession. His mother Kate went first, and he was suddenly struck—as if he had never seen her before—by how aristocratic she looked. Almost as tall as his rangy father: elegant, intelligent... *beautiful*, her face slightly shadowed by the navy hat she had chosen for the day. His father followed, his arm immediately and possessively around her waist. Inexplicably wistful, Michael stepped into the aisle behind them.

Then, looking past his parents, he saw two women he had only glanced at before: on the bride's side—also pausing at the end of a row of chairs before returning down the aisle. A mother and daughter, by the look of them. The mother looked like none of the others on the Hogarth side of the church; she was hatless, her greying hair neatly combed but rough-looking, and her skin weathered prematurely, he judged, by whatever sort of hard life she lived. He guessed she was in her fifties.

He caught the eye of the young woman who was with her, and saw a faint resemblance between this girl and the bride. The same well-defined cheekbones and oval face, even though the colouring was different. Unlike Clare, she had wide brown eyes. Her face was ringed by a mass of dark curls, and she gave him a warm, if fleeting, smile, with perfect teeth. She looked so full of life that he expected her to pirouette down the aisle. Instead, she rather sedately took her mother's arm and moved on without looking up again.

Out of the corner of his eye, almost without turning, he could see his brother's eyes swivel to follow the younger woman. Ian was staring openly at her, making no effort to veil his interest and curiosity. He finished the appraisal with a slight twist to his mouth, his eyes narrowing slightly. Moving very slowly with the procession, she was still looking at the carpet; but then as his brother continued to ogle her she flicked her eyes questioningly back to Michael's face. He wanted to smile, to whisper, *Never mind my rude brother,* but he was too disarmed by her to do anything except shuffle back towards the west door with the others.

They went out into the crowded porch. After the church's dimness, the August light outside blinded him for an instant. The two women were right in front of him, and he wondered if they could feel Ian's eyes—his own eyes—boring into their backs; if the younger woman would be as inquisitive about him as he was about her. London's close heat rose up to them from the churchyard's concrete pathway, and the mown banks hissed with crickets. Michael smiled to himself, shutting his eyes for an instant and breathing in the cut grass smell. That, at least, was the same as in the country.

The woman's mother was saying something to her that drove the colour into her cheeks and sent her eyes back to the Monaghan brothers. Michael heard her say, 'Don't fuss, Ma, I'm OK.' And when the mother tried to twist an escaping curl back behind her daughter's ear, she pulled away, annoyed, and obviously embarrassed. 'I'm not a little *kid*, for goodness sake!'

American. That voice was defintely American. He looked afresh at the two women. Well, people didn't wear their nationality on their sleeves, did they? There was nothing to suggest from their appearance that they were Americans. Now he was even more curious. *What part of the States is she from?* He knew he was staring, perhaps as rudely as his brother, now; though he doubted if his brother's thoughts were running—as his own were—on wide American cornfields, endless clouds of vibrant autumn leaves, and fat American farmland...

He smiled to himself, pulling himself up sharply. The other girl had deserted him only a week ago. *No more fantasies.* Women had caused him enough heartache already this year.

'Over here, please, family members.' A photographer was calling them unceremoniously from beneath a line of silver birch along the edge of the churchyard. Michael turned his eyes on Frank's shining face and the brilliant flowers in Clare's hands that seemed to echo their joy. Frank steered Clare towards the family gathering under the trees.

'Bride or groom?' the photographer asked Michael's father. The man was flushed and impatient, marshalling everyone as if they were on a school trip.

Michael disliked his bossy manner, the fussy way he was pushing them into stiff positions and coaxing fixed smiles from everyone. The shutter clicked and clicked again. In the crowd, watching as the groom's family photographs were taken, stood the curly-haired American girl. He saw her grit her teeth, cringing slightly every time the photographer shouted an instruction. The shutter snapped again; the photographer darted about once more, twittering instructions.

The American women were next in line for photographs.

'Who've we got here?'

'Williams,' the mother answered levelly. 'I'm the bride's aunt—Rita Williams. And this is Clare's cousin, Marie.'

Marie Williams. He could not take his eyes off her. He kept trying to draw them away, focusing on the haze of outer London that whitened the sky, then on the tinkling birch leaves that framed the bride's group ... but then again only on Marie.

When all the photographs were taken, he hoped he would be able to find and talk to her, but somehow the milling guests separated them; and as everyone walked across the churchyard to the reception hall, he found himself following others, instead.

Aunt Peggy Bernard found him before he had time to feel disappointed. 'I'm Frank's mother,' she said unnecessarily. 'And who are you, my dear? Has my forgetful old mind lost one of our relatives?'

Michael warmed to her. He remembered her lenient ways with the Monaghan children—her own and the many cousins. He softened, hearing again the thick West of Ireland brogue she'd never lost, not as his father had largely lost the Belfast accent he used to have. He smiled at her. 'No, you've not forgotten anyone, I'm sure. I'm one of Jack's sons. Haven't seen you for a wee while.' It was hard not to start talking as she did. Then, hearing himself, he added quickly, 'Michael, that is.'

She looked closely at him, and for a moment he thought she was going to make some remark about Ian, and *what a good-looking young lad he is, and how unlike him you look* ... as they all did. But she only smiled, her eyes misting over. 'Jack's boy—aye, Michael. I recall who you are, right enough. Have you a kiss for your old aunt, now?'

He stooped and kissed the soft skin of her cheek. 'Of course I have. And this is a happy wedding.'

His great aunt wiped her eyes and tucked in a stray hairpin. 'Lord love you, it is indeed. It's been too long in coming. Have a wee chat to the bride, if you see your chance. Clare's lovely altogether, so she is.'

He glanced at Frank and Clare, now moving among the guests, kissing and shaking hands, wreathed in smiles. 'I'm sure she is,' he murmured, but he was thinking of the American again, already.

'Not many people of your own age, I suppose.' Peggy Bernard's watery eyes wandered over the crowd. 'A cousin of Clare's, from New England, that's all. Marie Williams. Have you met her?'

Startled, he wondered if the old woman could read his mind. 'No, not yet.'

'You will, surely. And if you like wee folk, there's a deal of them here. Scampering in and out the tables like ragamuffins. The grandchildren... all of them.' She smiled indulgently. 'Ah, it's grand, so it is, to see them all here at once.' Then her eyes wandered off again. 'Sorry, sweetheart. Frank's after calling me, so I'm away for now. Have yourself a fine day, won't you all?'

When she'd moved away, Michael felt as if the hall had cooled; the old woman's warmth was almost tangible. He could see Ian, with Stacey still firmly attached, working his way round some of the other Monaghan relatives with his most charming smile. It would only be a matter of time before Ian found a way of losing Stacey for a moment and finding Marie Williams... unless Michael could find her first.

He quartered the big hall for her dark, shining head, but did not see her until they were seated for lunch.

Someone had arranged the seating plan for the wedding meal so that relatives and friends of Frank and Clare were mixed randomly— or so it seemed to Michael. As a result, here he was with Rita Williams on one side, next to the bride, and Stacey on the other. Opposite him sat an array of relatives and guests he did not recognize. Marie, he saw now, was on Stacey's other side... but she was also next to Ian. His brother grinned smugly from the end of the table, ogling both Stacey and Marie. *I can watch over all the local talent at once,* his eyes seemed to say.

Michael tried to catch Rita Williams' attention, but she had turned towards Clare. Stacey too was avoiding his eye, drinking deeply from her wineglass. He could almost feel her resentment at being separated from Ian again. 'We'd better make the best of it, Stace,' he said drily. 'Come on, it's not that bad. You've got me for company, after all.'

'*Great* company,' she said into her glass.

He stuck his tongue in his cheek. 'Oh, come on. I'm sure Ian would like you to feel part of the family.'

She measured his sincerity with a flick of her pencilled eyebrows. 'Ian might, though I'm not even sure about that—the way he's eyeing that woman on the other side of me. And your mother would rather I disappeared completely, I don't kid myself about that.'

He felt sorry for her again, and murmured some nonsense about her imagination.

She gave a strange shrug of one shoulder, her mouth twisting bitterly. Her tone was ascerbic. '*You're* all right, Mike. The groom's cousin. But I'm not anyone's cousin. A hanger on. Persona non grata. Ian's girlfriend, that's all. And not even that, if your mother gets her way.' Her face changed for a moment. 'I liked that—the photographer, I mean. Calling her "Mrs M"! I bet no one's ever called your dear mummy "Mrs M" in her whole life!'

He was appalled, suddenly, by two things simultaneously: that he understood her dislike of his mother, perhaps even sympathized and might sometimes have agreed with what she was saying; and that Ian had picked a girl so damaged, so defensive and bitter. Then he was appalled that those things appalled him. Mutely, he just stared at her.

'Well, so much for the great company.' She dropped her voice to a theatrical whisper. 'I think I'll have a chat with this woman on the other side, before Ian's eyes pop out of his head and he forgets about me altogether.' And she presented her back to him.

He had to act quickly, before she could speak to Marie. He leaned so close to her that he smelled the musky heat of her thick perfume, saw the lines of new, dark growth at the nape of her white neck, below the bleached strands of her old hair. 'Wait,' he whispered, 'maybe we can do each other a favour. If you swap with Marie, then we'll both be happier.'

She swung round. Her eyes had hardened. 'You don't waste much time, either, do you?'

He saw her throw another speculative glance at Ian and heard his brother say smoothly to Marie, 'Ah, so you're the lovely American lady we saw in church.'

To his relief, Marie sparked back, quite deadpan, 'Er—no, you must be thinking of my mother.' She turned to Stacey. 'Did I hear some kinda discussion about changing seats? I think *you* were with this young man—I guess there's been a mix-up in the seating plan.' And without any hesitation, Marie stood and offered her chair to Stacey.

Michael crowed with laughter. Ian had met his match, this time. He liked the way she'd said 'this young man'.

Stacey flashed her teeth at Marie in what almost passed for a smile, and suddenly Marie was sitting in her place, beside him.

'That's better,' he said. Ian's head was now bent close to Stacey's: gold next to dyed blonde. He felt a surge of relief.

'Better for whom?' Marie quipped, laughing back at him.

He wasn't sure he was witty enough for her, but he loved her quicksilver smile, and the glint in her eyes as she'd mocked Ian. He hoped he would not sound too intense. 'You're Marie.' He offered her his hand, then regretted the stiff Englishness of the gesture.

Her hand was dry and warm, small in his. He let it go quickly, as if he'd been burned. Her cheeks coloured, though there was nothing demure about her. 'That's me.'

'Stacey wasn't happy in your chair—it was my idea you swap.' He felt he was blundering, out of practice. It was a long time since his first meeting with a girl he liked. He reached frantically for something to say. 'You look a bit lost.'

'Me? Lost? No, not really.'

'I also heard you tell someone you're the bride's cousin.'

She smiled. 'Yes, and you're the groom's nephew—Michael. My, we *did* have our ears out on stalks.'

Michael grinned back. 'Not quite his nephew. These family dos confuse me no end, but I know I'm not Frank's nephew. What does it matter? Second cousin? Third cousin? Removed cousin? Who cares? I'm here. You're here. And very pretty, too.'

She blinked in surprise, and he felt surprised, himself, at the way he had spoken to her. 'Thanks.' She smiled back at him, apparently losing her bearings. 'I guess I'm here, OK.'

'All the way from the States for a wedding.'

'All the way—from the USA.' She said it like a silly rhyme. 'I've been looking forward to this for a long while.'

He nodded. 'You wanted to see part of England?'

Her face changed. 'Always. In Boston you grow up knowing where the roots of the city reach to, and you want to go—it's something you gotta do at least once.'

'Is it just roots, d'you think? I'm sure that's got nothing to do with it. You see pictures in a travel magazine, and you want to go, however mad and unlikely it seems. Surely that's it?'

'Maybe, maybe not. It's to do with belonging, I think.' She shrugged, suddenly looking self-conscious. 'I guess Americans don't have a history as old and deep as yours. We want to find it—find where we belong.'

He remembered the mental debate that had begun for him earlier in the day. *Time to find out where I belong, and who I am.* 'Yes, I understand that very well. But, roots or no roots, I'd certainly like to go to your country one day.' He knew he sounded too serious now.

She put down her fork. 'Did you ever go before?'

'No. Seen lots of films and whatnot. That's what I meant just now about pictures and magazines. It's one of several places I'd love to see.'

'Anywhere in particular?'

'I'm interested in agriculture,' he said shortly.

'That's the truth!' Ian's most boorish voice interrupted, and Michael winced. Leaning against Stacey with affected playfulness, his brother went on, 'Most people have blood in their veins, but this man has slurry.'

Michael glared; Ian just wanted to wind him up. 'Talk to Stacey, will you?' He pulled his eyes back to Marie. 'Any agricultural area would do me.'

Her eyebrows rose. 'You're a farmer, then?'

He hesitated, waving his hands in dismissal, then suddenly realizing what they looked like; his nails were still ingrained with some of the dirt from his work in the shed and the fields the day before. 'A farmer? Yes, will be one day. Not now. Too much to learn, still.'

Marie had noticed his hands too. He caught the quick movement of her eyes from his face to his hands, and back again.

'Yes, I know. Farmer's hands.' He was proud, suddenly. 'I hope, at least.'

She was obviously unsure what to say next. 'What sort of farming?'

'We live in Kent.' He had to remind himself again that she was American. 'Garden of England, it's called. Dairy and fruit. I used to think I'd want to grow hops, but I've discovered I like animals better.'

'Your father's a farmer, then?'

He shook his head. 'I wish he were. No, he's a social worker. Used to be a carpenter. You'd think he'd sympathize that I want to do practical work—' He dropped his hands. He wondered if she would understand. Well, he reasoned, there was little to lose in telling the truth. 'But Mum's the driving force in our house. And she wanted us both at university.' He looked down. He was saying too much, after all, and too quickly.

'So what will you do?' she asked.

He was uncomfortable talking so much about himself. She hadn't given him a chance to question her much about herself. He dropped his voice lower, so that she had to bend nearer to him and he could feel her breath on the shaved skin of his jaw. 'I'm working for the summer on a farm a few miles from home. There aren't any other jobs this year for students. No one can complain about what I'm doing or stop me.'

'How long for?'

He realized that her questions were drawing him out to express the plans that had been slowly forming in his mind since the beginning of the long vacation. He hesitated again, almost superstitious about articulating them. Especially since he had not yet plucked up the courage to come clean with his parents about his intentions. 'I'll work on that farm as long as I need to. Then I'll decamp some time in the autumn. Itchy feet. Not sure where yet.' He forced his eyes to meet hers. 'But you might inspire me.'

A small band struck up on the far side of the hall, and a few couples got up to dance. The bride and groom went out first, and Marie drifted away from him for a moment, watching them with what he interpreted as envy. Then she seemed to register what he had just said. She blushed. 'Don't spoil it,' she said quickly. 'I'll write you off like all the boys I know at home, if you start talking like that.'

'All right. Sorry, I can take a hint.'

'What you want,' she began, talking fast and speaking lightly, 'is an escape through a free and magic tunnel into Massachusetts. Plenty of fruit farms near us, and northwards, as well, into Maine or Vermont.'

He felt he would have to fly to keep up with her. 'Not fruit, I said.'

'A New England dairy farm, then.' A strange look crossed her face, as if her mind had suddenly jumped sideways, and she had thought of something else.

He looked her up and down again, attracted, fascinated. 'I quite fancy an escape into your part of the world, Marie.'

She groaned, blushed again, and laughed. 'You sound so corny! Don't be crazy. There're more seafood farms than dairy farms around my neck of the woods.'

At last he would find out more about her. 'Is that what your dad does, then? Seafood? No—don't tell me. He runs one of those seafood restaurants I've seen pictures of. You know, the backdrop of red New England autumn—I beg your pardon—*fall* leaves, and fat pink lobsters on the tourists' plates. Outside a converted fishing hut, naturally. You know the kind of advert I mean.'

She looked slightly pained, as if he had said something mildly offensive. 'No, no. We own a marina,' she said simply.

'Ah.' He felt nonplussed.

The smile returned. 'There! Now you don't know what to say.'

He reached into a back pocket and found a torn piece of paper. 'Oh, no hesitations,' he said. 'You never know what might happen. Just give me your address, and I'll look you up next time I drop in for a lobster meal in Boston.'

She paused. 'You're a little hard to take seriously. Still, OK... you do that. I won't be able to offer you a lobster dinner, but you could always rent one of our boats and sail off to the farm of your dreams.'

'I might do just that.' Then, *No more fantasies,* he said to himself again. All the same, he passed her the paper.

'Crazy loon,' she said gently, writing her address for him.

'Now your telephone number.'

'Crazier and crazier.' She wrote that for him, too.

He read it, nodding. 'You Americans have such neat handwriting.'

She snorted. 'Not according to my old teachers.'

His eyebrows rose. 'I thought you said—'

'I'm a year out of school. Just finished my freshman year at college. The marina's not even half mine. In fact—'

He had guessed she was in her early twenties. 'I thought you were older.'

'So, now you know.'

He grinned again. 'Never mind. I'm not cradle snatching; I'm an old man of twenty myself.'

'You're not cradle-snatching anyway,' she fenced, 'as far as I know.'

'I thought my intentions were quite clear. Honourable, as well.' He glanced down the table at Ian, regretting the priggish words as soon as they were out of his mouth. 'I'm not like my brother, you know.'

She undercut him, chuckling. 'All sugar and jam tarts?' Then her eyes went back to the dancers on the scratched wooden floor.

'Watch yourself!' He thought he knew what she wanted, and what he wanted, as well. 'Come on, I'd like to dance with you.'

'I'm not much of a dancer.'

'Yes, you are. Or I'll show you if not.' He pushed back his chair and held out his hand. She wouldn't turn him down now, would she? 'Come on. Who knows when you'll be able to put your arms round an Englishman again. I'll teach you to dance. One day you can teach me to sail.'

'If you only knew,' she said, hooting with laughter.

He felt Ian's and Stacey's eyes on their backs as they left the table. *It doesn't matter now,* he thought. Smiling into Marie's eyes, he held her lightly and guided her round. She kept stepping on his feet and losing her balance, but that only gave him an excuse to hold her a little more tightly, and she raised no objection. The day had turned out better than he had dared hope.

His parents glided past. He saw Marie watch them, her face growing rosy and her eyes a little dazed. Then Ian and Stacey swept by, steps perfectly matched, golden heads bent close together.

'Like dancing with an American filly?' Ian grimaced at him. He and Stacey whirled away, but not before Michael heard him add, 'All teeth and legs, poor girl.'

Michael gritted his teeth. 'Don't listen to him.'

Marie flushed but still looked amused. 'See? You're wasting your time. I'm worse than a carthorse.'

His hand on her back pressed her a little closer. 'Not at all.'

'I'll give him a sampling of American horseflesh, if I get half a chance.' Her face was animated, her eyes still following Ian and Stacey.

'Oh, never mind him.' He bent and touched his mouth to her hair. 'I'm enjoying this wedding. Aren't you?' The words sounded inexpressive and hollow to him. He felt piqued by her, but there was no way to say that. The song ended, and he had to release her.

She opened her mouth to say something, but a bevy of small girls erupted from the side of the room where his great uncle and aunt had been sitting. Their faces were bright with excitement, Laura Ashley bows bobbing, hair shining and pink mouths open to demand attention like so many baby birds. 'Look out,' Michael said. 'Here come the Bernard grandchildren. Now we're for it.' He remembered Peggy Bernard's request that he keep half an eye on the children; but he hadn't even thought of them.

'Michael! Michael!' one of the little girls shrieked. 'Dance with us. With *us*.'

'Why should I?' He was ridiculously pleased with their affection.

The girls eyed Marie and stopped, uncertain.

'Girls!' Mrs Bernard was calling them. 'Come on over here, would you? I think Frank and Clare will soon be away on their honeymoon. Come on, I've some confetti for you.'

The children turned away again.

'Saved by granny,' Michael murmured, cupping Marie's elbow with his hand.

She looked bewildered. 'They're leaving already?'

'Frank and Clare? Must be. I'll get you some confetti.'

She shook her head and laughed. 'Not for me, thanks. Ma and I bought something else to throw—American style.'

'And—?'

'Just a minute.' She disappeared towards the door of the hall, into the crush of cousins and aunts from both sides of the family.

He followed her, seeing her just outside, her head bent close to her mother's. Around them, a few hankies fluttered and mopped at tears, and the bridesmaids fussed with their ribbons and posies. He watched her, and in a moment she doubled back to him.

'What's all this?'

Out of a box she poured grains of rice into his hands. 'Yours to throw over them,' she said. 'Don't miss.'

He felt clumsy beside her quick loveliness. 'I hope the sharing of rice has some deep and eternal significance,' he said, laughing into her eyes.

'Not that I know of.' She sounded dry now: a stranger, after all.

Within moments the bells in the church tower had begun to peal. The bride and groom, now dressed to travel, had emerged from a low doorway at the side of the hall and were running the gauntlet between the showers of tears and confetti.

Michael scattered the rice high and wide. He felt it rain down and watched, laughing, as it landed on Frank's shoulders and Clare's bright hair.

'Be happy, happy!' Marie called.

He picked a few grains from her hair and took another couple from his own mouth.

'You too, Marie Williams,' he said. 'And one day I'll see you in Americay.'

'Crazy as a rice pudding,' she told him.

4

When Frank and Clare had disappeared with empty tins clanking and bouncing on the road behind the car, Michael turned to find Marie; but in the crush of wedding guests at the gate she had moved away. Her mother seemed to be standing guard beside her.

He felt the heat prickling under his collar but knew he couldn't dispense with his tie yet. He watched Marie turning to talk to some of her Hogarth relatives and saw how easy she was with anyone she spoke to. He wanted some of her happiness, as if he could rub it from her and see the genie of it curl up and enfold him.

At last, with a few words to her mother, she turned her head again and gave him a quick smile. He felt the familiar tug of desire in the pit of his stomach and for an instant closed his eyes against it.

'Michael?' Her voice was somewhat uncertain. She had come to stand beside him again.

He wanted to divert himself from all the feelings that welled up and unbalanced him—feelings he'd rather resist after the disappointment of the week before. 'It was a lovely wedding,' he said, clutching at the first words that flew across his mind.

Her eyes were shining. 'Different from American weddings. Beautiful.'

Still he did not know what to say after her abruptness of a few minutes ago. He needed to think about her, get his bearings again. The sense of anti-climax rolled over him.

'What'll you do now?' she asked.

'Oh—go back to Kent, I suppose.' It was easy enough to answer that sort of question, at least.

'With your family?'

'Of course.' He took a deep breath. 'With my brother and his girlfriend, anyway. My parents'll want to stay longer and talk with the Bernards. We didn't come up together, anyway.' He gave her a pale smile. 'What about you, Marie?'

'Back across town with Ma and Aunt Edie, I guess.'

'Will you stay in England much longer, then?' He knew it was pointless to ask. By tomorrow he would be back in the shed splattered with cow muck, relieved to be away from his intense, impossible to understand family, working in a world of animals he did understand. Happy in his own way, though he wouldn't see her again.

'We're flying home on Tuesday.' She wrinkled her nose.

'I've got your address.'

'Yup.'

'I'll use it.'

'You'll be lucky to get an answer. I don't even write my brothers. I've never been famous for writing letters.'

He felt excluded again, somehow, by those few words. She belonged in a world he did not know at all, whatever he had said to her about converted fishing huts and tourists eating lobsters. She and her family moved in foreign circles where people talked of putting their boats to water and partied in season at the marina and out of season at the exclusive yacht club next door—or so Marie had described things. He did not even know her brothers' names.

'You could always start now,' he said lamely. 'At least—' He stopped, then made himself go on, 'I could write to you first, if you like.'

Her face softened. 'Try, then. Maybe you'd better give me your address, too. You never know when I might come back to England.'

To your relatives in London, he answered her silently.

'Don't look at me like that! I'll send you a card, at least.'

'Very good of you.' He knew he sounded sceptical. All the same, he scrawled his address on the other half of the paper that now showed hers, tore it off and gave it to her. 'Here you are.'

'It's been nice meeting you,' she said.

He wondered if that was a line all Americans used, automatically, when they met someone new. It had tripped too quickly off her tongue. He met her eyes directly. 'I was glad to meet you, too,' he said steadily.

Without any warning, she reached her arms round his neck as she had done on the dancefloor, and hugged him. Surprised, he breathed her perfume, wanting to remember everything. He knew he wouldn't kiss her, only hold her in his arms, as she was holding him, lightly, for a moment.

She looked over her shoulder and past the gate to the car park. 'I gotta go,' she said.

He released her. 'Goodbye, Marie.'

'See you. Oh—look—Aunt Edie's waving for me to hurry. Sorry.'

And she was gone, weaving between the others, a thread of brightness and definition in among the predictable pinks and pastels. He felt blank, lost. Then, thinking further, he decided he was over-reacting. *Weddings!* he thought irritably. *They turn everything into soft focus.*

He searched the crowd for his brother. Ian was leaning against a tree, his jacket slung over his shoulder, his face bent towards Stacey's as usual.

Michael worked his way through the crowd. As he passed his parents, his father nodded at him. 'We'll see you back at home.'

'All right. I think we'll be off in a minute.'

His father grinned. 'Go easy on the way home, will you?'

He grinned back. 'You know I will.' Then he caught his brother's eye.

'Ah, the chauffeur, at last, Stacey.' Ian looked away from her and smiled mockingly at Michael.

He grimaced. 'Ready to go?'

'*I* am,' Stacey said imperiously.

'Are you driving, or am I?' Michael asked Ian.

'You are, of course,' Stacey snapped.

He shrugged, and they made their way to the churchyard gate where he had said goodbye to Marie moments before. Without thinking, he opened the front passenger door for Stacey.

'I'd rather sit in the back with Ian, thanks.' Her voice was crisp. As he closed the door again, he felt something small and hard bite into the skin of his back, under his shirt. *Rice,* he thought.

On the far side of the car park, he saw Marie's dark head dipping down as she got into a car with her mother and aunt. She did not even look up and smile. He ached a little, thinking of the last smile she'd thrown in his direction, moving away with her mother outside the church gates. He was just another face in the crowd for her, he guessed. It should have felt the same for him, but he felt pulled towards her on a string, like a puppet. She was the kind of spontaneous, happy girl he still hoped to find one day... but there she was, driving away, then flying away... to the other side of the Atlantic.

At least he had her address warmly folded into his pocket. Still, it seemed unlikely he'd ever see her. Or even that she'd write to him. So it was silly to think of her any more, he resolved again. *No more fantasies.*

Ian pushed past him and got in beside Stacey. 'Day dreamer,' he said.

Michael steered the car thoughtfully and resolved not to look in the mirror any more than was strictly necessary. All the same, he noticed his brother wind down the back window and heard air bursting in from outside. Idly Ian flicked a grain or two of rice through the window and shut it again. 'So who was today's wonderwoman, little brother?'

Michael did not answer.

'Who was she?' Ian repeated. 'I couldn't make any sense out of what she said.'

'Her name's Marie Williams,' he said reluctantly.

'Marie Williams,' Ian echoed, and the name sounded foreign from his lips. 'But who was she anyway? All I found out was that she was an American.'

'Slipping, aren't you?' Stacey said sourly, and Michael heard the click of a compact; then, in spite of himself, caught sight of her in the rearview mirror applying fresh lipstick to her pouting mouth. 'She was the bride's cousin, didn't you know?'

'Look, Ian, Stacey—I don't want to talk about her.' Instead, he focused on the journey ahead.

Driving the familiar roads, he let his mind range free again. He made the turnings on first the South Circular, then the A20, quite automatically. He looked at the sweep of Kent's landscape with the eyes of one who had seen it a thousand times, but now saw in an altogether different direction.

He returned to his earliest memories: saw the low, grey-blue mountains of Ireland with their shrouds of watery mist, saw Lough Neagh dropping away below the aircraft as the family had left County Antrim for the last time. It was surprising, even to him, how clearly he remembered that last sighting of the narrow waters of the lough, then the wide waters of the Irish Sea. Remembered the smear and blear of tears as Ireland melted behind and beneath them into the wadded clouds, and they landed then in dreary England in the rain. *Our new home,* his parents had said, but he had felt nothing except a sense of empty bewilderment. England *wasn't* his home. It might be his mother's—God knows she seemed glad enough, relieved enough, to come back to England. But it wasn't his father's home, who had been born in Belfast. And it wasn't even his brother's. No, he and Ian had both been born just outside Londonderry, within view of the Donegal mountains.

He understood why his parents had been forced to leave Ireland. It hadn't been safe, he now understood as an adult, for a Catholic and a Protestant, married to each other, to stay in the North. So his parents had chosen to come to England.

He had nothing against England, but he had grown up with the feeling that it wasn't his country and that he didn't belong. The feeling had crystallized at primary school, where the other children called him 'Mick' and told him he should go back to the shanty shack where he was born. But even in those early days of living in England, he belonged neither there, nor back in Ireland.

Not so with Ian, however. Ian had lost his accent quickly and had generally charmed and smiled his way through school, ever popular, usually disassociating himself from his older brother. In spite of their father, there *had* been fights. More than once, Michael had intervened to rescue Ian. A pointless, foolish rescue. Ian had always come up from the bottom of the pile of bodies grinning and smacking his enemy on the back as if they were friends. Michael recalled how, ironically, it had been he himself who had gone home with a bloody nose to the rebukes of his mother.

'Why can't you ever get on with the other children?' she would say sadly, sponging his face.

'But boys will fight, love,' his father would say, laughing easily, remembering (he knew now) the uncles in Belfast, years before, who had fought and scrapped in the schoolyard. And in Michael's own ears would ring the taunts of the English children, *Go home, you bloody Mick. We don't want you.* Taunts that went on into secondary school, until his thick accent melted and blended into the softer sounds of mid-Kent; then things became better with the other children—though not with Ian.

He thought now that the move from Ireland was probably when the seeds of conflict in the family had first been sown. That move had been a dislocation for them all. The sense of injustice had begun then, sharpened in the unequal treatment by teachers and by other children, as well, he sometimes felt, as by his mother. Injustice—but not rancour. He knew again and with slight surprise that he was not jealous of Ian. His brother might tease, irritate, sneer, show off—do all the things calculated most to rouse his temper . . . but Michael still felt no jealousy. He just felt hurt; he just felt the outsider.

He was the outsider now, with Ian and Stacey cuddling in the back seat, and he did not know what to do about it. He felt too weary to want to banter and argue with them. He sighed. *At least another hour to go.*

'Big sigh, Mike.' Ian sounded more conciliatory, for a change.

'I'm tired,' he said simply, letting down his guard.

'Fancy a drink, then?'

In the mirror, Stacey brightened visibly.

'A coffee, anyway,' he said.

'What a good idea.'

'I'll stop at the next greasy spoon.'

Stacey scowled. 'Shows what you think of us,' she said petulantly.

'Oh—are you paying?' he asked mildly.

'There's a roadside cafe up by that pub.' Ian was leaning forward, pointing out of the front of the car.

'The pub would be nicer, wouldn't it?' Stacey suggested.

'Good idea,' Ian agreed.

'No. The cafe's fine,' Michael said.

'Rubbish. It'll be just as you said—a greasy spoon. Let's hit the pub. Stacey's right.'

Michael gritted his teeth. 'The cafe was your idea in the first place, and there aren't any tables outside the pub. It'll be far too hot.'

Stacey suddenly leaned forward and shouted in his ear. 'Oh, for goodness sake call it off, you two. Always quarrelling over nothing, like a pair of dogs. I'm sick of it.'

It was the first sensible thing she had said all day, Michael decided. 'So am I,' he said. Grinning, he drove into the cafe carpark.

'Oh, what a perfect place for our Michael.' Ian was opening the door before the car had fully stopped. 'Look at those cows in the field on the other side, will you? Right at home, you'll feel, so you will, so you will.'

'Stop taking the Mick,' Stacey laughed.

A commuter jet bound for the airport roared low overhead, wheels down for landing. The cows went on munching, not even lifting their heads. He watched them affectionately, smelling their warm smell in the breeze, imagining the feel of their sleek summer coats.

'Always did like cows better than people,' Ian heckled.

He resigned himself to more sniping and backbiting. 'What'll it be, Stacey? Or is my ever-generous brother providing the feast?'

'I couldn't eat a thing after all that wedding cake.' She patted her flat stomach theatrically. 'Just coffee—that's great.'

'I'm certainly not paying,' Ian said abruptly. 'You're the one who wanted to stop.'

'I thought it was your idea.'

Stacey groaned. 'I'll pay in a minute and put you both to shame. You're brats, the pair of you.' She stood still on the dusty unevenness of the cafe carpark and got out a cigarette lighter. 'Let's not bother—just go home.'

'Anyway, it can't be all that bad here.' Ian ran his hand over the flawless black gloss of a Mercedes that looked as if it had just been driven from a show room. 'If there's clientele like this, the coffee must be pretty damn good after all.'

Michael pushed his fingers wearily through his hair. Once again he felt like walking off, driving off, and leaving them to find their own way home.

Ian made the decision for them all. 'Well, even if you two aren't thirsty, I am.' He elbowed past Michael, and the cafe door swung creaking behind him.

Michael and Stacey looked at one another and laughed. Some of the tension seemed to dissolve. 'All right, Stacey. Come on, I'll buy you a coffee.' He reached into his pocket and rattled the change. A few pounds remained from last week's holiday wages—what was left after he'd banked some of it and bought a wedding present—but enough to buy coffee.

Stacey smiled coquettishly and took his arm.

He stopped. 'Don't.'

'Why not?' Her black-rimmed eyes widened in dismay. 'You're such a dark horse, Mike. I always fancied you.'

He couldn't help laughing again, after all. 'Hedging your bets? Thanks. I'd keep the feeling to yourself, if I were you.' He unhooked her arm and held the door for her. He almost choked on the next words. 'Ian's better for you, I'm certain of that.'

Ian was sitting on a high stool, lounging against the counter, when they came in behind him. A young couple with children were eating jammily in one corner, and at another table, farthest from the counter, four men sat hunched intently over cigarettes and steaming mugs of coffee. Otherwise, the place was empty and blessedly cool. A couple of bluebottles roamed aimlessly, banging into windows and walls.

Stacey hung back. 'Are you sure you wouldn't rather go into the pub?' She puffed a nervous cloud of smoke into the air, almost as if she were waiting, Michael thought, for everyone in the place to turn and notice her.

'At six on a Saturday in this weather?' he said wearily. 'You must be joking, Stace. Look, I know this isn't the Ritz, but it'll do for a coffee, at least.'

Ian had ordered his and was now eyeing the girl behind the coffee bar with more than passing interest.

Michael shook his head and was careful not to catch Stacey's eye. 'Two more coffees, please,' he said to the girl, pushing the money across the counter.

'I'm not sitting up there,' Stacey told Ian sulkily. 'Come on, Ian. Let's find a table.'

Ian winked and shrugged in resignation. They clicked their way across the sticky floor and sat near the four men. An elderly couple came through the door, and Michael saw one of the men look up, then away again, quickly, at his companions. Beside him, Stacey and Ian bantered about the girl behind the counter. He only half listened, resentful of the situation, wanting simply to get away again.

Out of the unmoving haze of smoke that hung over their own table and the table next to theirs, he suddenly caught more than one American voice. His ear was acclimatized to the accent after those hours with Marie, and he began to listen, ignoring altogether what Ian and Stacey were saying to each other.

The men were obviously business associates. All four were fair, with neat, blow-dried hair and lean bodies in casual clothes. Except for the American voices, they might have been Northern Europeans. He caught the words 'deal' and 'payoff' first, then others that seemed to have no relevance: 'daisies', 'the ring'. He wondered idly what sort of business the men were in. They mentioned hospitals a few times, as if they were reps for a medical supply company, but as he listened more closely it seemed that there was nothing too unusual or interesting in what they were doing. He guessed they were fresh off the plane from the States, perhaps driving now to London. He glanced round with wry amusement. *What an ugly place to start seeing the sights of Britain.*

Their voices were growing louder; they began to argue.

'I don't trust him—never have.'

'Then you're a fool to carry on.'

'We have to trust him.'

'He'll have found the best connections here, sure.'

'It won't take us long to build the links.'

'...not so tight here.'

'Wait, I'm not so sure. Easier than SA, maybe, but—'

'No, it's a cinch. No sweat to bring the stuff into those sleepy southern ports we saw, coming in just now.'

'But what about the market? I got a bad feeling about all this. There's too many damn loose ends. It's getting too complicated to suit me. Holland's all very well, but the London New York run, well...'

Someone scoffed, and coffee was splattered onto the table. 'Loose ends? Don't talk crap. He's got it figured to a tee. Slick as an oiled seal.'

'Yeah, it's all *too* slick for my liking. Too damn obvious, if you ask me.'

'Too slick? That's Steve for you, every time.'

'Obvious, shit, it's meant to be. They'll think the merchandise is great. And you guys'll come across looking as straight as little Dutch boys with your fingers in the dam to stop the water coming in.' There was a crude laugh. 'Why else would Steve go for you? Because he likes your faces, you stupid asses? Come on, wise up. And drink up, as well. We gotta get going.'

Michael watched them as they scraped back their chairs and jostled, close together and still staggering slightly from what he supposed was jetlag, for the door.

In the entrance they passed two other men, both conservatively dressed men with clear eyes and straight backs. He saw the four Americans hesitate, heard their loud debate fall silent, and saw them veer past.

'Oh, look, little brother,' Ian said, grabbing his sleeve. 'There goes that Merc we saw out there.'

He craned towards the smoky, smeared window and saw a trail of dust and flying pebbles where the Mercedes had been parked.

'In a hurry, weren't they?' Stacey murmured.

Michael glanced at the two who had just come in. They were ordering a meal at the counter, uninterested in anyone around them. He thought of Frank again, and of Clare; then—inevitably— of Marie.

5

'Where's Ian?' Michael asked, pushing the door wide and standing on the threshold of the kitchen.

His father must just have returned from work. He was leaning back in a wooden chair by the kitchen table, the newspaper propped in front of him and a cup of tea at his elbow. His mother, meanwhile, was emptying supermarket bags, packing things quickly into the cupboard.

Kate Monaghan did not stop. She moved from worktop to cupboard and back again, slim and efficient, so that he felt gangling and awkward, in the way.

Jack laid down the paper and smoothed his hand across it. 'Your brother's out with Stacey again,' he said quietly. 'They'll be back in a little while, I'm thinking.'

Michael saw how tired his father was, how spent by the day's work. 'Oh, it doesn't matter. I was just wondering—' He tried to gauge his mother's mood, and whether his father would welcome suggestions at this burned out end of the day. 'It's such a bright evening. We could go for a walk.'

A soft look passed between them, excluding him, though his father was quick to glance away from his mother and back at him. 'It is a lovely night. You're right.'

'I'm making a special supper for your brother.' Kate did stop now, her face determined. 'For his birthday, I mean.'

He had forgotten Ian's birthday, and her look reproached him.

Jack interposed. 'All the more reason to go a walk afterwards. The weather's surely going to hold tonight, Kate.'

She looked surprised, then turned away to the hob. 'All right, then, if that's what everyone would like.'

'You know Ian,' Jack said. 'He loves simple food.'

If he comes back to eat it, Michael thought. He was glad, though, that they would go all out together. It was a rare thing, these days, for them to do. He was still clinging to memories of damp walks over the Ulster border into Donegal, years before. Times when there had been peace in their house—or so it seemed; times when his brother was not always demanding—and getting—everyone's attention.

But this time he shrugged the memories away. *No, this is the day.* He would enjoy it now, not brood on the past all the time.

That image made him chuckle quietly to himself, and his father looked up from the paper again. 'Good day?' He poured himself a cup of tea and joined him at the table. 'Very good.' It was no use saying much more. How could his mother understand the satisfaction he felt with the fat line of cows swishing their tails, milking units attached to udders, mouths munching the dry feednuts? And how could his father understand, whose grandparents had been dirt poor potato farmers in Ireland—and who had wanted nothing better than to escape the farm life he now coveted?

His mother looked at him sideways. 'You're not going to sit in here long in those smelly things, are you, darling?'

He grinned at her. It would be easy to provoke her with offers of clothespegs for her nose, but on Ian's birthday jokes might not go down too well. 'No, Mum, not long. I'll have a bath.' But he felt in no hurry; he could share one little triumph with them, at least. 'I learned how to treat mastitis today. One of the cows was ill, and we had the vet in. He let me watch him.' Ian, he knew, would say, *How perfectly fascinating can you get?* But Ian wasn't there to comment.

All day, except when the vet had arrived; all day, as he had slaved mindlessly in the barn with the farmer and the unloader, stacking the bales from the second cut of hay and later driving the cows into the milking shed; all day he had been thinking about his plans. Things had come to him slowly, over the past weeks since the Bernard wedding. He had discovered that his bank balance was better than he expected after the summer's farm work, and that if he were going to make an escape it had better be now, at the time when his parents expected him to return for his last year at the university. He couldn't afford to wait any longer to tell them what he was going to do. Surely it wouldn't be too hard?

The kitchen was peaceful: a slight rustle as his father turned pages; the slap of cake batter in the bowl as his mother beat it. So often she worked alone in the kitchen, had finished cooking a meal scarcely before anyone had noticed she had started, before anyone could even offer to help. And she rarely spoke when she cooked, except to thank anyone who had managed to catch her in time to do so. She was silent now, and he was tempted, in this unusual moment of peace between the three of them, to tell them now what he had decided. But no, they would be more relaxed when they were out of doors, later.

He would do it this evening.

He stood up, groaning under his breath. His muscles had stiffened after the day's work. He winced, knowing it would be a long time before he would be as hardened as his employer. His father looked up and seemed to read him, for he reached up and rubbed his hand gently across Michael's back. 'Take it easy, son,' he said.

'I'm going to have that bath,' he said, expecting—and getting—no reply.

Soaking in the hot water, he began to think again. In the beginning of the summer, when he had first returned home, the decisions he would have to make had presented themselves to him. Either he could remain at university until he had finished his degree, working to save as much as he could for agricultural college. Or he could opt out altogether, make just enough to start a new life on his own—and move on. But that was before the worst of the tension with Ian, before the wedding, before he had met Marie; and now he was even more determined.

The decision seemed clear. He would go to America, stay with Marie's family for a while, then travel the States and see what opened up for him there—or, if not, back in Ireland or England.

At first the plan had seemed utterly crack-brained. But the more he had thought about it, the more he considered being forced to spend any longer with his brother, the more he dwelt on the unhappy thought that his parents seemed sometimes indifferent to his presence in the house, the more he remembered about Marie—the more he was sure that going to America was a good idea after all.

He knew others who had gone, and he had heard their stories: adventures in Arizona, moments of fear in Mississippi, sunsets in Nevada, concerts in the park in Philadelphia, festivals in New Orleans, fishing in New England. But he saw no reason why he should not make a break now. Saw too that if he did not use the freedom here, this very moment, he might never have it again. He would have to take the leap into the unknown, then trust for the rest.

He towelled his hair dry, dressed, and returned to the kitchen. His father had gone into the garden, cutting flowers at his mother's request, and Kate herself was setting two steaming circles of cake onto a wire rack.

'You look brighter,' she said.

'Should do after washing away half an inch of dirt.'

She almost smiled.

He tried to sound casual. 'Ian still not back?'

Her face fell, and she turned her back again, stirring what was an already perfectly stirred bowl of icing. 'Not yet. I can't think why.'

I can, he thought. Absently he began taking knives and forks from a drawer and laying them on the table for supper. Forgetting, he said, 'Probably held up in traffic.'

Her voice was dry. 'On foot, dear? I hardly think so.'

He felt stupid. 'He'll be back the minute you serve the food. Smell it a mile off, he will.' Now he got plates from a shelf and pushed them into the bottom of the oven to warm, set fresh bread on the board, ready to cut.

Kate stood wiping steam off her glasses and did not look at him. 'Yes, yes, of course.'

He almost wished—then felt guilty for wishing it—that his brother would not come home at all. 'You worry too much about Ian,' he said. But he knew it wasn't worry: just disappointment, and not for the first—or last—time.

'I don't *worry*,' she said fiercely.

Jack came and stood at the doorway as Michael had done before. He was wiping earth off his hands, and Michael smelled the rich, bright smell of dahlias on him. 'You don't *worry*, love,' Jack echoed softly. 'Just fret yourself to death, that's all.'

She folded an invisible strand of hair back into place. 'Perhaps.'

Jack went to the sink and washed his hands. 'Is supper ready yet? I'm hungry.'

'Yes, it's ready. All except icing the cake, and I'll do that shortly.'

Michael saw her distress. 'I'll make tea, shall I?'

'Do. That's kind.' His mother's cheerful tone sounded forced, but he felt foolishly pleased that for once she had noticed him enough to commend him. Now she was counting out birthday candles, reckoning the length of ribbon she would need for the edge of the cake, and cutting it with a precise clip of the scissors.

Sitting around the table a few minutes later, the three of them stared at each other uneasily. Michael made himself sit still, though it was all he could do not to jump up and rush out, away from the tension in his father's face and the unhappiness in his mother's eyes.

At last Jack said resolutely, 'Well, it's a pity, but we'll start without Ian, I'm afraid.' He made the sign of the cross, bowed his head, and blessed the food.

When Michael looked up, he saw that his mother's cheeks were wet. Indignation at his brother's selfishness filled him. No matter how hard to please his mother often seemed, he hated to see her hurt.

They ate in silence the aromatic curry and tossed salad that were Ian's favourites. As they chewed, he could see the clouds gathering both outside the window and on his father's face. The front hall clock ticked the minutes hollowly, chimed the quarter hours, somehow made the empty fourth chair seem all the more empty.

Afterwards, Jack got up and leaned over Kate to put his arms around her. 'Never mind, sweetheart,' Michael heard him murmur. 'He's just a silly, forgetful fool. Go on—get your jacket, and let's take ourselves for a wee walk, if we're going.'

He could see that his mother would rather have stayed at home, but she went all the same to the coat cupboard in the front hall and pulled out a light jacket and headscarf. Michael opened the door and breathed in the smell of rain on the wind.

His father stopped behind him. 'It'll blow over,' he said. 'Nothing much. Come on.'

They took his father's rattling car to the edge of the estate and parked it in a layby. The shower had stopped already. A grey stone marked the public footpath, and they climbed the downs steadily, the town dwindling behind them under the watery sky. The breeze was fresh, clouds racing overhead.

Michael went in front, stopping here and there to pick a few blackberries or to examine a plant he did not recognize. His parents followed close behind, his mother's scarf flapping like a flag in the wind. His lungs felt clean, his head clear of any anxiety he had felt before about telling them news they would not welcome.

They reached the waymark on the highest point of the Weald and stopped, breathing hard, beside it. There was no need to talk yet, he decided, and all three turned to look back. Below them and to the east, a string of horses in a field, and white stables bright in the sunshine that came fitfully between the clouds; ragged lines of oaks along the hedge of a field; straggling woods, thinned out by the storm of a few years ago, covering another ridge of the downs; to the west, harvested pea fields stripped, stems flattened by the breeze and the machines. Kent: home for his parents, but still not for him.

His mother's face was flushed pink from the climb, her eyes full of delight. Had she forgotten about Ian for a moment?

He took a deep breath. 'There's something I need to say to you.'

Jack dropped into the rough grass beside the marker. He looked cheerier, restored by the air and the climb.

'Isn't it wet?' Kate asked.

Michael stretched out beside his father. 'Only a little, Mum.'

'Say on, Michael.' Jack was looking at him closely.

Michael saw a tremor of anxiety cross his father's face. 'Not with Mum standing up there so uncomfortable—please, look, here's my sweater.' He pulled it off before she could protest, and reached to lay it on the other side of his father, so that she would not sit close to him, would not be able to intimidate him with her frightening blue eyes.

Reluctantly, Kate lowered herself to the ground. She didn't look at him, however, turning instead to let her gaze rest on the fields below.

He was relieved. 'You're not going to like this.'

Jack smiled faintly. 'Get it out, then. I knew you had something brewing.'

Suddenly he didn't know where to start. What else could he do but blurt it out, whatever way the words came to him? He had never been a mooth talker, like Ian—at least, not with his parents.

'I've decided I'm not going back to university.' He paused, hearing his mother's sharp intake of breath. 'I know it was what you always wanted for me. And I can't make a big speech or argue my case like a cleverclogs—sorry. But it isn't right for me. That's all I know.'

Again he knew what his mother would say almost before the words were out, and she said them, right on cue. 'Have you prayed about this?'

'Of course I have, Mum.' He made his voice gentle.

'Go on,' Jack urged.

'This job I've done this summer—I've never been so happy. It's the best time I've had doing anything.' He remembered Marie, dancing with him at the wedding. 'Well, almost. And I've had it with exams and books. Biology's all very well, but I'd rather do it than learn it.'

'Things are different these days, Michael.' Jack spoke quickly. 'You need a degree, so you do. Farmers are managers and thinkers, not just peasants like my people were.'

'So everyone says. But I've thought about it for weeks, and I know what I want to do more than anything. And it's not going back to Brighton, believe me.'

'I thought there was a girl there.' Jack gave him a half smile of encouragement.

He looked into the grass beside him and watched a small creature travelling arduously across the jungle of greenery. 'There *was*. Not now. She's getting married—leaving, in fact.'

Kate's voice was sharp. 'I hope that's not why you want to leave, is it?'

'Nothing to do with her. But I'm not going back for the last year, Mum.'

He knew they would not try to twist his words or make him feel guilty—whatever else they might do. There would be no reproaches about how he had not considered them, about the sacrifices they had made … there would be no waving of tearful white handkerchiefs to send him away guilt-ridden, submissive, with his tail between his legs. Yes, they might be angry, disappointed; they might spend hours trying to talk him round to their way of thinking, but they wouldn't do anything underhand.

'Go on then,' his father prompted again. 'Let's hear your reasons before the next rain's on us.'

Michael looked up at the clouds. If anything, for the moment, they seemed to be rising, blowing away. 'I've earned almost enough. Another week or two and I'll be ready. I'm going to the States.'

His mother sat very still, her eyes still on the valley below them. 'And what gave you that idea? Would you mind explaining? Michael, I know you're old enough to make up your own mind about things.' She leaned forward and flashed a look at his father. 'We'd be the last people to stop you becoming independent, self-sufficient. But America … why?'

Jack picked a tuft of grass and pulled out the sweet inner stalk. He sucked on the end of it and eyed Michael shrewdly. 'Not just why. What about when? I mean, when did you come up with this idea?'

He felt suddenly embarrassed, caught in what he knew his mother, at least, would think was arrant sentimentality. It was his turn, now, to look away at the melting horizon. 'Three weeks ago,' he said carefully.

'It wasn't around the time of Frank's wedding by any chance, was it?'

'Yes.'

They said nothing for a minute. They didn't have to. Ian had mocked and teased him about Marie for days after the wedding, and they must have seen the stamped airmail letters sealed and ready for the post. *Michael—the man who never writes letters.*

He decided not to wait for them. The initiative was his. The future was his, too. 'I know what you're thinking,' he said. 'And I have to admit it, I like Marie. That was part of it. But not all of it. Dad, Mum—I need to get away.'

'But a degree will open up so many things for you, Michael.'

'It might have. But it's making me unhappy, too. I'm going nowhere with biology. If I did stay, it'd be a third class degree at best—and that's not good enough, is it? There's nothing for me there. Nothing.' He held up his hands. 'This is how I want to work. Dad—' He directed a look of appeal at his father. 'Surely *you* understand?'

His father's eyes were softer than his mother's. 'In a way. Only I did it all backwards, and maybe you will ... Well, it wasn't easy going back to the books at twenty-five. Discovered after a few years of carpentry that I had a brain after all—and wanted to use it.'

Michael felt he was gaining a slight advantage. 'And are you using it with those kids? Are you using it in the really messy bits of your work?'

'Yes—and no. Not obviously. But without a degree I would never have thought through some of the important issues I face daily, these days.'

Michael shook his head. 'I can't believe that. I don't think you believe that either. You're only saying it because you know what Mum thinks.' He could hardly credit that the words were out. He had never before dared to be so blunt to his parents—especially about themselves, his perception of them.

He found a small stone under his hand and tossed it down the path. It rolled, bumping on the chalky dirt, and disappeared. From the woods behind them a warbler cried, answered by one nearer, in the gorse bushes below them. 'I've got to get away, that's all.'

'And see Marie,' his father persisted.

'I want to see her, yes.' Then he remembered stories they had told him as he was growing up, stories of how they themselves had met and fallen in love. It was hard to resist the opportunity those stories gave him now. 'Just a minute. I seem to remember that you both thought there was no chance for the two of you—once.'

'Michael!' His mother was shocked, slightly amused.

'It's true, isn't it?' he pursued.

Jack suddenly lay back and laughed, laughed hard, putting his big hands over his face. Then he sat up and grabbed Kate's hand. 'He's got us there, you know.'

'You told me—' he began, laughing himself, infected by his father's dancing eyes and mother's flushed face. 'There you were, Dad, bound for the priesthood. In Derry, right near where we used to live, wasn't it?' He knew perfectly well where it was, and how badly the Monaghan clan had first reacted when Jack had told them about his mother. 'And you, Mum . . .'

'Don't.'

'Let the eejit prattle on if he wants,' his father said. 'I'm rather enjoying this conversation.'

Michael grinned at his father. Now he was enjoying himself, too. 'I seem to remember hearing you were the very proper daughter of the manse, Mum. Not exactly a candidate for a good Catholic wife. And Grandfather Hamilton—'

'Hush!' Jack's back straightened, and his face turned serious. 'That's taking it too far.'

He trod more carefully. 'But you knew what was right for you. They would have said, surely, that you were too young. But you weren't.'

'Your mother was, at least.' The leprechaun wit of his father showed itself again, irresistibly, and Michael crowed with laughter.

Kate took it seriously. 'You're right. I was too young. But God is merciful, very merciful. And what we did was right.' A note of defiance that he recognized and appreciated crept into her voice. 'We were right for each other, no matter what anyone said.'

Michael pressed his advantage. 'I can't say I've got any such conviction about Marie. Of course not. Look, I'm not a fool. But I'm quite certain it's time I was out of this house. You don't want to stop me going—you've said so. You don't want me to go to America—you've said that too. But it's only for a while. How do I know what I'll find there, or what I'll do afterwards? And whatever happens—' He stopped, fumbling for the words. 'It's farming for me. Just like it was college for you both, then social work for you, Dad, and teaching for you, Mum. You both knew what you had to do. And I know what I have to do.'

'Simple as that,' his father said wryly.

'Simple, and very complicated as well,' his mother amended.

He didn't want them to follow that argument too far. 'I've thought it through—the practical things as well. I can tell you about them any time—once I've booked the flight.'

Jack's hand came and rested on his shoulder. 'Now you've told us what you want, don't be in any mad rush to book the flight—tomorrow, or some daft thing like that. I can help you. We'll pay for your ticket—an open return ticket. You save your money for the expenses you'll have when you get there.'

He shut his eyes and sighed. So they had accepted it, perhaps even anticipated it.

'You can't depend on Marie's family for long, and you can't live on nothing.' His mother was more grudging than his father. 'I could write to Deirdre and Liam and see—'

He wanted to escape their influence completely. 'No! For once I want to do things completely on my own. I've never met your friends the Donnellys in my life, and I'm not going to wash up on their doorstep like some old piece of flotsam and ask for a roof. I've got other plans, as I said.' He scrambled up, dusting off the chalk. He wanted to seal the conversation and set it aside, get on with living, not talking about it. But all he could think of now was something irrelevant and trivial. 'I wish we'd brought a box for the blackberries.'

His mother, for once, seemed willing to abandon the argument for the present and to take up the new thread of his thinking. She actually laughed. 'All right. I've got a bag in my pocket. I'll make a pie with them tomorrow.'

It began to rain as they zigzagged down the path again. The fields below looked smudged, the stables commonplace and dirty. They didn't bother to stop for blackberries, after all.

Michael's hair was plastered to his head by the time they reached the car again, and they fell dripping into the car, relieved by its dry warmth, hearing the rain splatter and patter on the metal roof.

'Ian'll certainly be home by now,' his mother said. She pulled down the visor mirror and began wiping her face and hair with her headscarf.

Twilight seemed to have come, brought tonight by the clouds, not the lateness of the day. The garden looked murky, drenched, the flowers drooping even where Kate had tied them up. But when they stepped inside, the house felt pleasantly warm. Michael could be detached now. It was as if the conversation had not happened—now that they had talked of blackberries and birthdays; yet everything had changed.

The downstairs was silent. No lights anywhere.

He switched on the hall light and caught the bleak expression, naked on his mother's face, because Ian wasn't at home after all.

Then the telephone shrilled. He picked it up. Someone wanting his father—a crisis at the children's home. They'd been trying to reach him for an hour. Could he come—and right away?

'I'd better be away out, Kate,' Jack said.

'I know. Go on, then.'

Michael was stabbed with tenderness for his mother. Ian's birthday. His cake cooled and perfect for a perfect icing, waiting on the kitchen table for him. A meal shrivelling in the oven. *Ian's a thoughtless so-and-so,* he thought—wanted to say it. But didn't.

He saw his father take his mother in his arms; heard the whispered, 'I'll be back as soon as I can. And Ian'll be back, too, love.' Then Jack opened the front door.

Kate stood framed in it, the darkness beyond her shadowing almost everything. 'It's stopped raining again,' she noted mechanically.

Michael felt so sorry for her. He stood hovering behind her, watching his father duck under the watery syringa leaves and step out onto the pavement.

'The moon's coming up,' his father called back out of the darkness. 'Look, both of you!' And he went off whistling some Irish tune Michael did not know.

Kate shut the front door and leaned back against it looking ten years older than at supper time.

He did not know what to say and so grabbed again for the first silly question that crossed his mind. 'What was that he was whistling just now?'

His mother gave him a thin smile. Her cheeks were still pink from the walk. She seemed to be thinking of something a long way off. 'It's "The Rising of the Moon",' she answered.

He went into the kitchen and made them another pot of tea. As the water boiled, he heard her footsteps on the bare wood of the dining room—a room they hardly used because the broad kitchen table was easier. Then he heard the lid of the piano go back, and the first notes of 'Moonlight Sonata' drift magically from her fingertips to his ears. The piano—always her place of comfort, her refuge.

He slumped in an easy chair in the front room, listening, full of an unnamable kind of longing. Beside him, the tea grew cold, and his mother played on.

Later, in bed, and after his father had returned, he heard the front door and knew Ian had come back. Their voices came up the stairs: his mother's sad, his father's terse, Ian's cheery, then defensive. He couldn't hear more than a few of their words, but it wasn't hard to guess what was being said.

He rolled over, away from the door, to block out the sound of them. Tomorrow they would eat a birthday meal together and cut the cake. Ian's selfishness would be forgotten. His own small efforts to please his mother would go unnoticed again. It would not matter that he was leaving—even though it would matter very much to himself. It would not matter because when Ian was at home his parents seemed quite contained and content. *Outsider,* he thought. He sighed in the dark. *Time to get out!*

When he came downstairs to the kitchen at five-thirty the next morning, ready to go and help with the milking, the birthday cake was cut to pieces, half burned candles strewn on three plates and on the tablecloth. They had eaten it without him.

6

For the second time since the taxi driver had left him on the corner, Michael stopped and lowered his bags to the sidewalk. For the second time he pulled out the crumpled paper on which he'd scribbled the directions he'd been given at Logan Airport. For the second time he reread them, wiped away the sweat that was trickling down his neck, then went on. His two bags felt leaden, his feet swollen from the long journey.

For a late September day, the heat seemed unnatural, stifling. In the parched yards on either side of the wide street autumn flowers bloomed, but the grass looked spindly and dusty. An unearthly quiet hung over the suburbs—parents at work, children at school, rusted leaves hanging limp in the still air, and no birds singing. He glanced up at the brassy sky. What the city needed was a good thunderstorm.

He counted the numbers, wrought iron and ornamental enamel, that were fixed against the clapboard walls and mailboxes of each house. One thousand and fifty-eight, one thousand and sixty. The street was far longer than he had expected... *One thousand and ninety-six.*

He stood at the foot of the paved path that led to the Williams' front porch. His tongue stuck to the roof of his mouth, and his stomach felt hollow. He saw that their driveway was empty of cars, and he felt a wash of unexpected relief. The meeting he wanted but dreaded would be postponed just a little longer. He wouldn't have to listen, yet, to her uncomfortable excuses about why she hadn't answered his letters. He wouldn't have to explain, yet, why he was standing outside her house.

It did not occur to him to ring the doorbell. Instead he went down the path at the side of the house. He would wait in the back yard. In the stillness he heard only the soft pad, pad of his trainers on the hot stones. His head felt disconnected from his shoulders, his body tense with jetlag, anticipation and anxiety.

He rounded the corner of the house. Dressed in a ruched swimsuit and big sunglasses, Marie herself was stretched on a garden chair at the back. Books, some opened, lay scattered on the patio beside her. Another book was just sliding out of her hands; she was half asleep.

He hesitated in surprise. His daydreams suddenly crystallized into reality.

He saw her stiffen, fling the book aside, and make for the sliding doors. Without a word she was inside, the screen clicking behind her, before he could step onto the patio.

Suddenly he felt exhausted. On one shoulder the sleeping bag weighed on him like a roll of hot, damp dough. On the other his holdall seemed to bend him to one side. He could see her shadow inside the screen door, and he could not understand her reaction; he had made no effort to conceal his approach. Surely she must have recognized him? He heard her gasp, and he came right up to the dark mesh of the screen. He could not yet make out her features on the other side, but he had seen enough of her, lying there, to know he'd made no mistake about the address. 'I frightened you. I'm sorry. I didn't think you'd be here.' It was like speaking to a disembodied creature, and he found himself gabbling something else about expecting the house to be empty, before she found her voice.

'Michael Monaghan!'

'Marie.' Now he pressed his face against the screen, put his hand to the catch to push it open; but it was locked. He tried to collect himself.

There was a rustling noise, and he saw her make a quick movement. Then she slid the lock across and rolled the screen door to one side. 'Michael, you—what? I mean, what—why? How on earth did you—?'

Now that he had finally arrived in Massachusetts the conversation he had rehearsed for so long in his mind did not seem so daunting after all. He lowered his bags to the stones and laughed up at her. In a loose wrap that she had thrown round her body, she stood in the doorway with her mouth half open. 'I said I'd drop in when I came to Boston. Remember?' He felt his face burning with the pleasure of seeing her again.

She was stuttering with confusion. 'But you didn't say—you didn't tell me you were—what *are* you doing over here?'

He threw his hands out. It would be easiest to give the bare facts, to start with. 'Well, it's quite simple, really. I've just come from Logan Airport. Before that from Heathrow.' He heard the dry, teasing note in his own voice, but then he panicked. She would think him obsessive, strange. He faltered somewhat, felt the colour draining from his face again. He was tired, unsure of his welcome.

Her face changed, full of pity. She stepped aside, and reached for his arm. 'Look, I'm sorry. I don't know what I'm thinking of. Come in. Just come in, will you? I'll fix you a cold drink. You can crash out if you want, talk if you want—whatever.'

'I didn't expect to find you at home.'

'It's Monday,' she said airily, as if that explained everything.

'But you said you were at college.' He let her lead him to a recliner, and she insisted on moving his bags into the front hall.

'I'm not on vacation, silly. No classes on Monday afternoons, that's all. I usually come home to study. Today I couldn't resist the call of the sunshine . . . I fell asleep. Then you—'

'Woke you up. Sorry. I hope I'm—' He stopped. *A pleasant surprise.* No, he couldn't say it, too uncertain of her reaction.

She perched on the arm of a chair on the other side of the family room, and he scrutinized her face. She looked bewildered, a little annoyed, but she was smiling with surprise and pleasure, as well. 'You've knocked me out, arriving like that.'

'Good. That was the whole idea. Now, what about that cold drink you mentioned?'

She jumped up and disappeared through louvred swing doors into the kitchen. Through the slats he could see and hear her moving about: the fridge opening, ice being cracked out of a box, water running, a cupboard shutting, a ceiling fan turning lazily in the heat. *Take it slowly,* he prompted, still not believing, himself, that he was sitting in her house at last.

He took the iced tea she offered, gulped it fast, then realized it was quite bitter, unlike anything he'd tasted before. He pulled a wry face, then laughed. 'I'm not sure I like this, but it's certainly what I need just now. I feel as dried out as your front lawn.' He rubbed his jaw, felt the rasp of stubble against his palm. 'It's mid-evening on my clock, you know, but it feels more like midnight.'

'I guess it would.'

He rested his head on the back of the chair, and a wave of sleep towered over him. He could not give in yet. 'Where do I start?'

She returned to her perch on the arm of the other chair. 'I was wondering the same. Go on. Explain.'

He looked up at her, taken aback by the sudden assertiveness in her voice. For a moment she sounded sharp, not unlike his mother, and he didn't like it. But she was right. He couldn't land in her house like a beached whale without a convincing story to explain himself.

He swirled the ice cubes in his glass, drank again, then took a steadying breath. 'I'd already decided to make the break from home some time soon. I think I told you that, when we met.' Images of the wedding unreeled in his head. They seemed to belong in another life. It was impossible to imagine now that that he had ever considered anything else but coming to America. 'I was due back at university now—this week. I couldn't face it.' He shrugged. He was sounding defeatist.'No, it's more than that, Marie. University doesn't have anything to do with what I want for my life.'

She flashed him a mischievous smile, white between the golden planes of her cheeks. 'Being on the move does, though?'

He shook his head. 'Not travelling, per se, that's not it.' Somehow it was even harder to explain it to Marie than to his family. He reached for the words, but they slid away, and what he said came out disjointedly. 'It sounds mad, perhaps... I don't know yet where I want to be, where I *should* be. Oh, I do know what I want to do, though. Farming—I told you.' He stopped, and she nodded. 'I'd decided that I'd have to leave home soon if I was to find out. Meeting you—' He caught her eyes directly for the first time since she had stared at him through the screen. 'Meeting you was like a catalyst.' *There*. He had got out the most important thing he wanted to say.

She eased off the arm of her chair and sank into the seat, giggling. 'I bet you say that to all the women you meet.'

He wished she could take him seriously for a moment, wished he knew how to make her *hear* him. 'No—no,' he stammered. 'I don't, not in the least.' He felt he was losing ground, that what he wanted to say— that all he was grasping for—was slipping away. 'I remember telling you I would quite fancy this part of the world. I'd only thought of it in passing before. Never considered it properly until then. After the wedding, I thought, well, why not?'

'If you didn't go right away, you'd never get away?' Her voice was flat. 'Yes. That's it, exactly.'

The corners of her mouth twisted slightly, sceptically. 'But it's not too practical, is it? I mean—'

He didn't want to wait for her to state the obvious. 'Of course I can't stay here. I know that as well as you do, and I won't sponge off your family. But d'you think your mother would let me stay for a bit—until I can work out what's next?' His pulse beat thickly in his throat, clotting his voice.

The house was quiet except for the slow whirring of the fan blade in the kitchen. His question hung heavy in the air. He felt again the weight of emotion that had impelled the question, the weeks of hoping and dreaming, as real to him as the weight of his bags, when he had walked down the street to her house.

He saw her turn everything over in her mind. The look of faint alarm melted into fresh cheerfulness. 'I'm sure you can visit here a few nights. Mama won't care. She's out all day, most days. I'm usually down at the community college. You can have the run of the place. She may have some ideas for you.'

His hopes lifted, and he sat forward in the chair. He was still fighting off sleep, but feeling now like a schoolboy let loose in a huge new playground. 'That'd be good.'

She eyed him shrewdly. 'Listen, it's none of my business, but d'you have enough cash? I'm not sure what Ma—'

He frowned indignantly. *What kind of a bloke does she think I am?* 'I wouldn't have come if I hadn't enough for a few weeks, at least, don't worry.'

'Things are more expensive here—even more than in London.'

'I said don't worry.'

'Fine.' She stood up. 'I'll see which of my brothers' rooms would suit you better.' She glanced at the clock above the fireplace. 'Ma will be home any time.'

He shut his eyes. Time to give in to the cresting tide of sleep. 'Thanks. I'm shattered, all of a sudden.'

'You want to sleep now—not wait and crash out at the same time as we do?'

'I could sleep till the crack of doom, the way I feel now. Nothing'll stop me, I'm afraid.'

She left him dozing in the chair, and he heard her mount the stairs, somewhere in the distance.

'There's a room sort of ready for you—upstairs. My older brother's.' She was standing over him, had given him a small shake.

He surfaced reluctantly and heaved himself out of the recliner.

In the narrow hallway upstairs she pushed open a door. 'Welcome to Jack Williams' room. He's long gone. Would probably be glad to know someone was using it. I hope it's quiet enough for you. This house has thinner walls than most.'

'I'm sure I won't hear a thing.'

A faded quilt was tucked loosely onto the mattress, and though the shelves were dusty, the books that had been left behind were arranged tidily on them. Baseball and football pennants decorated the room, but they were curled at the edges; they had hung on the walls for years. The carpet's pile was still in neat stripes as if the room had been vacuumed, then no one had stepped into it for weeks.

Marie had opened the windows and put fresh towels on the rail by the sink. He felt pathetically grateful for these small marks of hospitality, then foolish for thinking that way. Quite plainly, she had spared little thought for him since the wedding. Her life had moved on without him. She was a self-contained person; she would not want him, would not need him—not the way he wanted her, at least.

His mind shut down. He couldn't analyze and wonder any more. Only sleep.

Nothing—not the arrival of Marie's mother, not the thunder that later growled over the rooftops—nothing woke him until the morning.

Voices below, from the family room and kitchen, dragged him to consciousness. At first he could not think whose they were; then he remembered. He rolled over and lay still, his mind working slowly. His body told him that it was the middle of the day, and that he should get up immediately. But the thin morning light that filtered through the curtains told him it was still early. He recognized Rita's voice, then Marie's—more bell-like—in answer. They must think he was still asleep, and were making no effort to speak softly.

'I don't care if he's around for a few days, Marie.'

'You sure?'

'Sure I'm sure. He can go with me to the marina, if he wants. He won't want to sit around here all day while you're down at the college. There're several projects he could take care of for me.'

'Like what, Ma? Listen, I don't think he came—'

'Then what did he come for, Marie?' Rita's voice was unexpectedly ascerbic. 'As far as I'm concerned, if he's going to be here a few days, he can lend a hand. I'll pay him, naturally. A little more cash ought to come in useful. I don't see how he's gonna work out where he wants to be just bumming around Bedford, do you?'

Michael shifted uneasily. Rita's words had a relentless and frightening logic to them. The plans he had made just to get himself to Boston now seemed shallow and unformed; he hadn't properly thought out the next step.

'OK, Ma. You're right, I guess.'

'He can lift all the summer flowers out of the windowboxes for me, for a start. There's some painting I want done round the back of the office, and a couple boats need scraping down before they go up for the winter. That'd keep him busy till the end of the week, anyhow.'

Michael pictured himself, for a wild moment, as a peasant boy in a medieval folktale, slaving for the hand of a princess he loved. But then the images came shattering down.

'He's not visiting here long, though.'

'Fine with me.' Marie sounded uncomfortable.

'But I thought—'

'It was his idea to come here.' The answer came quickly. 'Not mine.'

'Just as well, honey.'

'But he's very cute, don't you think?'

Michael smiled to himself, the lopsided smile that he'd always been teased about… it appealed to Marie. At least there was one point in his favour.

Rita sounded prickly. 'I wasn't so unaware at the wedding that I couldn't see that for myself, Marie. I do have eyes in my head, you know.'

'We can hardly turn away a sort of cousin, now, can we?'

'Shirt-tail relation, I suppose. But that's not the point. I hope we can offer at least reasonable hospitality when a man comes asking for it. Anyhow, what'll he do next?'

Michael wished again that he couldn't hear. He was torn between putting his hands over his ears and sitting up, overcome with curiosity, to listen even more closely.

Marie sounded thoughtful. He could picture her shrugging, sitting on the arm of the big chair as she and her mother called to one another from one room to the other. 'I'm not even sure he knows himself. Travel, that's for certain, though he's says that's not the only motivation. Find work on a farm. Oh, I don't know.'

'Well—' Rita's voice fell lower. 'He's not our responsibility, not really. I'm happy to help you set him on his way, but that's all.'

There were more murmurings as they moved in and out of rooms downstairs, their words now indistinguishable. But he had heard enough. He was welcome for a week. No more.

Someone came upstairs, paused outside his room, then went down again. He heard the front door open, heard quick steps across the wooden planks of the front porch, then the door closing again. Marie was shouting something about the morning paper.

He found his watch. Rita would want to talk to him, would need to leave for work. Wide awake now, he pushed back the bedclothes and looked outside, as he always did first thing in the day. The weather had changed completely. A storm had chased away the late hot weather and left the world cooler and more crisp. A light frost edged the bushes below the window, and he gaped at it, dazed by the abrupt transformation.

He showered and shaved quickly. In the mirror above the sink, he looked critically at his own blue eyes and white-gold hair. Familiar, but somehow different this morning above the lather of his equally familiar shaving cream. The light was different; that was it. He stuck his tongue out at his reflection, grinned, and began to sing so that he could concentrate well enough to avoid cutting himself. *You can work this out,* he thought. *Just getting here, escaping, that was half the battle.*

In the kitchen Marie was buttering toast and reading the *Boston Herald* at the same time. The washing machine swished in the background. Her head was bent so that he could see the soft nape of her neck, the dark sheen of her hair.

'Hello. You look nice.' He was dazzled by her.

She reached for another slice of bread and rammed it into the toaster. She was brusque, almost guilty, as if she guessed he might have overheard all they had said. 'Thanks. Sleep well?'

'Like the dead.'

She looked relieved. 'What have you decided?'

He tried to keep a straight face. 'I'd like to take up your offer and stay.' He held up his hand. 'Look, don't panic. Just for a few days, while I think about things.'

Rita swung into the kitchen, bringing in a draft of cold air. Her arms were full of flowers. 'Well, Michael! You're up.' Her smile looked genuine enough, and he would have warmed to her if he had not heard their conversation. 'Welcome to Massachusetts.'

He shook her hand but knew his politeness sounded strained. 'Thank you. I'm glad to be here, Mrs Williams.'

'I've just been out back. You brought the fall weather with you, Michael. Look—these daisies and chrysanthemums are the only thing the frost didn't wipe out.'

He murmured something non-committal and helped himself to the bread Marie had sliced. Rita ran water into a vase and stuffed the flowers anywhichway into it. He watched her, imagining his mother's painstaking method of flower arrangement, the careful way she cut each flower, balancing it for length and colour.

But Rita had other things on her mind. 'Marie, what time will you be back tonight? Any idea?'

Marie flushed. 'Since when do you ask me stuff like that?'

'It's just that tonight—after supper—the senator will be here for a while.'

Michael waited for the toaster and went on watching the two women. He wondered why Marie's face suddenly had a distant look, as if she were remembering something or someone, not thinking at all of what her mother was saying.

'He's coming again? What does he want?' Marie asked. 'Does it make any difference if I'm back when he comes?'

'We've got—it's business. He may—' Rita stopped on the verge of saying more.

'Oh, well, I'm sure it's nothing to do with me, anyhow.'

'Maybe you and Michael could—'

Marie threw a quick look at Michael that made him feel acutely embarrassed. 'No, Mama,' she said firmly. 'I gotta study. And Michael wouldn't want to go out on his first night here.' She was talking fast, as if to forestall them both. 'Especially if he's been slaving all day at the marina.'

Slaving. He laughed. 'So that's what you've planned for me?'

Rita was not meeting his eye. She said quickly, 'Yes, if that's OK. Just this week, to set you up.'

'Those jobs you gave me "set me up" all right,' Michael joked later when he and Rita returned through the front door. He had spent the day stretching from a ladder to paint the back wall of the marina office. Now he was thirsty, his shoulders ached—but he felt Rita had half accepted him—for a few days, at least; he knew he had been useful to her.

She gave him a weary smile. 'You were great, Mike.'

He did not trouble to correct her. 'I enjoyed myself.' He scowled. 'Well, some of the time, anyway.'

They followed the smell of Italian food into the kitchen. Marie stood with her back to the door, her shoulders as taut as his own. She said 'hi' but did not look round.

He could not help eyeing her up and down appreciatively. For a second he thought of the way Ian looked at women, but the memory melted away like the steam from the boiling pasta. 'Something smells lovely.'

'That's what you're supposed to say.' She turned. Her face was pink, her apron splattered with spaghetti sauce. 'I thought I'd have this ready for you, Ma—with McEnroe coming, and all.'

Rita nodded and poured herself a mug of coffee. 'For you too, Michael? Thanks, honey. We're both bushwhacked.'

Michael sniffed. 'Onions. Tomatoes. Good stuff.'

'Tom*ay*toes,' Marie laughed.

'Tom*ah*toes.'

Rita frowned. 'Quit it, for pete's sake. The senator will be here before we know it.'

At the formal dining room table, so much in contrast with the battered old kitchen table he was used to at home, Michael told Marie what he had seen and done at the marina. 'I'd never make a sailor,' he said eventually. 'Give me the earth under my feet.'

'You just don't know till you've been out in a boat,' Rita said simply. 'It's a contagion for a lot of folk we know.'

'Not me. I'm immune.' He looked at Marie.

'You'd rather be up to your knees in a barn, I'll bet.' She winked.

He looked away from her through the front window, thinking of Ian again. Some of the old conflict bit into him.

'Sorry,' she said unhappily. 'That wasn't kind. But I thought you wanted to learn to sail, anyway.' Her face coloured again. 'That's the deal we made at the wedding. You would teach me to dance, and I would teach you to sail.'

'Believe me, I hadn't forgotten.'

'Mind you, I'd be a useless teacher, anyhow.'

Rita laughed. 'Yes. We had kind of a—'

'—close shave. This summer. Rachel McEnroe came out with me in "The Harrier".'

'Both nearly drowned.'

Michael felt bewildered by the way they spoke, breathlessly finishing each other's sentences, completely attuned to each other, even when the conversation veered off in a new direction.

'The McEnroes' granddaughter,' Rita explained. 'You'll see the grandfather this evening. Remember I told you about him on our way out this morning?'

Marie's eyes were suddenly shuttered; her lips thinned.

Michael swallowed his next bite uneasily. Had Rita confided in him things she hadn't even told Marie? Here were puzzles he did not understand. All he had learned was that a few years ago Bert Williams had died; the two sons had left; and Rita was in constant worry over some sort of scandal that had rocked Lynn Harbor at the same time. He had felt unable to ask her about it, and clearly Marie also was in the dark about things.

He sighed heavily. There was no future here, whatever he might have wanted to think, whatever he might have hoped and dreamed.

The doorbell made them all jump.

'I didn't hear a car,' Rita said. She pushed back from the table. 'Clear up, would you, kids? I'll take the senator round the yard for a minute, to give you time to pick up in here. Then I want to sit in here, with the table, while the senator's with me.' And she hustled into the front hall.

Marie looked directly at Michael. 'I've had enough of this. Even Senator McEnroe knows what dirty dishes look like. And I want to know what the heck's going on.' Her face was mutinous. 'I'm not leaving this room till I find out.' Again Michael felt bewildered by the sudden change in temperature. The room was full of electricity that had nothing to do with Marie's attractiveness. Something unhappy was going on behind the scenes.

'You can do what you like,' she added. 'Sit or move. Up to you.'

He stood up. 'Of course I don't want to be in on any private conversation. I'm sorry I'm here now, at the wrong—'

'No.' She looked chagrined, waving her hand in dismissal. 'No—there's been something bothering my mother for a long time. Especially since the middle of the summer, this year. And before that, as well.'

He wanted to put his arms round her, hurt by the anguish he suddenly saw in her eyes. But he knew it would be a clumsy and unwelcome gesture. 'Marie—'

'I'm OK,' she said.

'You don't look all right at all.' He felt miles away from her, and he knew her mind was following a very different course from his own. 'I feel like an intruder here. I don't mean to.' Then all his doubts came tumbling out. 'It seemed such a brilliant idea, at the time, to come and see you at home. But you're obviously very busy people. I won't be staying long.' Some of the joy had gone out of him.

She sounded savage, suddenly. 'Oh, don't put yourself down like that. This business Ma has with Julius McEnroe is nothing to do with you, nothing to do with anything in my life before, for that matter. But it bothers me how it affects *Ma* so much, whatever it is. I hate to see her so preoccupied and worried all the time. Things have started to get to me—not knowing, I mean.' She looked down. 'Especially when I sometimes think Ma talks to others before she'll talk to me.'

He stood up and pushed his hands into his jeans pockets. 'You needn't think she's said anything to me.'

'Maybe not. But she talks to McEnroe almost every week now, or to McEnroe's wife.' Marie shook her head, suddenly. 'Gee, I shouldn't be talking like this. Shouldn't be saying anything at all.'

'All right. I don't want to complicate things any more for you than necessary.' He moved to the door.

She looked at him as if she pitied him. 'You're not—not really.'

He stepped quickly, but not quickly enough, into the hall.

Rita was ushering a man through the front door. He seemed to fill the hall, his hair silver in the evening light, his head only inches below the tiffany lamp that hung just inside the door.

Behind him, Marie came dutifully to the door of the dining room and shook his hand. 'Senator McEnroe.'

'Great to see you, Marie,' he said. 'Prettier every day.'

Rita looked irritated that they were all caught together in the hallway. 'Er—McEnroe, I thought we'd just have a stroll outside while these young folk pick up for me. This way.'

The old man seemed unhurried, and curious. 'And who's this?' He nodded to Michael, smiling a slow smile.

'One of our ... relatives,' Rita answered. 'Michael. He's over from England for a while. Michael, this is Senator Julius McEnroe.'

A big hand reached for his. 'Michael. Glad to meet you. Nice name. You a Williams as well?'

Beside him, Marie sniggered. He felt the nervous tension that she radiated. 'No. The name's Monaghan. Just related by marriage, that's all.'

'You over here for long, son?'

'I'm not sure yet.'

Rita shuffled impatiently. 'Marie—make us all a cup of coffee, would you?'

Marie did not stir. She was apparently sizing something up, preparing to take a leap into something frightening.

'Go on!'

She seemed to reach a decision. Very quietly, she said, 'No, Mama. I won't be relegated to pouring your coffee.'

Rita bridled, throwing an uncomfortable glance at McEnroe. 'Why, what can you mean, Marie? Now listen here—'

'Mama, you listen to *me* just this once. You think I'm fresh outta elementary school! I'm not. D'you think I don't know how hard these last few years've been? It's been tough as anything, and you won't let me help with anything that matters. Bring the coffee. Make the supper. Clean up the kitchen. Gee, I've sure got more to offer than that. That's why I'm here, for goodness sake, and not away at some college in California or someplace.'

Michael stirred beside her. 'Please excuse me.'

'No, son, let's wait a minute.' McEnroe held up a restraining hand. He was obviously used to having his way, and Michael stopped. 'Now let's get to the bottom of this. Rita, she deserves a proper hearing before anyone jumps down her throat.'

Marie appealed to McEnroe now. 'Sir, I don't know why you're always coming here. But I'm sure as sure can be that something scary's going on. And I'm old enough to be involved.'

Rita's jaw was tight. 'You don't know what you're talking about.'

McEnroe shook his head slowly. 'Old enough to do one thing, at least.'

Marie stiffened. 'Mind my own business. That's what you're gonna say, I guess.'

They had all forgotten him, Michael realized. He heard in her voice the same defensiveness he sometimes heard in his own when he was at home in Kent. He felt sorry for her.

'No.' McEnroe's shaggy eyebrows curved upwards. 'No, no. I wasn't going to say that.' With a questioning look at Rita, he reached into his breast pocket and slowly lit a cigar. The hall misted with smoke. 'But you're old enough to listen.'

She folded her arms. 'To a lecture,' she snapped back.

He laughed. 'Honey, honey. Don't go all aggressive on me like that. C'mon. Let's sit down like sensible adults and talk this out.'

Rita's mouth compressed. 'I don't want Marie involved. I was surprised when your granddaughter was in on your discussions in the summer. But not Marie. I won't—'

'Let's just sit down in there,' Marie said tersely. 'Like the senator said.'

The dining room door shut behind them, and Michael fled into the family room. For the second time that day, the thin walls of the house gave up their secrets to him.

In the other room a chair scraped and dishes were clattered into a heap. Rita was apologizing about the mess.

The old man said, 'Marie, I just want you to hear me a minute.

111

You're worried about your mother? Well, you listen, and listen like you've never listened.'

'Are you sure—?' Rita's agitation was mounting.

'She should know, Rita, damn it all.'

'I'm listening,' Marie told him.

'You do that. Your mother's in on something I've been pursuing a long, long time.' He drew out the words. 'But neither of us knows exactly what's going to happen next, or when, or what the authorities will do. I need to explain. I don't know if you ever heard about it—you're too young—but my daughter Eleanor died of a drug overdose.'

'I heard rumours, but I didn't know.' Marie sounded quite cool, quite collected.

'She was trying to catch up with her lover, down in Miami. His name doesn't matter, Marie. He had a dozen aliases. Still does. A drug pusher, a big time peddlar doing a very dirty racket all the way up the East Coast. He came from Peru and made good in the cocaine rush of the sixties and seventies. But he was clever, and though the DEA sometimes caught up with his associates—never with him. Since then he's gotten lucky with crack and amphetamines, *frighteningly* successful.'

Michael was rivetted.

McEnroe's voice broke a little as he told the old story of his relentless pursuit of Ellie's killer. 'But Marie, he's back again. I'm out of legal things these days—officially—except for the fight I can wage on the senate floor on behalf of all young people hooked on those damn poisons, but there's one thing I'm not out of yet.' His voice became harsher. 'I can't rest while Eleanor's lover is still roaming this world looking for more poor fools to rob and dupe. The latest news is that he's got little cottage industries set up, duplicating bona fide amphetamines that used to be prescribed for dieting, and are still used in some decongestants. Perfect protypes of the stuff that comes out of the pharmaceutical industry. And as if that weren't enough, he's back to his old tricks of hiring kids—some as young as thirteen—to sell powdered amphetamines on the street—the same way he used to sell crack.'

For a moment McEnroe seemed to dry up.

Michael strained to hear. He knew he should have gone back upstairs to his room and shut the door, but this was compulsive listening.

'So how is Mama—what's all this to her?'

'We've been interviewing all marina owners, Marie. Not just your mother. We want everyone from Miami to Newport and on up to Lynn Harbor on the alert. This man's smooth as Corning glass. He'll sail in one day, debonair, full of slick talk, and get himself set up on shore again. We've got reason to think he may be up in the North-east again—operating something between here and Europe, we think. Everyone has to be watching. See, small marina owners are more vulnerable than the conglomerates. I didn't want your mother frightened any more than necessary. I wanted to talk to her myself. Give her some guidelines. Advise her on security. Offer some help with that security, if it's what she wants.' He cleared his throat. 'And every week, as I come over here or your mother comes to us, there's some little bit of news or progress.' He waited a moment. 'That's why I'm here again. That's why I wanted to talk with your mother. So now you know.'

Marie sounded stunned. 'I'm sorry. Maybe I was too inquisitive.'

'You were right to be.' The old man's voice had softened. 'Your mother needs to talk to someone she can trust, sometimes. You might be a pretty good candidate. I'll bet she's glad you're around.'

Silent for several minutes, Rita spoke then, now more relaxed. 'Thank you, McEnroe.'

'Marie,' the old man asked, 'Did all that make any sense to you?'

'Yes.'

'It's ugly, but it's the way things are now.'

Listening, Michael felt he had leapt from one world—the world of relatively smaller concerns for his future—to a different world: where people stole, betrayed each other, were imprisoned, and even died. An urban nightmare he wanted no part of.

A chair scraped again. 'Mama, I'll just—'

'Yes, go on and talk with Michael. I'll bet he's wondering what's going on.'

Michael picked up a magazine and tried to make sense of the print. He had never felt so foreign—or so useless to protect and help someone he cared about. He wished he could blot out some of the frightening things he had just heard, find something to laugh about, anything to restore his equilibrium.

He heard Marie hovering in the hallway, indecisive, so he got up again and stood in the doorway. Gently, he offered to make coffee for everyone, as Rita had requested earlier.

'Thanks.' She followed him across to the kitchen and pulled the curtains with a shiver. Darkness had fallen outside. She stood watching him dumbly. Michael thought she looked shell-shocked.

He filled the old-fashioned percolator as he had seen Rita do at breakfast, and the scent of coffee filled the room. Marie gave him a troubled smile. They did not speak, and he understood that he shouldn't break the silence.

Marie took steaming two cups into the dining room and returned immediately. 'Let's just sit for a while, can we?'

'Would you like to be on your own? As I said, I don't want to intrude.'

Her face was full of mute appeal. 'No, I'm kinda glad you're here, if I'm honest, after all.'

Warmth spread through him, but he didn't let himself hope too much.

After a while came the sound of the dining room door opening and the chink of coffee cups. Senator McEnroe stood in the lighted doorway, two cups in his big hands, and looked from one to the other. 'Didn't mean to intrude,' he said, winking at Marie, misreading the situation entirely, Michael thought.

I feel like an intruder, Michael had said. Now he smiled sadly at Marie.

'You're not,' Marie answered the old man quickly. 'Here, let me get those for you.'

'I'll tell Rachel I saw you, next time I call her,' he said. 'In fact I think I'll be seeing her in a few days.'

Marie brightened. 'Sure, OK. I owe her a letter. Tell her I'll write soon.' She flung a glance at Michael. 'Well, I'll try to, anyhow.'

He wondered who Rachel was, obviously so important to them all. Perhaps they saw the question on his face, because Rita interposed, 'Mr McEnroe's son has a farm in Western New York. Rachel's his daughter—a friend of Marie's.'

A farm in Western New York. He felt his heart speed up. 'Western New York? Is he a grain farmer, then, or a fruit farmer?'

McEnroe looked suitably impressed. 'My, you've done your homework,' he said. 'But it's neither. He's a dairy farmer.'

The room went quiet.

'I'm looking for a dairy farm,' he said slowly. 'I wonder—'

The mood in the room changed. Marie clapped her hands. 'Why didn't we think of it before? Rachel! Of course.' But then she looked at the senator. 'Wait, I guess Rachel's dad has enough going without someone arriving out of the blue and ...' Heat flared suddenly into her neck. She threw Michael a shamefaced glance and stopped.

McEnroe seemed to see nothing amiss. 'I'm sure he does, but don't pass up that idea altogether. You never know what's on the next green.' He grinned affably. 'Well, Rita, kids—' He rubbed his neck. 'It's getting late for an old guy. You gonna show me out?'

For the moment, Marie seemed to have forgotten the real occasion of the senator's visit. She was beaming.

Her mother came back from the front door. 'Now you calm down, girl,' she said. 'There's enough excitement around here already.'

Marie ignored her, laughing into Michael's eyes. 'It'd be the perfect plan. You need a farm. It's not that far—only five hundred miles.'

He flinched as if she had struck him. It had already become clear to him that American perceptions of distance were different from his own. *But five hundred miles ...!*

Rita sounded exhausted. 'Marie, there's a project for you.'

Marie looked momentarily deflated. 'Haven't I got—'

'Oh, don't get bent all out of shape! I mean—call McEnroes tomorrow for Michael, why don't you?'

He knew they meant well, but he also knew they would be relieved to see him settled somewhere else. He felt the familiar sting of rejection.

He sat alone in the family room for some time after the women had gone to bed. He would not sleep, now, with all he had just learned, with the possibilities they had just dreamed up battering his brain. Was it possible his old prayers were being answered in a way he could never have predicted? His last thoughts, when he did eventually turn off the light upstairs, was not of drug rings or even of Marie, but of a farm in a yet unknown country where he might find a place to belong at last.

Part Two

Ring of Roses

AUTUMN 1992

7

Michael had not been sorry to leave England. A pang as he looked back over his shoulder outside passport control at Heathrow airport. Just a slight pang as he saw his brother send him away with a mock salute and then link arms with both his parents. He would not miss a lifetime with them, he knew, the way he would miss Marie after only a few days.

It was McEnroe's fault, he decided, coming to the house on his second evening in Boston, full of news for Rita and Marie. News that echoed in every room, news that had distracted and worried them, so that he was no longer welcome. No, that wasn't fair, after all. It was the talk about the McEnroe family in Arcade that had spurred them all on. And above all it was Marie, her acrobatic mind flashing from one idea to the next, making a few phonecalls, *organizing* him . . . and before he knew what had happened, he was sitting next to a stranger in a narrow seat and waving goodbye to Marie and Rita through the tinted glass of the bus.

He couldn't have objected. He had arrived unannounced; the Williams were busy people; he knew he couldn't expect them to do much for him. He was too unsure of exactly what he wanted, too proud to ask, anyway. They had been kind enough for five days: just brisk about encouraging him to move on.

Except for the brief stop in Albany for a change of drivers and a cup of bitter tea in a fly-specked all-night cafe, he was unaware of the first part of the journey from Boston. He slept deeply through the Greyhound's grinding gears and shuddering hill climbs. He was exhausted. In his hand he clutched Marie's letter to Rachel, a fat envelope she had given him at their brief, half-embarrassed farewell.

When he did wake it was to blue half-light over unknown hills. In the shadows, they were like long-backed animals crouched on the horizon. He pressed his face to the cool glass, felt the draft of air-conditioning running down the glazing, and looked out onto miles of black trees. The night had bled the forests of all colour. Leaves, trees, trunks: all merged into cauliform black shapes. They in turn climbed the hills and melted into a vague sky; thin strands of mist hung over some of the slopes.

A few of the passengers stirred when a child began to wail wretchedly. Overhead reading lights came on.

Michael craned stiffly away from the window, careful not to wake his travelling companion, to look up the aisle.

'Five-thirty, nearabouts,' the driver announced in a low voice, to anyone who wanted to know.

There was a murmured response from one of the front seats, then everyone seemed to wake at once. Blinds went up; lights came on; people stretched, groaning, and pushed hair from their faces.

'We've got a scheduled stop about ten miles up the road,' the driver said, louder now. 'Rest stop and early bird special.'

Michael groaned. *You're an early bird,* Marie had said.

The man next to him woke. He squinted at Michael, frowned incuriously out of the window, then shut his eyes again. 'Nearly to Utica,' he said; he sounded jaded; he had made the journey a thousand times.

In the diner he sat among the other passengers but kept to himself. The place was coolly air-conditioned, antiseptically clean by comparison with the Albany small hours cafe. People talked in hushed voices, as if testing the day. He stared out of the window and saw a new, empty canvas. What strokes were painted on it, he reflected, were up to him. He had a sense of doing something very important, of starting on a journey that might change the course of his whole life; but at the same time a parallel sense of the ordinary: a seedy bus, a clean family restaurant full of tired people, a sky streaked with the hesitant early light of an autumn day.

119

October. Yes, he realized, on Monday it would be the first day of October. Now he looked outside more carefully, recalling the sharp bite of the air in his nostrils as he had strolled from bus to diner. Sure enough, there had been another frost. Not a heavy one, but enough to rime the yellowing blades of grass that poked up in cracks between the blocks of concrete outside; enough to bend the heads of french marigolds that rather pathetically adorned the walkway into the diner, enough to signal the end of the year's growing season.

It was fully light when they boarded the bus for the last stretch, to Buffalo. He sat alert, wide awake after strong coffee, and watched the alternation of forested hills and smoggy suburbs. The bus stopped more often now: Rome, Syracuse, Rochester, Batavia, a parade of towns with strangely metropolitan names that in no way lived up to their namesakes, sprawling greyly across the hills and valleys and linked by endless miles of concrete highway. He stared out, bemused, as yet unable to see himself in any of it.

Goldenrod and burning sumac bushes lined the roads, and stonebedded creeks ran northwards along the old glacial lines. He counted off their names as they crossed the labelled bridges that spanned them, wondered if they ever flooded, and watched all the time for dairy farms.

At first he saw few grazing cattle. Out of the towns there were vineyards and forestation schemes on steep slopes. The land grew more mountainous as they neared Buffalo, the hills darker and more threatening. He tried to imagine them in winter, and failed. 'It's very cold country,' Don McEnroe had told him on the telephone. 'Are you certain you want to spend any time in a place like we've got here?'

'I can only come and see, if you'll let me, sir,' he had said.

Buffalo bus station was a tumult of engines running, babies crying, and families shouting at each other over the roar of buses pulling in and out of the bays. He collected his luggage from the hold under the bus, grateful to be moving about after being cramped for so long, but hating the thick smell of diesel and the deafening noise, magnified tenfold by the canopy over the bus bays.

'I'll meet you at the depot in Arcade,' Don had said. 'Just catch the bus marked "Olean". They leave Buffalo every hour or so. Call me when you know which you'll be on, and I'll be there.'

He fumbled with the unfamiliar change and after losing a quarter in the machine worked out how to place the call to Arcade. The phone rang and rang. He waited. What would the farm look like? What would Don McEnroe be like, and the house? How long would he stay?

He shrugged the questions away, and at last a boy's voice came on the line. The formality of the words were belied by youthfulness of the voice. 'This is McEnroes' residence.'

'Hello? Hello. I'm hoping to speak to Mr Don McEnroe.'

'He's not here right now, and my mother's out the back. Can I take a message?'

He wasn't sure how to talk to the boy, guessing that he was about sixteen. 'It's Michael Monaghan.'

'Oh, you're the guy that's coming over today, aren't you?'

'I'm on a public phone. Can you just tell one of your parents I'll be on the bus that gets into Arcade at ten-fifteen?'

'OK. That's fine, Mr Monaghan. I'll tell them.'

He was surprised at the boy's courtesy. 'Thanks—I don't know your name yet.'

The phone went dead before he could answer.

When he saw the older, smaller bus that would carry him to Arcade pulling into the bay where he would catch it, he suddenly felt sick with excitement. More than anything, he realized, he wanted this visit to lead to something worthwhile, something that would matter, something that would make him feel he did, after all, have a place in the world where he was valued. Almost superstitiously, he reassessed everything he was doing, as if watching another person going through the motions. Getting on the rattling bus. Seeing the grey fungus of Buffalo fade into the brilliance of scarlet maples and yellow aspens. Counting down the roadsign miles to the place where he would live for a few weeks, at least...

121

'Where're you bound, kid?' An old man was peering at him from across the aisle. 'I saw you in Buffalo.'

'Western New York.'

The man's eyes narrowed, and he cackled harshly. 'You're here, then, sonny. Beautiful, ain't it?'

Michael hardly knew how to answer. There was a glint in the old eyes that suggested mockery; he wasn't sure how to take him. 'It's where I want to be, anyway.'

The old boy appraised him more closely. 'You're forrin, intya? Canadian, yeah?'

'English.'

He was met with a guffaw. 'What a hell hole to come to for'n English guy, eh? What, did'n anyone tellya? Preddy out there right now, ain't it? But colder'n hell in a few weeks, let me tellya.'

'That's what they said.'

'Oh, well, no false pretences, then.' He said the word 'pre-tences' with the accent on the first syllable. 'Yous're bit late for fruit picking.'

'I'm here to help a dairy farmer.'

'Poor bastard! Mind you, farmers up here tougher'n any this side of the Mississippi, sure as I'm sitting here. Hev to be.'

The question was inevitable now, though he had been hoping to avoid it. 'Are you a farmer then?'

'No thanks! Usta bust my ass working on someone else's land, but that was before I got more sense.' The old man laughed wheezily to himself. 'Naa.' He twisted the grimy baseball cap he was wearing jauntily to one side. 'I finished with that game a long time ago. Professional armchair sportsman now. The old gal passed on a few years back, and I go see my daughter now and then, like now, but I'm through working, thank God . . . hey, you say you're gonna work on a farm? Yeah, yeah. Thought that's what you said. Well, you ain't come to the best place. Farms up here git washed away, blown away, poisoned away, sometimes. Thinnest topsoil in any county this state. Planted and grazed to death. Fertilized to death. Sick land. It won't be worth a brass nickel in fifty years.' He eyed Michael again. 'Say, why you wanna work here?

Big guy like you—you could have your pick of it, surely?'

Michael felt he couldn't explain why he was coming to Arcade. 'It's where I want to be, though,' he repeated.

'Why not Idaho or Indiana, for pete's sake? Good grain states. Or how about Wisconsin, if you want a real fat dairy state?'

Michael glanced out of the window just as the bus shook and roared its way past the Arcade town limit sign. He smiled rather desperately at the old man. 'We've arrived, anyway, I think.'

Perversely, the old man grinned, shrugged and gave up arguing with him. 'That's what I like. You stick to your guns. Go for what you want, sonny.' Then, under his breath, 'You'll get licked into shape soon enough here, anyhow.'

And then they were there, the bus's gears scraping horribly, the brakes squealing as they pulled into a depot that looked like an old aeroplane hangar. The hiss of air as the bus came to rest, then the ringing echo of voices and other buses under the metal roof as he alighted.

His anxiety had returned. He thought how naive he had been to take the Williams' word—not farming people after all—that Western New York was a good place for him to spend time. But then he pushed the doubt out of his mind. If the land were as worthless as the old man had said, Don McEnroe would never have deliberately left New England to buy land here.

Half comforted, he retrieved his bags and turned into the small waiting area. It reeked of fried onions and hamburgers cooking on an open grill behind the lunch counter. A swift look round told him that Don McEnroe had not yet arrived.

He waited. Tiredness crept up on him again, his eyes scratchy from insufficient sleep, his stomach churning the dawn breakfast uneasily. The digital clock above the passenger entrance clicked away the minutes, and the meeting area emptied. At least Don would have no trouble recognizing him; apart from the waitresses and the short-order cook, he was the only person left now.

He went into the men's room and washed out his mouth, combed his hair, and splashed water on his face. Automatically, he checked his jeans pocket. There were still plenty of dollars and some travellers cheques; whatever happened now he would manage.

When he returned to the waiting area, a small, stout woman and a gangly, spotty-faced boy were the only new occupants. They looked at each other uncertainly.

'We're late meeting someone.' It was the woman who spoke first. 'You're not Michael Monaghan, by any chance?'

He felt a wave of relief and gratitude. *I've arrived,* he thought. He dropped his bags and offered his hand. 'Yes, that's me.'

Her eyes crinkled at the corners as she smiled. 'Michael. Well, that's good news. Maggie McEnroe. Come on. Billy will carry your bags. The car's out front, double-parked.'

The boy leapt on the luggage before he could protest, shouldering the holdall, showing off.

Michael smiled at Maggie. Her face was open and relaxed, rounded, like the rest of her, and although her thick brown hair was untidy, she did not look like a woman who was indifferent about her appearance; she just looked happy, easy to be with. He liked her immediately.

He wanted to say how glad he was that the journey was over, but the words got stuck somewhere, and he felt uncertain about calling her 'Maggie' so soon.

She seemed happy enough to talk for him. 'You must be wrecked. I'll see that you get some quiet when we get in. Don couldn't come … got stuck on the phone to the Co-operative, that's all. But Billy wanted to come with me.'

She led the way outside, to where cars passed in a desultory fashion and leaves, scraps of paper, eddied in the wind. He tried to take it all in: white clapboard houses with delapidated verandahs and the occasional picket fence, open front yards with few flowers, an open level crossing gate and single-gauge railway track; a wide, dusty main street overhung with a single light that flashed yellow, yellow, to slow and warn the already slow traffic. It was like no town or village in England that he could remember, but it was exactly how he pictured smalltown middle America.

'This is where we come for groceries and bits of things,' Maggie said. 'But you'll have time to explore later.'

He let her carry him along in her wave of energy, and the three of them drove off in a cloud of dust and litter. He sank back into the deep seat, allowing Billy's chatter to wash over him. 'There's the cemetry, see? And that's where they used to show movies, but it's closed now. We have to go to Orchard Park or Buffalo if we want a good movie. There's our church—that one, yeah. And in a few minutes...'

'Hush, Billy, he's tired.'

'You'll see a line of conifers. That's where the south pasture ends.'

He roused himself. Maggie was turning the car left off the main road and onto a narrower, more uneven road with deep ditches on either side, but no hedges to mark the field boundaries.

What Billy had called the south pasture was a mature field, the grasses now yellowing towards autumn, grazed by Holsteins. The animals looked content, tails swishing, hides glossy, bellies nicely rounded. The sight of them filled him with delight and anticipation. For a while, at least, these would be his animals, as well.

'Welcome to "McEnroevia West",' Maggie said, her voice full of laughter.

'That's what Pa calls the farm. After Grandpa McEnroe's house in Boston,' Billy put in.

'Don used to mock out his parents for their fancy house, that's all. Called it "McEnroevia". So when he bought this place, he dubbed it "McEnroevia West". Real annoying for my mother-in-law, though I think she's gotten used to it now.'

He was slightly dazed by the way they talked, firing one after the other, in volleys, much as Marie and Rita had done.

'Yeah, Pa says when he got the farm GraMar wouldn't come near the place if she could help it. Thought he was turning into a hayseed— a hick.'

Michael grinned briefly at Maggie. 'Translation, please?'

'Country bumpkin. I guess that's what you'd say. But don't you fret, we may be a long way from civilization here, but we aren't a bunch of, well—'

'Local yokels? That's what we'd say.'

'Whatever. Something like that. Now, most of this land you can see on the left is ours. Greys are next up the track, and Wilkinsons in back of us. I'm sure Don'll give you the tourist's guide when you're ready.'

'It all looks good to me.'

Maggie's voice was softer now. 'Well, I wasn't born to any of this, but I sure love it up here.' She signalled left again, swinging the car through a set of broken stone gateposts, one of which was half covered with creepers. 'Anyway, Michael, welcome.'

He smiled. 'Oh, I feel more than welcome. I just hope I can be of some use to your husband.'

'I'm sure you will.'

He had noticed on the bus ride how tall American silos were, and how many more of them there were than at home. Now as the car jolted along the farm track he looked up at the farm's two towers, painted light blue, that stood by the edge of the south field. Beyond them was a ramshackle shed that might have any use—he couldn't tell—and there, around a corner, a double barn which, like the silos, was cleanly painted and well maintained. Then the car pulled into a dusty area at the back of the farmhouse. Two mongrel dogs ran out of the shed, barking furiously and circling the car, then lost interest and slunk away. A light breeze lifted the leaves of two young maples that stood at either end of the house, like red sentinels. Hens fluttered away cackling as a door on the back porch slammed. Two men came out—one young and the other middle-aged.

'Look, here's Pa,' Billy said. 'And that's Joel. Named after Joel Wilkinson.'

'Our neighbour,' Maggie added.

A tall, heavy-set man with a streak of silver through his dark hair came bounding down the verandah steps. He was followed closely by a gangly boy of about seventeen who had a shock of fair curls on his head.

'Hi!' Joel was the first to the side of the car, wrenching open the door before Michael could move to open it. 'You must be Mike, right?'

Mike. That's what Ian had always called him. 'No—Michael,' he corrected. Then he heard the severe tone he'd used, and winced. 'Sorry. I don't like the name "Mike".' He smiled. He wanted to get on well with these boys. 'You're Joel.'

Joel seemed more interested in Michael himself than in showing off the farm to him, as Billy and his mother had been doing. Before Michael knew what was happening, Joel was sweeping his bags out of the boot and begging him to come in for a cold drink. 'C'mon. I'll show you where you're staying.'

Don laughed, flicking his hair out of his eyes and throwing a quick glance at Maggie. 'Hey, just a minute, buster, not so fast. You hear me, Joel?'

Michael turned and met him, and both of them laughed.

'Don't let the boys carry you along like that, will you? Boys, this man's here for me, for the farm, understand? He's our guest for as long as it takes him to get over the trip, then it's down to business for as long as we're all still friends.' Don shook his hand hard. 'How's that sound to you, Mr Monaghan?'

'Michael, please. It sounds great. I'm thrilled to be here.' He saw pale scars on Don's hands and wondered what they were.

'You got a good report from my father. He called last night and asked if we'd struck any kinda deal. Said you'd be good news for me.' The blue eyes looked directly into his, appraising, but not cold. 'You look tough enough. I'm sure glad you could make it just now. You know what it's like at this time of year. So many things to get done before the cold sets in. And, like I said, I've been short of help for weeks.' He stopped and bent his head slightly to one side. 'Ah, but you're tuckered out. C'mon, we'll get you a bite to eat and some shuteye.'

Michael followed the McEnroe family up the wooden steps of the back porch. The boys clattered into the house first, throwing off their sneakers behind them, and disappeared. Don and Maggie went next, his arm loosely over her shoulder, smiling, saying something quiet to her. He stopped on the top step and looked around him again. He could see a pond away to his left, and, nearer to that side of the house, an unfamiliar tree with lush fronds that hung limply in the chill air.

He bent to take off his own shoes, observing the clutter of shoes by the back door. As he did so, he noticed a bank of red and white roses that he had passed without noticing, beside the steps. They grew thickly on either side, where the house sheltered them. The night's frost had not touched them, and the perfume of the flowers rose richly into his nostrils.

As long as the McEnroes wanted him in this house, on this farm, he could be happy here.

8

With the windows and screens closed for the first time in weeks, the house felt strange. Rachel glanced from the muddle in her room to the side window, wondering at the sudden change in the weather. Gone was the stifling heat of one of the driest Indian summers her father could remember; now the mimosa outside her window bent sadly, and only one late blossom remained among the ferny leaves. The sky was still clear, but it was a chill blue, not the pale chalk-blue that came with the heat of late summer. Fall would come sharply this year, frost succeeding frost; and then the interminable snows.

She turned back to her packing. At least she would not have to endure a New York winter this year. If she had gone back to college in Ohio, as she had first expected, the weather would have been equally unmerciful; but now the plans had changed. Instead, she would be flying to England in a few days. She sighed, half smiling, not quite able to believe it was true.

She stacked a set of zoology and chemistry textbooks neatly into the wooden chest her father had found for her. The shelves above her bed were somewhat bowed from the weight of books—everything from *The Little Engine That Could* and *The Three Little Pigs* to *Introduction to Psychology* and *Flora and Fauna of Western New York*. She would need to choose carefully.

'All the stuff you take weighs something,' her mother had reminded her simply. 'And you have to carry it. Just the bare essentials, Rachel, that's what you should take. Excess baggage will be excess in more ways than one.'

Rachel heard the echo now, as she made her decisions. Going to medical school in London wasn't like going back to the state university in Cincinnati. She couldn't empty out her bedroom in Arcade, as her friends would do each fall, and take everything that made her feel at home: the fat teddybears, the big cushions, the pots of geraniums and spiderplants, the pictures, books, and knicknacks of nineteen years. Her biggest suitcase and a wooden chest would contain the most that she could take. The rest would stay here, waiting for her.

'You'll doubtless come back with half of Windsor Castle and the Tower of London,' her father had teased.

She had laughed and told him she wouldn't have time for any sightseeing, not if the St Stephen's Hospital timetable they had sent her was anything to go by. 'I'll be lucky if I have time to talk to the other kids on the programme,' she had retorted.

She opened the top drawer of her desk and began to sift through the contents. Papers, letters, cards, scribbled notes, torn envelopes— the flotsam of the last few years brought back a thousand trivial memories. Resolutely she bundled most things into the trash basket, saving only what belonged in the chest.

Thumps and shouts at the back of the house told her that Maggie and Billy had come back from the bus depot. Typically, she could make out Billy's voice above the rest. He would be telling tales to the Englishman about Joel and herself. Her mother would be brewing coffee, trying to keep her father from dragging the newcomer straight into the barn.

She chuckled to herself. *What a family!*

She felt no curiosity about Monaghan, except to wonder if he would be able to give her some tips about survival in London. Those would be helpful. But perhaps, if he were a country man, he would know no one in London, would know nothing about it.

She began to hum a country tune she didn't like, an inane song that had wailed at her out of the radio late the night before when she had started packing. It was one of those annoying songs that got stuck in her brain and held on like a barn-owl with a mouse. The words were mawkish, sentimental, sung in a nasal whine. Unforgettable in the worst way.

Downstairs the voices abated. She heard the crash of the screen door on the back porch; that would be her father going gratefully back to work. Then the sound of voices on the stairs: her mother's, bright and welcoming; and Monaghan's, deeper and quieter than she had somehow expected. Probably coming up so that Mom could show him the guest room. She held her breath, strangely reluctant to go out and say anything friendly or look him in the face. *I need to concentrate on what I'm doing,* she told herself, opening the second drawer.

In a moment she had forgotten everything at home and was on her knees looking again at photographs that had recently come back from the printer. Her grandmother's birthday. She studied them slowly, lovingly, seeing under the Kodachrome gloss the breeze-blown figure of her grandmother, holding the armful of roses she had picked that day; the careworn smile of her grandfather—both of them looking right into the camera, straight at her. *I'll be seeing them again in a couple days,* she told herself happily. *What a good kind of send-off for England.*

She dealt the photos onto her bed one by one. The picture of her grandparents was best, but there were others she liked. She flicked past the snaps from Ohio to others from GraMar's party. One of herself with her mother on the patio behind 'McEnroevia': easy smiles and floral print dresses. Another favourite had been taken by McEnroe; he had snapped her with Marie Williams, their heads bent together, laughing, the sun shining on their hair.

Marie. She had enjoyed those two days with Marie as much as any she had ever spent in Boston. She still remembered clearly the terror of the storm and the boat tossing uncontrollably on the ugly waves. But more than that she remembered Marie's relaxed smiles, happy laughter, and openness. Definitely someone to look up whenever she was staying in Bedford.

How strange that Marie herself had been instrumental in directing Monaghan first to McEnroe, then to the farm. Life seemed to go in rings and circles; there were patterns and purposes.

The creak of floorboards outside her room and her mother's knock at the door brought her to her feet. 'Rachel? May I come in?'

'Of course.' She moved the photos so that her mother would have space to sit down, and pushed in the drawer she had been sorting.

Maggie's head came round the door. 'I wasn't sure if you wanted to meet Michael. He's just arrived. Oh, honey, what a jumble! Gee, that's not like our Rachel.'

She grinned back. 'No way to pack without making a mess, Mom.'

'Looks like you're making progress, anyhow. But what about meeting Michael?'

Rachel tried to see past her mother into the narrow upstairs hallway that divided the bedrooms.

'He's starting to set himself up after his own journey. Funny, really. Him *un*packing, and you packing like crazy. He's met everyone else. I'm sure he'd like to meet you.'

She swung her hair back. 'Yeah well, I'd sure like to talk to him, but maybe not right this minute. Let him catch his breath. Doesn't he want to sleep?'

'I guess he will for a while.'

'Plenty of time, then.'

Maggie opened the door wider. 'He gave me this.' She held out a thick, crumpled envelope. 'It's for you, he says.'

Rachel laughed. 'Mom, you look nosey as can be.'

'No, no—'

'Oh, it's from Marie. A great long letter. Good! She said she'd write me.' She held out the photo that was still in her hand. 'See, I was just looking at this picture and thinking of her.'

Maggie smiled. 'Nice girl. And I guess you might see her next week.'

'If I could . . . but she'll be back in college. It might not work out.'

'You'll want to see as much as you can of Grandpa and GraMar, anyway.'

'I'm looking forward to that.'

Her mother looked suddenly wistful. 'My gosh, I'm sure going to miss you, honey.' She patted the empty space on the bed.

'Don't stand out there, Mom. Come on in. Have you got time?'

Her mother smiled again, a little sadly. 'Sure, a few minutes. Your father's outside until lunch, and the boys are out there helping him a bit. A quiet Saturday for me, for a change. I'll get some work done in the garden, maybe.'

Now it was Rachel's turn to feel wistful. 'Life goes on, doesn't it. You and Pa always so busy, never an end to it. And I won't be here, now, to help with any of it.'

Maggie put her arms around Rachel. 'Ah, sweetheart. I know. You must feel so mixed up inside. One minute you were looking toward going back to Ohio, practically next door, and before we know it you're off to *England*. But, Rachel, we knew that when you applied for the scholarship. It's surely a chance of a lifetime. You're not going to back down?'

She shook her head, bumping her mother's shoulder. 'No, no way. I'm excited about going. It'll be great . . . But it's frightening to think of how different everything will be. And what I'll miss at home.'

Her mother expelled her breath in little amused gasps. 'Go on. That's crazy. "What I'll miss at home"? Heavens, think of it, Rachel. You'll miss the cows busting out of the pasture and trampling all over the track or getting themselves bumped off the highway. You'll miss the chickens scratching up my flowers for the hundredth time. You'll miss the harvester breaking down and nitwits falling off ladders. You'll miss Pa being trucked off to Jamestown or Buffalo hospital with half the farmyard in his hand.' She was laughing now. 'You'll miss the boys arguing and teasing you. You'll miss Pa and me fussing at you to help around the place. You'll miss the eternal mess in this house. Sure you'll miss all that.' She held Rachel away from her but still smiled into her face.

Rachel felt her eyes grow moist. 'Yes, Mom, but I'll miss other things, you know.'

Maggie had regained her self-possession, now. 'I'll ask you what if you don't turn to marshmallows on me.' She detached Rachel's arms from her neck and sat back a few inches farther.

Rachel swallowed. 'Well, one thing's for sure; I won't miss the winters we have here. I guess England'll be raw, but not freezing.' Her eyes wandered to the window again. 'No, what I'll miss is the space here. And the peace.'

Maggie's eyebrows rose. 'Peace?' she scoffed. 'Rural life couldn't be much noisier than it is. Cows bellowing. Dogs whining and barking. Machines thrashing and chugging all day. Menfolk shouting. Cocks crowing.'

'That's nothing—you know what I mean. The slow way the cows come out of milking into the pasture. The sun setting behind the barn. The crickets at night in the summer when we sit on the back porch. The sound of the wind in that tree out there. Those dumb ducks quacking on the pond. The shine on the corn when it's rising in July. Oh, everything—just the atmosphere of the place.'

'I do know what you mean. What you love here is what I've always loved.' She squeezed Rachel's hand. 'Oh, it wasn't easy those first winters up here, not after Boston. It hasn't been milk and honey all the way, you know. I couldn't get used to the people up here.' She grimaced. 'And probably most of them couldn't make me out, either. But certainly I wasn't about to let it all get the better of me—any of it.' She spread her hands. 'And now look at me, two decades on. Your grandpa would say I'm as much wedded to this farm as your father, and he's right. There's nowhere else I'd rather be.'

Rachel laughed and began to sing 'On the Street Where You Live'.

Her mother kissed her. 'Your Aunt Ellie used to sing that to me,' she said thoughtfully, 'when I was missing your father and thought I hadn't a hope that he'd ever fall for me. But you'll be OK, daughter of mine. You'll discover all the urban genes in you that I left behind in Boston. I'll bet you love London.' She stood. 'You read that letter, now. And for goodness sake keep going. It'd be nice now you're done studying for a while if you could put your head out of this door and make friends before you go half way round the world.'

'I get the message. Will do.'

Her mother softly shut the door. Alone again, Rachel emptied and sorted her third drawer, then turned to Marie's letter.

It began with gushing apologies that she had not written sooner. '*I've had a great summer*,' Marie had written, '*but not much time for letters.*'

Rachel read slowly. Marie described the jobs she had been doing all summer. She wrote about returning to college after her trip to

England, and about the marina. She wanted to know how Rachel was enjoying college.

'*Clare's wedding was wonderful,*' the letter went on.

> *I never knew until we came through the clouds over England how green it is compared to dusty old Boston in August. Barking wasn't very special—that's where Clare grew up, and where my aunt still lives. But the place where Clare got married, out in West London, was full of trees and fabulous shops. Everything quite old, but not trashed and spoiled the way some of the old bits of Boston are. I can't explain it, but it made me want to go back to England one day and see what it would be like to live there.*

Rachel laughed quietly to herself, remembering that Marie did not yet know her news, did not know that she herself would be in England long before Marie ever had the chance—not in Ohio after all. *I hope I like England as much as Marie does,* she said to herself. Then the thought of dropping through the clouds over a strange city, however beautiful and full of history, suddenly made her stomach knot. When she flew into London she would know not one person in the city. All she would have would be her suitcase and a wooden chest, the address of the residence hall where she would be living while she trained at St Stephen's, and a thick packet of papers about the course she was embarking on. Nothing familiar. Everything to learn. It would be like starting life from the very beginning, all over again.

But I don't need to be afraid, she reminded herself. She fell on her knees, suddenly, hugging Marie's letter to herself and feeling strangely torn between laughter and tears. She thought of a song they often sang at the church in Arcade. 'Come walk with me on stormy waters. Reach out your hand, and I'll be there . . .' She sang it under her breath now, repeating it like a talisman. *No one on earth, nowhere on earth,* she thought, *is walking in a strange land. The whole earth is the Lord's.*

She dried her eyes after a while and sat back on the bed. From downstairs came the smell of baking; the men would soon be in for lunch. The familiar pattern of life went on no matter what—as she had said to her mother.

She went back to Marie's long letter.

I'm going to ask Michael if he will bring this letter with him. I know I could have mailed it, but I hoped this might somehow start him off on the right foot with you. I figured you'd be home from Ohio for some weekends and would get it from him when you walk in the door.

He's a nice guy, Rachel. He likes me a lot, and I like him a little, too, but not in the way he likes me. I was kind of hoping he'd like you, you see.

She laughed out loud. 'What a schemer!'

Here's a joke for you. I met Michael in England, at that wedding. A relative of his married my cousin Clare. Honest, I never gave him much thought afterwards, but I guess he thought about me, and the next thing you know he arrives on our doorstep, this Monday afternoon, and wants Ma to help him find a job. Ma gets totally geeked out. He's a farmer, not a sailor. Would you believe he wanted me to teach him how to sail—as a trade-off for trying to teach me how to dance? Crazy, yeah?

Well, I'll tell you, I didn't get far with the dancing, and he sure didn't get far with the sailing. Ma took pity on him and gave him four days of odd chores down at the marina—enough to earn a few dollars. And on Tuesday this week your grandfather had business with Ma . . .

The letter was smudged on that line, then resumed in a different ink, as if Marie had been interrupted as she wrote.

We suddenly thought of your dad's farm. I guess you've worked that out by now! Anyway, you can blame it on me that Michael's now adding to what you said was chaos in your house. I miss my brothers a bit (though I wouldn't say so to Ma), but I wouldn't trade with you now, for the world; I wonder how you'll get on with both your brothers still at home and now a third guy clattering around the place as well!

When you read this you'll have seen Michael. Please write and tell me what you think of him. I'll be on suspenders till you do. And write me about Ohio, too, would you? Maybe I'm too late with this and you've met the guy of your dreams in Cincinnati—like the song, 'By the banks of the Ohio . . .' But I hope not. Michael's a real down to earth guy, like I guess your dad is, and I just have this feeling . . .

The handwriting deteriorated, then, from a neat copperplate to a wild scrawl.

Sorry. I've got to go. It's way past my bedtime, and when I get back from college tomorrow it'll be Michael's last evening here. Take care, dear Rachel. Heaps of love from your new friend,
Marie.

Folding the sheets of paper, Rachel smiled again. She had spent such a short time with Marie, but she felt they knew each other quite well, and already she could almost have predicted that Marie would be a matchmaker. How surprised Marie would be to know she would be in Boston next week, while Monaghan was left here! *So much for the schemes!*

She cleared a path to the door of her room, through the stacks of books and notebooks, clothes and shoes. Now she felt even less interested in meeting Michael Monaghan. She imagined a spaniel-like young man, with soulful brown eyes and a sorrowful face, a romantic—what a pity Marie didn't like him—she's just as bad!—a sentimental guy who must have followed Marie around for five days before giving up and hopping the next Greyhound to Arcade. Yes, perhaps he would be likable—even Marie said as much—but dull. Shy, withdrawn: that's how she imagined Englishmen. And it wouldn't matter what he was like, she decided. She would be leaving in two days.

She closed the door on the junk of her room and went slowly down the stairs. She could hear Billy's loud voice in her father's office, next to the kitchen, and Joel answering. They were arguing about whether it would rain in the afternoon.

The back screen door slammed, and now her father's voice joined the others. 'Sure it'll stay dry, boys. Colder, but still dry. We've got to see to the fence this afternoon. And we better get the storms up, as well, before it *does* rain.'

Rachel went into the kitchen, grinned at everyone, and automatically set five places at the table.

'Where's Michael eating?' Joel challenged. 'In the barn with the cats?'

'Quiet, Joel,' Maggie said.

Rachel set another place, and Billy began ladling soup into bowls. He was smirking.

'Tell Mr Monaghan lunch is going on the table, would you please, Joel? Since you're so concerned about him, that is.' Don was laughing at him.

Joel thumped up the stairs, and Rachel poured cold water into all the glasses. She was filling the last one—Michael's—when he followed Joel into the kitchen.

Don guided him to the table. 'Michael, I hope you're hungry.' He patted his stomach. 'I sure am, and Maggie's no slouch in the kitchen. Come and eat. Oh—I don't think you met Rachel.'

She set down the jug and looked up. Her father was a big man—thickbodied as well as tall—and Michael stood shoulder to shoulder with him. She noticed right away, though, that despite the powerful shoulders, he was much leaner than her father.

For an instant she looked into his face. He was smiling at her: an uncomfortable, slightly crooked smile; and he looked very tired. Violet shadows smudged the skin under his eyes, a surprising contrast to the sunshiny lightness of his hair.

She looked away, then caught Maggie's watchful eyes on her face. 'Rachel?' Her mother seemed to see beneath her carefully controlled face.

'Oh—sorry. Yes.' She managed a smile at Michael. 'Glad to meet you.'

He seemed too tired to notice her, or perhaps too overwhelmed by the journey and the sudden crowded attention to know how to deal with one more person.

As usual it was her mother who made the rough place smooth. 'C'mon, you all,' she drawled, 'the muffins're getting cold, and I'm getting old just standing here watching you. Let's eat, for pete's sake.'

Rachel did not bow her head as her father said the grace, but she saw that Michael did, as if he were used to the same custom at home. As the 'amen' was said, she bent her head shamefacedly and was slow to look up again. Michael faced her, four feet away, across the table.

She marvelled at the way he spoke to her brothers, the tactful way he deflected their enquiries about what he would be doing on the farm, and for how long. She knew what was behind their questions: an unspoken anxiety about someone only a few years older than they were, an outsider, coming in to work on the farm *now*, now when they were still too young to take up the reins—as Billy at least wanted to do—beside their father. But Michael seemed to understand the silent politics. He was gentle with them, tolerant of their loud impatience and personal questions, sensitive to the anxiety they concealed so poorly.

Later she could not remember anything specific from the conversation, only her general impression of someone carefully attuned to the undercurrents at the table; only her impression of an intense, quick-witted, and kind man—beautiful to look at, too. She remembered nothing except that at the end of the meal her father had invited Michael to go with him round the farm, and the two of them had gone out, closely followed by her brothers, to do what her mother called 'the grand tour'.

When the house was quiet again, she went back to her packing with her soul in a tumult, completely unable to concentrate, taking things out of the chest, putting them back in, and rearranging the contents five times before she gave up.

'I'm going out,' she told her mother in the middle of the afternoon.

Maggie was hoeing the rough soil in the garden at the side of the house. She stopped, wiping her face on her sleeve. 'OK. Will you be back for supper?'

Rachel looked distractedly at the wheelbarrow her mother had piled high with garden rubbish: tufts of brown grass, big stones, dead cosmos flowers that had grown so tall in the summer that small birds had nested in them. And leaves—dry maple leaves, red heralds of the cold. 'Supper? Yes, I'll be back long before then. Er—d'you know where Joel and Billy are?' In fact she did not want to find her brothers at all, hoped they were out of the way.

'Your father sent them up by Greys' property—where he had alfalfa this summer, remember? They're supposed to be checking the fence. He's—who knows where. Showing Michael where everything is ... Rachel, you look pale. You OK, sweetheart?'

'I'm fine.' And she turned past the corner of the house before her mother could ask any awkward questions.

The yard was deserted except for a couple of motley kittens who had fallen asleep, warm in the lee of the hen arks. They lay in a tight ball, the mother cat nowhere in sight. Normally she would have stopped, scooped them up, and gone in search of the mother in the barn. Today she walked straight past the hens and across the drafty space to the barn. She could hear two dogs barking at each other: one of her father's, and one, farther away, that might have belonged to any of the neighbouring farms.

Dustmotes danced in the afternoon light that came in from the pasture beyond. Outside the huge double doors at the back of the barn the clay-heavy soil of the collecting yard was churned and dried into ruts where the cattle had trodden in and out for milking every day this summer. The feedbunk was empty, a few stray stalks of hay sticking out, but the cows were foraging anyway, farther down the pasture.

She followed the dirt track that flanked the hayfield and ran down towards the creek. At this time of the day, if the boys were doing the fences, and because it wasn't time yet for afternoon milking, her father might be anywhere.

Her head was empty of any idea of what she would say when she met them, only that she wanted to be with them.

In the end she found them on the path between the oatfield and the alfalfa fields. Bruce, the younger dog, was sitting at her father's heels, alternately scratching and cocking his head on one side whenever Michael spoke. The two men stood with their backs to her, hair ruffled sideways in the wind, facing down the gentle slope to the creek. She stopped out of sight of them and listened to their voices on the stiff breeze that blew across the stubble.

'The corn's finished, really, by August,' her father was saying. 'It was a great crop this year—did real well. I'll show you when we get back to the feed stores. We brought it in a little early for a change.'

'No maize for human consumption?'

'None at all. Not worth it. The kids complain about it, but you can buy a dozen ears a dollar at the side of the road this time of year. Why bother? Anyhow, my neighbours—Wilkinsons, that is—grow plenty of corn for foodstores. Sally's likely as not to bring my wife a bushel basket that keeps us going quite a while, at least.'

She stepped closer, her shoes catching in the grasses along the edge of the path. Hearing her, they both turned.

'Had it with packing?' Don waited for her, then reached his arm round her shoulder and pulled her close.

'I sure have. Thought I'd come and see what everyone's up to.'

Bruce whined, panting, and began to weave round Michael's legs.

Her father grinned at Michael. 'You're honoured. This girl has hardly had time these last five years to put her head out of the door of her room. My own dogs don't know who she is these days.'

Michael gave her an acknowledging nod. 'Working for your exams?'

'Studying my head off.' She laughed nervously. 'I'm glad it's over for a bit.'

Don squeezed her shoulder. 'But Rachel, it's just beginning.' He looked enquiringly at Michael. 'Did we tell you Rachel's off to your own country in a few days?'

She gritted her teeth, fighting back the colour she knew was rising into her face. 'Pa, I think everyone's told him fifty times by now.'

'Rather you than me,' Michael said ruefully. 'I've had enough of books for a while.'

Don kicked at a clod of loam, and a fine cloud of dust rose round their feet. 'Don't blame you. I used to feel the same. Studying's all very well, but in the end you gotta get your paws dirty.'

A shout came from their right, then a second.

'That sounds like the boys,' Rachel said, frowning. 'Where are they now?'

'Where we left them, I hope. Top end of the alfalfa, by the fencing.'

'Pa! Give us a hand!' Joel's voice carried over the brow of the hill more clearly now.

Don slipped his arm from Rachel's shoulder. 'You'll excuse me. I'll just go make sure they haven't wound themselves in barbed wire, or some dumb thing.'

Rachel shuddered. 'We'd better—'

'Nah, you stay with Michael. Take him down to the toolshed and the feed stores, would you? We haven't seen those yet. I need to get going, anyhow.' And he was gone, running in a shambling gait across the uneven rise of the field, then out of sight towards the boundary of Greys' land. The dog loped behind him, barking.

'It's a good farm,' Michael said easily.

She saw that he looked less tired now, his eyes full with pleasure. 'I've always liked it,' she said.

'You all do, don't you?'

'I guess so.' She shrugged. 'It's not something I think about very much. If you've always lived somewhere, you're just *there*. You don't belong anywhere else.' Then she heard the words afresh, in her head, as if someone else had said them. *What do I mean—'You don't belong anywhere else.' Then why on earth am I going away?* It was something she'd have to puzzle over, later.

They went down and walked along the edge of the creek to where the path widened into a broad track for farm vehicles. Late dragonflies hovered and darted through the weeds on the water's edge, and purple loosestrife lined the borders of the oats, where machines never cut and no seed was sown.

Rachel looked up at the cloudless sweep of the sky. 'This is how I'll remember it when I'm away,' she said. 'I don't want to think about the cold. Oh, I know it's cooler than yesterday, and tomorrow will be cooler again, and the frost will get thicker and thicker until it's snow ... but I'd rather remember this.'

He nodded, stopped to pull out a stalk to chew on. 'You've always lived here, you say?'

She laughed. 'I was born right in this house.'

His eyebrows rose. 'Isn't there a hospital?'

'Miles away. Mom wanted a midwife and a home birth, but the doctor said no; I was supposed to be a big baby, and a first, as well. But they never made it to the hospital.' It had been one of her favourite stories as she grew up. 'They got as far as the pickup truck, and Mom refused to get into it. Pa said she was acting like one of his cows—I can just imagine the scene! So back she went and got into bed. She figured if Pa could deliver an eighty-pound calf then he could deliver an eight-pound baby.'

She stopped, laughing in embarrassment, but picturing everything as clearly in her mind as if she could recall her own birth. Then realized that she was talking to a newcomer, and blushed.

Michael looked at her curiously but seemed not to notice her confusion. 'Do all your family talk as much as they seem to?'

She knew he was teasing but felt a shadow cross her. 'Only when they're uptight,' she said. 'Sorry. It's because you're new here. Pa needs you to be happy here for a few weeks until Larry's OK. Maybe we're all over-reacting.' Her jaw seemed to go stiff as she answered him, and she kept her eyes carefully on the track. Now she wanted to run away. He would see more than she wanted him to see in her face if he kept examining her that way. His perception had been apparent enough at lunchtime.

His reply took her by surprise. He spoke abruptly, but with a depth of feeling that she couldn't fathom. 'Well, it's nice to be wanted here.'

They walked on in silence for a moment. Rachel turned over what he had just said, presuming he was thinking of Marie.

'You couldn't stay with Williams, I guess.'

'No. I knew that when I flew in, though I would have liked to stay longer.'

She decided it was pointless to play games with him. 'You—you liked Marie.'

He smiled, and this time she did look at him again. 'I couldn't help it.' His mouth twisted slightly. 'I suppose she told you all the gory details in that long letter of hers—you got it?'

'Yes, Mom gave it to me.'

'And she told you—.'

Rachel swallowed. 'She said you were a nice guy.'

'But—?'

She shook her head. 'Oh, Michael, don't hurt yourself.'

He shrugged. 'Stupid of me. Yes, you're right. No future in transatlantic relationships. To meet *my* parents, though, you'd know there was a God who could work miracles across far bigger distances than the Atlantic . . . a God who's over and in us all. Around us. Making patterns with us.'

She stared at him in amazement. Was it only a few hours ago that she had thought the same . . . *Life seemed to go in rings and circles. There were patterns and purposes* . . . Then she thought wistfully how many unfamiliar things must lie unseen behind this face that was already growing familiar to her: things she would never know about. But questions about his family could wait. What he had said about God made her look at him freshly. 'You believe in miracles—in a God of miracles?'

'I certainly do.' His eyes looked very blue now, and steady. 'But miracles can't be engineered by human beings. I believe that as well. They're God's department, I think.'

'Yes.'

'And I was trying to engineer things.'

'By coming over here? Is that the only reason why you came—for Marie?' It was painful to ask, but she wanted to know what was going on under the calm cadences of his English accent.

'What a question!'

'Oh—I don't mean—' She stammered into silence.

'But no reason I can't answer.' His eyes fixed on hers, and for a moment she thought that, had they known each other better, he might have touched her arm, or her shoulder. 'You ought to understand. You're going to England to study medicine—that's what your parents told me. And how have people reacted when you told them that?'

'Dumb amazement!' She laughed, thinking of their neighbour Sally Wilkinson's openmouthed response, and of her own brothers' shrugs of dismissal. *Rachel's gone nuts!* 'But in my case I'm going because—'

'I don't imagine your thinking was much different from mine, was it? You've had a dream all your life, surely?'

She nodded.

'And so have I. It wasn't to be in America—not at first. It was just to learn everything I could about agriculture. There I was, right in the middle of university, like you, but I wanted to start *now*, not wait the years of study that wouldn't have any relevance for me. Meeting Marie set me thinking. I was getting a lot of flack at home.' His voice was suddenly sad. 'I needed to get away, as far away as I could. It fell into place in my mind, and so I arranged the flight.'

Rachel remembered what Marie had said in her letter about his arrival. 'But Marie had no idea you were coming?'

'None. That's where I was guilty of "engineering".' He shook his head. 'But in the end, I'm sure something good will come of it. The God who does miracles in drastic circumstances also solves smaller problems in simple ways.'

'Larry the Ladder, poor guy,' Rachel laughed. 'And here you are.'

He held open the gate at the foot of the track. 'Then what about you? Your journey to England—is that something you were expecting, or what?'

She could smell the sap of the fir trees as they passed them. She breathed deeply, storing it up for when she was away. 'I've been at the state university for two years—Ohio. But I wanted more. I applied for St Stephen's, London. Just filled out the forms, then put it out of my mind. I was going back to Ohio. It was all fixed. Only now I'm not.' She spread her hands.

'How long for?'

'Eighteen months for the Bachelor of Medicine course. Very intensive, the prospectus warns me. Then several more years, I guess, depending on my options. What about you? Have you booked a return flight?'

'Some time within the year, that's all I know. I feel very lucky to have the chance to work for your father. It's solved my problem as well as his.'

They were back on the edge of the farmyard again. It would be a simple thing to show him round the buildings, as her father had asked. She went through the spiel mechanically. 'This is the toolshed. That's what we call it, though I never figured out why. Not many tools in sight. Just all these big machines, as you can see.' She pointed through a crack in the weatherboarding at the back. There's a woodpile out back. Pa was splitting some of the wood this morning, for the fence.'

'Yes, he said he'd done that.' They went outside again. 'I do like your silos,' he said.

She wanted to laugh. '*Those* old things?'

'They're so tall.'

'We need a lot of wet feed in the winter,' she said. 'As well as the dry stuff.'

'A shorter grazing season here.' He was squinting up at the sky, taking it all in.

'You're probably right. Pa'll keep the animals out as long as he can. He hates the winter as much as I do. But then they'll need every bit of feed he's got—and some.' She thought of the extra grain her father would need next season because of the charity work he was getting involved in. But then she forgot it and glanced across the yard as the mother cat found her kittens and started rolling in the dust with them. 'Pa showed you the barn, I'll bet?'

'He was going to, but your brothers diverted us when we first went out.'

'Twice in one afternoon! Good going.' She was pleased that he hadn't seen the barn. 'Then I'll show you. I can't explain all the technical stuff to you. Pa'll do that. But I'd like to show you anyway.'

They walked past the big rolling doors. The barns were still empty of cows, the freestalls clean. Water was dripping in the automated drinking system, and down the far end two pens of calves bawled and pushed for attention.

'This is the part of the farm I like best,' she said.

He smiled, his teeth very white in the dimness of the barn. 'That's something I understand very well,' he said.

'I used to come out with Pa and watch him milking. Pour out the feednuts sometimes, or throw down the bales.'

He seemed to look at her differently, for just a moment. 'You do love it here.'

'It's the animals, mostly.' She couldn't meet his eyes.

'You'll miss it.'

She moved and put one hand on the fieldside door of the barn, turning her back to him. The lead cow came snorting inquisitively past the collecting yard and up the baked field, her mouth leaking torn yellow grass, and snuffled at her other hand. She felt the warm, grassy breath from its nostrils on her palm, the heat rising from the black hide. 'Yes,' she said, 'I needed to escape, but I'll miss it all like crazy.'

9

Don came through the office and into the kitchen. 'You're ready at last, Rachel? Everything all set?'

She looked up from the basket of apples she and Maggie were peeling. 'Yes, Dad. I actually saw the boys onto the schoolbus this morning, for a change. That sure embarrassed them.'

Don chuckled. 'I'll bet!'

'She's giving me a hand.'

'So I see.'

Don filled three mugs with coffee from the stove and sat down beside the women. 'Here—get your tonsils round this ... So, Rachel, how d'you feel?'

She went on peeling, watching the thin russet skin curl away from apple and knife under her quick fingers. She found she couldn't look up.

'Mixed up, I think,' Maggie said. 'Isn't that right, honey?'

The knife slipped, and a trickle of blood stained the white flesh of the apple in Rachel's hand. She dropped both and ran her hand under cold water. 'Yes,' she said after a moment. 'That's about how I feel.' She knew her mother meant well, answering for her, but a small note of irritation crept into her voice. 'It's a long way to go, Pa. I can't come back any time soon.' She staunched the blood with a clean towel, then mustered a smile. 'And I'm going to miss everyone.'

'Sure you will,' he said.

Maggie gave her a long, speculative look, which she avoided, blowing into her coffee.

'But don't you start pining and moping, girl,' Don said. 'We'll all be fine here, and you have an exciting job of work to do. You're doing just what you wanted.'

'Only it's in another country,' Maggie added hurriedly.

Rachel smiled. 'It's OK. I'll be fine, too. Mom—you don't need to worry for us both. And Pa, of course I'm looking forward to it. It's just…' How could she explain the confusion of feelings? For weeks she had looked forward to going, but now she was beginning to realize that to leave for England would not necessarily be an escape; she would miss the farm; it wasn't the cluttered, claustrophobic place she sometimes considered it. And how could they understand that it would be worse now that Michael had arrived? She couldn't explain any of those things. It was safer to occupy herself peeling apples and chatting about nothing at all until it was time to drive to the airport.

'Where's Michael?' Maggie asked a few minutes later.

'I left him replacing one of the cables on the barn cleaner—with Tony,' Don said.

'How's he doing?'

Don sat forward. 'He's damn good, Maggie. Makes me wish I'd had someone like him around years ago. It's all very well with guys you've known for years like Larry and Tony, but we're all getting on now.' He grinned ruefully. 'Larry and Tony especially! And when I watch the way that boy shifts the muck after milking—Lordy, I remember what it's like to have *energy*.'

Maggie pushed up her sleeves, laughed, and winked. 'Oh, you're not over the hill yet, McEnroe.'

'Don't you McEnroe me, Maggie Fuller.' He drained his cup. 'You should see him work, anyhow. And he picks things up fast. I like that. Reminds me of Joel a few years back.'

'Our Joel?' Rachel asked, surprised.

'No, you loon, Joel *Wilkinson*. Used to help us quite a bit in the early days. Before old man Wilkinson started pushing up daisies—you remember. Michael's the same: strong as a horse, willing as a young dog, and he never complains.'

'I like him.' Maggie threw a penetrating glance at Rachel which fell on her like a shattering piece of crockery. The silent words in that look were so loud that Rachel wondered if her father could hear them.

Mom's psyched me out again, she groaned inwardly, then chopped another apple into pieces and threw them into the pan.

'And another thing,' her father mused, 'There's none of this insincere crap you get from kids these days: the "Yessir Mr McEnroe" and "Nosir Mr McEnroe", then "I'll do as I damn well please Mr McEnroe". None of that! No, he just asks a quiet question, nods, and gets on with it.' Don shook his head. 'If he hadn't told me he'd grown up with a teacher for a mother—' He stopped, grinning at Maggie, 'and a social worker for a father, I'd swear he'd been born with a cow on one side and a bucket and boots on the other. It's all second nature to him.'

'Maybe the Monaghans were farming people, back in Ireland.'

Don guffawed. 'Maybe, but I don't believe all that nonsense about farming being in the blood.'

'There you are, then. He's just got a passion for land and animals and hard work. The same as you've got, and always had.'

Don laughed. 'Yeah, and I guess law and politics were as good a home training ground as any for farm work.' Rachel felt dazed by the conversation that washed around her and over her head. *Law and politics ... what do either of those things have to do with farming?* But she was glad that her mother had stopped those quizzical looks, and that they were now arguing about farming in the abstract, nothing that impinged on how she was feeling.

Her father stood up and stretched. 'I'll get out there for just a little longer, before we go.' He turned to Rachel. 'That's if you don't object, honey?'

Maggie stirred cinnamon into the mound of apples and squeezed in lemon juice. 'Leave enough time to clean up before you get in the truck, would you?'

Rachel grinned at her father. 'Yes,' she agreed, relieved by the mundane turn of the talk. 'Let's not take half of Allegany County into the pickup and have everyone in the airport staring and running off.'

'Watch your mouth, Rachel McEnroe. Anyhow, it's only corndust.' The office and storm doors banged behind him.

Maggie gave her a conspiratorial smile. 'Never changes,' she said.

Rachel went back to peeling and chopping. Maggie poured honey in a thick stream from a bucket they kept in the corner. She set the pan to heat on the stove. Rachel began dropping pieces of apple into the second pan, heard them fall with a soft thud against the empty metal. The sweetsour smell of the apples filled the kitchen.

Then suddenly everything hit her at once: the enormity of leaving home, the vastness of the Atlantic, the arduous study that lay ahead, the way she would miss everyone at home. Even the way she would miss the chaos of this kitchen. She felt tears prick at the corners of her eyes and push out, running against her will down her face.

Her mother looked up and saw them disappear into the apples. 'Hey! What's this? I didn't tell you to put salt in there, did I?'

She answered with a shaky laugh, not trusting her voice.

Gently her mother took the knife from her hand. 'You've done marvels in here this morning. Quite enough. You won't sleep much tonight. I think you oughtta get some fresh air, Rachel. Here.' She passed her a paper handkerchief from the copious box on the dresser. 'Go on out for half an hour.'

She felt herself caving in. 'Yes, I'll do that.'

'Say goodbye to everyone, while you're at it. Tony'll be sore if he doesn't get at least a peck on the cheek.'

She wrinkled her nose and sniffed wretchedly. 'OK, Mom.'

'And go see all the animals, as well. You might as well remember them as they are on what's an otherwise perfectly ordinary Monday morning. Go *on*.'

She was at the door, pulling on boots, when her mother followed her into the office. 'And see if you can find Michael,' she added.

Rachel watched her own fingers hesitate as the boots went sliding onto her feet. If she answered, there would be questions. Pretending not to have heard, she let the doors crash behind her just in the way her father and brothers did twenty times a day. Then she ran down the steps as if someone were chasing her.

The wind had come up, clouds rolling in from the northeast. Perhaps there would be rain, now, after weeks without it. The farmyard was empty except for her father's rusting pickup, Tony's clapped out Chevvy, and some Rhode Island Reds scratching for corn grains beside the night arks.

She went to watch them. They were used to her and paused only to eye her beadily, crooning in their throats. Gently she stooped and picked one up. The bird was fluffed against the wind; Rachel bent her head and smelled the familiar scent of warmth and feathers, felt the soft, layered silkiness between her fingers. The hen crooned and nodded, her red wattles shaking, seeing all with sharp black eyes.

Rachel closed her eyes, remembering the first time she had held chicks, the stab of fear and wonder she had felt at the peck-pecking of their beaks against her palm. Other images, painful and happy, crowded in then: her father having to wring the neck of a chicken that was sick, before the whole flock could be infected and die; hand-rearing a chick that the hen had rejected for some strange reason, and hearing it peep-peeping across the kitchen floor behind her, bewildered and afraid; collecting eggs with her mother in the morning, before school—her hand closing in the nesting box around the warm, stone-like smoothness.

She set the hen back on the ground and sighed. Then she climbed to the highest point on the farm, the ridge where the hayfield ran parallel with Route 39. She loved the feel and smell of the enormous field at this time of year, the way the stubble lay gold in one direction and brown in the other, where the machines had cut in opposite swathes; the sound of the sharp dead stalks brushing her boots; the acrid scent of autumn in the air and on the ground. Her father had been lucky with the third cut this year, and would have to buy less dry feed than usual from the Arcade feedmill.

From the ridge she could see the whole farm—grainfields, tracks, the creek, the silos, the buildings, and the burnished trees on the north side, where Greys' land abutted the lower hill that marked that edge of the property. It all lay sleepy-looking under the smudged sky, everything except the trees losing colour in the turn of the seasons.

A figure moved in the yard, behind the house. She heard the thin echo of the storm door slamming, a fraction after she saw it shut, then she realized that Michael was crossing the yard. He was making for the path by the toolshed.

He stopped at the corner of the yard, looking to his left across the south pasture, no doubt watching the cows, and then to his right across the home pasture. He seemed indecisive. She wanted to call to him, to say, 'Come up and see the kingdom,' but all she could do was to wave.

He caught sight of her, then, and came at a slow run up the track from the foot of the field. She walked down through the stubble to meet him, her heart lightening, and a smile starting on her mouth. All the pictures she had first formed of him, after reading Marie's letter, crumbled and lay in pieces around her. He was beautiful. She melted inside, felt everything turn over, and back again. They had hardly spoken to each other, but she had lost herself completely.

'Apple sauce to you,' he said, when he reached her.

She sighed with relief. 'Saucy yourself.'

'Your mother suggested I keep you company for half an hour. Told me the coffee was finished, and if your father wanted me to have a break, then I'd better do as I was told. But I could see a new pot brewing on the hob. What's she up to?'

She felt like laughing. 'Blessed if I know.' It was a convenient saying of McEnroe's.

'Where are you going from here?' He turned and stood beside her. 'Ah, I see why you came up here.'

'Didn't Dad bring you up here on Saturday?'

'No. Just waved an arm and said, "Hay this year—and most years" and took me down into the other fields.'

'Typical! Then you missed the best view.'

He pointed to the trees on the far side of the farm. 'Those are what I always wanted to see. American trees in the *fall*. I can't get over the colours. The land over there looks as if it's on fire.'

She faced him shyly. 'We haven't long,' she said. 'How would you like to go get a closer look?'

Something electric crackled between them. She wanted him to take her hand and run breakneck with her down the hill, laughing and rolling and running to the bottom like the rabbits she had seen playing in the pasture last spring.

'All right,' he said. 'Come on then.' He strode off, and she had to hurry to keep up with him.

'You've lost your shadow, I see.'

'That dog Bruce? Yes. Every time I turned around I fell over the beast. Your dad tied him up, and your mother threatened him in no uncertain terms—the dog, I mean—with a bath if he gets into any more trouble.'

They cut between the home pasture and the grainfields. The track dipped into an old watercourse of the creek, then rose gradually until they came to the fence and the narrow band of woods along the northern boundary.

Michael stopped, just ahead of her, and stared. She heard him inhaling deeply, then breathing out slowly. *In a few days,* she thought, *he will be able to see his breath when he does that.*

'The red's brilliant—like nothing I've seen in England.'

'On a brighter day, it's even better.' She tried to see it with his eyes. She had always loved fall, but as she saw Michael's appreciation, she felt more of an observer than a participant. His pleasure in everything was fresh, her own somehow diminished.

He led the way to a small gate, one that was partly overgrown with creepers and was rotting from age and disuse. 'Could we go through?'

'Of course.'

'What's to see in the woods?'

She felt the press of time; within an hour she would be climbing into the pickup and going to Buffalo airport. 'Not much.'

He looked at her sceptically. 'I don't believe a word of it. I may not get much chance to see it, so if you've still got a few minutes, let's walk around.'

She wondered what he expected to find. No animals except for a few possums or foxes, well hidden at this time of day. Perhaps even a stray deer, though that too would be resting in the brush, cleverly concealed. But it did not matter; she would be with him.

Without answering she followed him along the overgrown path. It occurred to her that she should be leading the way; the woods, after all, belonged to her father, and she knew the twists and turns of them; knew where the foxes ran and dug dens; knew where the first wild arum lilies turned gold in April, where the dandelions and dog roses showed in May, and where larkspur winked out its blue stars in late September. But it was he who wanted to see the woods, and she felt at ease following him between the red and yellow branches.

He lifted a long, hooped bramble out of her way and gave her a quick smile. 'Aren't you glad we came in here?'

She was more glad than she could tell him.

'I like the smell of these woods. It's different from home.'

'How different?'

'Sharper, colder. The undergrowth even smells different.'

He was moving quite swiftly now, and once or twice where the path bent she lost sight of him in the leaves. She stumbled over a root and heard him stop. He was very still, and she quietened her own movements as she caught up with him, saw the muscles of his back ridge and tense under his shirt.

'Ssh. Can you hear—?'

The sound of her own breathing was loud to her now, and she could feel the beating of her heart. 'No—nothing,' she whispered.

'I can hear an animal. Listen.'

She strained but heard only the breeze in the leaves and in the cobwebs strung between them. She shook her head.

He bent back, put his mouth to her ear, his voice more urgent. 'It's in pain.'

She winced, turning her head away from his to hear. Then she heard it too, a soft whining. 'A fox.'

'In a trap?' He was frowning. 'Your father wouldn't set a snare, surely?'

She felt the colour flood into her face and raised her voice indignantly, 'No, he sure would not.' She broke away from him and crashed over fallen boughs and bare bushes in her haste. 'Whatever it is, we'd better find it.'

He was right behind her. 'A cub, perhaps?'

'At this time of year?'

They stopped again to listen, but the woods were silent, only the wind moving through the dry end of summer. Rachel felt foolish. She should be back at the house, putting things into the truck for the journey; not walking around the woods looking for a fox in an imaginary trap.

Michael stood frozen. 'There it is again!'

She heard the same low whining, nearer now, to their left. 'Yes, there is a fox's run on that side. And something's caught, all right.'

They slid their way down an overgrown bank. She could see midday light through the trees ahead of them; they were near the northwest corner of the woodland, where Greys' grazing pastures adjoined her father's land, and where the creek twisted for a hundred metres into the woods, then out again.

'Here!' Michael had reached the foot of the bank and was stooping just in front of her. 'Oh, you poor creature.'

A dog was huddled miserably in the thick brush where foxes usually ran. Rachel knelt beside Michael, her hand to her mouth.

'It's one of your dad's, isn't it?' He was putting out his hand to it.

She grabbed his arm. 'Stop! Don't! That's *Wally*.'

He tried to push her away. 'What—?'

'Not like Bruce. He's half wild, savage. Won't let anyone touch him except Pa. Didn't they tell you? And look, he is in a trap.'

The dog shivered, twitched, and struggled frantically. Its hind leg was caught in a fine, shining wire.

'He'll cut his leg off if he keeps on like that,' Michael said.

Rachel saw that the colour was draining out of Michael's face. She gritted her teeth. 'I'd sure like to know who did this.'

'Never mind who did it. Let's just get him out.'

The wire was attached to a strong stake that someone had driven into the ground. The wire had been invisibly looped across a twig on the other side of the foxes' run, and Wally had gone right into it.

As Michael went closer, the dog showed the whites of its eyes and bared its teeth furiously. Michael drew back, laughing uneasily. 'I'd better think about this a minute.'

Rachel hesitated beside him. Wally would know her voice, but the dog had never liked her and would certainly turn on her, especially now he was in pain. 'Wally,' she said, 'Wally, you'll be OK. Oh, I should get my father ... but there isn't time. Pa could get him out.'

'Then you'll miss your plane. And if we leave him, he may chew his leg off and bleed to death rather than stay in this hideous trap.'

She was sickened. 'Then we have to get him out, no matter what.'

Michael looked her up and down. 'Any gloves in those pockets?'

'No—oh, I wish.'

He took off his jacket and wrenched at the sleeves.

'What are you doing?'

'Making myself some protection.' He ripped out the sleeves and pushed his hands into them. 'I'm going to try and slide the wire off his leg.'

She looked doubtfully at Wally's leg. The dog was straining against the wire, already bloody where he had fretted and pulled it into his flesh, biting it and clawing at it with his front paws. 'You'll never—I don't see how—' The adrenalin surged through her as she thought how she would have to treat Michael's hand as well if Wally ran true to form and clamped his jaws shut.

Michael seemed to forget everything except the dog. He inched forward, his voice slow and soothing. The dog panted, then lay still, his liquid eyes fixed on Michael's face, almost hypnotized. 'That's it, that's it. Easy does it. Silly old Wally. Silly dog, and well named, you wally. You'll be all right, dog.'

Rachel held her breath, waiting for the horror of Wally's long teeth, snapping jaws, and the dripping of more blood onto the leaves.

But the dog didn't move. Michael's hand stroked the dog's rough coat, slower and slower, until, watching, she felt almost hypnotized herself. His hand went nearer and nearer to the injured leg, until his fingers slid out of the torn sleeve and closed on the wire.

The dog growled low in its throat, teeth showing. Still Michael talked and stroked, stroked and talked, easing the vicious wire out of its bloodied groove and down over the animal's hind paw.

Even when the snare fell empty onto the leaves, the dog didn't move.

Michael lifted his hand away gradually, then eased the sleeve off it. 'I'm going to tie this round his leg,' he whispered, without turning back to Rachel.

She backed away, expecting Wally at any moment to leap up and attack Michael or herself. But the dog lay strangely passive, as if transfixed by the gentleness.

She watched Michael bind up the leg and edge backwards, standing slowly. She was shaking with relief.

Michael wiped sweat off his upper lip. A streak of blood smeared his face and there were dead leaves in his hair, but his blue eyes were full of light.

Wally seemed to come alive. He scrambled to his feet, tail between his legs, and limped stiffly to where they stood. He whined again, head on one side, his eyes fixed on Michael. Slowly Michael extended his hand to the dog's muzzle.

He's licking him! Rachel stared in blank amazement, laughing shakily. 'You're wonderful,' she breathed. 'Just look at him.'

Michael's face was inscrutable. His smile had faded immediately. 'Come on, he'll take care of himself. You'd better get back to the house.'

The dog limped close to their heels all the way back along the meandering track to the gate. On the edge of the home pasture, Michael stopped. 'Is he all right with cattle and poultry, this one?'

'He sure should be. It's people he doesn't like.'

'Let's go through here, then.'

They cut across the field. The ground felt firmer, as if the night's frost, now in fact melted, were already taking hold for the winter. The grass was shrivelling, she noticed. Her father would have to bring the animals in for winter, any day. Everything growing in the pasture seemed to have been suspended. Plants along the fence line drooped.

'It's all dying,' she said.

'It's almost winter here,' he said shortly. 'What d'you expect?'

By the corner of the barn, though, in the shelter of it and out of reach of cows' voracious mouths, a clump of yellow daisies still stood up bravely. Michael pointed them out to her, stopping her with a hand on her arm. 'Not quite all dying,' he said.

She looked at the daisies, then back at him, dumbly, and they walked on.

The ducks had left the pond and were congregating near the chicken ark honking and quacking, apparently upset. They fled for the water with a trail of white feathers and flapping wings when Rachel, Michael and the dog rounded the corner of the barn.

Michael gave her an amused half grin. 'Wally's taken Christmas dinner here out of season, has he?'

She shuddered. 'I hope not. Mom would have a fit.'

The dog shouldered past them, ignoring the birds, and sank down by the stake where Don had tethered Bruce. There was more whining and licking, and Bruce yipped and barked, sniffing at the torn cloth tied on Wally's hindleg.

'I'll sort them out later,' Michael said, following her anxious gaze.

Maggie came out onto the back porch. 'Oh—good. You're back. You need to go, Rachel.'

'I know.'

Her mother nodded towards the pickup. 'Your father's upstairs getting washed up. He's packed your stuff in the truck. You about ready?'

Rachel saw her eyes dart over Michael's face and back to hers. 'I guess so.' She wanted to say something to Michael but didn't know what. 'I'd better run in and check my room one last time.'

'Did you see Tony out there?'

Rachel stopped guiltily beside her mother on the top step of the porch. 'My gosh—no, I forgot. Didn't see him.'

Her mother's eyebrows rose.

'We were in the woodland. We found Wally in a trap.'

'*A trap?* What trap?'

'There was a snare in the woods. There may be more, Mom. If we hadn't gone up there, Wally would have—'

Maggie was rooted to the spot. 'But who would set a snare in those woods? Not your father. I know there're foxes, but they don't trouble us much. And why would Wally go foraging up there, anyway?'

'The foxes, Mom. He'd be after a fox himself. The trap was on one of their runs.' She hugged herself. 'It was horrible! Dad should go up there and see if there are others—find out who laid them.'

Maggie looked distressed. 'Well, yes, we'll have to do that. We'll keep the dogs tied until we find out what's going on. But Rachel—'

'I know. I'm going.' She burst through the back doors. Her breathing was ragged, and she was still trembling. Now, though, she was shaking with emotion, as well. In the dimness of the familiar staircase, she shut her eyes and saw Michael's hand moving slowly, slowly over Wally's hide to move the cruel wire. She saw the way the dog slunk back and licked his hand, whining in gratitude. She saw the light in his eyes.

She toiled up the stairs, her fingers like claws on the banister, holding on to it as if all reality would slip away otherwise. *Michael,* she thought, in panic and longing. *Oh, but I'm going away.* She felt shattered, as if light had broken in on darkness and loneliness she had never even been aware of—happy with her family—until now. It would burn her, heat her through, but because she would not be with him, it would not comfort her.

When she came back to the top of the stairs a few minutes later, she heard her parents talking in the kitchen below. It was Michael's name that arrested her.

'I'll speak to the old man about him,' her father said. 'See if we can do it legally and work out some way round the immigration issue. I won't find a worker like Michael again in a hurry, whether Larry's back on the job or not.'

'You want him to stay, then?' That was her mother.

'As long as he wants to, but I don't suppose he'll stay long. Got all his life ahead. He'll want his training, and he'll be off on his own like Joel Wilkinson was—like I was. But I like him. We owe him a fair bit already.'

Rachel heard her father exhale heavily.

'I couldn't afford to lose Wally. And that's just for starters.'

A few simple words, and Michael would be staying for a while.

Rachel felt numb, confused, unbalanced. It would be painful but easy in some ways to walk down the stairs, kiss her mother goodbye, and drive away with her father. But nothing was the same any more—neither in Arcade, nor in herself... nor therefore in London.

In the kitchen three large pans of apples hissed and bubbled on the stovetop. The sweet autumn smell filled everything. That, at least, was the same, and would be next year, when she would still be away. She noticed as she went down the porch steps behind her parents that last night's cold had finally caught the roses. Their petals were blackened, at last, by frost. She stepped past their drooping heads and down into the windy yard. Michael was still there, sitting on his haunches beside the two dogs. White padding was pushing out of the torn armholes of his jacket, but he was oblivious.

'Rachel's off now,' Maggie said unnecessarily.

He stood and came towards her. She wanted him to hold her but remained stiffly beside her father, hating the moment, hating her own inability to speak.

'I hope it goes well, Rachel,' he said.

'You too,' she managed.

His voice was dry. 'Give my greetings to London.'

Somehow she found a cheerful tone. 'Kiss the runway, like the pope, when I land, you mean?'

'Don't bother.'

She wished she could ask where his family lived, could do something to tie a thin thread between them across the wide, wide waters. All she had was an address in Kent she could not possibly use—he had scrawled it for her earlier in the day. 'Goodbye Michael,' she said.

'Cheers.'

Her father took over, then. 'Michael, would you take a shovel out of the barn and go back up to the woods? Ask Tony to go with you, for safety's sake, and dig up that stake. Have a look for any others. Heaven knows, I don't want to lose anything else up there.' He pulled off his cap and pushed his hair out of his eyes, a gesture as familiar and endearing to Rachel as anything she associated with him. 'Why, even the cows get in the woods sometimes. It doesn't bear thinking about. And when I get my hands on whoever set that thing...'

'Don!' Maggie called over his mounting voice. 'For pete's sake!' She tapped her watch. 'You'll miss the flight, honey.'

It was all happening too fast. Her mother's arms went round her, pulling her close. 'Sweet Rachel.'

'Oh, Mom.' She closed her eyes and smelt her mother's familiar scent. At the same time she saw as if printed on her retinas the clumps of yellow daisies Michael had pointed out to her in the field.

'I'll miss you so.'

'Pa'll look after you.'

Rachel just wanted the goodbyes to be over. As the truck pulled out of the yard, she looked back and saw her mother waving from the porch, her face wet, and Michael walking away from the house as if he had already put her out of his mind.

But that's the way it'll have to be, she told herself.

She looked down into her lap at her hands folded into a tight, cold knot. Where she had cut her finger doing the apples, the blood had now clotted.

She thought of the blood on Wally's leg and Michael's face. She thought of Michael's cornsilk hair and blue eyes. Then she turned in her seat to look out at the familiar landmarks retreating behind them, one by one.

But she did not see them.

10

Rain fell in dark curtains onto the yard. Michael stood between Maggie and Don in the kitchen and watched it.

'About time,' Don said gruffly. 'It's threatened long enough.'

'Wasn't it raining when you did the milking this morning?'

'Splattering, Maggie, that's all. So I guess we got that last hay cut in at just the right moment.' Don sipped his tea and went on staring out of the window. 'Trouble is, I reckon we'll lose some of the barley now.'

Michael peered out. 'D'you think it'll rain all day?'

Maggie laughed. 'Around here, honey, when it starts raining, it generally rains for *three* days. We'll be lucky, the way the temperature's dropped, if it doesn't snow by the end of the week.'

'Surely not!'

'Snow in October's common enough up here. When the weather breaks, it breaks hard.'

He could see, now, why both Don and Rachel had seemed so morose about the onset of winter.

'Aren't there any jobs you can do in the barn this morning?' Maggie's face was lined with concern. 'You don't want to be out in *that*.'

Don grinned across at Michael. 'No. This is where I see what this guy's made of. Larry's still on his back. Tony's got the day off, and like it or not I've got to get up and do some more on that fencing. Michael can help.' His face darkened. 'Don't want Grey round here again with a bill for his dratted *bull!*'

Don pulled on his boots, and Michael followed suit. Ducking their heads as far as they could inside their jackets, they ran with shoulders hunched across to the toolshed.

'May's well go in comfort,' Don panted. 'C'mon.' He jumped into the cab of the tractor and motioned Michael to follow him. A moment later he had jumped out again, shouting about the trailer.

'Just in case the boys missed anything, let's take all the equipment with us.' He opened a ramshackle store cupboard and rummaged about. Michael just watched, knowing where nothing was. 'Wire cutters, gloves, pliers, iron bar, mallet... ah, Michael. Could you bring as many locust posts as you can carry? They're out back—in the woodpile. The thin ones, sharpened already. And a shovel or two, from the barn.'

Michael found the posts and hefted a big bundle back into the toolshed. Rain made the wood heavy and slippery. Don was bent over the back of the tractor hooking it to a trailer. 'Good job. We'll need more, though. Get them on our way round.'

'The spades—?' Michael felt slightly uneasy. For all his bulk, Don McEnroe moved fast, grew quickly impatient, and was a man of great energy; he wondered if he could keep up with him.

'That's OK. Get them now. I'll be done in a minute.' He knocked the pin into place and was still clanking safety chains when Michael went out.

He trudged across the yard again, his boots sliding. The dust left even after yesterday's hosing was turning into the mud of early winter.

The barn was dark and quiet but looked spotlessly clean. He pulled down the string that turned on the light by the door, then searched until he found the shovels among the other cleaning tools kept near Don's desk. As he turned to go out, he heard an ominous growl from the corner, and a dog crawled out, belly flat, ears pricked... and hindleg bandaged.

He stopped. 'Wally. It's me.'

The dog hesitated, looked ready to spring. Michael felt his throat go dry. He kept utterly still.

Wally crawled closer, sniffing and growling. Then he lay down, put his muzzle on his front paws, and began to pant, his mouth open in what was almost a smile.

'Wally?' Slowly he bent to the dog.

There was another faint growl, then once again Wally licked him. He wanted to stroke the dog, but contented himself with more soothing words and a quick examination, with his eyes, of the injured back leg. Then he stood slowly again and moved carefully to the barn door.

Don was back in the cab of the tractor, which he had driven up to the pond end of the yard without Michael having heard its engine. 'What took you so long?'

He threw the shovels into the trailer, opened the side door of the cab and climbed in beside Don. 'Wally was guarding the barn. I had to placate him to get out without a hole in my trousers.'

Don laughed. 'You've scored a hit there. Tony's used to him, and keeps a civil distance. Wally knows if he ever sank his teeth into my wife or either of my men I'd have his hide for kitchen carpet. Joel and Billy keep their distance as well; they're not around enough for him to remember all the time who they are. Like you said, he might take a fancy to their backsides.'

'He likes you, though.'

'Yeah, I feed him. He and Bruce were in the same litter, and I rescued them from a neighbour of mine who had more puppies than he knew what to do with. He would have taken them down to the Cattaraugus and put them in a stone-filled sack, if I hadn't come along. I think Wally had been beaten as a pup. He trusts me, but that's all.' Then he added cheerfully, 'Looks like he might trust you, as well. Could be useful. You keep in with him, if you can.'

'I'll try.'

Michael admired the way Don handled the tractor so smoothly, taking the corner of the home pasture in an easy curve. The windshield wipers swept to and fro in front of them, the rain dancing madly on the thin glass, and muck from beneath the wheels splattering up into it. The cows were huddled, backs to the wind, in the most sheltered corner.

The tractor began to jolt as they left the big pasture and hit the machine ruts on the track that divided the fields. They bounced against each other, laughing.

Don's mind seemed to be travelling a new path. 'By the way—did you and Tony reckon you got all the traps in the woods yesterday?'

Michael had gone back into the woods the day before, after Rachel had left, and searched for snares. No more stakes or wires anywhere. 'I think there was just the one, as I told you. We really combed the woods.'

They were passing the broken gate now, where only twenty-four hours before he had walked with Rachel to look at the trees.

'Well, fine. I hope you're right. I'm going to make a close check of that stake some time and try to work out where the snare came from.' Don gritted his teeth. 'I know there're foxes, but I've no time for people setting traps up here. They're not necessary. And on my land...!'

Michael tried to read his face. 'Any idea who might have set them?'

'I've got my theories, let's say.' Don stopped the tractor at the edge of the now empty field, in the middle of the line of fencing. 'I want to go over the fence along here especially carefully,' he said, 'even though we were up here a couple days ago.' He gave a short, dry laugh. 'Time for a history lesson as we go.'

They swung out onto the sodden stubble and looked up briefly at the drenched trees; all the leaves were darkening from red and yellow to rust and brown. 'History lesson?'

'Yeah—the story of why we're doing this work now, and maybe even why... no, that's not fair, until I have more to go on.'

Michael shrugged and followed as Don made his way slowly along the fence, pulling and pushing at the posts, and examining every bit of barbed wire. He waited for Don to explain. 'It's a long story, but Elias Grey was thick as thieves with the man who owned this land before we bought it—Davies by name. Grey's got the property north of us.' He waved his hand towards the woods. 'Other side of those trees. When Davies sold to us because his boys didn't want to follow him, Grey disliked me from the start. I was the city boy, the outsider, the "book farmer" who had to prove myself.' He paused by an unsteady post and knocked it in more firmly with the mallet. 'Well, one way or another I couldn't seem to make any headway with the guy. He was a cunning old fellow—still is. Confused me by coming on quite friendly when we had some serious trouble—' He stopped and wiped the rain out of his eyes. 'Not something I like to talk much about. Ask Maggie. She'll tell you. Anyhow, Grey let me use his facilities for milking my cows for a while, when I needed to. I wasn't crazy about the man, but I thought we'd get on OK once we knew each other better.'

Observing Don's purposefulness both with the fence and the story, Michael felt redundant, except as a listener. 'And you didn't?'

''Fraid not. Things improved generally after three or four years up here, when Rachel started nursery school and we got to know some of the other families in town. Wilkinsons—they're west of us, on the other side of the creek—have always been allies. Not Grey, though. Any chance he could put the knife in, whether it was at the feedmill, or with the town gas company, or when some of us decided to get together to make a parish grain donation to charity, or at the Co-operative—anywhere—he did it.'

'But why? Why would he want to do that?'

Don moved on. 'If I could've figured out why, maybe I could've done something about it.' He waved his hands. 'Maybe I was a threat to him because I wanted most things done the modern way. I wanted it state of the art, and I rang my tech adviser for advice; that was my sin. I didn't go down to the Agway and chew baccy and straw with the good ol' boys for half an hour to figure out a problem. So I guess they didn't trust me, didn't know me, and couldn't like me.'

'But surely all that was a long time ago?'

Don laughed sadly. 'Twenty years. A long time to bear a grudge, or to be on the receiving end of it. But this is the sticks. Twenty years counts for nothing. And Grey seems to be like that. He holds on to what he's got, including his grudges.'

'He's your age?'

'No! Heavens, he was sixty when we came. Must be eighty now, I should think. He clings on to life as tenaciously as he does everything else—cantankerous old man that he is.'

Michael thought vaguely that under cantankerousness there was often a layer of softness. Don seemed to overhear the thought. 'And don't imagine for one moment that he's one of those characters like leather on the outside and velvet on the inside. Not a chance!'

'So—' Michael looked farther along the line of neat fencing and saw nothing wrong anywhere. 'Has he complained about the fencing? Is this a check you have to do extra, because he's made accusations? And what about the fencing on the other side of the woods—if it's yours?'

'It's mine, all right. And I'll be checking that, as well, believe me, as soon as possible. And yes, he's complained about the fencing. Calls me at least once a week, but the guys can never find anything wrong. Yet just let us leave off the checking for a few days, then sure as taxes, something goes wrong.'

Michael had been turning over everything he'd said. 'Was this the man you bought the dogs from, then?'

Don guffawed. 'Yes, that's another little thorn in his flesh. Like I said, one of his bitches whelped, and I happened along when Grey was getting out the sack. I think the old villain would have liked to drown the pups anyway, but he could hardly argue when I said I'd relieve him of a couple. Maggie says I'm soft, and I felt soft as butter when I saw those poor mites ready for the riverbottom. They're sheepdogs, really, but I like having them around. Bruce is useless, too dumb for anything. Wally's another story—fine guarddog, except when he's after foxes! Grey might wish he'd kept that one, at least.'

They reached the corner of the field and turned back towards the tractor.

'Looks good so far. But up there—' Don was pointing, then dropped his hand. 'Wait, I see something.'

Without elucidating, he half ran, half scrambled down the bank above the creek. Michael saw that they were very near now to where he and Rachel had found Wally in the snare. They went farther, though, along the edge of the creek, to where it curved sharply and then turned into a finger of Greys' land where the trees petered out.

'I can see it!' Michael ran forward abreast of Don. 'There *is* a hole. Look, the fence's broken here.'

In a small hollow, out of sight of all but the most scrupulous inspection, one of the posts was uprooted and the wire bent useless into the ground. Blurred animal tracks from Grey's land and from the woods made it clear that the fence had been down for some time.

Don stood still, pushed back his cap, and wiped his eyes again. He let out a low groan. 'Ah, nobody's perfect! This is what I get for sending the others out and not checking so well myself. Damn it, this explains *everything*.' He turned to Michael. 'Want to hear more of the story?'

Michael felt cold and wet, but he wouldn't grumble and give in. And he felt curious. 'Of course.'

'How about you stand here and keep watch? I'll bring the tractor down as far as I can, and we'll fix this once and for all.' He took stock of the posts he and Michael were carrying betwen them. 'Yup, that's what we'll do. Not enough tools here after all. I want this fence to stand till the last trump.'

Michael shivered but stood his ground. McEnroe was back within minutes, the tractor chugging and sliding across the softening field. Don turned it along the contour of the slope; then they unloaded the trailer and set to work on the repairs, Michael steadying the posts while Don drove them in.

'It all makes sense now,' Don said. 'Remember I said Grey was a stickler for the old ways?'

'Yes—go on.' He felt more useful now, and as he dug the next post-hole with the iron bar, the way Don had shown him, sweat mingled with the rain around his collar.

'He's the only guy round here, would you believe, who still keeps a bull. Won't use the AI service at the Co-operative. Well, I understand some of his thinking, but it's not economic. I couldn't afford to do it that way, at least. And his bull's a pain. Folk can't cross his pastures for fear of getting gored. Oh, the same might be true of my land, with Wally around, but it's not *quite* the same, I reckon. Much worse when a bull gets out.'

Michael looked at the old tracks in the mud. 'You think his bull got out?'

'Must have done. I'll tell you why. This corner here, on my side, was left for grazing last year. I used it all the summer and into the fall.' He frowned. 'Then in the spring, on the first good days, before I would plough it up again for this alfalfa, I put one of my prize heifers in here.'

Michael nodded. 'Oh-oh, I can guess.'

'Sure you can. She was coming up to two, prime for showing, and I didn't want her in calf for another six months. I had her in here a few days at the beginning of March when we had some early sunshine—put her in with the cows I was drying off. I never knew what happened, but when the cold came back and I brought them all in, I soon discovered she was in calf.'

Michael frowned. 'Grey knew she was a special animal?'

'I doubt it. But he sure knew I'd asked him to keep his bull off this end of his land.' He pointed at the creek bed. 'Any time the water went down, I figured it was a short walk for a horny bull round onto this pasture.' He shook his head. 'Shouldn't have trusted him to honour his word and keep the bull elsewhere. And, obviously, he didn't. That bull didn't have to walk even as far as the creek. Oh, I can just imagine! Must have come across my heifer that week. Sure, I'll get a good price for her calf, but I couldn't show *her* as a heifer. Worse than that, when I complained to Grey that his bull must have "walked on water" to get round into this field, he said if the heifer was in calf he wanted a fee off me. For his prize bull!'

Don straightened his back, walked over to the tractor, and began to set up a block and tackle. 'It'd be funny if it wasn't Grey. The whole thing's just typical—dirty from start to finish. And I'm not even convinced my men missed the hole. Hate to say it, but I wouldn't put it past Grey to open up the hole himself and wave the bull through! I'm mad at myself for not checking this section, but I'm madder than anything with Grey himself.' He took a deep breath, then grinned. 'There. Does that fill you in?'

'It certainly does.'

'Right. Now we gotta stretch the wire. C'mon, this is the nasty bit.'

Michael helped him uncoil the lines of wire. 'Wouldn't the pliers do the trick?'

'Not strong enough here. OK on a straight bit of fencing, but not where it's all so uneven, like here.'

For the next half hour they worked in concentrated silence. When the fence was at last fully repaired, Don grinned and stood back.

'Now I defy anything short of a herd of buffalo to get through here.'

They climbed back into the tractor and lumbered back the way they had come.

'Now you see why I always say politics is good training ground for farming,' Don began again. 'Lots of backstairs manoeuvring and lobbying and cheating goes on. You can never figure out if it's your own ineptitude or someone else's skullduggery.'

Michael wanted to say that he doubted Don's 'ineptitude' was a frequent problem, but he refrained. *It'll sound too like flannelling.* He smiled. He thought of Grey and the heifer. 'So did you pay the bill for the bull?'

'Ha! Bill for the bull! No way. Figured the old goat owed me a thing or two, so if I get a prize calf out of it, he could always buy it from me.' He chuckled to himself. 'Poetic justice, don't you think?'

'I'd like to see that!'

'So would I. He won't, of course. More likely to come down with his wire cutters and demolish the whole fence when no one's looking.'

'Could he have set the trap, then?'

Don did not look at Michael as he answered, and the words came out measured, cautiously spoken. 'I was thinking he might.'

'You seriously think—?'

'I don't believe he would open up the fence on purpose. I was joking about that. If the bull wanted that heifer, it wouldn't have taken much for him to trample down a weak bit of fence like that. There you go! Too bad for him that I didn't mend that fencing before. But the snare, yes. More than likely.'

'What'll you do?'

'Nothing, right now. Make sure, first.'

'What would he have been after?'

'Foxes. There's still a bounty on their pelts up here. But he had no business trapping in my woods. The foxes don't bother him any more than they bother me. He wouldn't have been after possums—not worth the trouble.'

'Bears?'

'Hardly any bears round here nowadays. But it doesn't matter what he thought he was trapping, not in my woods. If it was Grey, and if this was his crazy way of getting back at us for the bull, then I'll have his guts for garters. Wilkinson—any of the guys—would have laughed and chalked it up to nature having its way. But of course, like I said, no one else is nuts enough to keep a bull... Enough of that. Let's get us some coffee.'

The kitchen was warm, untidy, but—for the first time since Michael had arrived—empty of people. Already he had become used to the way the family spent most of its time at home in the kitchen. He felt at ease there in a way he had never felt at ease in his mother's kitchen in Kent.

'Your wife's gone out, has she?'

'Might be down at the store, but her car was outside. I doubt it.' Don went through to the hallway and shouted up the stairs.

Maggie came down, then, fussing over them, taking their wet clothes and pouring coffee. *Mother hen,* Michael thought, warming to her.

Later Don went out to catch up with paperwork at his desk in the barn. 'You rest up a bit,' he told Michael. 'There'll be plenty to do tomorrow.' He nodded to Maggie. 'I've been giving this man a potted history of a few things. You're better at that, sweetheart, than I am.' He glanced at Michael again. 'If we haven't already talked his ears off, tell him some more.'

The doors slammed behind him. Maggie wiped the table and poured more coffee. 'Won't be too many lazy, quiet days like this, I assure you. Make the most of it.'

'I'm happy as can be.'

'That's good.' She sat down again, opposite him. Her brown eyes were direct and bright. 'What's he been telling you?'

'Mainly about Mr Grey and some of the problems there. The heifer, the dogs, the old enmity between them.'

'Ah, it makes me sad, that.' Her brow creased into a frown. 'The McEnroes are used to having enemies, but I don't like living like that. I'd love to have peace.'

'What about Grey's wife?'

'Dead for years.' Her smile came back again. 'I like to think a woman would have made him different, softer. But you *do* have to be tough up here, and that's why Grey's lasted so long. Without the wife, I had no way in, for sure. God knows it was hard enough to get into conversations with the women when we first came, let alone the men.'

'But it's better now?'

'Most of the time.' She looked away.

When we had some serious trouble . . . ask Maggie. She'll tell you. Don's words pushed to the front of his mind.

'How did it start? Your husband—'

'I know. Hates to talk about it. In fact we came closer to losing the farm in the first year—in fact even before we were together—than at any other time.' She assessed him shrewdly. 'You interested?'

He smiled. 'More "history lesson"?'

'That what Don called it? Well, if you like to hear, I don't mind talking all day.'

He laughed. 'Not used to company?'

'It's rare now the kids are older.'

Something made him think of Rachel, and the words were out of his mouth, dangerous between them, before he had thought what he was saying. 'You'll miss Rachel.'

Her eyes filled, and he glanced down, embarrassed, wanting to bite his tongue. 'Yes. She's a good friend, a loving daughter. The boys spend most of their free time with Don. Man's men. Always have been. Unless they change when they're through school and college, they'll like nothing better to take this farm when we retire—Billy especially. Second generation farmers—they'll have none of the sense of isolation we had at first. They grew up into it, and they love it, thank God. That makes Don happy, so I'm happy, too. But Rachel's absence makes a big hole here.' She stopped. 'No, we won't talk about her.'

He studied the grain of the worn table. 'Tell me about the early days here—if you don't mind.'

Her words came pouring out. He listened carefully, thinking all the time that he might one day be telling a parallel story to someone else, of how he himself had begun the path towards working his own farm.

'Like I said before, neither of us was bred to this, you know. I guess you met Don's father, so you know maybe that McEnroes are a family with old money and plenty of clout in New England.'

Michael nodded. 'Yes, I like your father-in-law.'

'Well he's changed. He was disappointed, at first, that Don didn't follow him into law or politics. In the end, though, I know he's proud. Don's done things as well here as McEnroe did in court, all those years. And McEnroe's an outdoors man, at heart—always loved golf. If you think about it, it's not so surprising that Don would want to work outside for life. The cows . . . well, that's a far cry from the State House and the county courts—' She grinned ruefully, 'Though Don might tell you otherwise on some days when they're being ornery as heck, digging their hooves in, giving us a hassle, or breaking out somewhere.'

They both laughed.

'Don went to agricultural technical college over in Massachusetts. I met him while he was studying—through his sister.' Her face grew serious. 'Ellie was my closest friend. We stuck together through high school and, later, college. I was from a very ordinary family—middle class Catholic and no skeletons in the closet. I was pretty awed by the McEnroes at first, but I think Ellie and I did each other good. When she finished high school, we stayed together in a little apartment off Boston Common. But she died—she was a drug addict.' Maggie stopped, holding up her hand.

Michael debated telling her what he had overheard at the Williams' house, but thought better of it. He saw the distress in her eyes as she continued.

'No, don't say a thing. It was a very painful time, for years, but we got through it. And out of the ashes of that friendship came all this.' She swept her hand round the room and pointed out of the window. 'Not a way I would have chosen to start the real beginning of our romance, but that's the way it was.'

He shifted uncomfortably on the wooden chair. He had not expected this baring of her soul. He didn't understand yet, either, how this story fitted in with the tension between the McEnroes and the Greys. But he waited. He was used to listening, after years of Ian and Kate talking at him, demanding his attention. And he found he didn't feel the same about listening to Don and Maggie, anyway, as he did when his own family was talking.

She smiled sadly. 'Am I saying too much?'

He felt even more uneasy at her sharp perception. 'Oh—no, not at all.'

'Well, then.' She hesitated but seemed to believe him. 'It was before I was up here. Don had just bought the place. There was still so much to organize. I was teaching—finishing the semester in Boston—when I got a call. He was in hospital. There'd been a fire.'

Michael swallowed. 'Here—in the house?'

'No. There was an old double barn out where our big barns are now. Don was in here eating supper. He'd just been in the old barn bringing feed down for the heifers. The cows were in stanchions in those days. A fire started in the hayloft. It went through the barn like a flash.'

Michael watched her face.

'It's hard for Don to talk about it, because he had some burns on his hands. He says now he reacted rather than thought what he did. The cows were chained in, you see, and he couldn't bear to see them die that way. So he let them out first, but he lost his heifers—all of them. The yield was down for months, and he had to milk at Greys' place.'

More pieces of the puzzle slotted into place. 'His hands—was that serious?'

'Not physically, not for long. It was more the loss of confidence. He worried he wouldn't be up to the work. He had terrible nightmares about the animals. And he worried for a while that he had been at fault. It was a relief when we found that he wasn't, but people still claimed he was, and it was hard to live under the barrage of suspicion and innuendo. And of course there were money worries.' She appraised him. 'We're both Catholics—Don's got more faith than I have. But without knowing God's love and help, neither of us would have made it.'

He thought again of the years when he had wanted to leave home and escape the sniping and sneering of Ian, when he had longed to show his mother and brother that there were some kinds of achievements more important than doing well with music exams and books at school; when he had clung desperately to his own faith, and waited. 'I understand that very well,' he said gently.

Her eyes were still moist. 'I was slow to discover the source of all the love I felt when I was with Don or his father, I admit it. But that's another story!' She rallied. 'Meanwhile Grey hadn't a good word for anything Don was doing. We had the assessors in, of course, and they said it was a wiring problem, but Grey and some of the cronies he had then—all dead now—started talking. Stories went round. Some folk wouldn't speak to us.'

'How did you manage?'

'Lonely. But we weren't going to be *cowed* by that sort of trashy talk.' She grinned.

'We started from scratch again—spent a lot of time at auctions and investigating loans. Then we did a big PR exercise when the new barn went up. It helped our credibility with some folk, but not all.'

'What about Grey?'

'Things got worse with Grey. Don couldn't wait to bring the cows back here. The cows weren't easy out of their familiar space, and we lost money like water down a drain. Without some good advice from the tech and some realistic loans, we would've gone under. I took it harder than Don.' She smiled. 'He's such an optimist, such a worker. I might have given up. The Wilkinsons helped us, as well. Christian people worthy of the name.'

'I'll meet them?'

'I hope so. Bound to, sooner or later. Pity the old man's gone, but you'll like Joel and his mother. Good people.'

He rubbed his hand up and down the grain of the table. 'Perhaps I'll have a story like that myself, one day.'

She laughed and went with the coffee things to the sink. 'Oh, I hope not! I wouldn't wish it on anyone.'

Marie came to his mind then, and he wanted her there. *If only she had heard*... But no. It was no use pretending. And by the time he had a farm of his own, perhaps in England, things would be different in many respects. He could think of no towns in Britain quite as isolated and parochial as Maggie had made Allegany County sound. He saw now that it wasn't just physical toughness the McEnroes had needed; they had needed emotional resilience as well.

The doors swung open then shut with the usual crash, as Don came through the office and into the kitchen with his boots still on. Maggie looked up in surprise. 'I thought you were in the barn.'

'I was.' Don waved a familiar stake—from the snare. 'But I got to thinking about that trap, and I wasn't going to sit there any longer with that on my mind. I ran over to Wilkinsons.'

Maggie was frowning. 'But what's Joel Wilkinson got to do—?'

'Nothing. He sure didn't set this thing. I just thought he might be able to help me figure out who did.'

'And?'

'I didn't put any ideas into his head. Tried to tell him how they found it, and where, in a neutral way. Didn't want him to prejudge things the way I've been afraid of doing.'

Maggie looked pointedly at Don's boots but said nothing, and Michael could guess that he was too excited to know he was still wearing them in the kitchen.

'It's pretty clear Grey's to blame.'

Maggie sighed heavily. 'I was afraid of this.'

'Wilkinson was down in the lumberyard a week ago. Said he saw Grey there, buying split wood for fenceposts.'

'Nothing unusual in that.'

'No. Course not. Except that Grey doesn't hold with locust posts the way we do. You know why I like locust; it lasts almost for ever. But Grey likes the old way—uses ash or maple.' He tapped the stake on the table. 'This is ash. Joel doesn't use ash, I don't use ash, and there's no ash trees hereabouts where just anyone could have split this—except at the lumberyard. And look, it's unseasoned wood. New. Not long out of the sawmill.' He drew a steady breath and went on, 'That wouldn't be enough to go on, but I called the lumberyard to ask about their ash stocks.'

'Do they keep much?'

'Cut it to order specially, every two seasons—just for one customer. Guess who.'

'Ah.' Maggie looked more and more unhappy.

Michael leaned forward. 'What will you do now?'

Don grinned. 'Think hard before I do anything ... Well, I'm tired. Any more coffee left?' He slumped down beside Michael. 'Good thing Rachel isn't here to get the news. She'd be as upset about the discovery as she was about the trap.'

In his mind Michael pictured Rachel's frantic eyes as they found the trap and she warned him back. He remembered the way her hair fell forward over her face as she tried to stop him get the dog free. He recalled, too, the savage, terrifed expression of an animal in pain.

He knew he would dislike Elias Grey, even before he met him.

1 1

Rachel was swept into her grandfather's arms as soon as she walked off the ramp and into the main concourse of the airport. Over his shoulder she saw her grandmother's smile, the blue eyes crinkled in pleasure.

'Honey! Great to see you!' McEnroe gave her a another squeeze and released her.

She greeted Marianne next, seeing out of the corner of her eye the silvery brightness of the platinum daisy ring as her grandmother put both hands on her shoulders and drew her close. 'Dear GraMar.'

'Gee, we're so happy to see you.'

Rachel beamed at them both. 'Seems like yesterday.'

Marianne laughed. 'My birthday, you mean? No—it seems a long time ago to me.'

McEnroe took her hand luggage. 'C'mon. Let me have that. Where's the other stuff? Your mother phoned and said you had quite a load.'

'It's not too bad. Luggage carousel, I guess. Down there.' She linked arms with them both. 'Oh, I'm glad I could come here first. It's like a resting place.' She still had Michael at the back of her mind. 'I'm going to miss it all so much.'

'They'll miss you more, I'm sure,' McEnroe said.

She let him lead the way as usual, shepherding them, asking her so many questions about her journey and about St Stephen's that she could neither keep up with him nor answer.

As usual, people in the concourse stopped and stared at them, pointing and whispering. 'Isn't that Senator McEnroe?' Marianne was used to the attention that was always turned on them, but stiffened

179

against it. McEnroe nodded briskly in acknowledgement and kept up his quick pace. Rachel just smiled. She had never got used to the goldfish bowl that her grandparents lived in, and it surprised her every time she visited them.

But soon she forgot the rude stares, relaxing as the Oldsmobile passed the hulls and masts of the naval shipyard, dipped into the tunnel, and began the long trek through the city. Her grandfather could, she knew, easily have opted for a state-owned chauffeur-driven limousine to and from Boston; but he had always disdained it, preferring to drive his own car wherever he went with the family. It was one of the things that endeared him to her, that he had always tried hard to protect what little privacy and normality they did have.

Cambridge, Somerville, Arlington, Lexington—the familiar names and landmarks fell into place one by one, and she recalled Christmases, birthdays, and anniversaries when they had *all* made the trip to Boston to stay with the grandparents. But it was strange to be arriving in the city now, on a Monday afternoon when everyone was coming out of school or still at work; when her grandfather would usually be in his office in the State House.

She strained against the seatbelt to rest her chin on the back of his seat. 'How come you're not working today?'

'Oh, I was in there this morning, you may be sure. There's a lot on.'

'Always is,' Marianne's voice was brittle.

'But when my best granddaughter arrives, I know where my priorities lie.' He caught her eye in the mirror and grinned at her.

She melted with love for them both, but then sank back against the padded softness of her own seat and realized afresh the ache of knowing that it would be a long time, after this, before she would see them again.

The car telephone buzzed imperiously. Rachel caught the glance that went between her grandparents as their heads turned in surprise; saw the indignant pursing of Marianne's lips and the tic that began in McEnroe's cheek.

'I sure wish you didn't have that thing,' Marianne said.

'So do I, honey. But sometimes it's necessary.' As the phone continued its insistent buzzing, McEnroe pulled the car into a truckstop and picked up the handset. 'McEnroe.'

Rachel watched the Fords and Buicks and Cadillacs cruising by and wished she did not have to hear the call. She felt her grandmother's tension.

McEnroe leaned his head against the window as he spoke. 'Yup, yeah, I know... No, not now.' He sounded weary and slightly short of breath. 'I'm on my way up to Bedford—you knew that. Give me about fifteen minutes, willya?... No, no can do right now. You stay there. I'll call you right back.'

He replaced the phone in its bracket, gave Marianne a rueful smile, and eased the car back into traffic.

'Who was it?'

'Just one of the guys in the office. He'll have to wait.'

Marianne sighed.

'No honey, please don't get upset.' McEnroe flung out one hand. 'Do you see *me* getting upset? Listen, that's just the way it is, some days. You wouldn't have known a thing about it if I'd been in there, now would you?' His voice was calculated to sound soothing, Rachel thought, but she didn't miss the sudden rigidity of his shoulders and neck.

They flashed past the sign that proclaimed the city limits of Bedford, and McEnroe slowed the car. Rachel shut her eyes and wondered what the call meant and why both her grandparents seemed suddenly uncomfortable. It was not like McEnroe, she thought, to let matters at the State House drag him so quickly into irritation. Then she remembered the summer, and her anxiety for him. It wasn't just state business that he had on his mind these days.

She felt afraid again, did not want to know what was going on, not now when she was travelling to Britain and could not share in any way in his concerns. She had looked forward simply to following McEnroe around the golf course or going to the wildlife refuge with Marianne, for the short time they would have together. She wanted to empty her mind, before she caught the plane to England, of all except what her new life would bring.

Already, however, she was discovering that it wouldn't be possible.

Her mother's sorrow had run down her own cheeks. Her father's woebegone expression as he waved her onto the plane was on her own face again. Michael's indifference was imprinted in her mind. And now her grandfather's worries came crowding in.

Leaving America would not after all be leaving the ones she loved. There was no leaving the people you love, she decided, until God claimed you. In his scheme of things, the Atlantic was a little speck of water. Space did not divide her, not emotionally, at least, from the ones she would be parting from this week. A blessing and a bane.

She opened her eyes as the car slowed even more, knowing without looking that they were now very near the house.

'Here we are, sweetheart,' Marianne said brightly.

McEnroe signalled to turn left. Cars came in a steady stream in the opposite direction, and behind them the traffic built up in an impatient line, horns honking.

'OK, keep your shirts on,' McEnroe chuckled.

Rachel sat forward again and looked left down the treelined avenue that led to 'McEnroevia'. *Home east,* she said to herself, glad again to be here.

'Here we go, folks.' McEnroe slipped the footbrake and inched forward as a gap appeared in the oncoming traffic.

Suddenly there was a squeal of tires and the ugly smell of burning rubber. As if out of nowhere came a low-slung black car, engine roaring, straight towards them. In an instant, Rachel heard the simultaneous intake of breath, a scream from her grandmother, and a shout from her grandfather.

Marianne grabbed for McEnroe's sleeve. '*No! No, don't!*' But the Oldsmobile was already half way across the junction. It lurched as McEnroe's foot went flat down on the gas, pushing the car forward. Rachel was flung back against the seat, her shoes cracking against the bottom of the seats in front, her stomach muscles wrenched by the impact. The world seemed suspended, in slow motion, as the black car braked, slid, and came bearing down on them.

McEnroe grunted, his shoulders massed in concentration. The Oldsmobile shot into the left turn.

A grinding crash, and the hideous tinkle of glass. The black car had caught them on the rear fender, and both cars swung round violently. Instinctively, Rachel covered her head and ducked. Her grandmother's scream went on and on. Then there was another great crunching thud, and both cars came to rest at the side of the junction.

The world went utterly quiet. No more horns blared at them. No engines were running. Rachel found herself drenched in sweat, and shaking. They sat in stunned silence.

'Out—fast as you can.' McEnroe was galvanized. It was the voice of a major general, and they obeyed without thinking, shoving open the doors. Though Rachel's had buckled in the middle, it opened immediately.

Marianne fell into Rachel's arms on the side of the street, and they both slumped against the silvery bark of a large birch. 'Thank God,' Marianne breathed. 'We're all OK.' She was shivering uncontrollably.

McEnroe was slower to join them on the verge. His normally weathered face was chalk-white and trembling; Rachel watched him sway as he moved.

The driver of the black car was jumping out too, a man by himself, and young. 'What the hell?' His voice wasn't slurred, as Rachel had expected.

McEnroe turned and faced him. 'You were about forty miles an hour above the speed limit,' he said bluntly.

'*You* were turning across oncoming traffic,' the other accused.

A crowd was gathering by the side of the street.

'We won't settle things like this, honey,' Marianne urged. 'C'mon—let's just do the necessary and get ourselves home.' She was shaking with shock, her eyes feverish and her hands clutching at McEnroe's jacket.

'I saw what happened, Senator.' A woman pushed forward. 'It was just like you said.'

'Senator?'

Rachel caught the frightened look on the other driver's face, then the dawning recognition.

McEnroe pulled out his driver's licence. 'Here. But who I am is hardly the point. We had an accident, and we both need information.' He turned to the gathering crowd. 'Please, ladies and gentlemen— don't hang around unless you saw *everything* and you're willing to witness.'

Taking her cue, Rachel gently led her grandmother along the street. 'Let's leave the men to work it out,' she said. 'I'm going to wrap you up and get us some coffee.'

Marianne's eyes swerved to hers. 'I was just going to say the same.' Her voice was high, her teeth still chattering. 'But what about your baggage, dear? We need—'

'It doesn't matter now. We're safe. You must let me look after you, GraMar.' Behind them, Rachel heard McEnroe telling someone to redirect the stalled traffic and asking for the other man's licence. 'He'll get it all straightened out. Come on.'

Marianne's fingers on her arm were like a bird's feet: small, and hard. 'Yes—but, oh, he's not himself right now. I worry ... And you— you're off to England. And now this.'

Rachel stopped. 'It doesn't *matter*. Really it doesn't. It's only a car. No one was hurt.'

'But the media ...' Marianne had turned as if to go back.

Rachel knew her grandmother had always hated the press. 'The police will check it all out. Please, GraMar.' She knew she couldn't insist, and so tried to make light of it. 'Please—we've gotta get you treated for shock. My first patient.' She thought of Wally, then, and Michael, but put her arm firmly around her grandmother's slight waist and led her on.

The wide sweep of the driveway in front of the big house was so normal, so quiet behind its tall hedges and open gate, that Rachel almost wanted to weep with relief. The housekeeper had been watching for them, but looked taken by surprise when they came in on foot, without McEnroe. Still, she bustled them into the family room and brought coffee and cookies.

'You eat these right now,' she insisted.

Rachel and Marianne submitted to her cossetting, and Rachel wrapped her grandmother in an afghan that always lay on the back of the sofa. The sweet cookies tasted good, and they both fell back into the sofa and stared at one another, as if seeing each other for the first time, now, rather than at the airport.

Rachel tried to gather her thoughts. Reluctantly, she began, 'So what's happening here?' Marianne met her eyes. 'A lot he can't talk about.'

'Even after all he told me this summer? Oh, but he seems more strung out than I can ever remember. That accident—'

'May very well have been his fault.' Marianne dropped her head onto her wrist and sat motionless. 'Dear God, it all happened so fast.'

Rachel had been replaying it in her mind but could not reconstruct things properly. Had McEnroe pulled across the junction before or after the other driver appeared? 'Yes, it was like a flash.'

'But I don't know, Rachel.'

'There's something else bothering him. He went to pieces when the phone rang.'

Marianne looked up sharply. 'You mustn't exaggerate, honey. And you mustn't try to figure him out. You may be starting your training as a physician, but you're no psychiatrist.'

She felt small. Marianne had never spoken so abruptly to her. 'I'm sorry.'

Marianne smiled faintly. 'Me too. I didn't mean to raise my voice. We've so much been looking forward to today. Too much pressure for your grandfather at the moment—we wanted to have the time with you free and easy, and forget the rest.'

Rachel slid off her seat, knelt by Maraianne's lap, and took her hand. 'Let's do that, then. An accident is nothing if everyone's OK.' Her mind reached for something, anything, to distract them. 'Let's talk about something else. Tell me the family news.'

Marianne rallied a little. Family gossip was something that never failed to arouse her interest. 'Your other grandmother called yesterday and wanted to know why you weren't visiting with *her*.'

Rachel groaned and sank her cheek against Marianne's perfumed arm. 'Oh, no ... I didn't even think of—'

Marianne's face creased momentarily into a naughty smile. 'It's OK. Your mother was one jump ahead and called her when you were on your way. Told Laura you were only passing through for England. When Laura called me I told her she was more than welcome here for supper—either day.'

Rachel waited, searching her face.

'She declined.'

Rachel tried to mask her relief, though it had never been a secret between them that she had always found Grandma Laura hard to get on with. 'But we'll be having another visitor, for lunch tomorrow.'

Rachel thought of Marie and brightened. 'Oh—Marie Williams?' Then she remembered that Marie would be back in college.

Marianne looked blank, then surprised. 'Rita's girl? Oh—no. Guess again.' She smiled. 'Someone you'll be specially pleased to see.'

Rachel could think of no one but her family in Arcade, and Michael. 'I give up,' she said finally.

'Your Uncle David's in the city for a medical conference. Boston General. I guess your mother told him you'd be staying here a couple nights, and he says he'll come over tomorrow. He can cheer you on your way to London.'

For a moment the accident—and even the cause of her long journey ahead—fell away. Rachel leapt to her feet, her face warm. 'Oh, that's great!' She began to think of the delight she would have in showing her uncle some of the papers from St Stephen's; and how he might be able to explain some of them to her. More than that, he would be able to share her excitement about the opportunity of studying medicine in London—an excitement she knew he would well understand.

She slumped back into the sofa with her grandmother. 'Now that is good news.'

In a few moments they heard the double doors at the front of the house open and close quietly, then muffled conversation and heavy footsteps on the carpet of the lobby.

He's home, she thought.

Marianne was watching the open door, her face drained again. 'Ah, sweetheart.' She stretched out her hands as both McEnroe and the housekeeper came in.

Rachel thought her grandfather looked older than he had looked only an hour before. He had already lit a cigar, and she watched him set it in an ashtray a few feet away, his hand shaking slightly, before he came to them. As she had done before, he knelt in front of them, leaned over the sofa, and took them both in his arms.

For a moment he said nothing, his large, silver head resting between their shoulders. Then he raised his face, kissed Marianne, and stood up stiffly.

'You're OK, the two of you?'

Mrs Watowski had discreetly withdrawn, leaving more coffee and another plate of cookies. Now the sight of both made Rachel feel sick.

'We'll be fine,' Marianne said.

McEnroe assessed them with that shrewd look Rachel knew so well. 'Sure?'

'Sure we're sure,' she said lightly, pressing her grandmother's hand again. 'But what about you?'

He shrugged and took up a cup of coffee. 'Me? Oh, I'm a tough old so-and-so.'

Marianne wiped the back of her hand across her face, smudging her lipstick. 'That man—how about him?'

'He's a young guy, wiry and resilient. No problem for him. He's learned a lesson all right.'

'Had he been drinking?'

'I doubt it. No odour of alcohol. His mind seemed crystal clear. He was going too fast, that's all.'

Rachel felt her grandmother grow tense again, her muscles contracting as if she were ready to burst out in distress, or jump up from the sofa and shout in protest about everything that had happened. She felt, too, the control that Marianne was exercising.

'It was strange,' she said in a flat voice, 'the way he just appeared like that. It was—oh, Julius, please sit down, honey.'

McEnroe turned away from them and retrieved his cigar. 'Listen,' he said, without turning around again, 'it was a nasty business, but it's over now. I'll be on to his insurance company this afternoon, and the police have got several reports. Apart from that, and apart from knowing that you're both fine now, I don't want to think about what happened any more.' A cloud of smoke left his mouth and wafted, blue and aromatic, around his ears. He faced them again. 'Do you understand?'

Rachel saw something she rarely saw in her grandfather because he so rarely exploited it in his own family: the aura of power and influence he so naturally carried with him into the State House and the courtroom. For an instant she was almost afraid of his fierce eyes.

His face softened, then, as if he saw what she was thinking. 'Honest to God, I've got enough else to think of, as it is.'

Marianne was murmuring in sympathy and understanding, but Rachel felt powerless. *What have I come to, this time?* she wondered. *Why are they so edgy, and where is the resting place I hoped for before the long journey?*

McEnroe drained his cup and smiled faintly at them both.

Marianne sat forward. 'You're going back to work, are you?'

Rachel could tell she was trying to hide her anxiety.

'Not exactly. Like I said, I'll call the insurance companies. The car's outside until the adjusters have been. We'll have to use yours for now, honey. And I've got that other call to deal with, as well.' He glanced at his watch and then smiled again, this time directly at Rachel. 'Dear girl,' he said. 'This wasn't much of a welcome back for you. But don't you worry, it'll improve.' He was trying to put a brave face on it, and she saw his resolve. 'If you'll excuse me.'

The joy they might have had that afternoon was shadowed by what had happened. For the first time in her life that she could remember, she felt slightly claustrophobic about being in her grandparents' house. Marianne needed some time to rest, and after the accident she felt in no mood to call Marie Williams and begin a conversation about trivia.

Instead she wrote her a note, not mentioning Michael, telling her in glowing terms about her impending flight to London. The letter lifted her spirits and restored her perspective, and by supper time she felt better, as if she had got over the shock of the accident; more able to help her grandparents. She lay soaking in a hot bath thinking about the future and letting the last few hours—the parting from her family and from Michael, the accident, the fact that there was nothing she could do to help her grandfather—drain away with the bath water.

'Boy do I have news for you,' McEnroe said when they sat down for supper together later in the evening. He was freshly shaven, his thick hair more ordered than usual, and his eyes as bright as if he had slept for part of the afternoon.

Rachel caught the swift exchange of looks between her grandparents.

'What's that?'

'I'm coming with you.'

She set her spoon in the soup. 'You're *what*, McEnroe?'

He was grinning hugely, his eyes dancing. 'You heard me right,' he answered gruffly. 'I'm flying to England with you.'

'You're kidding.' She looked at Marianne for confirmation, but her grandmother gave nothing away.

McEnroe, too, was straight-faced. 'Business summons me to Britain for a short while. That's partly what that call in the car was about this afternoon.'

'But what'll you be doing?' She gaped at him.

He shook his head and bent to break a bread roll over his soup. 'That's something I can't discuss, as you'll appreciate. Don't ask, please. But I need to go, and I need to go soon. Something may be falling into place at last.' His face was sober now, the laughter gone completely from his eyes. 'So I want you to tell me your flight details.' He nodded at her. 'We might as well travel together, I reckon.'

The worries were forgotten now in the keen pleasure she felt. Memories flooded back to her, of times when McEnroe had held her in the circle of his arms after she had fallen and hurt herself, of the safety she had always felt, with him. And now they would be travelling together to a place unknown to her, but familiar to him. He would be carrying something of the world she knew into the world she did not know. He would be making a difficult place easier for her.

He told her the next morning that he had booked a seat on the same flight as she would be taking. 'No seats left in economy class,' he added, almost as an afterthought. 'I cancelled your seat and booked us both onto first class. I hope you have no objections? I'll pay the difference, of course.'

She did not know what to say, only smiled at him and nodded. But it came to her later, when David had eaten lunch with them and they were sitting together on the patio drinking coffee, that McEnroe might simply have manufactured an excuse to go with her, perhaps out of concern for how she had felt after the accident. She turned her eyes back to the french windows of the house, not seeing him, and tried to understand. But then she knew, as clearly as if he had told her, that he would not have gone all the way to England with her out of any sense of guilt or worry; more likely he would have wanted to stay at home with Marianne and ensure that *she* was safe and well.

Her uncle was in an expansive mood. She listened to him, finding so little in common between her mother and her uncle. Where her mother would have reminisced, had she been trained as a doctor, about her days at medical school, David was one to look forward.

'Are you thinking, yet, about what your specialty will be?'

She laughed and brushed the hair off her face. 'Not at all. It seems so far away. I don't think I'd *want* to specialize. General practice, I guess—if I'm forced to a decision now.'

'I wouldn't dream of twisting your arm like that.'

She loved the way he always spoke to her as an equal; she felt more adult when she was with David. 'The only thing I might want to get into is ob-gyn.' She smiled. 'Babies—it'd be something very positive.'

David nodded. 'Most of the time, anyhow. But not always. And appalling hours.'

'Well, I guess so. But I'll let you know when I decide,' she said.

'You glad McEnroe's going with you?'

'Very.'

He frowned slightly. 'I'm surprised.'

'Surprised that I'm glad, or surprised he's going?'

'Not surprised he's going. I may not have seen much of the old guy, but whenever I see him he's on the move. Like the sea's in his blood or something.'

'That's not a very medical observation, Dr Fuller.'

He grinned. 'No, but I'm quite surprised you're pleased about flying out with him.'

'Ah—then there're things you don't know about me.'

'You always come across so independent and purposeful.'

She looked across the wide lawns, past the cedars and flaming sumacs, and thought again of home: her parents, the animals...and Michael. She knew she had always presented herself as he had described her, and sometimes to her cost. 'Independent? Do I?'

He was silent for a moment, and she felt his eyes on her. 'Well, maybe I'm wrong.'

'Oh, I know what I want to do. I've known it for years. You know that. And I'm not *afraid* of going to England, though it's a big step. But I love McEnroe. And I don't know when I'm coming home again.' She heard her voice waver, and steadied it. 'He'll "ferry" me across the water.' She shaded her hand against the mellow autumn sunshine that came at an angle across the patio, and looked her uncle in the face. 'When I'm with McEnroe, I feel somehow... I can't explain... that God is...' She stopped.

David only smiled. 'I think your mother used to feel the same, even before she knew it.'

She did not understand what he was saying but felt that it didn't matter whether she understood or not. 'David—'

'Yes.'

'Something's wrong with McEnroe, I'm sure of it.'

David's face was unreadable. 'What makes you think so?'

She let her mind roll back over the past twenty-four hours in Bedford. Saw the tension in his neck and shoulders in the car. Heard the shortness of breath and weariness in his voice. 'He looks run down and exhausted a lot of the time. More than could be explained by all he's got on his plate right now.'

David frowned again. 'No more than usual, as far as I've noticed. He's always had that weathered, tired look.'

'But why?'

'Used to drink far too much, for a start.'

She could not imagine it.

'Also, don't forget that being a hard-working guy of seventy plus is no picnic in the senate *and* the courtroom, even for someone who's done it for years and knows the ropes. There must be a lot of stress.'

'I'm sure there is.' In her mind, she heard the car phone ringing.

'And he used to be much heavier, years ago, when I first met the McEnroes. I think it was Ellie's death that checked him. It clinched something for the whole clan—your mother as well. They all changed. Nothing was the same after Ellie died.'

Rachel recalled what her mother had said on the subject, many times. She had grown up with that sentiment echoing in her mind, and it had stuck. But Ellie's death could not explain everything in her family history. It might explain part of McEnroe's state now, twenty years on—his compulsive desire to catch the drug dealer—but it surely didn't explain everything.

'Everyone says that,' she sighed. 'But he seems different this time. He's uptight in a way I can't remember.' *And vulnerable,* she thought.

David looked shrewdly at her. 'Are you sure it isn't just that you've got your antennae out too far? Or that you've grown up so much since the last few visits you had with him that you see things now that you didn't see?'

She sipped the coffee; it had cooled. 'It could be that, I guess.'

'Truly, I don't think you need to worry about your grandfather. He's a tough old bird. He can take care of himself. He can take care of others as well.' He smiled. 'As you know, as you've felt, and said a moment ago.'

'That's what he always says, that he's tough. But he seems more frail than—' *Frail. Vulnerable.* How foolish those words sounded in reference to her grandfather. But, somehow, they seemed true, now.

David set down his mug and grasped her forearm where it lay on the edge of the garden chair. 'Stop being such a worry-wart, would you? Listen, you. One of the first things a young physician has to learn is that she can't heal the world single-handedly. The whole planet is not going to be your practice, Rachel. God puts us in a corner of it, that's all.'

'And Grandpa McEnroe's in my corner.'

'So are others. Open your eyes, Rachel. Listen to me, I said. McEnroe's a busy, intelligent man. There'll always be something happening in his life that makes him uptight. Why don't you look at your grandmother?'

She spilled her coffee, then, and set the mug on the flagstones between them. 'What d'you mean?'

'It's your grandmother you should be watching—and McEnroe should be watching. Have you looked carefully at her, lately?'

She thought of the scream in the car, and of what her grandmother had said after the accident, how it had shocked her. *That accident may very well have been his fault.* Then of the way her grandmother seemed already to have completely forgotten about yesterday, to be preoccupied about other things. But she remembered, too, the birthday luncheon, and her grandmother's radiance. *Will you look at this ring? Your grandfather gave me this.* The daisy ring, and the ring of light that seemed to glow from her grandmother that day.

She said, unsure, 'Yes, I look at her all the time. It's hard not to. Always so lovely, so pretty. What are you saying, David?'

'It's not like Grandma Laura's case. We all know what's wrong with her—the Parkinson's. It's a terrible and sad illness, and as I said to you in the summer, I think it won't be long before we bring her out to the island with us, where she'll be safe and cared for properly. But it'll be different with your other blessed GraMar, I think.'

She felt chilled. 'Why won't you tell me what you're getting at?'

Apparently avoiding her eyes, he bent over the side of his chair and put his mug next to hers. 'Because she's not my patient, and I can't go nosing into a Bedford doctor's bailiwick or pull McEnroe aside and tell him what I think, either.'

'But can you tell me?'

He looked at her steadily. 'I don't know. I don't think so. You'll be with McEnroe a long time on that plane.'

She sat up indignantly. 'That's not fair, then. You shouldn't have mentioned it.'

He hung his head. 'No I shouldn't. I was trying to divert you from worrying unnecessarily about your grandfather. But you're absolutely right—very unprofessional. Anyhow, you should watch her yourself.'

Tears pricked the back of her eyes, and her throat felt furred and thick. 'How can I?'

'No, I realize that. I'm sorry.'

She felt older than she had felt the day before, at the airport. Felt the twisting knife of surgery cut back into herself, felt the first anguish that a doctor must feel for a patient she has grown to know and even love. She leaned down, picked up the coffee mugs, and stood up. 'It's getting cold out here. And I just hope you're wrong, whatever it is,' she said.

David stood as well. 'I often am,' he said softly. 'And you can at least monitor your grandfather on the trip over to London.' He was smiling now. 'Please, forget I said anything. I'm in and out of Boston—just like this week. I'll keep a watch on them both for you.'

She returned the smile. 'I'd been thinking too much before of how McEnroe would monitor *me*.' She shook her head, wanting to clear it. 'Very selfish.' She looked down at the puddle of spilled coffee where it was slowly drying on the stones, and at the rings left by their mugs.

And I was thinking, too, how I might still feel, when I'm with him, as if I did belong somewhere. Not just suspended mid-Atlantic in noplace.

Now, she was not so sure.

12

She had hoped to see the great pyre of New England's leaves burning, dwindling away beneath the wings of the 747 as they left Logan Airport. Flying into the city only two days before, that's what she had seen: that, and the combers of the North Atlantic creaming in against the harbours and beaches of the North Shore. This time, when they took off, the sky was already deepening from pearl grey to mauve, and because they were flying east, it grew dark immediately. Then there was only the drone of the plane's engines, the muffled crying of a baby in the economy class, and for the first part of the long night the glare of the plane's overhead lights. Later, there was darkness, quiet, and nothing else.

She felt again the strange sense of suspension between one world and the next. Even with McEnroe breathing heavily beside her, his head dipping onto his chest or against her shoulder with the faint motion of the plane, she felt quite alone. *Who am I? Where do I belong?*

Almost all the other passengers seemed to sleep, but she found she couldn't and grew cold inside the thin blanket the steward had brought. Seeing her sitting bolt upright and open-eyed, the cabin staff had pressed her to more champagne, warm washcloths to wipe her face and hands, and glasses of orange juice; but she refused them all and sat in rigid stillness, waiting. She resented the closed blinds of the portholes, wanted to watch the stars washing past, wheeling in their constellations as the plane turned steadily north and east; but had to be content with the shuttered cabin.

McEnroe stirred and muttered in his sleep: something indistinguishable about the seventh hole. She smiled to herself.

Where was he playing golf, sleeping now over the greens and fairways of the Atlantic?

When dawn came up, the passengers shuffled and shook themselves like old dogs. Blankets were thrown into the aisles and blinds pushed up. Rosy light pierced the portholes on the left of the plane. She frowned, forgetting for a moment that they had flown over the Pole and were now bending southwards again. Then breakfast came, and she left behind the long loneliness of the night in the croissants and coffee that came to them on small trays decorated with carnations and baby's breath. McEnroe smiled when he saw her blink at the lavishness of first-class travel, but they didn't speak, both too full of what lay ahead.

She expected to see endless miles of rich green fields when the plane came through the clouds. All her friends who had flown to England before had told her of that first startling sight. But as when they had left Boston, nothing was as she expected or hoped. The plane was late, the captain ominously announcing that theirs was the last flight permitted to land until the fog had cleared. 'It might be a little bumpy,' he said, 'but I'll get you there.'

McEnroe smiled inscrutably. 'They will too. It's always bumpy, anyhow.' Then the brilliance of the sun above the clouds was lost to the plane as it skimmed into them. Rain drummed on the roof of the aircraft and spat on the portholes. The clouds thickened into soupy greyness, and they went down, down through them, as if there were no land below them, nothing to receive them except more cloud, more fog.

A tiny runway light pricked the murk outside, and then the plane had landed, still enshrouded in fog, on a dim and rainwashed runway. Behind them, they heard the passengers in the main body of the plane cheer with relief.

McEnroe squeezed her hand. 'Welcome to Europe, sweetheart. An old new world for you.'

She stared at him dumbly, wanting to weep, but feeling that it was futile and would upset him as well as herself.

They parted outside St Stephen's at about eleven in the morning. McEnroe had rented a car at Heathrow, and they had driven, still half dazed, round the airport ringroad, onto the M4 and finally into London. Rachel marvelled at the way her grandfather navigated what seemed to her the backward traffic patterns of British roundabouts and entry ramps. Marvelled at the way his hawk eyes seemed to see the roadsigns with ease, even through the thick fog.

'Will I see you at all while you're still over here?' she asked, before he kissed her goodbye. 'You haven't said when you're flying back.'

'That's because I don't know when. But I won't see you, honey, I'm sorry.'

She wanted to hold him back, her last thread of contact with home. 'Then is there a number I can call you? Some way I can at least say "hi" and ask you the news—' She looked into his face, which had grown grim. 'Or at least tell you my own news.'

His blue eyes were full of compassion but his mouth set in determination. He shook his head. 'I think it's better not. Let's just say the State House and the CIA know where I am. That's enough. You can always call home, you know.' He hesitated. 'But—of course, forgive me—are you OK for money here?'

She rustled open her billfold. 'Dad saw to it that I got some currency before I left. It's OK. The scholarship is very generous.'

He reached into his blazer pocket and pressed some notes into her hand. 'Here, take this as well. You just don't know when you'll need it.'

'But you'll need it yourself, surely?'

'I'm fine. Expenses, you know.'

He had winked at her, but behind his cheerful tone she heard something else: more anxiety. Not about money; it couldn't be that. But about the job he had come to do. She looked carefully at him, storing him up for the next time they would see each other. She saw droplets of the fog clinging like dull beads to his hair; saw him wipe them away and pull his collar higher round his neck. She shivered, herself. Out of his familiar Boston world he looked somehow smaller.

McEnroe flung a glance over his shoulder at the hired car, which was double-parked. 'Can you manage that baggage? I hate leaving you here like this, not even seeing your rooms, or anything. But I can't figure out where to park, and I need to get to my first appointment.'

Rachel waved vaguely at the chest and bulging suitcase on the steps behind them. 'Yes, I'll be OK.' She reached up and put her arms round his neck.

'Don't you fret, honey. You're going to do real well. I know you are.' He hugged her hard against him.

Two students passed them, striped scarves wrapped thickly round their necks, and stared as they stood in each other's arms. The men were laughing at some private joke, and their English voices jarred strangely in Rachel's ear. They did not sound at all like Michael, though one of them was similar to look at.

'I'd better go,' she said reluctantly. 'Thanks for everything, McEnroe.'

He lifted a thick strand of her hair off her cheek. 'Godspeed, Dr McEnroe,' he said. He took her head between his hands and bent to kiss her once more. Then he was gone.

She stood on the hospital steps watching the diminishing foglights on the back of the car. She did not feel frightened, and nor, now, did she feel sad. Just completely alone.

After a dazed moment she turned back to her luggage. Her medical students' manual had advised her that there were porters in the reception area, and without thinking further she left the chest on the steps and hoisted the case through the revolving doors at the front of the building.

Sure enough, a bedraggled porter was standing just inside. 'You just got 'ere?' His voice, too, grated on her ears.

'Yes.'

'That's all you've got?'

'No—there's a chest outside.'

He raised his eyes skywards. 'Gawd 'elp us, a Yankee-doodle. Don't you know there's bomb scares every day in this part of London? Can't go leaving your luggage on every corner you know. Come on. Where is it?' He sounded jaded, even in mid morning, but also used to the vagaries of medical students in their first week.

Meekly she followed him, and soon they were trundling with a trolley through a labyrinth of corridors, then finally through a door at the back of the main building, where the smell of cooking hovered and steamed through open windows, and where geraniums dripped and drooped miserably in the damp. They went down a stone path to a smoke-grimed Victorian building behind the hospital.

''Ere's your medical school. Rooms in 'ere, to start with, anyway,' the porter said laconically. 'Lectures down the steps, over there.' He pointed first one way, then another, bewildering her. 'And there's a med students' union as well, where most of them seem to waste their lives and spend their readies.' He eyed her with a droll expression. 'No doubt you'll do the same, once you know what you're doing. They're a rum lot, you'll soon see.' He chuckled to himself. 'In more ways than one, 'n all.'

It was a bleak welcome, she reflected as she closed the door after him. On the fourth floor, her room was shoehorned between two others by thin partitions that divided what must once have been a generous, if cold, room. A draughty, uncurtained sash window near one corner of the little box was sliced in half by the partition wall and rattled with the roar of traffic that came clearly from the bridge. Fog slid down it, impeded only by smuts and the sooty grime left by years of neglect.

A radiator blasted heat into the cramped space but seemed to have no impact on the draught. The carpet was threadbare and the walls torn by tape pulled off by previous posters. In one corner a small sink gurgled as if it had swallowed spiders, and she heard the rush of water descending the pipes on the wall outside from another room nearby.

She tugged off her jacket, pulled it back on hurriedly, and slowly lowered herself onto the bed to take it all in. *What have I done?* She had exchanged an airy, bright room in a Western New York farmhouse where a mimosa tree waved outside in the breeze ... for a cramped, stuffy box at the back of a dirty old hospital. Or, looking at things another way, she had exchanged the efficient, purpose-built dorm rooms of the pre-med students at Ohio for *this*—an ugly, dark place on the wrong side of the Atlantic.

Suddenly the sleeplessness and the emotions of the past four days caught up with her. Abandoning her things altogether, she sank onto the bed and let the tears come. They came in raw sobs that shook her whole body. They came with the harsh, animal sound of bewilderment. Then they stopped and she slept, and remembered nothing, falling into a furrow of sleep so deep that she would not have cared if she had never climbed out of it again.

A crash outside the door sent her bolt upright, the world spinning round her. The room was shadowed now, as in twilight. Michael was standing in the doorway, a huge grin on his face. She was dreaming. No, it wasn't Michael, for the voice was someone else's, and she was wide awake, instantly.

'Oops, sorry. wrong room. Better lock your door next time, sweetheart.' As if to mock her, for he was like Michael, he grinned again, saluting her. Then turned away.

She rubbed her head sleepily, everything flooding back to her. Stiff from sleeping without any movement in one position for who knows how long, she stretched. Her mouth tasted foul.

She found her watch, still ticking faithfully on Boston time, and sat on the edge of the bed to alter it five hours. Then she busied herself with the familiar, unpacking her washing things and setting them on the shelf above the sink. She would buy a hot water pot so that she could make tea, and she would repaint the room to brighten it. This would have to be home for a few months, at least.

The door flung back again, startling her. She hardly had time to think that she had not, in spite of the warning, locked the door, when she saw that it was the same student as before.

'Hello! Here I am again, darling. Right room after all. Aren't you glad to see me?'

She saw now that he was one of the students who had passed her on the steps of the hospital, when she had noticed his face less than his voice. Her heart was beating oddly, and she felt the blood soar into her face. 'Should I be glad to see you?'

He pulled a quizzical face. 'Oh—you're American. I saw you looking like the maiden all forlorn, so I thought I'd come and rescue you. New, aren't you? Silly moo, of course you are.'

'And you're not.'

He was holding out his hand, his scarf still absurdly round his neck. 'Christophers,' he said. 'Charlie Christophers. The obstetrical surgeon of the twenty-first century. Naturally I have a special interest in the women here.'

She laughed. 'Naturally.'

He cocked his head to one side. 'Er—I didn't hear your name.'

'I didn't say it.'

'Be a devil, then.'

'Rachel.'

'Ah, an angel.'

'No. Just one very tired woman.'

'Fresh off the boat?'

'Yes.'

'Just how I like them.' Mockingly, he rubbed his hands together. 'What a pity you didn't get here in time for our exciting induction week!'

'Didn't plan to,' she said shortly, wondering privately if that had been a mistake. Now she didn't know how to get rid of him. She thought of her mother, suddenly, and the way Maggie could reduce most people with sarcasm, when she wanted to. 'Mr Christophers—or are you Doctor?—I'm trying to unpack and get my bearings. Please—'

'Oh,' he said blithely, 'I suppose I'm being a most tiresome boor. Of course, you want to freshen up—isn't that what you people say?— before you face the mob in the canteen. Shall I come back later, then?'

'Don't come back at all.' But she was laughing.

'Ah, don't say that. You might not meet another human soul until you hit the first lectures tomorrow. Come on. This is your great chance.'

She stood with one hand on her hip and her other full of things from her case. 'What exactly did you have in mind?'

'Well, before I knew you were a Yank, I thought you might like an outing to the nearest watering hole. And now I know you're a Yank, well, I still think you might fancy an outing before we get our tea. Wet the new year's head, if you see what I mean. Start as we mean to go on, and all that.'

She didn't see what he meant, at all, but she was glad of his bright face and cheery voice, after all. 'OK,' she said. 'Give me half an hour. That'll be enough; I'm awake now.' She came and peered past him into the dim corridor. 'So all these dorms are mixed?'

'Dorms? Oh, wouldn't that be fun! Halls of residence, dear, that's what we call them. And yes, they're mixed. Well mixed, in fact. Lunatics on one floor. Drunkards on the next. Boffins on another—we keep them locked in their rooms so they preserve their happy little illusions that everyone else works as hard as they do.'

'And which floor am I on?'

'Oh, the lunatics', of course. With me.'

'Thanks for warning me. Now, please scram.' She held the door wide.

'I'll be back in half an hour. That's a promise.'

He came back precisely thirty minutes later wearing a spotted bow tie, tuxedo and scarlet cummerbund. Opening the door to him in a thick sweater, dark skirt that brushed her calves, and stockinged feet, she felt undressed, and burst out laughing.

'I'm not exactly arrayed for Buckingham Palace,' she said. 'I presume that's where you're headed.'

'No. This is how I dress every time I take an American girl to the pub.'

'Woman.'

'Oh, blast it, you're a feminist as well as an American. How very difficult this will be.'

She didn't bother to argue with him, and he swept her away like a dervish through the long corridors, across the wet courtyard, and out again onto the steps at the front of the hospital.

'Now you know your way through that lot,' he said.

'No I don't.'

'I told you that you should have come to induction! Well, then, you'll have to get your guide through inferno from the door that says "Dante". It said "four-twenty", once, but I had that room last year as well and thought "Dante" was far more poetic. Don't you?'

He took her across the bridge, walking fast over the swift-flowing black waters of the Thames, to what he said had been an old coaching inn. 'This is our favourite boozer,' he told her. 'You'll never be lonely if you come here.'

'Assuming I have dollars in my pocket.'

'Sterling might be more useful here, my love.'

He introduced her to a crowd of students whose names she knew she would not remember beyond that night. Women her own age or a little older, and men of all ages. All medical students, they assured her. Many of the women had severe, clever faces, their foreheads already lined, their hair pulled back tidily or cut into straight bangs in the front. She thought they looked dowdy, but their conversation sparked and rippled around her, and they laughed at jokes she couldn't understand. The men were different, more relaxed, some of them already dipping down the path to inebriation, their eyes red, their pullovers old and full of holes; but their mouths generous, and their words to her kind. The hospital scarf seemed de rigeur, both for fashion and for keeping out the penetrating cold which seeped even into the cosy bar where they sat and ticked away the hours until the pub closed and they went rollicking back across the bridge to the hospital. 'To begin life in earnest tomorrow at nine,' Christophers told her morosely.

She fell asleep that night rocked with the picture gallery of their faces and the waters flowing, flowing under the bridge. She thought of Michael, whose face was already merging in her memory with the irrespressible Charlie Christophers', and she wished he was in London to explain things to her, and to talk with her.

Tomorrow, she thought, *I will look on the map and see where Kent is... so I know... so I can one day see it, perhaps.*

The next day, however, she had no time to pull an atlas off the library shelf and peruse it leisurely, daydreaming. She found herself in a herd of others, mostly British but a few Asian and African, galloping from anatomy to physiology to pathology... taking notes while all the time realizing afresh that she should have arrived at the beginning of the week so as to have all her equipment ready and to know her way round the place. Christophers, however, stuck with her. She found out that he had failed his first-year exams and was starting again. 'Daddy says it's make or break year,' he told her. 'So I'm going to get serious this time.'

She could not believe him, but was still, for want of meeting anyone else, glad of his company.

She sat next to him in the first pharmacology lecture at the end of the second day. He was shredding his notebook with the tip of his ballpoint, drawing juvenile cartoons, and generally doing all he could to distract her. She was scribbling frantically, still unused to the British intonation and having to strain to follow the lecturer's line of discussion.

He leaned over and wrote on the margin of her paper, 'How about the hop tonight?'

She looked at him blankly, losing the last words of the tutor.

'Translation,' he hissed, 'the *disco*. It's Friday, don't you know?'

'It hadn't escaped my notice,' she whispered back irritably. 'Please, I'm trying—'

'Goody two shoes,' he muttered, going back to his own notes.

When the lecture was over, the lecture theatre emptied into one of the few places in the hospital grounds where Rachel felt at home—the grassy courtyard between the buildings that the others called the 'ambulatory'. She was making her way unthinking, as she had already learned to do, between the geraniums and towards her hall, when Christophers caught up with her, grabbing her sleeve.

'Hey! Didn't you hear what I said?'

'Oh, Charlie—'

'Look at me with those melting eyes of yours, Rachel, just once more.'

'The name's Beatrice,' she said waspishly, unable to resist it.

'Oh, excuse me. Wrong room again, I guess.'

'You were saying?'

'The hop.'

'Yes, the hop. Disco, whatever.'

'You want to go.'

'I'm not sure.'

'Look, I know you said you grew up on a farm, dear Beatrice, but surely you went to a prom, or whatever, didn't you?'

She thought quickly of the cost she had paid to be high school valedictorian, packing a four-year course into three years. Then of the first two frantic years at Ohio. She had not been to a single dance. Had deliberately missed the homecoming dance and the senior prom that traditionally sent everyone back from college in a haze of nostalgic, sometimes drunken glory. But she didn't want to admit those things. Not yet, at least. And be classed as an odious boffin, relegated to the dim corridor where no one stirred from the room except for library, labs, or lectures.

She looked at him uncertainly. 'I—'

'Aye! That means yes. You're on.'

She laughed and decided to give in. 'Do I need a ballgown and glass slippers?'

'No. Just the sexiest thing you can lay your hands on—apart from me, of course.'

'I do have a little black dress...' His enthusiasm and persistence were catching.

'Just the job. I'll pick you up at seven-thirty. Just make sure your door is locked, this time, or I might feel obliged to ravish you first.'

'Er—I don't think so. A most un-Dantelike idea.'

'Very ungallant, yes. But very natural.' He tipped her chin up. 'Be there. You're gorgeous, Rachel.'

She went off to her room wondering if she had made a mistake, but so many things seemed to sweep her along here in London that she didn't have time to think about everything she was doing. Fleetingly, she wished she had begun to befriend some of the women in Christophers' group, so that she would not feel quite so dependent on him in these first days; but it was perhaps too late to think of that now.

She was standing behind her locked door, still brushing out her hair, when someone knocked. 'It's Dante.'

'Hold on a minute. Beatrice isn't quite ready to navigate the inferno.'

'I'll wait as long as I have to.'

She groaned, then caught sight of her reflection in a small mirror she had attached to the door of her cupboard. The silly smile she saw implied too much. It was stupid to confuse him with Michael just because they were both English and looked similar. They could hardly be more different. And it was ridiculous to involve herself in his fantasies by referring to herself as Beatrice. She had come to London to study medicine, not to embroil herself the very first week in a relationship she might regret later. That much she told herself rather sternly as she finished her hair, then smiled at her own sententiousness.

When she came out into the dim corridor, he bowed and presented her with a tiny nosegay of heather and everlasting.

'I'm not used to all this,' she said in what she hoped was a cool voice.

'You're kidding! American men are so gallant.'

She thought of Larry and Tony, her father's farm hands, and of her father himself: rough diamonds all of them with their muddy boots, muck-splattered plaid shirts, overalls and skewed caps; she thought of the gangly, gauche boys in Ohio; and she laughed. 'Don't believe everything you see in the movies,' she said.

He was either too ebullient or too thick-skinned to mind her barbs for more than a second. 'Come on. The hop's this way.'

He led her past the now empty students' union lounge and the crowded, shouting bar. Outside the double swing doors of the dance, he turned and took her by both arms. 'Listen, sweetheart, I invited you to the hop. But I should have levelled with you, since you've no way of knowing, being a foreigner—' He grinned and raised his eyes skywards in mock contrition. 'But these dances do tend to be a bit of a cattlemarket.'

Her mind flashed to her father again, bidding against the other Allegany County farmers for farm stock, or selling his calves at veal auctions. Undeterred, she met his eyes. 'I should feel right at home, then.'

His mobile face was for once almost serious. 'You might. But stick with me.' It was like a watchword with him, *Stick with me.*

'All right, I'll do that.'

'Then in case it's too bloody noisy in there for me to ask you in a civilized fashion, what can I get you to drink?' He reached into his trouser pocket and rattled a handful of loose change.

'I'm buying,' she said blithely.

'Not a chance—well, not the first time.'

'Too proud?'

'Damn right I am. You can buy the second one—if you insist. I'm having a pint of bitter, so name your poison.'

She was unused to drinking. So many towns in Allegany County were dry. Not that Maggie and Don had kept her from alcohol, and not that she had gone without cold beers with friends in Cincinnati. But it was humiliating to explain these things to him, so she searched for the first safe thing she could think of. 'Oh—I'll have a cola.'

His eyebrows shot up. 'That's all. Or with rum in it?'

She could see that his budget wouldn't have run to rum and cola even if she had asked for it. 'It's OK,' she said, smiling into his eyes, 'I just want a cola.'

He shrugged. 'Suit yourself.'

The hall swayed and rocked, the lights scintillating like sequins from the turning ball on the ceiling. Inside the door, they stood still for a moment to adjust to the darkness and the crashing, vibrating sound. Rachel looked around and saw a few candles flickering on tables pushed to the sides of the room, circles of faces bending towards the flame, palely flickering, themselves, in the half light; cigarette ends glowing in the twilight. The music beckoned, but no one was dancing yet.

Charlie leaned so that his mouth was against her ear. 'You wait until the Rugby Club hop. It's even worse than this.'

She nodded abstractedly. Worse in what sense? But he seemed cheerfully unperturbed, steering her to one of the tables where a crowd of men hailed them loudly.

'Hey, it's the poet himself!'

The men looked her up and down and one of them pulled a face at Christophers. 'You're a dark horse, mate.'

Charlie grinned. 'Shut your great Aussie face. I'm going to buy Rachel a drink. Behave yourselves while I'm gone.'

Rachel felt irritated. 'I can look after myself, thanks.'

There were the usual exclamations—which by now she'd come to expect—about her transatlantic origins. But that didn't last long as a source of conversation; one man was from Cairns in Australia, *Hot as Christophers' flamin' inferno,* he assured her; one was from Manchester, *Might as well be the Antipodes, for all these stupid southerners know about the home of the greatest football teams on earth,* this one commmented loftily; and another from an obscure island in the Hebrides, *Wherever those are, dear lady,* she was instructed, is *certainly of even less interest to the average Londoner than the whereabouts of your own fair city.*

She relaxed, puzzled by their strange mixture of bonhomie and rivalry. In many ways more urbane and worldly wise than the young men she had left behind in Ohio, they were, she thought, still oddly innocent and even childish in the way they behaved. When Christophers came back, the men quarrelled over football teams and boat races, only occasionally catching her eye: loud and self-conscious. She was perplexed by them, wanting to be included but aware that she couldn't belong; she was a woman, for a start, and far more of a 'foreigner' than the Mancunian or the Hebridean—no matter what they said.

At first she could see no reason for Christophers' description of the hop as a cattlemarket. She looked up again and again, expecting to see the floor fill with dancers and the old rituals—familiar on either side of the Atlantic even to an ingenue like herself—begin. But song followed song, and all the students seemed bent on doing was shouting, smoking, drinking, and scrutinizing each other.

When the gloom cleared and her eyes became completely accustomed to the smoky dimness, she saw that, except for herself, all the other women were sitting at two tables in one corner. Their chairs were drawn into a circle, *Like a waggon trail pulled up against the Indians,* she thought unexpectedly, amused. They talked earnestly, but their eyes were less on each other than on the tables full of men. Who were the cattle here—the women or the men? she wondered. She recognized one or two faces from the evening in the pub by the bridge, but she could remember no names. She felt uneasy, then, suspecting that she should be with them rather than at Christophers' table.

She pulled idly at the little bunch of flowers he had given her. They felt dry and stiff in her hands, and one of them crumbled at her touch. They were old, she realized; something Christophers might have picked up from outside a patient's room.

'You're here to learn to mend things, not break them,' he said, following her look of dismay as the dead petals sifted to the floor.

She grinned ruefully. 'Sorry.'

'Ah, don't be a bully, Charlie. She's just a new chum.' The Australian winked and leered at her.

Christophers ignored him. 'So much for chivalry. Now, you mentioned a second drink...?'

She laughed. 'Subtle, or what?'

He shouted into her ear. 'Just give me the money. I'll see if I can get a discount.' She put a five-pound note into his hand. It still felt to her like Mickey Mouse money; she was unused to the feel of English money, and alarmed by the speed it seemed to disappear—just as the porter had predicted.

Christophers ambled off towards the door. 'That's the last you'll see of him, if he runs true to form,' the Australian told her knowingly. 'Better watch that galah. He has a slick way with the sheilas.'

Another of the men elbowed the Australian. 'You're a fine one to talk. Stop your artificial Aussie chitchat, Basden. Can't you see she's a lady? You've got to address her in *English*.' He caught Rachel's eye. 'Don't listen to a word off his lying Aussie tongue. Not for nothing he's called "Crock"—and we're not just talking about Crocodile Dundee.'

The others guffawed, but she was lost in their laconic humour, looking again at the women. She wanted to join them. She wanted Charlie to come back. She wanted to dance. Anything rather than sit in this bewildering circle and listen to a language she only half understood.

She thought of McEnroe then, facing a task in London he did not relish, then bit her lip uncomfortably, rejecting the self-pity that snapped at her.

The Australian stood up suddenly, and pushed a loose shirt into his jeans. 'Mizz Rachel, please do me the honour.' He held out his hand to her. 'I don't normally go for pommy women, but I guess you don't count.'

The others drew noisy, showy breaths of apparent horror. 'Asking for it, Crocky.'

'That's my worry. Coming, Rach?'

Torn between amusement at his brashness and the definite feeling that she was being somehow patronized, she stood up slowly. She threw a last look around the hall but could not see Christophers. 'Sure.'

Basden was a heavy man, but he was light on his feet. From the shadowed tables, others watched, and a few drifted out to join them.

'I don't know how to dance—not for real,' she found herself saying apologetically.

'No worries. This isn't dancing, anyhow. Just an excuse for necking, that's all.'

He drew her to him. She smelled the heavy aftershave he wore, felt the rasp of his skin on her face as he crooked her head onto his shoulder. But did not feel afraid so much as annoyed that she had got caught in this way; that she had let Christophers go off with the money; and that she was the only woman in the hall without other women for company. As they meandered around the floor, it soon became obvious that Basden knew as little about dancing as she did, but enjoyed it more than she did. Christophers passed them, another girl in the circle of his arms, staring straight through them as if he had never seen either of them before, blankly.

'That's typical,' Basden hissed at her. 'I saw his routine a thousand times last year. Only normally it's with poor young nurses who wouldn't know any better. Not fledgling doctors who would.' He eyed her glassily. 'Or would they?'

She felt hot with indignation, but laughed uncomfortably all the same. Then she excused herself, reclaimed her handbag from the table to the accompaniment of banter and teasing shouts, and took a deep breath as she crossed the hall to where the women sat.

They greeted her with polite indifference, their conversation lapsing for a moment as soon as she pulled out a chair and sat down with them. A couple of them asked her name, wanted to know what she was doing at St Stephen's, and otherwise ignored her. One of the women then resumed a long and ghoulish account of an operation she had witnessed in theatre that morning, and another began to talk across her about a string of episodes she had enjoyed—or perhaps not enjoyed—with various men in the hospital. 'All worthless scum,' she concluded, cleaning her red nails indolently with an orange-stick.

Rachel sat wondering why the women were there, if they didn't want to dance. They seemed bored and listless, jaded, evidently all entering their second year—the main exam year—of studies. They had seen it all, done it all, tried it all. Sitting among them, she felt naive, foolish, and still alone.

The atmosphere in the hall changed abruptly when the last recordings were announced. Those who had been covertly watching the men before, including the one who vowed indifference, sat forward and observed them with even greater attention. In turn the men stared back, and within a few moments had stampeded the women's table. All were snatched up, grabbed and groped as they spun onto the floor, and she retreated into the shadows, feeling even more wretched. It was a painful and novel sensation—to be shunned like that, and yet to feel that the attention the men gave was not what she wanted anyway—and she hated the self-pity that suddenly returned to her.

Basden and Christophers left before the last song ended: laughing and shouting loudly as they went. Christophers gave her a jeering wave, his face contorted with irony, as he escorted one of the other women out of the door.

Suddenly she couldn't bear it any more: the isolation, the lack of real friendliness, the harsh music and pale, flickering light. She stumbled unnoticed out of the swing doors and fled into the draughty corridor.

The doors of the students' union bar stood open. Through the pall of smoke, she heard shattering glass and braying laughter, then the sound of someone running for the door, pursued by sarcasm: 'Poor wee man. Can't hold his booze. Oops, lost our supper and drinks, have we?'

What have I come to? she thought, hurrying on.

She found that she was trembling like someone in shock. Her heart beat furiously in her throat, and she felt sick, herself. *I'm still jet-lagged,* she thought. But it was no use going straight back to her room, after all; there would be no sleep for her in that bleak place.

She turned aside into the hushed lounge with its deeply padded chairs, some of them in oily leather and others in faded chintz. Closing the door after her, she chose the chair farthest from the door and dropped into it, waiting until her breathing returned to normal. The lamps shed a weak light onto tables littered with medical journals and sports magazines, and the big room had an air of womblike security about it that was vaguely comforting. Even the commonly pervasive smell of cigarette smoke had dissipated, and though the room's ashtrays were overflowing as usual, she was happy to sit there, shutting her eyes, and let the peace soak into her.

After a while she opened her eyes again and looked around more carefully. In two days she had already spent several coffee breaks in the lounge, but there were things she had not noticed before, in daylight, that caught her eyes now. Someone had closed all the curtains in the room—it was one of the few places in St Stephen's that was curtained—and the pattern on them arrested her.

Daisies.

Her eyes filled. She thought of Marianne, and of the daisy ring that McEnroe had given her. Something she was pleased would one day be hers, though she felt no sense of ownership or possessiveness about it. She loved GraMar too much to wish her time away.

And she thought of Michael, and of their walk only a few days before— now a world away—back from the woods to the farm; of the clump of yellow daisies bravely standing against the frost on the corner of the pasture.

I can do this thing, she told herself, gritting her teeth, *because I know it's the right thing for me to be doing, however hard it seems at first. And because it's what I've wanted—for months.*

Her wet eyes followed the spiralling swirls of daisies on the dusty curtains: round and chaotically round, yet the pattern repeated itself in a way that did mean something.

At last she got up and retraced her way into the courtyard again. On the floors visible above her, she knew, patients slept and doctors on call dozed fitfully or worked with the night nurses. Her turn would come for all that.

I can't let myself get so far down—never again, she resolved, pushing open the residence door at last.

Someone had taped a notice to the battered paint of the door.

Joy! Joy to the world!

She had rarely felt less full of joy.

Come and join the Christmas madrigal singers. Come all ye, whether ye'll be here for Christmas or no, come and sing St Stephen's celebrations. Practise every Thursday till Christmas, 8 p.m. in union lounge.

Yes, she thought, *that's something I can do.*

She fell asleep instantly, forgetting everything. In the morning there were no lectures to attend, and for the first time since she had arrived the sun was shining palely into the mist outside her window. *Saturday.* This, then, would be the real beginning of her life at St Stephen's.

When she crossed reception later in the morning to check her box for mail, she found a note telling her to stop at the desk.

Flowers waited for her there: a great spray of budding, blooming chrysanthemums and asters.

'From Christophers?' she murmured, half to herself, and half to the porter who handed them across to her with a wry smile. Perhaps Charlie had felt contrite about abandoning her the night before.

But no. The flowers were from her grandfather, with a short note in his large handwriting, and a boldly scrawled, familiar signature at the foot, *McEnroe.*

Dearest Rachel

I'm thinking of you and hope you're happy and cosy as a cricket at your new place. Since I won't be in London much longer and can't, I guess, call you, here's a floral greeting for a lovely granddaughter. So I know what's going on in your new life, keep in touch with the family, won't you? Love as ever.

She clutched the flowers to her. 'Keep in touch with the family.' Well, *of course I will.*

Part Three

The Family Ring

WINTER 1992–93

13

Michael stood hosing down the yard. Gusts of wind blew the icy water from the nozzle so that it flew back and trickled into his clothes and boots. His hands were turning numb, but the yard looked cleaner than it had half an hour before. 'I want it especially clean and dry before everything freezes,' Don had said, squinting at slate-grey clouds scudding fast over a windy white sky. 'Ideal day, I reckon.'

As he worked, Michael watched the crows tossing about like black rags in the wind that raked over the farm. As soon as they alighted in the maple, they were torn out and thrown back into the air, somersaulting and cawing, the sound curiously softened by the wind. A few gulls had flown inland from Lake Ontario, and they too were buffetted and powerless, banking in the gusts.

Don and Tony came out of the barn, both splattered with muck. Michael turned off the water at the wall and wiped his hands on his overalls. They felt huge and clumsy, deadened by the cold.

'I'm afraid we gotta go to Buffalo.' Don waved some papers he was carrying. 'I promised one of the guys at church that I'd get some of the paperwork finished on that shipment of grain we'll be sending to Second Harvest. And Tony's going after some parts up there, as well—it's those new cables for the barn cleaner. The ones we just installed were no good.'

Michael did not take in, at first, what Don said about the grain. He looked up unhappily. 'Was it the work I did on the—?'

'No, Michael. I guess the cables were just poor quality. No reflection on your work. But I gotta see to them right away, or we'll be breaking our backs before the week's out.'

Tony scuffed his boot on the ground, leaving a smear of muck. Then he caught Michael's startled expression and grinned. 'Sorry, kid. Didn't mean to mess up your good housekeeping. I've had my eye on a farm auction just outside the city, as well—I wanna check it out if we have time. This is a good chance, before the vacation, and before we're cut off with the snow and whatever else God sends this year.'

Michael looked from one to the other and realized what all this news meant. His stomach lurched with excitement.

'So I guess you're on your own this afternoon.' Don's eyes crinkled at the corners. 'Think you can manage?'

'I'll do my best.'

'Get the milking done, that's all I ask. Don't go tackling anything else on your own. I'm not expecting much. You can always check with Maggie if in doubt. Thanksgiving tomorrow, anyhow; things should be quiet.'

Michael couldn't follow the elliptical reasoning but swallowed Don's instructions anyway, immediately forgetting his cold hands. Don and Tony roared away in the pickup truck about ten minutes later.

In the middle of the afternoon, an hour before milking, he decided to survey the farm again. Since Rachel had left there had been no time to look closely at things. He often wished he had spoken more to her in the two days they had both been in Arcade. She could have told him so many things about the farm—things he could only guess at now, things Don wouldn't perhaps think to mention. In those two months he had come to love the place, although he never forgot, day or night, that Larry Harper would resume work one day, and Don would have to let him go. He tried not to think of that more than he had to, quietly working out what might come next.

The wind came up again with a great sough, and he pulled his shirt collar higher, wondering how much colder the weather would get in the winter Don warned was still around the corner. The wind stung and burned the skin around the edge of his ears; it was a kind of cold he had never known, keen as daggers.

ELIZABETH GIBSON

Wally shambled out from under the porch to follow him, as usual. He had grown used to the dog's presence, shadowing him everywhere.

They went first to the silos. He opened the low door at the bottom of one, then the other. The wet feed was ripening nicely—rich and rancid as old cheese. Standing near the unloader at the foot of it, he almost felt the weight of the silage pressing down on him. But the smaller silo, for grain, smelled quite different—dusty and golden, redolent of summer. *That shipment of grain we'll be sending to Second Harvest.'* Don's words had skimmed over him, but they came back now. *I wonder what that's all about.*

Wally trailed him next into the milking parlour. He looked over the machinery he had now become so familiar with, then did what he had seen Don do almost every afternoon for two months: went up on the stepladder by the tank to check the milk level inside it. He raised the cover and lifted the dipstick; yes, the Co-operative truck had been to empty it. He breathed in the soapy warmth that hung in the air of the parlour, even on cold days.

When he climbed down again, Wally began to whine and snuffle beside him, pushing his muzzle into his hand and making funny little yelps that Michael had never heard before. 'What's up, boy?' he said, stopping. Absently he went back up the ladder and filled the scoop that hung there. Moving carefully he climbed down again and filled a bowl kept for the barn cats. 'Here—have a swig of this.'

The dog slavered but ignored the milk, barking, wagging his tail and dropping his forelegs lower on the ground, as if he wanted to play.

'Not now,' Michael said. 'Work to do.'

He turned into the other part of the barn, to where the summer heifers were penned next to their older sisters. The young animals were curled in their clean hay or standing up, pushing their noses against the wooden gates that surrounded them, snuffing through their soft nostrils as he stood watching: used to him.

He leaned over the gate and patted a few of them on the neck, let one of them suck on his fingers like the overgrown baby it still was. It lowed woefully; there was no milk on his fingers now, as there had been when he had bucket-trained it two months before. He moved over and climbed another ladder to where the alfalfa hay was stacked,

218

sweet and dry, above the calf pens. He felt the rough baler twine bite into his palm as he tossed down one of the bales. Then he jumped after it, untying the twine as the calves butted and pushed him into the tight space between the manger and the gates. Laughing, he roared at them to move away so that he could escape.

Wally began to yelp again, and bounded off to the larger pen nearby. It was then that Michael became aware that one of the older heifers was bellowing with distress: a spasmodic, desperate cry he recognized as that of a heifer about to calve. *Freshen,* Don called it.

Sweat broke out inside his collar. He searched his memory of the farm in Kent and the few times he had helped the farmer there calve the cows. The pictures were no longer clear.

For a moment he stared at the heifer in dismay. His concern doubled when he realized that it was Don's favourite heifer—the one Grey's prize bull had cornered down by the woods. *Why didn't I check out here before? Why didn't I realize?* He fled to the desk where all Don's records were kept, running his finger down the table that showed when cows were served, dried off, or due to calve. On all lines except that of this heifer, dates were written neatly and precisely, but in this case Don had written 'ca. Jan 1'.

He groaned again. *Six weeks early.* He wasn't sure what he should do. *'Milking...don't go tackling anything else on your own.'*

Trying to calm himself he returned to the heifers' pen and moved the gates carefully so that the one heifer was in a smaller pen, isolated. She rolled her eyes and bellowed again. He wanted to shut out the sound so that he could think.

Then suddenly it seemed quite clear and simple. *Phone the vet, of course!*

He spoke to the heifer and smoothed his hand over her bulging, heaving side. She flinched and lowered her head threateningly.

It took him a few more anxious moments to find the vet's number among the papers on the barn desk, but when he did, the line was busy. Standing at Don's desk he rekeyed the number twice, his finger trembling, so that he missed the number and had to punch it in yet again.

The vet on call was out at another farm and would drive over as soon as he could, the receptionist told him in a bored voice. 'Isn't there some other line I can reach him on? We could lose one of our best heifers. This is an emergency.'

The woman sighed. 'That's what they all say.'

At the sink he washed his hands. When he went back to the pen for the third time, the heifer had rolled onto one side and was breathing raggedly, her eyes wild and terrified. Michael could see the calf's hooves beating against the birth sac. *At least it's alive and kicking.*

Wally whined and yapped.

'Go on—out of here, or I'll have to tie you in the yard.' He pushed the dog away with his boot. 'Not now. Go on.'

Squeezing between two of the gates, he re-entered the pen. Bloody water suddenly drenched the straw behind the heifer, and at the next contraction the calf's hooves appeared.

The vet would never make it in time.

He tried again to remember the calvings in Kent—the way the farmer had worked to ease the birth by turning and pulling on the calf's hooves. 'It's no gentle job,' he had said. 'Often you need cords—and a lot of courage.'

But then he calmed himself. So often a cow dropped her calf without any help from the farmer. No need to worry after all.

He grasped the hooves and pulled. The heifer lowed again, thrashed and twisted on the straw. She sounded exhausted, weaker now than when he had discovered her. Her head went down on the floor of the pen, her breathing rough and unnatural. He remembered nothing like this at the other calvings.

He scrutinized the hooves, and with a chill recognized that the calf's back hooves had been born—not the front hooves, as usual. Beginning to shake, he knelt and spoke to her again, pushing his hand into the birth canal to try to understand what had happened.

Something's terribly wrong.

He felt the convulsion of the calf. It was still alive, but its position meant that it would only be born alive if the vet arrived in time to do a caesarean.

'Should I try to turn it?' he muttered to himself, as if someone else were standing beside him, prompting him. *But how?*

Blindly he reached further inside, past the back legs, for the head of the calf. The heifer seemed to have given up. She neither fought him nor made any sound except the uneven breathing.

He pictured diagrams in the agricultural books he had bought at the Smithfield Show a couple of years before. Awkwardly he struggled to shift the calf into what he thought might be the right position, then stood up again. He was afraid to pull any more, in case he tore the heifer.

Outside the barn, the wind had temporarily dropped. He heard the drone of the schoolbus making its sluggish climb over the rise on the side-road that led to the farm. In a few moments Joel and Billy would be home. Earlier, he might have thought wistfully of the end of his brief reign over the farm; now, all he felt was relief. Perhaps they would even be able to help him.

The heifer moaned again. Michael watched her, praying, thinking all he could do now was wait.

Soon Joel and Billy found him. His first, irrelevent thought as they tramped in, calling for their father, was how clean they looked in their bright ski-jackets. He himself was dirty and splattered, his overalls caked with mud and straw.

'What's up, Michael?' Joel was usually the first to greet Michael, but this time it was Billy who took in the bloodied overalls and worried look on Michael's face. 'And where's Pa?'

'This heifer's got stuck. Premature birth, and it's breech,' he answered shortly. He felt oddly defensive, as if it were somehow his fault that the animal was calving early and had got into difficulties. 'Come and see for yourselves, and if you know what else I can do, give me a hand.'

Billy stripped off his jacket and bundled it into his brother's arms. 'Here, take this, willya?' He knelt next to Michael. 'Gee, Michael, she sure doesn't look too happy.'

He grunted. 'I had a go at turning it. Not sure I have. Any idea what else we can do for her?'

'Did you call the vet?'

'Of course. He can't get here for a while.'

'Pa'll kill us if she dies. This was his baby. Where is he, anyhow?'

Michael winced. 'I know that. In Buffalo—said he was sorting out his part of grain order for—I forget the name. Sounded like a charity.'

Billy was staring intently at the heifer. 'Oh, right... but I thought she wasn't freshening until Christmas or so.'

'So did your father.'

Joel came and hung over the gate. In a loud voice he said, 'Billy, you don't really know what you're doing. Michael—'

'Shut up!' Billy hissed. 'Listen, Michael. You've been here with her. It wouldn't hurt to try turning it again.'

'I'm not so sure.' He thought again of the calvings in Kent, and flotsam of textbook advice floated across his mind. *As much as possible, the animal should be left to follow the natural course of the birth, without rushing or unnecessary straining.*

So much for ropes! And why didn't textbooks tell a person what to do with a breech birth?

'Shall we try to pull some more?' Billy pushed his hair off his face, his forehead furrowed with the same panic Michael felt.

Joel said, 'I'm trying to think what Pa would do. No, if the calf's the wrong way round, we could kill her. Oh, darn it, where's the vet, for cripesake?'

A few loose pebbles in the yard scattered and crunched under someone's tyre wheels. *Don already?* It couldn't be. Nor would it be the vet—not this fast.

Michael rejected the temptation to vault over the gate and run harum scarum into the yard. Any sudden movement would terrify the heifer. Cautiously he squeezed back out of the pen, then jogged outside.

'You phoned for McEnroe?' A bald man, bag in hand, slammed the door of a new four-wheel drive.

'That's right.'

'Emergency, I was told.'

'Yes—in here.'

The man followed, looking at him curiously. 'Don't recognize you. You're not one of McEnroe's youngsters, surely?'

In turn, Michael eyed him uncertainly. He had met the McEnroes' usual vet only once before, but this man was unfamiliar. 'Oh—I'm here for Larry Harper. The McEnroe boys're in there. But please— never mind that. There's a heifer having trouble. She doesn't look good.'

Telling Billy to stand aside, the vet dropped his bag and went straight through the gates with an economy of movement that Michael watched with respect. He walked round her, murmuring reassurance, ran his hands and eyes over her. The heifer lifted her head with piteous eyes, but the dreadful groaning stopped, and she lay still. Michael found that he was trembling with relief.

Behind him, Joel drifted towards the barn door. 'Guess I'll go and shift my homework now the crisis is over.'

'Wait.' Billy turned. 'Tell Mom to come on out, willya?'

'I don't think that's necessary.' The vet was curt. 'In fact, why don't all you boys clear out and let me get on with the job? I'll come across when I'm through.'

'I'm staying here,' Michael insisted. The 'all you boys' rankled.

'Yeah, you better,' Billy said.

Michael bit back a sharp answer. He didn't fully understand the irritation that sometimes crept between himself and Billy McEnroe. With a heavy heart, he watched the brothers leave the barn and vanish into the yard. *I don't want all that with them, as well,* he told himself, thinking of Ian.

The vet stood up again and faced Michael. His mouth was grim. He gestured, thumb over shoulder. 'It's her—or the calf. Take your pick, son. She's been trying to calve since this morning, and there's no way she'll make it without drastic intervention. Someone should have called me before.'

'But Mr McEnroe was here this—'

'Hell, what does it matter who should have caught things? She's giving up, kid. It's too late for a caesarean now.' He swore. 'Make up your friggin' mind.'

Michael took an unsteady breath. 'Forget the calf. Save the heifer.' *Either way,* he thought, *Don'll have my guts for garters.*

'If you're sure then?'

'I'm sure.' He slumped against the gate and watched the vet pull on latex gloves.

'This won't be pleasant, son.'

'I'm sure it won't.' Swallowing hard, he stood his ground.

'I don't often have to do this—cut the calf up before it's born. But it's that, or lose the heifer. No other way to get this baby out.'

Michael flinched and nodded dumbly.

A few moments later a dead calf lay in pieces beside its mother, and the heifer had subsided with another groan onto the straw. Numbly, Michael looked at the glistening dark pelt of what only minutes before had been a living calf; at the staring eyes and open, drooling mouth. The calf was smaller than usual, but would have been perfectly formed. He thought of the warm pressure of the calves' mouths sucking on his fingers, and sighed. 'Couldn't anything be else done—wasn't there any way—?'

The vet shook his head, glanced back at Michael, then shot the heifer in the rump with a vial of antibiotics. 'Get some fresh warm water and clean rags. I'll see if she needs more stitches. Then you can do the clean-up.'

Glad of something he could do without thinking, Michael obeyed. His mind travelled ahead to what Don would say about the calf—about the heifer. To what the vet—obviously not a close-mouthed man—might say in Arcade about Don and himself. He felt raw and inadequate; but he could think of nothing else he could have done that he had not already done.

The office and kitchen felt oppressively warm when, half an hour later, he led the vet across the windy yard and through the storm door into the back of the house.

Maggie met them at the door. 'Michael—?' She was staring at the vet as if she'd never seen him before.

The vet elbowed past him. 'I'm Waterman. Your regular vet's away on vacation—I'm subbing for him. I wasn't far away—only at Greys' place—so the office called me. I came right over.'

'Thank you.'

'You've lost a fine calf, Mrs McEnroe.'

'That's what the boys thought.' She was restrained. 'Anyhow, won't you have a cup of coffee?' Michael could see that the mention of Greys had put Maggie on edge. Her offer sounded slightly forced.

'I don't reckon so. Listen, if I can just park myself at your husband's desk here a minute, I'll let you have the bill.'

'Right. Thank you.' She was speaking from between gritted teeth.

Michael passed into the kitchen, turning his back on the others to pour himself a mug of coffee, his hand still unsteady. Coffee slopped onto the stove and ran hissing away in gold droplets.

The vet's voice came harshly from the office. 'None of my business of course, but I heard quite a tale from old Mr Grey when I was leaving there.'

'Oh, really?'

Michael was not imagining the frost in her voice now.

'Told me your husband's prize heifer was in calf to his prize bull. If this is the one—man, he'll be upset, I'd guess.'

Michael hated the man's insidious, threatening tone, but Maggie was trying to keep her voice light. 'Well, Mr Waterman, if this were the same heifer, I guess he would. We're grateful for your service. But you're right—it's not your business. Nor is it Mr Grey's business what happens here, I dare say.'

Michael turned. He understood and shared Maggie's resentment, and he felt an unexpected wave of protective warmth towards her.

The vet scrawled his signature with a flourish, then stood up stiffly. 'You do your husband's accounts, I presume? Or do I give—' He waved the bill in Michael's direction.

'He does his own accounts. You can leave the bill with me, though. Thank you.' She did not so much as glance at it. 'The heifer's going to be OK?'

'I can call back tomorrow, if you want.'

She fairly bristled. 'My husband will call you if he thinks that's necessary.'

When the door finally closed behind Waterman, Michael returned to where Maggie stood in the doorway with the bill in hand. She unfolded it, hardly seeming to see it, and he saw the hurt at the corner of her mouth and eyes. He felt inadequate again. 'Not a pleasant man.'

'No.' She crinkled the bill absently between her finger and thumb. 'Twice the bill we'd usually expect, as well. Don'll be furious.'

Michael looked at her unhappily. 'I was thinking how upset he'd be.'

'Not with you, honey.' She gave him a quick smile. 'Not your fault the calf was early.'

'But Billy—'

'Don't mind what the boys said. They're as upset as you are—Billy especially. You know how he is about anything to do with the animals.'

'And I should've known what to do—more than I did.'

She shrugged. 'I'm sure you did all you could. It's just like that sometimes. Don goes out for a couple hours and this sort of thing happens.' Her eyes suddenly widened. 'But hold on, I've just noticed how dark it's getting. Surely you better get the milking underway?'

He almost dropped the coffee.

She grinned at him. 'Hey—it could've been worse! They might both have died. If you hadn't been here to handle it—just think.'

Don found him in the milking parlour an hour or two later as he was cleaning up. The ticking and pumping of the machines was still pulsing in his ears, and he had not heard the doors roll back or Don's boots on the cement floor.

'Maggie told me.' Don leant against one of the stalls and folded his arms. 'I just went round and took a look at her.'

He gave him a wan smile. 'I'm sorry.' There seemed nothing else to say, now.

'Michael, it wasn't your fault. You mustn't blame yourself. The heifer's gonna be fine.'

The McEnroes' patience was as unexpected as it was strangely hard to deal with. He would have known exactly how to respond to harsh words and criticism—or worse. But it seemed lame to repeat what he had already said to Maggie.

'Listen, Tony and I agree she'll be fine. You did right to tell the vet to save her. And when the test results on the calf's carcase come back from the lab, I'll let you know what we find out. Something wasn't right with that calf, that's clear.'

He felt vindicated, but not completely. 'I wasn't happy with the way I—'

'Michael, it was a chance in a hundred that she'd freshen today, and even more freaky that the calf was round the wrong way. I know how you feel. Remember about the fire we had here—Maggie told you?'

He nodded, reluctantly.

'I blamed myself for everything. Thought I'd dropped a cigarette. I used to smoke, you know. But it wasn't my fault at all. Bad wiring in the old barns. It's no use carrying the can for something out of your control. I learned that long ago.'

He nodded again now. He felt lighter. 'Thank you.'

Don surveyed the milking parlour. 'All done in here? Looks like it.'

'Think so.'

'You did fine, Michael. Thanks.'

'Let me know what else I can do.'

'Just relax. Forget it.'

'There's nothing...?'

Don gave him a dry half-smile. 'Look, if you're that desperate to do a kind of penance, take yourself up to the feedmill, would you? I could use a dozen more bags of feednuts. The usual—before the vacation would be quite handy. Have him put 'em on the slate. I'm in credit up there right now, but rather behindhand in placing my orders.'

He was glad of something so simple. 'It'll still be open?'

'Sure—till six.'

Michael hesitated, trying to gather himself. He saw the sagging lines around Don's mouth and the shadows under his eyes; he looked exhausted. 'I'll do that... But you haven't said how you got on in Buffalo.'

Don shifted from one foot to the other. 'Getting cold and getting a bit late for a long tale now—if you're going over to the feedmill. But it's all to do with the church.'

227

Michael frowned in surprise. Since the first weekend in October he had been to the village church every week with the McEnroes; they would never have thought of missing Mass. He had met the Wilkinsons there, and other families in the parish who cared about things far beyond the realm of Arcade, New York. But he could recall no mention before of farm products going out from the parish. 'What's the church doing?'

'It's working with Second Harvest—a group out in Chicago. I thought I mentioned it when you first came. They help food businesses and farmers get together and put food where it's needed. We've only been involved for a few months. It's a small thing to do—at least our involvement is. But it makes me feel...'

Michael warmed to him again. 'As if you're doing something worthwhile?' he supplied.

Don gave him a wry smile. 'Well, if you want to know the truth, even after all these years, I feel I'm doing something worthwhile every day as it is—just working this land. Don't mean to sound trite, but that's how I feel. But Second Harvest—that's another matter. I found out a while back that at least twenty per cent of the food produced in this nation gets wasted one way or another—bulldozed, burned, or trashed. That makes me sick. I decided I didn't want any part of big agribusiness that wastes resources. Someone at the church told me about Second Harvest. That was it. We signed up. Wilkinsons signed up. Almost everyone in the parish committed something.' Don's eyes wandered to the far side of the barn and beyond it to Grey's boundary. 'Almost.'

'Always grain?'

'No, but it is for us this time. We've got a deal with a mill up in Buffalo, who'll process a consignment of next year's wheat harvest and do it up in thirty-pound sacks of whole-grain flour. None of your white rubbish which—or so Maggie assures me—the rats even have more sense than to touch. It's good stuff, and it goes to school breakfast programmes in the inner city, and to food pantries for the homeless—to people like that.'

Michael's head was buzzing with questions. 'But don't the supermarket chains fight against what you're doing?'

'Some do. Others are in on it, right behind it.' Don held up his hand, smiling again. 'Kind of puts things like that calf in proportion, doesn't it? See—you've forgotten already! That's better. Go on. Take the pickup if you're gonna go. We'll talk more later.'

In the dark, the lights of the dashboard gave the pickup's cab an eerie, greenish glow. But the truck's stuffy warmth was strangely comforting, especially as the wind was still flattening the dead weeds along the margin of the highway, and shearing at the trees. Once again, he let the events of the afternoon sift away, feeling only the quiet pleasure of doing a straightforward task at the end of a tough day.

The wind caught at him as he bent his head inside his jacket and ran across the parking lot to the glass doors of the feedmill. Only two other pickups graced the wide space. Light from inside shed a wide path across the lot, and he ran into it, gratefully. The air inside was as cold as it was outside, but quite still, except where a draft blew across the cement floor of the entrance. The familiar scents greeted him: dry wood, dusty sacking, and the clean tang of new paint.

Dressed in a thick down jacket, the manager was reckoning up the till, a radio behind him murmuring the latest news from downtown Buffalo. He gave Michael a brief nod and went back with his work.

'I'm not too late?'

'Nah. Get a move on, though.' The man went on pushing buttons and muttering over the day's takings as Michael rolled a flat waggon between the canyons that separated the heaped up supplies, searching for what Don wanted. Above the rafters of the feedmill the wind rumbled and raged over the corrugated roof, but inside the atmosphere was dead, and he could see his breath. He began to whistle between his teeth.

Other voices came to him, then, from men out of sight behind the bags and sacks and boxes. In the relative quiet, their words were discernible to him. He heard heavy boots—of at least two men— then scuffing and shuffling as they stopped unseen behind the mounds of supplies.

'Told me this afternoon he lost the calf that rightfully belonged to Grey.'

'Yours?' A gurgle of sour laughter. 'What'd Donald McEnroe be doing with anything of *yours*, Elias?'

'You might well ask.'

Michael knew that cracked voice. It was dry as the whisper of frosty wind that blew under the main door of the feedmill.

'Well, go on. Haven't got all night. Tell us what happened.'

'You tell him, 'Lias.'

The old man cleared his throat. 'Vet was over my place doing some routine tests. Got called over to McEnroes' by that whippersnapper of an English kid McEnroe's had working there. Seemed his best heifer came on early—the one my bull covered, back in the spring.' He cackled. 'Kid couldn't handle it. Waterman was back an hour later with the bad news. Calf was dead. Idiotic ineptitude.' Grey's voice grew cruel. 'Typical of McEnroe. I would've crucified him to get that calf.'

'Paternity rights, yeah?' More of the same bitter laughter.

'Nothing I can do now. Anyways, it serves the bastard right. Never did look to his fences properly. By God, he will now, I tell you.'

The others laughed harshly. 'Heard tell your own fencing ain't no great shakes, Elias.'

'Maybe. But McEnroe's, now—'

'And that calf was nigh-on perfect, Waterman said. If he'd called before, they would both have made it, he reckoned. Wasn't even sure the calf was premature, as that English smart-ass claimed. Champion little bull calf. Still breathing when he got it out.'

Michael felt the heat rise inside. He did not wait to hear more but abandoned the waggon and strode straight down the nearest cross-aisle until he saw them: three old men in faded overalls, the 'good ol' boys' Don always spoke of. In his mind's eye they stood for ever in the town bar, or here, in the feedmill, sucking on straws, chewing tobacco, and spitting. It was a shock to see them as they were.

Until he stood right in front of them, he had no idea what he would say. Grey he'd already met, but the others were unknown to him.

The words splurged out, hot, indignant, and wonderfully satisfying. 'Don't talk that way of Mr McEnroe. Don't talk that way of me. You don't know what you're talking about. How do any of you

know what happened? You weren't there. I saw the calf for myself—
quartered, it was—by Waterman. Breathing! My gosh, it was done for.
Dead as—' He searched for the words, waving his hand wildly, in
frustration.

For some reason, Rachel's face floated in front of his brain—
illuminated by afternoon sunshine, her hand pointing to the daisies
at the corner of the home pasture. 'Dead as daisies in November. If that
calf was from your bull, Mr Grey—' He struggled to recover his
composure. '—then it must have been premature.'

They looked up with eyebrows raised in surprise. All three of their
mouths showed tobacco-stained and broken teeth; their crabbed,
leathery faces grinned in twisted amusement.

'Who's talking?'

Michael looked at the man who had spoken, one of the two he
didn't recognize. 'Michael Monaghan. Don McEnroe's farmworker, for
the moment. The "whippersnapper of an English kid" you were just
talking about.' He felt like adding, *You should know. You seem to know
everything else around here, before anyone else does—even the
exaggerations and lies of a so-called professional vet. A vet who should
have saved the calf if there'd been any way to do so.*

They glared, remained irritatingly silent.

He remembered what Don had said. *I wouldn't put it past Grey to
open up the hole himself and wave the bull through.* But he could hardly
sling accusations like that at the man. In fact Don had admitted he was
in the wrong about the fencing. But that didn't remove all
responsibility from Grey. The bull had been in the field right next
to the McEnroes' prize animals, and Grey must have known about,
could have told Don before about the hole in the fence...

He faced them, foursquare—taller than all of them but now
feeling self-conscious, melodramatic, and tongue-tied. He exhaled
unsteadily and lowered his voice. 'Mr McEnroe said there was no way
of knowing the heifer would calve early. You must've had breech
calves before now, surely. It could happen to anyone. The carcase's
gone to the lab, anyway. We'll know what's happening when we get
the results back.'

'Oh-oh! Willya listen to that boy shoot his mouth off? Kid, you're as wet behind the ears as the big Mac was when he came up here with his new-fangled notions and city ways. You don't know nothing. You'd best keep your trap shut. Waterman said you were as much use in that stall as a piece o' straw in the wind.' Grey was so full of derision that Michael expected him to spit on the floor.

He felt the heat of temper surging again into his face. He had caught the old men talking behind his back—behind Don's back. He had cornered them. No wonder they were out to savage him. They were like Wally: wily and vicious. And he suddenly felt the same, wanted to guard what was Don's good name; wanted to defend those he had come to respect.

He opened his mouth to answer them. Immediately, the lights flickered, faded to brown, then abruptly went out. The feedmill lay black and close and cold around them.

In the dark Grey began to curse. All of them stood still.

'Power out!' shouted the feedmill manager with unnecessary officiousness. In the dead air they could hear him scrabbling about. 'Stay where yous are. I'll have a flashlight going in a jiffy. Damn powerlines down again. Not surprised in all this wind.' The man went on complaining, then thin beams of torchlight wavered over the ceiling, sending wild shadows from the supplies. The wind howled outside like a demented animal.

'Over here,' Michael called, shivering. He separated himself from the others and moved towards the light. Somehow he must get the feednuts before the mill shuts for the Thanksgiving Holiday.

'That's blasted Allegany County for you,' Grey intoned from behind him. 'Power cut right in time to stop the womenfolk putting the turkey in for Thanksgiving.' He sniffed. 'Great, ain't it, fellas?'

Michael smiled to himself in the dimness as he went back and heaved the bags one by one onto the waggon. For just a moment, but only a moment, he almost liked Grey.

14

Rachel could not grow used to the early evenings: the way the darkness closed in before four, now that they were so near Christmas. A cold had dogged her since late November; and no matter what she did, she couldn't seem to shake it off.

The medics' library had almost emptied. A few other women—perhaps feeling as pressed as she felt—remained to pore over their textbooks and make notes on sheaves of papers that lay on tables and floorboards. All the other students seemed to have resigned themselves to failing the January half-year exams; or else decided that Christmas was reason enough anyway to abandon their work for the final days of the term.

Was she the only one staring at the ceiling and simply wanting the term to finish . . . so that she could sleep? She had been too busy for the past ten weeks to think beyond sleep to how else she might spend her time over Christmas. Nor could she afford the luxury, now, of pursuing that kind of daydream. She must shut out the whispered conversations she could hear from the gallery and the journal stacks at the far end of the library about family Christmases in English homes, with one-point-four brothers and two-point-one labradors, and a crackling fire in the hearth.

She must forget the letter from her mother that she had carried in her coat pocket for a week now, describing the family's plans for Christmas in Arcade and New Year in Boston, passing on to her ('just in case you can get away, honey') the Monaghans' address in Kent. She knew now that Kent was somewhere nearby, but she knew also that she would not have the courage to call Michael's family and foist herself on them. She had made that decision anyway, when

Michael himself had first given her the address. This year, she would be alone, and in London.

Like siren voices, everything clamoured for her attention. 'Get down to your studies,' the lecturers and tutors urged. 'You'll regret it if you don't. The eighteen-month MB goes frighteningly fast.'

'Blow the studies. Time to party!' the other medics—especially the men—insisted. Then spent their evenings in drunken revelry in and out of the residence halls, shouting from the ambulatory until one in the morning, vomiting on staircases, and careening like mad pool balls down the corridors outside her room.

'Don't miss this lecture!'

'It'll be a fantastic hop tonight.'

'Time for carol-singing rehearsal, Rachel.'

'We'd better go and check that experiment, don't you think?'

'Your tutor was looking for you.'

Hearing the voices echo in her mind, she rubbed her scalp wearily, then realized with a small smile that this was just how McEnroe rubbed his head when he was tired.

A woman's voice brought her back into the library again. 'I knew I'd find you in here. Rachel, you'll go mental if you spend any more time on that alternative medicine project—or whatever it is you're in the thick of now. For goodness sake, take a break!' Cecelia, a nurse who had befriended her in the Thursday night meetings of the madrigal singers, stood sternly beside the table where she was working and looked at her through thick lenses with a mixture of pity and disgust.

'You look like the sister in casualty,' Rachel teased. 'Fierce and formidable.'

The weekly singing practices were the one outlet she had allowed herself, once she had discovered that treks across the bridge to the men's favoured 'watering hole' were expensive and often increased her homesickness.

Cecelia leaned forward to make her point. 'Come on, it's the last practice of the term. We need you if you're going to sing on the wards. And I think you've forgotten the meeting this—'

'Now you sound just like that nutter Christophers,' she laughed; she had begun to use some of the words the English medics used. 'According to him, the rugby club *needs* me to cheer this afternoon. A game against Guy's. Meanwhile Dr Tate *needs* this project finished in two days.' She sneezed loudly and blew her nose. 'Sorry. This wretched cold.'

Cecelia scoffed and waved a plump hand. 'Go on with you! Our lads're an utter waste of space. Guy's'll slaughter 'em, even if the dean and the chief executive themselves get out there cheering. Besides, it's raining again.'

'Exactly. The perfect cure to the common cold.'

'But you could get to both events, Rachel.'

'I think I'll skip the game, thanks.'

'Well, never mind the rugby, then. But what about the meeting we were talking about yesterday? That's really what I came about.'

Rachel sat back and dropped the pencil she had been using for notes. She met Cecelia's dark eyes levelly, concentrating properly now on what she was asking. 'Wait, aren't you on duty this afternoon and tonight?'

'No. I'm on earlies tomorrow. I swapped. I didn't want to miss that lecture. Don't see why you high-flying medics should get all the useful lectures while we spend our lives emptying bedpans and strapping sprained wrists.'

Rachel snorted. 'Don't be crazy. You're good. Don't forget I've seen you in action once or twice. You do a lot more than that.'

Cecelia's short-sighted eyes seemed to withdraw further behind her glasses. Her mouth was set. 'Well, make up your mind. Coming, or not?'

Rachel turned over the papers she had been working on, and sighed. Her brain felt heavy with information and ideas she doubted if she would ever use. Suddenly she envied Cecelia her opportunities to work directly with patients—not just inspect tissue under microscopes, catalogue diseases in the lecture theatre, or cut up cadavers in the dissecting room—where medicine threatened to become an abstraction.

She began to weaken. 'It's definitely about the contribution women can make in ob-gyn?'

'You know it is.'

'Of course I'm interested, but...'

'Rachel! How often d'you get a lecturer as interesting as the president of the Royal College of Obstetricians and Gynaecologists?' Cecelia's round face softened. 'Look, it's Christmas. What better time than now to think of childbirth?'

Rachel chuckled. 'Just because your poor mama had nine children...'

'That's got nothing to do with it. This is daft.' Cecelia snatched up the papers. 'Just leave them here, if you're so determined to come back and work later. See, I've piled them up all neatly for you.' She pulled Rachel's coat off the back of the chair. 'Shift yourself, woman, or you'll feel my sharp tongue. Cuppa first, then we're going to this lecture.' She scowled ferociously. 'We'll contemplate the madrigals later. I'm not letting you get away with cracking your head like an egg all the time. You're already hard-boiled, according to my diagnosis.'

Rachel let herself be carried along by Cecelia's bossy determination. She waved her hands in surrender. 'OK, OK, you win.'

Only a few students dotted the lecture theatre, so that it felt colder than usual. The draft seemed to rake straight down the banked rows of seats to the front, and the students sat hunched against the cold, university scarves wrapped thickly round their throats, and coats still on. Even for an optional lecture, it was too small an audience, Rachel thought, glad now that she had allowed herself to be persuaded to attend.

The head of the department introduced the speaker, who looked round uncomfortably, and his attempted whisper came clearly to where Rachel and Cecelia sat at the back of the echoing hall. 'Isn't there another venue...?'

One of the second-year medics rose and stepped down to the podium. 'The students' union lounge is empty this afternoon, sir. There's a rugby game on, so the bar should be quiet, as well. If we could...?'

The senior lecturer nodded. 'Why not? You won't need the CCTV, will you?'

Everyone shuffled out and along the labyrinth towards the lounge. Rachel thought of the hop she had been to with Charlie Christophers, and how she had found refuge in the lounge afterwards, for the first time savouring its quiet. She had retreated there many times since, for the peace.

The room was stuffy as ever, but at least warm. Cecelia subsided into a seat in the middle of the room and motioned Rachel to sit beside her.

When the chatter ceased, the speaker leaned forwards. He began brightly, 'When you decided to take up medicine, you thought you were making a career choice. I wonder if you've discovered yet that it's nothing like most other careers. More like a vocation. Society expects you to be on call all the time. You're lucky if you can carve out a private life—let alone a family life.'

The professor was nodding sagely, but the Australian Crock Basden, sitting in the front circle of chairs, shifted irritably and muttered, 'Get to the point, mate.'

The speaker heard him and smiled rather sadly. 'Ah, my Australian friend, but it is the point. By all means stop me and we'll chat about it in a minute. But that's what I've come to present to you—women, especially.'

Unwillingly, Rachel caught his eye.

'We're talking here about a career based on families ... that doesn't allow for our own families.'

Rachel's concentration wandered to the daisy-swirled curtains. She thought vaguely of Marianne, and of Michael, then began twisting a thread on the cuff of her sweater as her half-formed imaginings brought her to Boston, to Arcade, then back to the lecture in the over-heated lounge. She was disappointed; the lecture was to have been women and obstetrics, not the general drawbacks of the medical profession. But she was too tired to whisper an excuse to Cecelia and escape to the library again. Out of sheer listlessness she stayed where she was, but her mind slipped gears again and returned to the alternative medicine project she had been researching. It was taking up much of her time now—a good way to stave off homesickness.

She knew it would be controversial. Dr Tate, her tutor, would raise his eyebrows in dismay and tut-tut over it, but she felt she had to go on. Since the beginning of October, since the first lectures in clinical medicine, she had been puzzled and alarmed by the conservative, sceptical line St Stephen's lecturers took on alternative medicine. Their ideas and practices seemed to be based on the view that all human disease was purely physical and therefore treatable only by physical means. She had made up her mind to resist the flow of their convictions, and the research she was doing as part of the project had given her the opportunities she had hoped for. 'Medicine and Materialistic Thinking' was the grand title she had given it—much to the other medics' amusement.

The way that lecturers and hospital staff usually spoke disturbed her. She and the ever-sympathetic Cecelia had talked about it, one night, after a madrigal practice.

'Did you ever notice the words people use in this hospital?' she had wondered, almost thinking aloud.

Cecelia screwed up her nose. 'Like what?'

'Sometimes when we're in the dissecting room or in theatre, it sounds more like a theatre of war than a place where healing might start.'

'What d'you mean?'

'Think about it.'

'You have, obviously. Come on, what are you driving at?'

' "Cut it", for example.'

'What's wrong with that?'

' "Burn it".'

Cecelia nodded. 'I get it—in oncology, you mean.'

'Or "Shoot it out"—more like chemical warfare than chemo-therapy.'

Cecelia frowned. 'But what are we *supposed* to say, Rachel?'

She shrugged. 'I don't have the answers yet. But I sure don't think medicine should be about frightening people. How can bodies heal if minds are in fear and turmoil? The hospital chaplains would agree—but that's about all. And what about the spiritual side of human beings? Do we ever address that?'

Cecilia shook her head and entered into the spirit of Rachel's argument. 'No. You may be right, come to think of it. I heard Sister talking to an anxious mother on the ward this morning. "We'll whack him in next week, Mrs Bloggs. Whip those tonsils out before he knows it. Don't you worry."

' "Whack him and whip him". Sounds good, doesn't it?'

They chortled uneasily.

'A brilliant recipe for not worrying! "Kill the bugs with antibiotics", "Choke off the blood supply on this artery, will you, nurse?" ' Rachel had raised her hands, palm up. 'No good, is it?'

'So what do you suggest?'

It was the question she had wrestled with most throughout the term. 'A different attitude.'

'How? What? You're losing me.'

She scratched her head. 'Well, for starters, the business ethic is creeping into medicine. Put in so much investment, and you get so much output. Focus on the costs, on the paperwork, and don't worry so much about the patients. If we have such and such funds for a hundred hip replacement ops, then that's our "output" from the funding. But what about the patients? Aren't they just production numbers on a doctor's output chart? Whatever's happened to the notion of a doctor as a healer who works with the *whole* person?'

'Watch it, Rachel, that sounds a bit radical.'

'Oh, baloney!' She had been thinking about it for weeks, and the words had spilled out. 'Medicine isn't business, any more than it's warfare. The Greeks knew that thousands of years ago. The church figured it out hundreds of years ago. Well, Jesus didn't say to the quadraplegic, "Up you get, friend. I've *zapped* you, and you can walk now." He didn't say to him, "I've come to the end of my NHS quota of scalpels and wheelchairs for you quadraplegics, so tough, you dumb fool." He told him his sins were forgiven. He wanted him healed body and soul, not just body.'

'You should have been a preacher.'

Rachel laughed. 'No women priests in our church, or yours, Celie.'

Then the RCOG speaker's voice penetrated again, indirectly tying in with her thoughts. 'We might as well be celibate priests for all we're allowed to enjoy our own families. And women doctors who make it to the top of the career structure and end up lecturing at hospitals like St Stephen's about the latest in midwifery and obstetrics haven't even seen the birth of their own children. They're childless. Here's my point: the baby's in danger of going out with the money spent on birthing pool water; the soul's in danger of going out of our profession.'

Some of the medics murmured in assent, and Rachel sat forward.

He caught her eye again. 'Look at yourselves. Fifty per cent in here are women. Fifty per cent of St Stephen's intake in the autumn were female. But only twelve per cent of all ob-gyn consultants are female. Why? You take time out to have a child, if you're sensible. But competition drives the machine, and you're left behind. The men at the top, if they've managed to eke out any kind of a life, probably don't have a satisfactory family life. And women who do have families have no chance of making it to the top.'

Rachel felt as if someone had punched her in the stomach. *Probably don't have a satisfactory family life...'* *'Probably don't have a satisfactory...'* *'Probably don't...'* The words writhed inside her like a sickness. *Oh, I couldn't stand that.*

She recalled learning in the term's first obstetrics lecture that Britain's birth rate was only a little short of three quarters of a million each year. But where were the specialists coming from who would cope? And would they—she reverted for a moment to her meandering thoughts on alternative medicine—be capable of taking into account more than just the bulge on the front of a woman's body, the mere physical fact of pregnancy?

She felt weary again with all the dilemmas. She wanted to work with real lives—not get lost in the mires of argument.

She rested a hand on Cecelia's arm and put her mouth to her ear. 'Sorry, but I've had it up to here. He's good, I agree with what he's saying, but I'm out of here.'

'All right then.' Cecelia's whisper was barely audible. 'I'll see you at the practice. No practice, no going on the wards to sing carols, remember?'

Rachel grinned. 'I know it.'

Things had seemed comparatively simple at the beginning of the term. Attend lectures and keep up with studying. Check on the current experiment in the lab. Grab a bite in the canteen. Go to weekly madrigal practices. She hadn't bargained on the welter of other demands on time and energy. She hadn't bargained on the persistent homesickness or the dogged grey drabness of London in winter; this, after all, was where she had *wanted* to study! Once, she had made the mistake of confiding in one of the housemen about how pressed she felt. Scornfully, he had told her to get off her 'self-pity trip'. She had long university holidays, didn't she? What more could she ask? How could she fuss when she didn't have to work days and nights on end with no holiday at all? And what did it matter if she were homesick if once she got beyond the pre-clinical and clinical courses she would have no more time to fly to Boston than she would to go home to Birmingham—if that had been her home. She had learned, after that, to push aside her feelings and get on with her work.

Cecelia found her later, back in the library. 'I've got something for you,' she said. 'Come on.'

This time Rachel brought her books and papers out of the library and followed Cecelia across the street into the nurses' home.

'I've made you some tea. Nothing fancy. Just fuel for singers.'

As they had done several times during the term, they ate beans on toast in front of the hissing gas fire in Cecelia's cramped room, then returned to the main hospital and to the madrigal practice. Next door, the bar was roaring like a rugby crowd.

'Probably is a rugby crowd,' Cecelia quipped. 'They actually beat Guy's, would you believe it?'

'Drunk as skunks all night. I thought we were supposed to be treating cirrhosis of the liver here, not offering ourselves as guinea pigs.' They laughed.

The practice was more focused than it had been all term. None of the usual shuffling of music. The conductor issued everyone with red folders, gave out the order of the carols, and led them through the singers' entire Christmas repertoire in two hours. As they sang, the noise in the bar next door dwindled to the occasional muffled shout; a few of the rugby players actually drifted in to listen, clap and even sing with them. And as they sang, Rachel forgot all the demands of the day and was carried away on the swell and surge of the singing.

By the end, she had relaxed. Cecelia invited her to go back to the nurses' home again for cocoa, but she declined.

'You're not going on with that dreadful project, surely?'

'No way! I'm going to sleep.' She touched her throat. 'I'm even more scratchy after all that singing. I want some voice left—to sing tomorrow.'

They pushed through the lounge doors and wandered companionably down the corridor.

'I'm back on duty at seven a.m. myself. So I'll see you when we start singing. Sister's letting me off for that—the ward's been pretty quiet.'

Rachel stopped. Something had suddenly clarified for her. 'What about Christmas Day? What duties d'you have?'

Cecelia looked down. 'I'm a bit like you, Rachel. Love to get away and have a real Christmas, but I've got no more leave until the New Year. It'll be the first year I've not got back to Ireland to see the mob at home. I'm on days for the whole of next week, and nights from New Year's Eve, would you believe.'

Rachel made sympathetic noises. Visions of the rarely used front room of the farmhouse danced across her mind: the conifer branches her brothers always cut to decorate the room; the tree twinkling with tinsel and ribbons in the corner, the bright pile of presents under the tree, and the smell of warm cider and eggnog wafting from the kitchen. Then there was 'McEnroevia', and her grandfather, with his arms out to her, shouting greetings of welcome; toasting the New Year, the city of Boston, the farm, the golfclub, the country club, the Red Sox, and everything else his quick mind could think of. But she mustn't think of those things now. 'I know how you feel,' she murmured. 'But I don't want to get sorry for myself, OK?'

Cecelia's smile came back. 'You're on. The wards are jolly as anything on Christmas Day itself. That can't be bad. They shut half of them, you know. Send as many patients home as possible, then make it fun for the rest of them if they can.'

Rachel took a quick breath. 'What if—I mean, would there be any problems, d'you think, if I came on with you?'

Cecelia's eyebrows went up.

'As an orderly, or a volunteer visitor or something. That's all. I wouldn't do anything official—I know I couldn't. But if people can go round with candy waggons—'

'Hospital trolleys, silly!'

'And newspapers and library books, well, why can't I go on?'

'I suppose I could ask Sister for you.' Cecelia looked doubtful.

Rachel sighed. 'I hardly dared think about how I'd spend Christmas Day. You maybe just solved my problem.'

She fell asleep that night more at peace than she had felt for weeks. In the next two days she attended her last lectures, finished the alternative medicine project, and sang madrigals to patients—all with a sense of satisfaction and completion. But she still looked forward to the long mornings sleeping in and taking her ease before the medical school ground into gear again.

Her first thought on Christmas morning was something that seemed to come out of nowhere. It was as if her mind had been turning things over and over while she slept. *There are McEnroes in Scotland. McEnroe's cousins. I could travel . . .*

She woke properly, sat up, and began to cough. The air in her room was bitter.

She reached for the radiator. It, too, was cold. *No heating on Christmas Day!*

Her sleepy mind went back to the half-dream of cousins in Scotland. She had seen pictures on television and in the newspapers of blizzards in the Scottish Highlands. It would be even colder there. Not as cold as Boston or Arcade, certainly, but at home people at least knew how to keep houses warm.

She shivered and sneezed. Going to Scotland was an insane idea.

In the dull mirror on her cupboard she caught a glimpse of her face as she bent towards the sink. Her cheeks were paler than usual, but her nose looked almost blue. She smiled to herself. *No wonder*, she thought, turning on the tap. *And the water's freezing, as well.*

Self-pity welled up again. It had followed her the way Wally had followed Michael down to the farmhouse on her last day at home. Right behind the heels, relentlessly. She pushed it away. *Only a little headcold,* she told herself. *And the people on Celie's ward today will be in much worse shape than that.*

It crossed her mind that she shouldn't go on the ward at all with a cold. *Hospitals are the dirtiest places in the world,* one of the lecturers had breezily informed them in the first pathology lecture. Well, she could always wear a mask.

She dressed fast, still shivering, grateful to be leaving the room for the main hospital. It would be warm enough in the canteen and on the ward, she knew.

Cecelia was nowhere in sight when she pushed open the swing doors of the men's post-operative ward. Some of the men looked up expectantly when she entered, then away again when they did not recognize her. Others slept, oblivious, heads turned to one side, mouths open, faces drained of colour. Several of them lay motionless with heads or legs swathed in bandages.

Without Cecelia for guidance, she waited with some trepidation in the corner of the ward, outside the sister's poky office. The door was shut, but through the glass door she could see a student nurse inside, her back to the door, nodding as the sister gave directions. She looked around more as she waited, taking in the festoons of rainbow-coloured hangings that the nurses had looped from window to curtain rail, from curtain rail to overhead lights. Visitors were already drifting in, some laden with poinsettias or wrapped presents. The big ward was bright and warm, but the hush of it seemed out of character with the day. There should have been music, she thought—however quiet—and the smell of turkey.

Bed curtains swished open at the far end of the ward to reveal a patient whose arm and face trailed driplines, and a houseman dressed cheerily in a Santa Claus hat and white coat adorned with tinsel as well as the usual stethoscope. The doctor's appearance and hearty parting words to the patient were strangely at odds with the patient's white, exhausted face. 'What you need, Mr King, is a damn good kiss under the mistletoe and a stiff jar of Bell's.'

Walking beside him, the staff nurse blanched. 'Doctor, I don't think...' But the houseman was already pulling out another set of case notes and moving to the next bed. His insensitivity grated on Rachel.

Beside her, the ward doors swung open again, and Cecelia appeared. Her face was flushed, and she was pushing a drug trolley. 'Rachel! Happy Christmas! I just went out to the drug cupboard. Sorry. I'd almost forgotten. What, Sister tied up? Come on—we'll get you kitted up in the linen room.'

'Merry Christmas to you, Cecelia. But—'

'I've already spoken to Sister. She's pleased to have you. Says you can at least pat pillows, rearrange the deckchairs on this little Titanic, and help serve the lunches. Guess who'll carve the turkey on this ward? No—it's simply too gruesome. The professor of surgery, who else? Comes in specially every year, they told me, complete with cracker crown and Santa gear... Just hold on a minute.'

Rachel watched her chain the trolley to the wall and check the lock. Then she followed her to the linen room just down the corridor from the ward. 'He'll have competition, then. The houseman's already playing the part.'

'Oh, him. What a wally! He'll be gone long before lunch, thank goodness. Never mind him—I've got some interesting titbits to tell you when we get a moment.'

Dressed in a mask and an ugly green overall, Rachel followed Cecelia round the ward. Cecelia's calm cheerfulness, cheeky banter with some of the patients, and tactful understanding of their feelings filled her with admiration.

'You're good with those people, like I told you before,' she said later, when they sat in the staff coffee lounge for a mid-morning break.

'No patronage or babytalk, but no nonsense either.'

Cecelia shrugged. 'It's what I always hoped to do.' She grinned. 'Even on Christmas Day. It's not too bad being on duty today, at all.'

'I feel totally incompetent. I can't believe I'll one day be telling nursing staff what dosages to dish out, ordering biopsies and IVs, or whatever. Seems impossible.'

'Or delivering babies, or seeing patients in your own surgery.'

'But so many things are geared towards *hospital* medicine here.'

'Oh, that's what you think! Wait until you get further in your training.'

Rachel set an empty coffee mug on the floor by her chair. 'So what's this news?'

'Idle gossip, I expect. But there're no newspapers until Tuesday, so we may never know. A locum registrar came in for the morning—over from St Thom's. Says something funny's been going on there the last few months.'

'Like what?' Rachel felt only slightly interested, eager to get back to the ward.

'Like drugs going missing out of double-locked cupboards to which there's only one key. Like patients having to wait while crucial stuff's rushed to them from Guy's, from here, or the manufacturers.'

'Careless stocktaking?'

'Could be. I doubt it. You know how tight they run that ship here. Everything counted, re-counted, and locked.'

Rachel felt the cold close in on her again. Inevitably she thought of McEnroe's battle with the East Coast drug dealers. She said slowly, 'What sort of drugs?'

'Apparently they're very selective. Not necessarily what you'd predict—you know, analgesics and opiates—that sort of stuff. But they've been lifting some of the more powerful decongestants.' Cecelia was enjoying the drama of her account and the effect it was having on Rachel.

'What do the admin people think's going on, then?'

'They've called the Met to find out.'

'Regular London police? Isn't there a special branch that—'

'That's what I heard. So-called "Violence Intelligence Unit". They're the people who look into drug-related murders and organized crime.'

'And?' Rachel heard her voice sharpening. *Is this why McEnroe was over here in the fall? Dear God, don't let it be why...*

'Rach—you've gone white as a hospital sheet!' Cecelia chortled. She touched her arm. 'Whatever's wrong?'

'Please, just tell me what else you heard.'

'Not much more, really. They're looking into it. Theft, almost certainly. And probably from inside. There's bound to be another security crackdown here, as well. It happens from time to time. Sister was very twitchy when I fetched out the supplies this morning—and I wasn't even getting any of the controlled stuff. More twitchy than usual, I mean. Anyway, we're bound to hear more on the grapevine, sooner or later.'

'It sounds scary to me.'

Cecelia wasn't taking things seriously. 'Could be fun and games. Apparently the undercover blokes are after investigating what's been going on in *all* the London hospitals. Sure, they'll be over here soon, nosing around.' She stopped and rubbed her hands together. 'Great stuff! I'd love to get my hands on a *healthy* male body for a change.'

Rachel sat back and laughed. The momentary panic subsided. This was Christmas Day, a long way from Boston, and Cecelia had a refreshingly funny view of things she herself took perhaps too seriously.

They were still laughing when the ward sister put her head round the door. 'My turn for coffee, girls. Back you go now.' She nodded at Rachel. 'Got a bit of a cold, have we? Well, thanks for wearing a mask. Back on when you go out. And Cecelia, move those chairs first, please.'

Cecelia looked flustered, but Rachel exchanged a small smile with her. She was still smiling behind the mask when they re-entered the ward, realizing suddenly that she had forgotten her self-pity and was entirely engrossed in Cecelia's world. Christmas or not, there was help she could give.

Her attention was again drawn by the man with the dripline. His sad eyes had been following her around the ward. 'Does that bottle need to be changed?'

Cecelia was moving chairs for a bevy of visitors who had come in and were clustered, talking in subdued voices, around one of the other beds. 'I'll check it now,' she said.

Rachel watched the deft movements as Cecelia unhooked the almost empty dripfeed and attached a new bottle. The patient's face did not change. He stared at them through torpid eyes, his hands lying slack on the covers and under the feed tubes the corners of his mouth turned down. Dressings covered part of his abdomen, but he seemed not to care about pulling his pyjamas over them.

She noticed that no one had brought flowers. His was the only bed in the ward not surrounded by cards, wrapping paper, or relatives. Moved, she whispered to Cecelia that she'd sit with the man for a while.

He frowned at her when she pulled up one of the uncomfortable plastic chairs supplied to visitors. Then he turned his head away, winced, and shut his eyes. His lips framed a couple of scratchy words, but she missed them.

Nonplussed, she waited with her hands folded in her lap and watched his face for another change. 'I thought you might want a bit of company,' she told him gently, 'seeing that it's Christmas.' She wondered if she should take his dry-skinned hand into her own, or if that would offend him.

The eyes popped open. 'You deaf?' His voice was loud and rude, now. 'Leave me alone, I said. Christmas means nothing to me.'

The staff nurse was beside her instantly, and Cecelia looked up anxiously from where she was talking to a patient several beds away. 'Lost cause,' the staff nurse said as she shepherded Rachel away. 'Best let him rest. Nice of you to try. We should've warned you. Mr King's a hopeless case.'

She remembered what the houseman had said about whiskey and a kiss under the mistletoe, and groaned. If she had cherished any illusions about being a sort of Florence Nightingale for the day, they were blown away now. 'Long-stay patient, is he?'

'That's right. He had a gastric malignancy resected last week. Not healing well. He's got a fistula under those dressings. But don't mind him.' She flipped up the watch that was pinned to her uniform. 'We'll be serving lunch in a few minutes, unless the surgeon's still running round the ambulatory trying to catch the turkey, or something.' She chuckled. 'Why don't you talk to Mr Petherton—over there. Family can't get in 'til later. He *would* appreciate you.'

The rest of Christmas Day passed in an alternating rhythm of rushed work and calm or laughing moments with patients and other members of staff. The surgeon who carved the turkey was familiar from some lecture or other, but he ignored Rachel as steadfastly as he ignored all the nursing staff on the ward, playing instead to the patients, and booming 'We wish you a merry Christmas' in a mellow bass voice when he helped serve the plates of steaming food. He was popular with all the inmates except the man on the dripline, who querulously complained that the smell of turkey sickened him. Cecelia shrugged and mimed 'There's one in every crowd' to Rachel.

Her feet were aching by three o' clock when Cecelia's duty ended. She could think of nothing else besides sitting down and—somehow—keeping warm until she fell asleep that evening. But Cecelia had other ideas.

'I know just the place for you,' she said as they brushed past more visitors in the corridor. 'We'll have a quick peep in the maternity wing, OK?'

Rachel wanted to clap. 'Great idea. I've never seen Christmas babies before.'

Five babies were lined up in decorated cots on the other side of a viewing window. Inside the unit, masked nurses moved from one cot to the other, adjusting covers or lifting babies to the window for fathers and grandparents to exclaim or gush over. The nurses wore red and green tinsel in their caps, and an air of talcum-powdered cleanliness and delirious happiness prevailed. Quite a different atmosphere from the shabby, bustling men's ward on the floor below.

'Are they all Christmas babies?' Rachel asked.

'Only the ones with the little stockings hung on the end of the cots. Look—that one must have been the first. They always give the biggest stocking to the earliest Christmas baby.'

A dressing-gowned young woman came shuffling to the window on the arm of her husband. 'That one's ours,' she told anyone who was interested. 'She's perfect, look.'

Cecelia grinned at them. 'What a present!'

Unexpected tears welled into Rachel's eyes. She thought of her father's delight every time a calf was born, and she wanted suddenly to hear his voice; or to be folded in her mother's arms and feel the familiar welcome of a Christmas at home.

'I'm off to my room, Celia, I think.'

'Already? But it's only half three.'

'I'm bushed.'

'But you said it was cold in there.'

'It was. But nothing'd keep me awake right now.' The desire for sleep had become like the pull of a tide—inexorable.

She parted from Cecelia outside the back door of the hospital. For once, the aromas from the kitchens smelled mouth-watering, but she had eaten as much as she wanted on the ward. Now she stood breathing in the cold air as Cecelia waved and trudged away on the path that would take her through the side gates and across the road to the nurses' home.

A funny way to spend Christmas Day, she thought. *But a good way, too*.

Her breath was white on the still air, and the cold pinched her nostrils. Twilight was already spreading over the hospital grounds; the street lights flickered on even as she watched. She blew her nose and started across the courtyard for the residence hall. Then, on impulse, she turned and retraced her steps through the deserted med school and ground floor of the hospital to the lobby. Of course there would be no postal delivery until Tuesday, but something prompted her to hope for just one more bit of human contact before she faded for the night.

The porters were drowsing in the heat of the radiators by the revolving doors. She recognized one of them as the same man who had been on duty when she'd arrived. Otherwise, the reception area was uncharacteristically empty of anyone else except a jaded woman selling flowers in the corner. She eyed Rachel hopefully, but Rachel passed her and went to the medics' pigeonholes on the opposite side.

A folded note fluttered out when she withdraw her hand from the box.

Startled, she opened it.

On the inside, in a spidery black handwriting, was a piece of headed notepaper dated December 20th.

> *My dear Rachel*
>
> *We're well aware that Michael is spending Christmas with your family on the other side of the Atlantic, and we've been wondering what you'll be doing. Please give us a ring on the above number if you'd like to join us for any of the Christmas celebrations. You'd be more than welcome—don't hesitate.*
>
> *All best wishes*
> *Jack Monaghan*

She read the note twice and felt the heat come into her face. then her eyes went back to the date at the top of the sheet, and she sighed. *But I checked the box yesterday . . .*

She turned the note over and saw that a different hand had written a PS in blue ballpoint on the back.

> *Sorry, Ms McEnroe. I was supposed to drop this note in when I was in town on 20th. I was back up here tonight (Christmas Eve) when I found it in my coat pocket. Best wishes anyway. Signed, Ian Monaghan Esq.*

The handwriting was bold and clear, the work of someone who was sure of himself; but the joky, careless tone of this note puzzled Rachel. She knew there was a brother, but Michael had mentioned him only in passing.

She re-read both notes again, then folded the paper. It felt warm in her hand.

Yes, she would ring Mr Monaghan after all. The family would perhaps welcome her for New Year's Eve.

15

Her weekend case banged against her legs as she negotiated the corridors and eventually passed out of the side gate of the hospital. Ahead of her the now familiar logo of the Underground gleamed red in the murk of a late December afternoon. In just over an hour, she would be in Kent, and she was glad.

The city seemed deserted. Since Christmas she had been surprised how, except in the hospital, many people seemed to have gone away for the entire week between Christmas and the New Year. The bustle and crush of Christmas shopping before the holiday had at least reminded her of downtown Boston or Buffalo. But now this end of London was eerie and unwelcoming. And still too *cold*.

She shivered and stopped to blow her nose. A chain of lights along the river winked into life; darkness was already creeping along the river.

At the head of the Northern Line steps she hesitated again to get her bearings. She felt the kind of mounting excitement that used to twist at her insides when the Cincinnati Greyhound pulled into the Buffalo bus station and she knew she would soon be home. She knew the difference, however. This excitement grew out of half-formed daydreams, not the solid reality of family, farmhouse, and well-loved fields.

She was just fumbling in her pockets with gloved hands for her ticket when her tutor came rushing up the steps. His greying hair and trenchcoat hung dishevelled on his shoulders, and the slate-blue shadows under his eyes told a tale of several nights' sleeplessness.

'Miss McEnroe! Sorry.' He had brushed into her and almost sent her case flying. He was out of breath but cheerful.

'Oh. Happy New Year's, Dr Tate.' She knew she sounded abstracted. In her mind she had already travelled the miles to the Monaghans' house.

'You look as if you're off to a party or something.'

'Just to friends.' *Friends.* And were they?

'How nice. Er—that ... project you handed in ...'

She did not want to think now about alternative medicine, or in fact about anyone or anything to do with St Stephen's Hospital. The only thing she could do was duck the question his rising tone and curious face implied. 'I hope you received it all right. You're on call, are you?'

'Yes—to both. Read your paper as well. Rather intrigued me. It struck me—'

She was anxious about what he might say. 'Forgive me.' She moved down the top steps. 'There's a train I need to catch out of Charing Cross. They stop early tonight, because of the vacation.'

'Of course. I only wanted to say I wasn't quite expecting a paper like that, Miss McEnroe. Found it *quite* readable.'

She would be rude if she slipped away after a comment of that sort without so much as an acknowledgement, but she also recognized thinly veiled criticism in his expression. 'Thank you, Dr Tate.' Her hand was going numb where she clutched the weekend case. She could feel time ticking past.

'It was just that your paper set me wondering if—er—you're on the right career path.'

Her heart lurched. He was tapping into some of her deepest worries. Reluctantly she turned towards him and set down her case. She resented being drawn into such a huge discussion now. 'How d'you mean?'

'You're pretty negative about the British medical establishment, aren't you? I noticed all your secondary citations were to *The New England Journal of Medicine*. All very well in its way.'

'But—? You weren't happy with the project?' Her voice sounded as cold as she felt. She couldn't stand meekly and let his challenge fly over her head, no matter how much of a scramble she might have to reach Charing Cross.

'On the contrary. I said I found it intriguing. I just wonder if you're in the right place and the right course. Have you considered at all ... ?' His hands finished the sentence with wild flourish.

Sure I have, she wanted to snap, irritated with his hints and with his dogged insistence in speaking to her *now*, of all places, about something so important. *Can't you let me be?* She felt the frost of the pavement under her boots penetrate to her toes, and she bit back the words. At the same time, one of the greasy overhead tiles began to drip onto her hair.

'Yes,' she said quietly, looking him straight in the eye. 'Yes, I've certainly wondered about that, myself. But I got a scholarship, and here I am. I can't just disappear the minute I disagree with things.' The tile dripped again, but she made herself smile and suddenly remembered one of her mother's sayings. 'Besides, when the going gets tough, the tough go shopping.' She swung her case up again. 'Well, partying, at least. Please, I really have to—'

He shrugged. 'Sensible attitude. Well, we'll talk about this in our first meeting next term.'

And with that threat ringing in her ears she fled down the steps to the escalators.

Small scraps of paper littered the Northern Line train, the windows grimed with winter. What few passengers were travelling dozed or buried themselves in tabloid news. Down one end of the carriage she heard American voices. She turned automatically, pushing Tate out of her mind, and watched her fellow countrymen with a sense of detachment. They were as unknown to her as all the Londoners on the train. If she could survive a solitary Christmas, then she could certainly fend off the doubts about her medical career and the homesickness of New Year's Eve, especially with the Monaghans' hospitality awaiting her.

The Network South-East train was even emptier than the underground train. Laughing at herself, she collapsed inside, breathless from hurtling across the platform. Immediately, the train jolted forward. Her heart lifted again. Through her own reflection in the splattered window she saw the lights of Charing Cross and

Waterloo East, then London Bridge and Peckham, melt into each other as the train gathered speed. She shut her eyes. When she returned to London in three days, she could look at the scenery then. For now, she would rest.

Later she counted the darkened stations—some of them too vandalized to be identifiable—and kept consulting her timetable. Wealdhurst actually came sooner than she expected, and she was still pulling on her coat as she trudged towards the barrier.

Michael's father had promised to meet the train, but no one awaited her at the barrier. She stood breathing warm breath into the raw dampness, and watched the road. The village shops adjoining the tiny station were shuttered for the night. A cyclist pedalled unsteadily past her, his red rear light wavering behind him as he faded into the fog—going home. A couple of cars swept by, one of them blaring like a ghetto-blaster. The sense of not belonging closed in on her again, as tangible as the fog.

Eventually a car bearing the label 'Wealdhurst Taxis' lumbered into view with its 'for hire' sign showing bright yellow in the gloom. Hopeful again, she flagged it down.

The driver rolled down his window. 'Sorry, love. I'm on me way 'ome. My mate should be along in a few ticks.'

She indicated the sign. 'But I thought—'

'Oh, aw' right then. 'Op in. But it's double on New Year's Eve, I'm afraid.'

She knew she had no choice, but she also knew she'd been conned; perhaps he had recognized her American accent and thought he was in for a generous fare. Sure enough, when he left her outside an overgrown gateway about five minutes and four pounds later, she knew she should after all have walked the distance.

She ducked under the bushes and bare branches that overhung the path and rang the lighted doorbell. An easterly breeze tugged at her scarf, and she shivered again. The excitement had vanished, leaving her with vague unease. She wondered whether she had made a mistake. No mistaking the address, *Fifty-five Ridge Road* ... but a mistake in coming at all to a place and people where she could not belong. The front of the house was shuttered against the wind. Night hadn't yet fallen, but curtains had already been pulled across the windows. A thin crack of yellow light filtered between one pair; the rest of the house lay dark.

Perhaps no one's in.

But the lock rasped, and the door opened. A tall, slender woman in her mid-forties stood framed in the doorway. Her hair—fair, but faded with grey streaks—was pulled into a loose knot, and her eyes behind thick glasses shone very blue in the light.

'Rachel McEnroe?'

She had expected an Irish voice, but Kate Monaghan sounded English. Her accent was cultured, assured. Someone used to being in command of her situation.

'Yes.' Rachel realized she was tired from the journey. Her eyes immediately left the woman's beautiful face for the well-lit hall behind her. She might have almost forgotten what he looked like, but she was childishly hungry for any sight or sign of Michael.

Kate held the door wider. 'Please come in. I'm alone at the moment, but the others should be back soon. My husband rang to say he was held up, so I thought I'd better wait here for you.'

The house enclosed her immediately, but it wasn't quite the sort of welcome she had envisioned. A cool formality pervaded the Monaghans' front hall that she couldn't associate with Michael's warmth. Oil paintings in plain, dark frames hung from a nineteen-thirties picture rail. Three doors stood firmly closed, and the worn carpet showed no sign of household pets, muddy boots, or any of the usual detritus of family living Rachel was used to.

She wanted to escape almost before she had set foot across the threshold, but there was no turning back now. She smiled wanly at Kate. 'Thank you. I'll be honest, I'm pretty worn out.'

Kate's face was immediately full of concern. 'Yes—and I can hear you've got a rotten cold.' She smiled, and Rachel saw that there was kindness, after all, though well hidden under the veneer of caution and stiff courtesy. 'I'll put the kettle on right away. Just leave your things here—' She motioned to an old-fashioned coat stand and mahogany bench near the door. '—and come through into the dining room when you're ready. Loo at the top of the stairs.' Then she melted away into what might be the kitchen—Rachel couldn't quite see—and left Rachel, rather bewildered, in the hall.

She stood still in the quiet. A radio was turned on low in the room Kate had entered, and the house was full of the smell of fruit cake or mincemeat. Somewhere behind one of the doors a clock ticked with a steady, dignified tick; she imagined a mantel clock sitting with fat self-importance over the fireplace, measuring out the ordered life of the house. Slowly she climbed to the first floor up stairs that bent half way and turned steeply onto a narrow landing. The upstairs doors were also closed, the carpets here thick-piled and new, deadening the sound of her feet across the floor. *So this is where Michael grew up.* But she saw nothing she could connect with him.

She was in the bathroom when she heard a crash. A young man shouted, 'Mum! We're home, Mum.' Below the bathroom, the front door burst open and was then slammed.

Smiling slightly, because at least the slamming door was like home, she listened.

'Hello, Ian. Oh, I see—' That was Kate.

'Mum, I brought Stacey round for part of the evening.'

Kate sounded subdued and taken aback. 'All right, darling.' No words of welcome for the unhappy Stacey, whoever she was.

'Hasn't that American woman arrived yet? Ah, I see some foreign gear left here. She has?'

'For goodness sake! Rachel's upstairs. She's tired. Come on, I'm making tea for us now.'

'I fancy something to drink, Ian.' A new voice—Stacey's. She talked with a slight whine in her voice. 'No tea for me, Mrs Monaghan.'

Rachel smiled to herself. Her own arrival was obviously not a source of unmitigated interest for everyone, even if Ian was as full of curiosity about her as she was about him.

Her heart began to beat faster. She wanted him to look like Michael, but she was afraid, too.

She smoothed down her hair, adjusted the chain of wooden beads she'd worn as a concession to fashion—something she'd had to forget during the first term of studies—and returned downstairs.

From the front room came the sound of Ian and Stacey talking with television canned laughter in the background. Rachel's mouth felt dry and her throat sore; she thought she would answer with a croak if they came out and spoke to her.

She tried another door and found the dining room. Bare wooden floor, polished like glass, and in one corner an ebony piano gleaming darkly in the indirect light from the now open door. The clock she had heard ticking before, only smaller than she had imagined. The room was chilled, and she shut the door again, with no desire to sit there alone.

The third door opened into the light and heat of the kitchen. A new fruit cake stood steaming on a wide table, and Kate Monaghan was at the sink with her hands in deep suds, washing pots and pans.

'Ah—you've found me. Do go and join Ian and his—er—friend in the lounge, won't you? I'll bring you all tea in a minute.' The words were polite enough, but Rachel saw that the woman would rather be left alone. Perhaps Kate sensed her discomfort, for she peered at her more closely and added, 'Or would you prefer to unpack first?' She dried her hands roughly on a towel. 'Yes, I can see you would. Come along, then.'

A puzzling mixture of relief and disappointment washed through Rachel. Michael's brother was only five yards away behind that closed door.

Then Kate surprised her. She crossed the hall in front of Rachel and went immediately into the front room.

'Ian, leave that rubbish off for a minute, can't you?'

Rachel hovered in her shadow, out of sight.

'I'd like you to show Rachel where she'll be staying.'

'Delighted!'

The door was thrown right back. Rachel saw Stacey first, curled on the floor with her spiky bleached and moussed hair a vivid contrast to the plump, dark furnishings of the room; her face was as shut and forbidding as the doors of the hallway. Then Rachel saw Ian, who jumped up from the sofa where he had been sitting beside the girl.

His likeness to Michael arrested her, but the way Ian smiled was quite different. His white teeth gleamed in the confident, broad grin of someone used to having his own way. 'Rachel? Well, hello!'

She laughed and tried to catch Stacey's eye. 'Hi there.'

His fair hair—almost the same colour as Michael's but more yellow—was just as untidy as Michael's. He wore the holey jeans and ragged sweater and grubby scarf that made up the uniform of all university enfants terribles. But the nonchalance was studied, not natural to him.

Kate was moving aside to let him through. 'She'll be in Michael's room.'

Ian registered amazement. 'Why not the spare room, Mum?'

'I haven't had time to clear it since last term.' Kate spoke fast and uncomfortably—a woman who generally had everything in perfect order.

'Lucky lady,' Ian told her, rolling his eyes. 'You get to sleep in my brother's bed. I can think of a few girls who'd love to do that. He probably wouldn't even notice if they did!'

Kate's mouth didn't even flicker into a smile. 'Ian, be pleasant, will you?' Her voice was resigned but slightly on edge.

'Don't forget I want a drink of some kind, Ian,' Stacey called petulantly from behind them.

Rachel had already forgotten the girl. Stacey's sulky eyes looked dismally at her. 'I'm sure I can find my own way,' she put in quickly, wanting to escape the tension.

Ian caught hold of her luggage. 'No chance. I'd never miss the opportunity of escorting a young lady up the stairs . . . Sorry Mum. I'll behave myself. Be right back, Stace.'

She followed him up the stairs. His shoulders were as wide as Michael's, his body as lean, taut and full of energy. The blood rang in her ears. She felt silly and over-excited about seeing Michael's room.

Ian pushed at the door of one of the front bedrooms and threw her case onto the single bed. 'Ta-ta-ra! Here you are. Big brother's room.'

She looked round eagerly. No rock stars as on her own brothers' walls, but white-framed watercolours of wide landscapes, hedged fields and apple blossom under cloudy skies, unfamiliar conical buildings standing sentinel by ramshackle barns. Home, but not home.

Ian followed her eyes. 'They're all of Kent.'

'It looks pretty. I couldn't see it from the train.'

'Didn't miss much. You're lucky, being in London.'

'Am I?'

'I'd say so. I'm up at Cambridge.' She didn't miss the arrogant note. 'Dead at night—you wouldn't think so, would you, with a bloody great university there? No nightlife like you've got.'

She smiled vaguely, thinking of madrigal practices and late evenings in the lab, or the roars of drunken students waking her as they made their way back to bed in the middle of the night. 'No,' she said quietly, 'I'm sure it's quite different.'

He was looking at her curiously and with the first suggestion of compassion that she'd seen on his mercurial face. 'Must be strange for you, being here.'

She thought of Stacey waiting for him downstairs and almost said, *Yes, your girlfriend seems to think so, too.*

'I mean, there's mad Mike living like a yokel on your father's— sorry, no offence, I assure you. He was always like that.'

She couldn't resist. 'Like what?'

He looked at her sharply. 'Crazy about farming. But I suppose your father's got a ruddy great machine of a farm with acres of rolling agribusiness wheat under a boundless blue sky. Am I right?'

She disliked his patronizing, sarcastic tone. 'No. It's not a huge place.' Her eyes watered, suddenly, and she looked away from him, feeling naked.

His lip curled. 'Well that'll just suit our Mike.' Then it seemed to strike him that he had given offence after all; his tone softened. 'No, I mean, here you are in our house, and there he is in yours. Given the laws of probability, it's quite a long shot over that kind of distance.'

'I guess so.' She couldn't keep the dull disappointment out of her voice. However much he looked like Michael, Ian was not the same. She began to understand how Michael might have become the self-sufficient, reflective man she remembered. Once again she wished she had not accepted the Monaghans' invitation.

'How's our man in New York doing, anyway?'

'Michael?' His name was warm in her mouth. 'I hear good things about him. He's been useful to my father.'

'Happy as a pig in the proverbial, I should think. Well, I'll leave you to it. I advise you not to let Mum's tea get cold, though.' He gave her a winning smile. 'And I'd better look after Stacey.' He stopped with one hand on the doorpost. 'She'll be jealous, Rachel. You're so attractive.'

Little comfort, Rachel thought irritably when his footsteps receded on the threadbare carpet of the stairs. She stole a glance at herself in a small shaving mirror on the windowsill. She looked washed out, anything but attractive.

Alone in his bedroom at last, she gently turned over each item in the room. Ornaments going back to childhood but free of dust, nevertheless: a homemade farm barn and rows of shiny china cows in miniscule stalls; a horse in a green cardboard field; and matchbox-sized tractors and waggons lined up beside them. The little farm was like a shrine left to his childhood. Obviously, like her father, he had never wanted anything else.

The books that lined two shelves above the bed were not unlike her own: botany, ornithology, chemistry. But French grammar books and large shiny reference books on rugby football also ranked among them. At random she took one off the shelf and opened it. A blade of dried wheat fell out, the kernels and husks pressed but still intricately textured and alive between her fingers. He had used it as a bookmark.

Now she picked up one of several silver trophies that were clustered on top of a chest of drawers. *Wealdhurst RFC, 1989-90. Michael Monaghan, captain.* And in larger letters below, *County Finalists.* She examined another with a similar inscription and wondered fancifully whether the Wealdhurst team would have stood a chance against the St Stephen's pack. She wished vaguely she had paid more attention to the rugby talk at the hospital.

The small silver bust of a swimmer caught her eye next. It was engraved with the words *Wealdhurst and Forest Hill Comp., 1990*: M. Monaghan. She thought again of Michael's wide shoulders and athletic build. He would slice cleanly through the water. She sighed and replaced the bust.

She would look at everything else later.

When she returned to the lounge, Stacey glared at her over the rim of a glass filled with what looked like grape juice but smelled stronger. 'Hello.' Her voice was as hospitable as the frost outside the house. 'I'm Stacey, Ian's girlfriend.' She leant on the last word.

Rachel sat down as far away from them as she could, on the other side of the gas fire. She wondered if Kate would applaud the stiffness she heard in her own voice. 'Pleased to meet you.'

Kate came in with a silver tray, teapot, and three delicate bone china cups. She frowned at Stacey's glass but said nothing.

'You can be mother, Rachel,' Ian said when the door had shut again.

If Joel or Billy had spoken to her in such an insulting, syrupy voice, she would have lost patience immediately. But it was Michael's brother, and she wasn't on home turf now.

Stacey bent her head back, indolently set her glass on a low table, and stretched like a cat. 'Ian tells me you're here for three days.' She dropped her voice. 'By the way, we're off to a party tonight.' She looked Rachel's loose clothes up and down. 'I expect you'd like to come.'

The nasal whinge in which she spoke begged for a 'no', but Rachel needed little persuasion to refuse. She would be far more content, she thought, seeing in the New Year with Ian's parents—if Jack ever got home—than with Ian and Stacey.

She poured the tea in a steaming curve and thought of her mother's stained brown coffeepot at home, and of the smell of coffee that always hung in the kitchen. 'A party? I don't think so. But thanks.'

'Hasn't she got a gorgeous husky American voice?' Ian winked and would not look at Stacey as he took the cup Rachel passed him.

Stacey inspected her nails. 'Don't wind me up,' she muttered.

The front door banged again. 'Anyone home?'

Ian and Stacey didn't move. 'That'll be Dad.'

'Who else?' Stacey mocked.

Ian pretended injury. 'I was only telling Rachel.'

Rachel rose. It was unbearable to sit in the same room with them. She went out into the hall in time to see Kate in her husband's arms, her head resting easily on his shoulder, and his cheek bent to hers.

They jumped apart like two adolescents caught cuddling at the back of a schoolbus. 'Oh—Rachel.' Kate's face went pink.

'So you're Miss McEnroe. Well done getting here tonight.' Jack Monaghan kept one hand on his wife's shoulder and held out another as big and capable as her father's. His hair was thick and straight, his wide smile genuine.

She relaxed immediately. 'Thank you.'

'Good journey?'

'Not bad.'

'Sorry I let you down. I had to do some overtime.' He glanced at Kate. 'Couldn't get out of it. Still, at least we've a wee time off now, thank God.'

Rachel warmed to him. 'I feel the same. I was tired when the term ended, and I think I'm still getting over it.'

'Is there more tea mashed?' Jack was pushing open the lounge door. 'Hello there, Stacey, Ian. Thanks, sweetheart, I'd love a cup along with the others here.' He let his long body slowly into one of the softer chairs. 'Come back in here and keep yourself warm now, Rachel. Been talking to Ian and his friend?'

She did not feel she could be ironic with Jack. Clearly, he and Michael were more similar than Ian and Michael. 'A little,' she said.

'So you're after being a great doctor?'

'Lay off the Ulster claptrap, Dad,' Ian moaned, raising his eyes to the ceiling.

'Better than Cambridge la-di-da,' Jack laughed good-naturedly. 'I'll talk how I please in my own front room, thank you.' His eyes returned to hers.

'I'm working on my MB right now,' she acknowledged.

263

'Bachelor of 'Mericans,' Ian said.

Jack ignored him. 'Where are you heading with that?'

'Some days I'm not sure.'

He grinned. 'Are you after staying in this country to finish your training?'

In October she would have answered unerringly, 'Love to', but now she was not as sure. 'I'm giving St Stephen's a chance,' she replied guardedly. 'I guess I won't make up my mind until I finish the MB.'

Jack questioned her in much the same way her uncle, David Fuller, had done in the autumn—about her field of interest, and how she felt about the hospital itself. As they talked, Ian watched her all the time. She was already growing used to his insolent scrutiny; she would ignore him.

Stacey got up suddenly and with enough noise to divert them all. She reached for a telephone nearby.

Jack cocked an eyebrow at her. 'Are you wanting the phone, Stacey?'

'Er—yes, if that's OK.'

His face was deadpan. 'Go ahead.'

'Or in another room?'

Jack smiled faintly. 'In our bedroom? I don't think so. This one works just as well.'

Stacey pouted. 'I'm just going to ring our friends about tonight.' She threw a quick look at Rachel. 'See if there'll be anyone nice for your visitor.'

Rachel moved to the edge of her seat. 'No—please.'

'Won't take me a minute.'

Rachel caught Jack's eyes but was at a loss for what to say. Obviously Stacey wanted to pair her up and get her out of harm's way.

Jack watched the interchange and frowned. 'Ian, is this necessary?'

'I'd much rather stay in tonight, anyway.'

'She's probably been on nights and everything,' Ian said lamely, arresting Stacey's hand on the receiver.

Rachel realized Ian knew nothing about first-year medical training, but she was not going to deny the escape hatch he'd provided.

'Never mind.' Stacey smiled brightly and put the phone down again. She gave Rachel a false smile. 'We'll see what we can organize for you for tomorrow. Lots of hangover parties, I bet.'

Jack was still watching her.

'I'm not sure—'

The door opened suddenly and saved her from saying more; Kate summoned them to supper.

At the table there was an uneasy silence as Jack blessed the food, crossed himself, and kissed Kate. Ian and Stacey exchanged glances. Rachel tried to focus only on Jack and Kate, but it was difficult. Ian picked at the food and found fault with everything, then finally said he wasn't hungry now and he and Stacey would eat at the party.

Kate's face fell, but Jack waved them off with a stern face. 'Away you go, then.'

Ian left the table with obvious relief. He bent to his mother and kissed her warmly. Rachel looked on. There was nothing articifical in that embrace. 'All right then, Mum, Dad. I'll wish you all a happy New Year.' Without so much as a glance at Rachel he took Stacey's hand and led her out.

Kate turned to Jack and murmured, 'I don't know how much longer I can go on being polite to that girl. She and Ian are nothing but bad chemistry together. It—'

'No, love.' Jack held up his hand. 'Rachel doesn't want to hear our troubles.' He turned to her with a rueful grin. 'If you've younger brothers, maybe you'll be knowing what a trial it is they're sometimes to their sainted mothers.'

She pictured Joel and Billy and felt the tension in the room begin to ebb away. 'I know it.'

'You don't have to go to any party tomorrow if you'd rather not. We invited you here for Michael's sake.' Kate was unfolding at last. 'I'd like to hear about your parents, about the family . . .' She leaned forward with her arms on the table, and Rachel saw again how beautiful she was.

It was like a balm to talk about home. She began where she'd always felt her life had begun—with her grandparents. The coolness she had first felt seemed to thaw, and Kate and Jack listened with full attention. They laughed when she talked about Joel and Billy, and nodded in recognition as she described the farm.

'Hasn't Michael written to you about things?'

They exchanged glances, and Jack shook his head. 'Neither of our two is much at the letter writing.'

She repeated some of the news in the letter from her mother that she had carried in her pocket since before Christmas. '… And he's happy with them—I know that.'

'Your father was very good to take him on,' Kate said, stiff again.

She looked back at him. 'Oh no. You don't understand. Dad would never take on anyone who wasn't right for the farm. It's nothing to do with kindness.'

Jack gave her a doubtful look. 'But Michael was sight unseen.'

Rachel met his gaze steadily. 'It may not be a big farm, as I was telling Ian, but he runs it businesslike. No messing. Michael wouldn't have lasted more than a week if he wasn't competent.'

'But when his worker comes back, Michael's on his own again?'

A prospect too bleak to contemplate. When she thought of the farm now, it was with Michael alongside her father. Though she couldn't see how it would be possible, she could not conceive of returning in the summer without seeing him there. Her eyes left Jack's face. She was remembering with a dull ache her mother's account of the calf that had died; how distressed Michael had been, and how he had stood up to Grey. Surely that would have drawn them closer together?

'I don't know. Larry Harper's got a ways to go yet, Mom says.'

Their questions left her wide awake long after midnight. They had sat talking until the bells of the Wealdhurst church and shouts of neighbours doing the conga in the street outside signified the New Year. They had toasted the New Year with a light wine that tasted sharp as if it had lain uncorked in a cupboard since the year before. The evening seemed a mockery—a long way from Boston and the party that would be going on in a few hours over there. Even further from other New Years' celebrations at home with the wood roaring in the log-burning stove and her parents laughing and weeping their way through 'Auld Lang Syne'.

She turned over and over in the bed that curved to Michael's shape and fought off the demons of loneliness.

Daylight restored some of her serenity. The house lay still when she woke. She wrapped herself in a thick dressing gown she had found in Michael's wardrobe and padded downstairs to make herself some tea. When she opened the kitchen curtains, the tentative light of January brought a little comfort. Anything was possible, she decided, after all. Raindrops frozen in glass droplets on the bare trees outside would thaw soon into buds and leaves.

Ian came into the kitchen first, already dressed, cheerful, and oblivious of the turmoil of emotions she had endured in the last twelve hours. Without Stacey, he was more friendly. 'Just look at that frost out there,' he murmured. His smile was sunny and engaging.

'Pretty,' she agreed. 'Quite mild for New Year's.'

At home, she would have gone for a walk across the yard and over to the pond. Billy might have put on skates and gone whirling and showing off across the ice. Or in Boston, she might have driven with her grandfather for a late breakfast at the country club. There would be hot muffins, steaming coffee, and talk of what would happen when the golfclub's greens and fairways were fit for play again. Talk that would have included her, even though she'd never swung a golf club in her life. Though the temperatures outside would have been much colder than in Kent, she would have basked in the warmth of belonging.

'Mild? It's bloody frigid if you ask me.' Ian shivered theatrically, stared at her, shrugged, and went out. 'Oh, by the way—' He returned to the doorway a moment later. '—we met some people at the bash last night who invited us for a lunch party today. You're invited, too.'

She groaned.

'What's the matter? Don't like parties?'

'It's not that, Ian.' She made herself use his name for the first time, though it sounded intimate and unnatural.

She understood fully now why Michael had scarcely spoken of Ian during the days they had been together in Arcade. He did not like his own brother, and his own brother was very little interested in him. He would, she guessed, feel more at home with her family than she felt with his.

If only he would still be there when she went home in the summer.

16

Jazz bounced and boomed across the low-ceilinged lounge. It was full of dancers. Michael watched Marie Williams on the other side of the room. He recalled now what he had forgotten since September: her sometimes offhand way. It was as if she couldn't focus on anything. As if she was still a long way from seeing things whole. Certainly a long way from recognizing him in the sort of way he had hoped she would. So what if there was only a year between them; he felt as if he had travelled much farther than she had in the three months since he had seen her last.

Under a net of brilliant balloons that would be dropped at midnight, she was laughing and talking with other women from her college. She had rushed the introductions, as if they had seen each other only the day before, not three months ago. Her voice had been light and friendly, but she hadn't wanted to look him in the eye. Breathily she had said, 'Girls, this is Michael Monaghan, from *England*. And Michael, here're Cindy and Laura-Lee and Sheri.'

Their names sounded, he thought, like so many dolls' names. Clever cosmetics painted their faces with doll-like brightness, as well. They giggled and nodded at each other, marionettes on invisible strings. They belonged with each other; he did not belong with them.

But he didn't after all want to be included, anyway. He couldn't associate this animated party girl and her friends with the vivid, spontaneous young woman he had fallen for at his cousin's wedding; nor could he associate her with the sober, frightened woman he had glimpsed on the night McEnroe had come to speak to her mother about the drug investigations. She was almost foreign to him now, no matter what he wanted, no matter what he had imagined.

Instead, he found himself gravitating to McEnroe—as they all seemed to call him. He saw the son in the father, attributed all Don's characteristics to him, then talked as freely with him as if he and Don were cleaning the barn together or driving to John Deere for a tractor part. As easily as if they had met each other many times, instead of those few minutes' conversation in the Williams' front hall—a conversation as brief as it had in the end proved important.

'You're happy at the farm, then, Michael?'

'I like it very much.'

'I'm glad we could get you the right papers so you could stay.'

'So am I!'

'It won't be for ever though, I guess.'

'No.' He did not want to think about leaving the farm. It would be infinitely worse than the disappointment he had felt in realizing Marie would pay him no more attention tonight than she paid to any other wannabes in the room. He shook his head. 'But when the time comes for Larry Harper to get back to work, I'm sure I'll know by then what I should be doing next.' He heard the confidence in his voice and wasn't sure it was his own.

McEnroe nodded. 'That's what I like to hear. Maybe not brass certainty, but positive conviction. God takes care of his people, you know.' From anyone else, the words would have sounded trite, but McEnroe was no pussycat. Michael saw him as an intrepid lion of a man with fiercely whiskered eyebrows and the shrewd eyes of someone who had seen and understood much.

'I believe that too.'

'It took me a while to learn it, I'll admit.' McEnroe blew a ring of cigar smoke away from Michael.

There was more to come, Michael knew. He waited.

'It wasn't easy to go on believing in God's care when my daughter was slowly killing herself.' His blue eyes probed Michael's face. 'Did anyone tell you about all that?'

He wanted to retort that he was most unlikely to have forgotten what he had overheard in the Williams' house. 'I do know some of what happened,' he answered levelly.

The old man's face was changing; he looked greyer, letting out a long sigh. 'Tell me.'

Michael wanted to restore to him the cheerful, expansive expression he had worn only minutes before. 'I heard you were doing some follow-up investigations on the drug-runner who caused you so much grief all those years ago.' Surely that was a tactful enough lead-in.

McEnroe's eyebrows bristled. 'Then you heard more or less right. Drug dealer, he was. *Is.*' His eyes roamed the room, stopping briefly at Marianne, Rita and Maggie, who had gone to the bar together to buy a tray of drinks for their party. Without looking back at Michael he added, 'Can't talk much here, of course. Can't talk much at all, in fact.'

'No.'

McEnroe stretched and blew another cloud of smoke towards the dancers. Abruptly, he changed the subject. 'How come you flew out here and Don's back at the farm, anyway?'

Michael had been curious about the investigations, but he found he was relieved at the change of tack. He smiled, remembering the discussions. 'Your daughter-in-law tells me he does this every year.'

McEnroe guffawed. 'Pretty much. "Cows", he just says. As if they explained everything. But it's not as if he hasn't got Tony and those two strapping grandsons of mine. So I guess he must have figured he could send you—let someone else have a break, even if he didn't want one.' He winked. 'And maybe he guessed there was a certain little gal you wanted to check up on while you were here.'

Michael grinned. 'Maggie just wanted company—that was it. The boys didn't want to come. And I feel very lucky to get a holiday. I wasn't expecting one at all.'

'You'd be ill if you didn't take one.'

'Maggie says you never take a holiday, Mr McEnroe.'

'McEnroe'll do fine, son. Me? Gee, what do I need a vacation for? Life's too interesting to tune out on some dumb Caribbean beach and soak up the rays, thanks a bunch. Far too much here I'd rather be doing.'

'Don never seems to take a holiday, either.'

'Not often, it's true. But the farm's his home. It's different. He never did much like this neck of the woods. Maybe he's more like me than I realized. His work and his family are his life.'

Michael examined the classic blue, white and gold decorations of the country club lounge, the understated elegance and wealth of the place, and he thought of Don sitting over a mug of coffee in the untidy farm kitchen. He nodded. 'I can't picture him here at all.'

McEnroe was quicker on the draw than he expected. 'What about you, son? You feel at home here?'

It came to him irrelevantly that although he would never feel at home in a country club, his mother would have been at her ease in this relaxed and sumptuous atmosphere. He smiled wryly, and the answer came before he had time to think more about it. 'Not *here*, perhaps. But with your family, yes. Very much so.'

McEnroe was assessing him. 'Like you did with Marie's family, I'll bet.'

Michael was taken aback by the way McEnroe kept changing his line of questioning, returning to the theme of Marie. The technique reminded him of his brother playing a Chopin etude, returning again and again to the melodic refrain. He could picture McEnroe better, now, in a court room or in the state senate. He would be a formidable adversary. The approach was oblique, but there was no mistaking the keen lawyer behind the friendly eyes.

He saw no point in dodging the questions—neither spoken nor unspoken. 'I would have loved to see more of Marie while I was here. I like her very much.'

McEnroe's eyes creased at the corners. 'Same age as you, I guess?'

'More or less.' He rallied. 'Oh—Maggie did warn me you were a bit of a matchmaker.'

McEnroe threw back his head and laughed. 'Did she indeed? Well, don't you say another word about her unless you want to.'

He looked back to where Marie had been standing with her friends. They had moved to join a group of shouting men who had downed too much lager and were showing off as much as the girls. They flung each other round the floor in a wild parody of fifties jive, and the jazz musicians responded by turning up the speakers and playing with even greater exuberance.

'Look at those crazy fools, willya?' McEnroe laughed indulgently. 'Marie's sure having a good time.'

'Marie isn't interested in me in the slightest,' he said simply.

'Too bad, but I think you're right about that.'

Michael felt it was time to turn the tables on him. 'But why aren't you dancing, sir? You've got your wife and Maggie and Mrs Williams for partners—so why not?'

Amused, McEnroe shifted in his chair. 'Much too old.'

'Nonsense.'

'Much too preoccupied, then. Anyhow, what about you? Any of those charming ladies would dance with a looker like you.'

He grinned at the old man. 'Thanks. I think I'll go and ask Marie, after all.'

He met Marie's mother on the way. Her lined face looked weary, and he wondered if she was still grieving over the husband she had lost a few years before; it was hard to be single in a room full of couples and laughing younger people on New Year's Eve.

'How are you doing, Michael?' She stopped, sizing him up. Her eyes were hooded, neither hostile nor openly friendly.

'Very well. Glad to be here.' He glanced around swiftly to see where Marie had gone; she was now in someone else's arms, swinging easily around the room; she certainly belonged here. Then he made himself look squarely at Rita Williams. 'But it feels a little different staying with the McEnroes this time—not with you.'

'Is that a hint, young man?' Rita's mouth thinned. 'Well, perhaps it's better that way.'

He thought how tough she was. Also he still remembered the sting of overhearing what she really thought of offering him hospitality when he'd first arrived; he did not know what to say.

She spared him the trouble. 'I'm sure you must be enjoying the McEnroes' company—here *and* at the farm—right?' He found he could not say to her how much he liked and admired them all. He turned his palms up in a half shrug. 'I feel very lucky. It's down to you and Marie that I met them.'

'Good friends for years... Now, you'll excuse me. I see the senator's on his own for a moment, and I want to bend his ear.' And with a light pat on his arm, she moved away into the crowd.

He stood at a loss for a few moments, then gathered himself and found one of Marie's friends for the rest of the dance. She leant against him provocatively whenever the music brought them together, but he held her lightly, keeping up a quick patter of empty conversation and biding his time for the next dance.

Marie caught his eye a few times as they turned on the floor. For a moment he thought she was looking at him in a fresh way, but it was only that his years of going to farmers' socials, rugby club dances and university hops had given him confidence dancing; it was something he never thought about, took for granted.

When the number ended he left his partner with all the haste that was decent and went straight to Marie.

'Hey, you're quite a mover.'

'In some ways, perhaps.' He winked, unable to resist the opportunity she had thrown him. 'Fancy a dance?'

'I'd love to.'

The quartet launched into a song Michael liked, and he whirled her away. 'Is this how you people spend New Year's Eve every year?'

'Not exactly. Maybe the McEnroes do—' She glanced over his shoulder to where her mother was talking with McEnroe. 'Mama's pretty shattered this time of year. We're home, usually. My brothers come over. Nothing special.'

'But I thought this would be a quiet time at the marina?'

'No. Boats to paint and scrape down. You got a little of the flavour yourself, back in the fall. Lots of bookwork to catch up on before spring and the end of the fiscal year. Spring promos to think about if she's going to get more custom next year.' She moved her shoulders.

'Stuff like that. And although things've gotten better lately with some new folk taking berthing space, Mama's gotten more and more tired ... since Daddy died.'

He murmured and dipped his face to hers in sympathy, but she pulled away. 'No Michael. I was talking about *Mama*. I accepted Dad's death months ago.' She stiffened in his arms. 'But I don't like what it does to Ma. That—and other things.' She looked back at her mother again. He decided he had been underestimating her. Either she was using her mother as a convenient excuse for holding him again at arms' length, or she was genuinely distressed on Rita's account, capable of more compassion than he had supposed. He said cheerfully, 'Then what's all this close conversation between her and McEnroe?'

Her eyebrows went up, and her voice was sharp. 'What are you saying?'

He stumbled. 'Well, is there ... I mean—'

'If you're inferring what I think ...' She broke away from him and stood two feet away, still now. The other dancers wove their way round them.

'I wasn't meaning to suggest anything.' He realized how tactless he had been. 'I'm sorry.'

She stood clenching and loosening her fists in agitation. 'There's stuff going on I'd rather not think of. Can't talk about it.' She searched his face, as if assessing how far she could trust him, or realizing that having gone this far she might implicate her mother more rather than less if she didn't explain further. 'McEnroe's trying to—there's been a problem. He's trying to help her, but also to find some things out.'

Her eyes filled, and he wanted to ease the pain a little by saying, *Look, it's all right. I know about some of that.* But he couldn't find the right words.

She went on, 'But damn it, I wish he'd leave her alone tonight, at least.' Her voice was passionate now. 'It's New Year's, for heaven's sake.' She waved her hand in the direction of her friends. 'I know the McEnroes invited us to this deal—' She threw her hands out impatiently. 'But that doesn't give the old man the right to grill Ma all the time. We should be *partying*!'

He put his hands on her arms to steady her. 'All right. I thought it was your mother who wanted to speak to *him*. But let's go and break up their little tête à tête. Simple. You ask McEnroe for a dance. He won't refuse you. I'll take your mother onto the floor. No sweat...as they say.'

Her quick smile broke like sunshine from behind clouds. 'Thanks, Michael.'

He had solved her problem, but now he'd be lucky to get another dance with her. And he knew, suddenly, precisely why McEnroe and Rita were in conversation. It was for the same reason that McEnroe had come to see her in September. It was for the same reason that he 'touched base', as Marie said, so regularly. It was because of the drug investigations they had just been speaking of.

He took Marie by the hand. Her palm against his own was damp and hot. She gave him a surprised, questioning glance, but did not pull away; even seemed glad that he had taken charge. McEnroe and Rita Williams sat with heads bent close together over the table. If he had not known why they were so engaged, he would have jumped to quite the wrong conclusion about them. McEnroe's shaggy hair had fallen forward over his face, so he could not read the old man's face or guess how he would react to being interrupted. But Marie's concern for Rita had infected him, and he would have done almost anything, then, to put some of the happiness back in her face. Even though he knew she wouldn't look back at him as the source of her relief.

He caught the words 'tentacles like an octopus—stretching everywhere and choking everything in their path'; then McEnroe saw them coming, gripped Rita's arm to stop the flow of their talk, and wiped his face expressionless. He reached for a glass and poured himself a bourbon from a newly opened bottle.

McEnroe spoke first. He seemed to melt when Marie dropped Michael's hand and held out her hands to him. 'Sweetheart, are you really serious about this?' His eyes were twinkling again.

'Senator? May I—?'

Rita glanced sharply from one to the other, and Michael stepped forward. 'What about you, Mrs Williams?' He hated the deferential tone he knew he was using. It came to him that he actually disliked Marie's mother.

She rose and offered him a dry, roughened hand. 'I smell conspiracy.'

'So did we,' Marie said pertly. 'You two gabbing your heads off. Forget the *business* tonight, can't you, Ma? It's party time!'

McEnroe grinned. 'She's right, Rita. Let's show the young folk how to boogie.'

Giggling now, Marie was rocked and rolled away at the old man's hands; Michael meanwhile found himself with his hand resting firmly on Rita's back and her grey hair grazing his chin. No rock and roll for them. Something more sedate would suit Rita, he thought. Her perfume—something musky and heavy that his mother would have hated—wafted into his nostrils. A heavy bracelet ringed with small charms tinkled in his ear.

They danced in silence for several minutes, then Rita opened her thin lips and fixed him with a hard stare. 'Did you come out here after Marie?' Her voice was harsh.

He hesitated. 'No.' It was the truth, he realized suddenly. He had been driven as much by curiosity about the McEnroe clan as by any desire to see Marie again.

'Don't believe you.' Under his hand, Rita moved her shoulders in a shrug of dismissal.

'The McEnroes offered me a short holiday here, as I said.'

'You're wasting your time if you still want Marie.'

'Thanks for the warning.' He felt that the cards were down on the table between them, now, and that it wouldn't matter what he said. 'I think I can work that out for myself.'

He wished he could account for the hostility that now glittered in her eyes. Her abruptness with him before, in September, wasn't far back in his memory, but this open animosity was something new.

'Why don't you just butt out of her life? We've had enough to deal with these last few years without someone coming all the way from

England like some white knight on a charger and wooing her this way. She's got college. She's with me, and that's what she wants. Best you stay out of it.'

She was worried about other things; it wasn't anything personal she had against him, he told himself. 'I understand,' he said steadily.

'You don't belong here, you know.'

Sudden rage rose in him like a red tide. He had never wanted to strike a woman, but he wanted to strike back now at the taunting face that was inches from his own. A picture formed in his mind of what his own face must look like: his teeth gritted, his eyes blazing, and he knew in a flash of insight that it was the same look of pure anger he had seen on his mother's face, sometimes, when he hadn't lived up to her expectations . . . and when Ian had.

He released her so fast that she staggered back into a passing couple and had to lunge for him to regain her balance. He held onto her like a vise.

Between clenched jaws, he said, 'You've no reason whatever to talk like that. Oh yes, you gave me a few days' token work when I came before, but you made it quite clear, Mrs Williams, that I don't belong here. So *you're* wasting *your* breath on that one. But Marie has free choice, and maybe she won't belong here much more, either. You can't keep her in a cotton-wool box. She'll go where she wants, with whom she wants.'

'Not with you.'

'Perhaps not with me, no.' He was cooling now. He felt unbalanced by his own anger. He wasn't sure how all this had started, or where it was leading. He wished he had left well alone and persuaded Marie to dance with him again, leaving the older people to their own devices. He was foolish to have let himself be dragged into Marie's anxiety.

Maggie, still chatting cheerily with Mrs McEnroe near the bar, caught his eye and smiled, then registered concern. She wouldn't have missed the look on their faces, he knew.

'So why waste your time?' Rita insisted.

It was no use, he thought, pretending to be other than he was. He pushed his hands into his pockets and faced her, still felt like fighting.

'I don't think I've wasted my time at all. I came because the McEnroes have been good to me—you were right about that.' Perhaps that would appease her a little. 'But when they said we were coming here tonight and that you and Marie would be here as well, I wasn't going to miss the chance of seeing her. Why should I?' He was carried along now by the force of his emotion. 'I fell in love with her at the wedding.' He wanted to add, *Maybe you've forgotten now what it's like to love and long for someone,* but he wasn't savage or angry enough for that. It would be a low thing to say, and the impulse to hurt her had gone as instantly as it had came. 'If you think I don't know Marie isn't interested in me, you're wrong. I was just saying so to Mr McEnroe, in fact. But there's nothing wrong in seeing her for a night, having a dance with her . . . then getting on with my life. The same way she'll get on with hers, I imagine.' He stepped back a pace.

Rita's eyes hardened. She sniffed. 'Well, if that's how you see things . . .'

He didn't want to hear any more. He would look for Maggie. 'Excuse me.' And he turned from her as the dance was ending, and walked away without looking back.

Perhaps Marie would hear of their argument. He cringed. Rita was right, after all. He was wasting his time with her.

Maggie moved towards him through the crowd, and out of the corner of his eye he saw that the senator's wife had found Rita and rejoined her husband. He would have Maggie to himself for a moment. It didn't matter what Rita Williams thought of him, after all.

It made him smile to realize how in only three months Maggie McEnroe had made herself into his confidante and mother hen. She warmed him, just by being near him.

'What's wrong?'

He gave her a rueful grimace. 'Just had a few words with Marie's mother, that's all.'

'Ah, well, them's the breaks.' She pulled a comical face. 'I thought you'd ask me to dance. I was watching you with those young girls before and thinking I've never seen such a smooth operator—for an aspiring farmer.' Her eyes were alight with mischief.

'Smooth!'

'Graceful, then.'

He began to laugh. 'That's even worse.'

'Marie looked as if she was falling over herself to dance with you.'

'So Mrs Williams noticed, as well. But she wasn't. Marie, I mean.'

'And that was the bone of your contention.'

'Something like that.'

'You shouldn't pay too much attention. She's always been a little waspish. She's OK really. Anyone who's been friends with my in-laws all those years can't be too bad, you know.'

'Then deliver me from OK people, that's all I can say.'

'Well, come on, aren't you going to ask me?' She hovered in front of him: small, her face upturned and eager, almost like a girl's. He caught a glimpse behind the plain features of what Don must have fallen in love with all those years before.

He held out his arms. 'Of course—let's boogie. That's what the senator said to Marie.'

She tsked against the fabric of his shirt. 'He would.'

'I think you've been stringing me along all this time. You're more of a matchmaker than your father-in-law.'

She pulled back a little and gave him a coy, innocent look. 'I doubt it. But Marie's got some growing up to do. Wait till she looks at you properly. Or hears you've met some other young lady at a parish dance. Then watch her run your way!'

'That's right. Comfort me with sweet talk. And you call *me* a smoothie!'

When the musicians broke for supper, Michael braced himself to go with Maggie and sit down again with the Williams and the McEnroes. It ought to be quite simple; after all the years of coping with Ian's animosity, he could surely somehow get through an evening at the same table as Rita Williams.

Noisemakers blared and bleeped around the room, a few balloons were popped prematurely, and party hats were unfolded and put on at rakish angles. There was no reason he had to speak with Rita at all—or Marie, for that matter—for the rest of the night. He would enjoy the McEnroe family, instead.

He found himself watching Marianne McEnroe now. They had been introduced briefly at the beginning of the evening. She leaned against McEnroe as they ate, turned to him often for confirmation of what she was saying, and repeated several stories without apparently being aware that she had done so. Her pale blue eyes found his more than once, with a little frown creasing her brow and her mouth opening in a slight moue of puzzlement, as if she couldn't quite remember why he was with them, or who he was.

He noticed her skin. While McEnroe's hung in folds and crevices round his face and bore the wind-grained lines of a man who had spent years playing golf, as well as years puzzling over problems in the senate, Marianne's was soft and still looked young. She wore a clever mask of naturally coloured foundation, and her hair was sculpted to perfection. While McEnroe was hugely larger than life, next to her husband she looked brittle: too fragile for life.

But something about her mouth—the curve of the lips, perhaps—made him think of Rachel.

He wondered where she was, and how she had spent New Year's Eve. He glanced at his watch. *Twenty to twelve.* In Britain it was nearly five o' clock in the morning on the first day of the New Year. Impossible to imagine that Rachel—his family, everyone—would be waking to January while he was still sitting here in the dying embers of December.

He shrugged the thoughts away. Place was something he understood. Time was another matter, too confusing to think about.

He came out of his reverie. Rita Williams was stirring and moving to the edge of her chair with her hands on the table.

'What is it, my dear?' Marianne McEnroe asked.

Rita's tired, hard face had relaxed. She turned to the others at the table, excluding him again, though not with deliberate rudeness this time.

'There's a couple I'd really love for you to meet—McEnroe, Marianne.' Her eyes slid briefly to Maggie's. 'You too, Margaret.'

'Well who's that, Rita?' McEnroe sounded cheery again, and Michael saw that he had poured himself another bourbon.

'Some new customers ... friends of mine. Think I might have told you about them back in the summer. But that was early days. Over there. Mr and Mrs Galloway.' She dropped her voice. 'Not long married—in spite of what you might think. Second marriage for her, I believe.' She stood and waved. 'See, they're coming over. Can we make room ...?'

McEnroe exchanged glances with Michael, and the two men stood to shuffle chairs and push another table against their own.

'I told you a new couple came to the marina. June it was. Gorgeous launch, they've got. And brought in some of their friends, too. Good business at the end of the summer.'

Marianne smiled vaguely. 'How nice for you, *dear* Rita.'

A well-groomed man and woman, both holding plates laden at the buffet, were making their way across the polished floor towards them. The man was in his late forties, the woman younger. Michael noticed immediately the expensive cut of their clothes and the gleam of bright stones on the woman's ringed hand.

'I told them Marie and I'd be here tonight as your guests, McEnroe. They were enchanted. Dying to meet you.'

McEnroe laughed affably. 'Don't gush, Rita. They might be disappointed.' He frowned. 'Is Galloway a member here? Don't think I've seen the guy before.'

Rita smiled back. 'Don't believe so. *I* wangled them a couple of tickets. Selfish of me, but they were so anxious to meet you. Seemed like a good chance.' She turned unexpectedly to Michael, all the animosity gone. 'And you might be interested to meet Mrs Galloway, Mike. She's English, as well.'

'Bit late arriving, aren't they?' Marianne observed querulously.

Galloway was quite clearly at home in the sumptuous surroundings of the country club, Michael thought. He was an unflappable, polished man with a shock of hair so dark that it looked as if the colour had come out of a bottle. Not tall—his fair-haired wife stood half a head taller—but nevertheless commanding attention.

He shook hands all round, perfect teeth flashing, and his eyes flickering over them all. 'Steve Galloway. Yes, glad to meet you. My wife Julia... Senator, we've heard so much about you from Mrs Williams.' Then he took Maggie's hand and made a small bow. 'And the younger Mrs McEnroe, too.'

Smoothie! he wanted to whisper to Maggie. *And you think I'm a smooth one. Well look out, Mrs M!*

McEnroe's face remained impassive, assessing them. He said drily, 'Glad you could make it.'

'D'you play golf, honey?' Marianne was gripping Julia by the arm and bending towards her with grandmotherly interest. 'So many English girls do, I know.'

Julia Galloway was as cool as her husband, Michael reflected. She held herself with the same sort of straight back as Kate—as if she had been to public school and expected people to look at and listen to her. 'No, Mrs McEnroe.' She spoke with a slight edge. 'I can't say I do.'

'But she sure can swing,' Galloway added for her, his bonhomie jarring.

'Er—do help yourself,' McEnroe was saying, as Galloway reached uninvited and poured himself a bourbon.

'Thanks—I have. You're talking to quite a dancer. Julia, I mean.'

Marie laughed nervously. 'You should dance with Michael, then, Mrs Galloway.'

'Please call me Julia.' The tone was silky and patronizing. She was English all right, but not the sort of Englishwoman Michael usually had any dealings with. She made him uncomfortable. Maggie, he saw then, was looking at him with quizzical interest and some amusement. Something mischievous made him want to stick his tongue out at her.

'He's British, too,' Marie added helpfully.

Julia flinched and turned sharply towards her husband.

'Really?' Galloway turned cold eyes on Michael and seemed to focus on him properly for the first time.

Michael stared back. The couple had obviously intimidated Marie, but he wasn't going to be intimidated. 'Yes, from Kent.'

Rita gave him a piercing look.

'Relative of Mrs Williams by marriage,' he added, nodding undeterred in her direction. 'But I'm staying with the McEnroes for a few days.'

Galloway eyed him over the rim of his glass and took a slow sip. 'How delightful for you. And what brought you from a beautiful place like Kent to this country—' He dipped his head slightly. '—if I may be so bold as to enquire?'

Marianne turned away from Julia and suddenly seemed to tune in. 'What perfect manners you have, Mr Galloway!' She beamed at him. 'Isn't that right, Julius? So unusual in young people.'

A twisted smile spread across Galloway's face, and Michael saw him catch his wife's eye again. 'I'm not sure if you're speaking of me, madam.' Galloway raked a hand through the thick hair. 'I hardly qualify as a young man nowadays.'

The atmosphere was overcharged. Even after his skirmish with Rita, Michael had been determined to make the best of the evening. But now the faces around the table were tense and watchful; only Rita was smiling, and he couldn't understand why. He crashed in with the first answer he could think of. 'I've always hoped to visit your country.'

Galloway raised his chin and curled his top lip as if he smelled an unpleasant smell at the end of his arrogant nose. Michael wanted to laugh at his pomposity; at the same time, there was something disturbing both about the way Galloway fixed his eyes so directly on everyone, and about the way he spoke. Michael searched for an understanding of what bothered him about the man. There was a slight burr in his voice—a variant on the American accent that he had not heard thus far. Idiosyncratically, Galloway rolled his 'r's' as dramatically as an operatic tenor.

He looked at him again. *Galloway*. That was Scottish, wasn't it? And he had learned enough already in up-state New York to know that the man's white skin and thick black hair could well mark him as a second generation American with Scottish parentage. But the accent wasn't quite right, not even for Scotland. Galloway's voice was musical, but with a gutteral edge.

'Michael's a friend of our granddaughter Rachel, in fact,' Marianne now informed him.

'Well—' Rita began.

Marianne had not heard her. 'Met Rachel at the McEnroe farm before she went off to London, didn't you, dear?'

Marie's face was bright with delicious enjoyment in the confusion. She winked at Michael, but he shook his head.

'It wasn't quite like that, Marianne,' Maggie corrected gently.

Disregarding her, Galloway leaned forward. He ran his finger around the rim of his glass. 'So—your granddaughter's in London.'

McEnroe flashed a look at Marianne that made no sense to Michael, except that he seemed to be warning her off. But Marianne's watery gaze fixed delightedly on the Galloways.

Julia was smiling, almost beckoning Marianne to continue. 'That's fun for her, Mrs McEnroe. London—such an exciting place for a young woman. I miss it, myself.'

'She's studying to be a physician. One of the big hospitals in the city—' Marianne's forehead puckered. 'Can't quite recall—'

'Guy's perhaps?' Julia supplied helpfully.

Marianne looked at McEnroe for confirmation, but he gave only a guarded half-nod. 'But it doesn't matter. She's a good girl. We all miss her.'

Maggie seemed as transfixed as Marianne by Galloway, but not with delight. She was mesmerized, as by a snake-charmer. She stared hard at him; he could almost see her mind processing the thoughts. *There's something about this man . . .*

Marie sighed and turned her wineglass round and round on its thin stem. Michael saw that she was bored and out of sorts, her eyes wandering repeatedly to her friends, who had returned to the bar. She was out of the limelight at this table—and didn't like to be.

McEnroe suddenly leaned forward, breaking the spell that seemed to have fallen over them all. He moved restlessly in his chair and rubbed the back of his neck uneasily. 'What about you, Mr Galloway? You a golfer?'

'In fact I am, Senator.'

'Where d'you play?'

'Oh—here and there.'

'Thinking of joining us at the Bedford club?'

Galloway looked back at McEnroe as if he suspected some kind of trap. 'Why, no. I'm not, actually. I've got friends round here, of course.' He smiled, but the smile didn't reach his eyes. 'As it happens, the waiting list for Bedford is rather a long one. I'm sure you're aware. But perhaps I will see you on the fairway one day. If I come as a guest, maybe.'

Michael expected McEnroe to offer his own hospitality, but the old man didn't take up the opportunity and instead turned to Marianne. 'Tired, gorgeous?'

Her answer was lost in the squeal of feedback from the band's sound system, followed by a shout from the club's chairman.

'Ladies and gentlemen. Please charge your glasses.' The band struck up 'Auld Lang Syne'.

'It's five of twelve. Then take your partners for our midnight waltz . . . or is that schmaltz?'

A chorus of groans answered him.

The McEnroes and Galloways stood up simultaneously. Marie slipped away in all the hubbub that followed to find her friends. Michael found himself facing the two other women left—Rita and Maggie.

He pushed his hands into his pockets. 'I'll see if I can find us some bubbly,' he said, wondering how he would afford it.

Maggie was at his elbow immediately. 'Don't worry. I heard McEnroe ordering it earlier. It'll be sent to us on the stroke of midnight. Before you turn into a white mouse and I turn into a pumpkin.'

'Thanks.' He smiled at her gratefully.

'I see you lost your chance with Marie. You want to dance with Mrs Williams?' There was a gleam in her eye.

'Not a lot. I suppose if I can't have Marie, the boss's wife'll do nicely.'

'Thanks. Now you *do* sound like a farmer.' She came into his arms, light on her feet for all her comfortable middle-aged plumpness. 'I promise I'll let you go at midnight so you can run right over there and kiss Marie.'

'Oh, don't!'

'That's better. Don't get set on her, will you, Michael.'

'That's what her mother said to me.' He grinned ruefully. It was better to talk about it than keep it all inside, worrying at him.

'Ah. You've got years, yet.'

'That's what all mothers say.'

When the din of midnight in Times Square was broadcast across the lounge over the singing of 'Auld Lang Syne', he somehow managed to find Marie in the crush. Women shrieked, men whooped. Balloons rained down around them and were burst by stilettoes and stamping feet.

Marie's friends were wrapped in their boyfriends' arms, and though her lipstick was smeared with kisses, she was alone when he reached her.

'My turn,' he said gently, pushing back the warnings Rita and Maggie had given him.

'Your turn, then.' She looked almost glad to see him.

He folded her against him, her dark curls brushing his hot face, and her mouth pliant under his. He wasn't dreaming. She was returning his kiss now, hanging on to him, warm and responsive, as she had been at the wedding.

But when he pulled away he saw that she had been teasing him. 'Happy New Year, Michael,' she laughed.

'The same to you, Marie.'

He turned and walked away from her. As he moved through the crowd, back towards the table where the others—all but Maggie—had sat down again to toast the New Year with champagne, he looked hard at Steve and Julia Galloway. Julia's diamonds sparkled in the oblique light, and Steve's arm was thrown carelessly around her shoulder. All of them were wealthy, good-looking, positive people. Men and women who knew what they wanted and how to get it. The men were talking about golf again, while Rita was steadily descending into the mists of New Year's Eve sentimentality, chattering to Marianne, who was even less coherent than she was.

He stood on the edge of the circle feeling the outsider again. No matter what she thinks, no matter how much she loves coming to Boston, he said to himself, Maggie doesn't belong here, and I don't belong here, either. On the farm, yes, but not in Boston society where there were social undercurrents he couldn't interpret the way he could explain the grudging acceptance of Joel and Billy McEnroe. Family tensions he understood only too well, but not the sort of tensions he had felt tonight.

Maggie came up behind him and cupped his elbow in her hand. 'Don't look so pensive,' she said. 'It's New Year's Day, Michael!'

'So it is.' Marianne rose suddenly and left the table to kiss Maggie. 'That's for being such a lovely girl,' she said. 'You'll do real well in London, I'm sure.'

Michael saw the miniature fire thrown out by a ring on her left hand. It was understated and pretty, nothing like the flashy brilliance of Julia Galloway's rings. Then he caught the pain in Maggie's eyes.

'Come on, Marianne.' She swallowed hard. 'It's time we all went home to bed, I think. Give me a hand, could you, Michael?'

You'll do real well in London, the old woman had said to Maggie.

17

Michael turned over. Marie swam before his eyes, white teeth a gleaming curve in her bright face, then her lips warm under his, returning the kiss he had given. He rolled over again.

Under his weight, the mattress hollowed perceptibly to a form that was not his own.

'This is where the young Mrs McEnroe used to stay—before she and young Don were married,' the old housekeeper, Mrs Watowski, had told him, ushering him into the bedroom where he was to sleep.

But he wasn't sleeping much. The hour had passed when he usually slid away into the mystery of sleep, and his thinking was too sharp now.

He pulled a dressing gown around his shoulders. The fabric felt scratchy on his wrists and ankles, but the deep frost outside had chilled the house, and he would need it.

He opened the curtains slightly. A frigid breeze had razored and sculpted the snow on the overhanging eves of the great roof. Below, tiny red and green lightbulbs winked by what looked like a covered swimming pool, and someone had decorated a cedar with more Christmas lights, as well as ribbons whose colour he could not make out in the oddly mottled dimness outside. A thick covering of snow lay over all, but there was nothing soft or pretty about it, like the rare snow at home. This snow was crusted like an old-fashioned sugar loaf, with harsh edges fit to cut any hand that dared touch. The contrast between the vivid heat and colour of the midnight dancing at the country club and the barren severity of the scene outside could hardly have been more marked.

He let the curtain fall and went out of the bedroom onto the darkened mezzanine. The house seemed to shift in the frost, the roof nails clicking and popping in the cold. It was an eerie sound, one he knew he would remember.

A faint aroma of cigar smoke still hung in the cool, dead air, and he stood motionless for a moment. When they had returned from the party, McEnroe had put his wife to bed with Maggie's help, then had retired grim-faced to his study. The door had remained shut when Michael went past it to climb the stairs himself. Through the polished panelling he had felt the old man's loneliness: invisible, but almost tangible in the thin trail of smoke that crept under the door.

'He won't want us to disturb him,' Maggie had said wearily—as if he would have dreamed of knocking.

As Michael descended the quiet stairs, the residual heat of the house rose around his feet to meet him. A pale dart of light showed under the study door. He hesitated, heard the sound of his own breathing, then a muffled cough from within.

He's still awake.

Michael was unsure in this strange house—so homely, but so imposing and heavy, tonight, too—what to do. No other sounds from behind the closed door.

He went on along the passage to where he knew the kitchen was, and after fumbling in the dark by the door found and pressed the knob for the lights. Their sudden glare and the blinding gleam of every spotless surface made him cover his face for a moment.

No one would mind if he helped himself to a drink. He thought of Don and Maggie and their nightly ritual of hot milk or cocoa. He had teased them about it, at first, but then joined them. It was comforting to sit with them at the grained wooden table in the kitchen and talk over the day's work; to feel like the son of the house, hours after the boys had gone upstairs to homework or bed. So he would make himself a hot drink now and hope that it would take the edge off the too-long day, leave him sleepy.

This kitchen was big enough, he decided, for a hotel. Sporadically aided by Marianne, the housekeeper kept everything in shining order:

copper-bottomed Revereware polished in rows; ladles, basting spoons and meat knives bristling out of a wooden pot; two eye-level ovens and a microwave with glass doors that shone; a glossy pine-panelled breakfast nook that spilled the scent of greenhouse hyacinths into the air; burnished brick-red floor tiles that felt faintly warm even through his slippers. Luxurious... but representing a time when Marianne must have been the most sought-after hostess, must have entertained for the senate, for local business men, country club members, and politicians.

It was not a world where she would be able to do much now, he reflected, except keep everything immaculate—for as long as she wanted to.

'We think she may be at the onset of Alzheimers,' Maggie had whispered to him.

He poured milk into a saucepan and watched it heat on the hob. Just as it bubbled up, heavy steps came down the passage and stopped in the doorway.

'Oh—it's you, Michael. What on earth—?'

He rescued the milk. 'Forgive me. I couldn't sleep.'

The old man stepped into the room, pulled out one of the breakfast chairs, and slumped into it. 'Me neither.' Except that his tie was now abandoned, he was still dressed, his mane of thick hair untidy and ruffled, as if he had been pushing his hands through it over and over again. 'I waited until Marianne was asleep—she goes so quickly these days—and thought I'd sit down here a while.' His eyes focused balefully on the pan Michael was holding. 'Anyway, what're you making?'

'Just hot milk.'

McEnroe snorted and stood up again. 'Come on. I'll give you a slug of something stronger than that. You haven't seen my study, have you?'

He wanted company, Michael realized. 'No, sir.'

'Don't mess with the "sir" bit. Bring that milk if you want to, but I've got some Scotch you can doctor it with if you want.'

'What about you?'

'Oh, I already had more bourbon tonight than in many a long year. Too much. It makes me maudlin, keeps me awake, as well. I don't want anything.'

'Not even cocoa?'

'You're worse than Don,' McEnroe guffawed. 'And you're starting to sound like Maggie, as well. Fussing over me. Stop it, you hear? This way—come on.'

Heat from a small log fire made the study warmer than the rest of the dark house. McEnroe's golf clubs stood sentinel by the door; shelves of leather-bound books lined the room.

'Law books, and Law Society info,' McEnroe explained with a dismissive wave of one hand. 'Not much good these days except for occasional precedent references, or for the duster, I guess. The kind of materials I need most nowadays are in the Boston Free Library or police records. Hardly touch this lot. There—sit down. Let me top up that white stuff of yours.'

Michael felt it would be churlish to refuse, though he was uncertain how well whisky would mix with the champagne of midnight.

McEnroe took a small log out of a basket on the hearth and threw it onto the fire. Without turning, he said, 'I saw you sneaking a peek at my clubs. Golfer, are you?'

'Not me. Rugby's my game.'

McEnroe returned the mug to him. 'Check this out, son.' He poured himself a long drink of tonic water. 'Rugby's not a game I know at all.'

Michael looked around at the overstuffed leather chairs and the family photographs. The room was comfortable, masculine, and quiet. A place where one might work out life's dilemmas.

'So—' The old man's blue eyes were fixed on his like steel chips. 'What's keeping you awake? Let me guess.' He took a slow sip from his glass and gave a wry smile. 'Girl trouble, right?'

Michael glanced at the clubs again. 'You just hit an albatross, or whatever you call it. Hole in one.'

McEnroe's smile widened into a grin. 'I would've thought you'd have it all figured by now. You were working on it at the party. I may have had a good pull on the bottle, but my head's still clear, and I remember that much quite plainly.'

Michael looked into the white bubbles nestling around the edge of the mug. 'I think I do have it worked out. Just decided I'm wasting my time hoping any more about Marie.'

McEnroe said nothing.

Michael suddenly felt uncomfortable under the continued scrutiny. He shrugged the embarrassment away, not wanting to think any more about the girl. 'But there's more to life than women.'

'Is there?' McEnroe's joviality was fading again. The old man was right; he *was* maudlin.

No need to answer. Let him do the talking, Michael thought. McEnroe had more on his mind, and more serious things on his mind, than he did.

'So—more to life than women, hunh! Well, I'm not sure about that. Seems to me this New Year's night that more than half the heartaches in my life have been women. I watched Maggie breaking her heart over Don all those years when she didn't have to, when he was still too blind to see what a gal she was. I watched Rachel deciding, though she could have had the pick of any med school in this whole goddamn country, that she wanted to go overseas to study. Well, gee, I guess that's no great problem, really. But Eleanor, my daughter, disintegrating under our very eyes—another story altogether.' He looked into the fire. 'And now Marianne. Never a sick day in her whole adult life. Never in hospital except for the babies. And now look at her.' He rubbed the back of his neck and went on as if Michael weren't there. 'It's a bitter pill to swallow. There's so much going on right now. I don't know how I can get through this year if Marianne's not—all there.'

Michael murmured something.

McEnroe looked up and registered his presence again. 'Ah, but I'm forgetting. You didn't know what she used to be like. So *radiant*. So gorgeous. Even a few months ago. And now this illness drives up on us like a train. Unstoppable. And she's under the wheels without ever knowing what hit her.'

Michael was out of his depth. 'I wish there were something I could say.'

'Of course.' McEnroe reached and opened the bottom drawer of his desk. He pulled out a large calendar, tore off a crackling wrapper, and flipped it open at January. A snowy landscape from somewhere in the state of Massachusetts topped the blank squares of the page. 'I look at this month—this year—and it's like the yard looks outside. All white. A frozen desert. It's scary, Michael, even for an old man who's seen a helluva lot of scary things in seventy-some years. I'm not ready for Marianne to leave me yet. Alzheimer's—if that's what it is—they're not certain yet—sure is cruel. Worse than death, because the woman I love doesn't know herself any more. Pretty soon she won't know me, either, I guess.'

A log shifted and fell with a shower of sparks into the base of the grate. McEnroe leaned forward and prodded behind the screen with a brass poker.

'We all think we're immortal. Even folks who love God and should know better. I guess I thought Marianne would outlive me, anyhow. Still might. But she won't properly be here for me to talk to about all that's going on.'

'There're Don and Maggie at the other end of a telephone.'

'Not the same though, is it?'

'No.'

McEnroe breathed heavily and smiled slowly again. 'But it's been great having you all here these last couple days. Takes my mind off things.'

'Even at about two-thirty on January the first?'

The room fell quiet for a moment except for the hiss of flames in the grate. 'Well, maybe not now. I never sleep well on New Year's. Guess I try to live my life ahead of myself too much. Work it all out before I get there.'

Michael knew he was being used as a sounding board. 'The sign of a young mind, perhaps.'

The old man laughed sadly. 'Gee, I wonder if that's true!'

Michael sized him up. 'Look, I know you don't know me, but I feel I know you—they talk about you all the time, in Arcade. You seem to live there almost as much as we do, you know. And I realize I'm young, but if I can listen, if I can do—' He threw his hand out, searching for the words, and it crossed his mind like a gleam of laughter that he was sounding like his own father.

The blue eyes were twinkling now. 'Good of you. Only God can change what's happening to Marianne. But I guess I can talk to you about other things, if you've really got the time to listen.'

Michael looked for a clock but could see none. 'All the time in the New Year.'

'Old men have to talk, but they bore younger men.'

'Young men talk too much and listen too little.'

'That's what someone said to me when I was a kid. He was right. I'm careful, have to be, whom I talk to. But too careful, maybe, for my own good.'

Michael felt he would sound sententious if he muttered something about professionalism. And there was more at stake, anyway, than mere professional conduct. If McEnroe was still investigating drug dealing on the North Shore, he would have to be close-mouthed all the time. For a man as sociable as McEnroe, that would be uncomfortable. 'You mentioned at the party that you were still chasing things on that—'

McEnroe took a deep breath. 'Yup, I am. And we're uncovering more and more. Makes my blood freeze more than this damned cold.' He stirred the fire again, and a wave of heat rolled across the hearth up to Michael's face. 'But you don't want to hear about that, I'm certain.'

Michael wasn't sure he wanted to hear about it, either. But he saw that the old man was eager to talk. He leaned forward. 'Yes, I do.'

McEnroe sat back and seemed to stare into middle distance. 'Well, then, why not?' He gave a dry laugh. 'The room's not bugged—at least I hope not. You can put all this down to the nocturnal ramblings of an old guy who can't sleep for thinking of everything. An old guy who sometimes needs to doff his professional hat and talk like a human being for a change. And then you can forget about it in the morning. Understood?'

Michael hesitated. 'I think so. My father sometimes shares his worries with my mother, or me.'

McEnroe's eyes refocused. 'Your father? He's a lawyer—solicitor—whatever the heck they call 'em?'

'Far from it. Social worker. Usually with too big a case load. That's all.'

'That's enough, I should think.' McEnroe chuckled. 'Well, and is he into any drug rehab work? If he is, you'll maybe know some of what's going on in Kent—that's your home ground, right?'

'In *Kent*?'

'Yes indeedy—in sleepy old sheep-and-apple, stockbroker belt Kent.'

Michael blinked. 'I mean, Dad's not involved, but I know there's a drug problem in Kent—same as everywhere else . . . but what amazes me is your knowing about what's going on *there* as well as here.'

McEnroe's laid one finger along the side of his nose and twisted his head to one side. 'Ah, if I knew everything going on here, I'd be in damn good shape. Unhappily for me, I don't. But I did learn a few useful tidbits when I was over in your neck of the woods this year . . . no, it's last, now.'

'I didn't know you'd gone.'

'Beginning of October. Flew with my granddaughter, matter of fact. Some of my contacts in London had uncovered some interesting things, and I wanted to track them down a little and see where they led. Looks like I may have to go back, as well.' He stopped and examined his big hands, clenching them. 'Maybe not, though. Your own Violence Intelligence Unit's quite competent, and they hardly want an old guy like me interfering on personal grounds, no matter what perfectly legit reasons I might dream up to keep it all above board.'

Michael looked at McEnroe's balled fists. 'I don't suppose you can—'

'Sure I can tell you. It's not classified, and you won't get rich on the information!' He chortled again, a spark of enthusiasm back on his face. Then he unlocked another drawer in his desk and drew out a thick folder. 'Learned a few statistics, for a start. Just in London—never mind the rest of the UK—there's four billion pounds of property theft each year. The Metropolitan guys told me they believe at least one third of that is drug-related crime. Maybe as much as a half.'

Michael whistled under his breath.

'Yeah, see what I mean? I had no idea until I flew out there how bad things'd gotten. Last I knew there was a fairly well-contained problem—back in the late sixties. The police mostly knew who the drug users were and had them taped. But I kinda lost track after that. Had my plate full here.'

'I wasn't aware of much, growing up, myself. Wealdhurst isn't exactly a big town.'

'Never heard tell of it. Near the coast?'

'No.'

'Then you wouldn't.'

'You hear on local news about drug hauls at the docks. They've been an issue for customs for ages.'

McEnroe shut his folder. 'Funny you should mention them. I learned a lot about what's going on in the capital, but I also dug into how the drugs get there—some of your court transcripts of drug trafficking offences committed in the ports. Interested?'

Michael was starting to feel sleepy, but the old man's face was so intent, and his eyes held him so directly now, that he nodded in assent.

'The first thing I stumbled on was through the Met boys. I had no idea you had a gangland problem in London like we have in New York and LA and Miami. There's Chinatown, for instance, and likely to get worse, as well, with the influx from Hong Kong when that goes back to Chinese rule.'

Michael stared at him blankly; he knew nothing of Chinatown.

'Your Chinatown's small, but almost as packed as the Walled City itself. Lots of businesses, and they aren't all Chinese. When businessmen move in, if they haven't been warned off, they're advised by men—they work in pairs speaking with newcomers—to register with a Triad gang for protection. Like the Mafia in Sicily or Chicago.'

Stories his parents had told him of their days in Northern Ireland suddenly jolted into Michael's mind. 'And like the paramilitaries in Derry and Belfast.'

'Exactly. And just as sinister. The Triad gangs offer a warranty of protection in return for free services and what they call "tea money" from the businesses. If people refuse to sign up, they're threatened with the chop.' He stopped, slicing his hand across his throat. 'Most people buckle, give in right away. It takes a rare bird to go public or tell them to get lost. And the Triads have a lucrative drug traffic going on right under people's noses because everyone's too scared to talk. The police can't get willing witnesses; hardly anyone ever gets nailed.'

Michael watched McEnroe's knuckles whiten as he talked, his fists clenching and unclenching on the folder he still held in his lap.

'The latest thing is that the Triad gangs are networking with some of the older traffickers. Not just drugs—arms dealers as well. Sophisticated guys who've been running stuff in and out of Amsterdam through the Kent and Essex ports for years. Guys who know what they're at. Guys who turn round and ship it straight in here. Or co-operate with South American barons and make hideous new drugs in clever little labs stashed away in hidden corners of Northern Europe. There's no end to it. And if things relax in Kent and London, now the trade barriers are falling, I say woe betide your poor little nation.' McEnroe shivered. 'And somewhere, probably near the middle of this international network, I'm convinced, is the man who with his cronies set our daughter on a course for disaster and ruin.'

Michael was riveted. He murmured, 'Eleanor.'

'Right. This man's name was Garshowitz one day and Garcia the next. Used to go by the name of Keith, though he's got dozens of other aliases. Bank accounts all over the shop, but never long enough for anyone to rumble him. And always behind a slick storefront. No fool... but we'll close in on him in the end. I just hope I'm around long enough to see justice done.'

The fire was dying now, the embers glowing grey-pink instead of gold-white. Michael watched them absently for a minute. 'You haven't told me much about the Kent ports.'

'Your own county courts were trying a big case when I was over there in the fall. One of the times when the customs guys got lucky and actually caught 'em.'

'But not the men you're after, I suppose.'

'No way, not yet!' McEnroe reopened the folder and shuffled through its pages. 'Under the Misuse of Drugs Acts '71 and Customs and Excise Management Act '79. They had police marksmen up on the roof of the courthouse all through the trial. The county town looked more like Chicago than the sleepy market town I'd heard it was. I sat in the public gallery and listened to part of the hearing—never sat in an English court before. Group of men hired a car and went across to France for a few days' vacation. That's what the defense tried to prove, anyhow. But it turned out they'd gone much farther—north into the Netherlands. The officers found a Dutch address under the trim around the dashboard. There wasn't a brass centime of French currency on any of 'em, but Dutch guilders—oh, plenty. Even more gratifying, they found bags of cannabis resin and cocaine hydrochloride in the back of the car.'

'That doesn't sound like a sophisticated operation, though, does it?'

'Only the tip of the iceberg. And it sure was a worthwhile haul. Forty-eight grand in US currency. That's not exactly part of a small-time operation. They were set up, they claimed. Fall guys for some outfit they wouldn't name. *Couldn't* name, of course, if they wanted to survive. Swore they didn't know the packets were there.'

'In the back of a hired car they had the only key for?'

'Defence argued that they'd mislaid the key temporarily in France and that the drugs must have been planted by someone intending to strip the car when it'd gotten back to Dover. Inside job, they tried to claim. Even tried to point the finger back at the Customs and Excise guys. But the prosecution unpicked that argument very quick, I'll tell ya, because of the mileage on the car's odometer, and the lack of defense evidence about the key. And the drugs were hidden *inside* the rubber of the spare tyre. No end to people's inventiveness, is there? The tyre was bolted under the car, in its regular place. No sign it'd been disturbed. It was even half deflated—the way most folks' spares are. No fingerprints on the trunk, either … as if four guys in a car wouldn't open the trunk during a week's holiday overseas, I ask you! They convinced themselves they'd thought of everything.'

'Then how did they get caught?'

'Four guys in a car on a pleasure trip—no wives or girlfriends in tow. Far more fascinating to an eagle-eyed customs officer than a family of four with two cranky kids in the back. Especially when someone's tipped them off. One of the men's contacts in Holland panicked after the drugs left the store, and he shopped them.'

Michael digested this. 'And that's only one case.'

'Like you say. But you can see what police and customs guys have to contend with. Small ports—well, I know Dover's not small to your mind—are soft targets. Same thing we've got up here all the way from Boston and up the North Shore. That's why I'm always after Marie's mother to be so vigilant, and why we keep each other informed, every chance we get. Think of it—miles of coastline—some of it rocky, isolated and hard to reach. Drug smugglers' dream. Sure, we get the occasional bust and lock up a few of those wasters, but people round here are half asleep. Dozing in their fat-cat retirements, playing a few holes of golf, and chewing the cud—' He winked. 'Pardon the comparison with those noble beasts of Don's—chewing the cud in their country clubs.' He grinned wryly. 'Kinda like me, huh?'

Michael laughed. 'Not like you at all.'

McEnroe shook his head. 'Sometimes wish I was like that, and could forget the whole damn mess. Then I look at my darling Marianne, and I think of all the sadness we've had over the last twenty years without Ellie, and I can't just sit cosy in my senate seat and do nothing. Some of the state officials can. I can't. Not me. Not while the terror goes on, Michael.' The old man dropped his eyes. 'Eleanor's story could be told by thousands of families here, thousands of families in Chinatown, London and Kent. Thousands more in Holland, Central America, South America—you name it.' He sighed. 'So now you know why an old man can't sleep on a long winter's night when anyone in his right mind is tucked up snugly with his wife and dreaming of the party he just went to.'

'But you can't do everything on your own.'

'Now you sound like Maggie again. She told me once I should stop playing at being God.'

The fire had dwindled to an uneven heap of ash and charred wood. Michael glanced at it again before he answered. 'I couldn't live at all, couldn't cope with anything—worries about the future, women problems—' He stopped. 'Sorry—that's nothing compared with your concerns—whatever it is, I couldn't cope if I didn't trust God.'

McEnroe moved his head in slow agreement. 'I may be an old sinner, but I couldn't, either.'

Michael was afraid of sounding simplistic. 'I do believe there's a pattern and purpose in everything, and that God is in and over and under and through and behind everything, even when I can't see him.' He looked up and found the senator's eyes—now red with exhaustion and drink—turned on his face. 'Rachel and I talked about that, too, when I first got to the farm.'

McEnroe stretched his arms above his head and twinkled at him. 'And she agreed, naturally... well, I'll try to remember what you've said.'

It was his cue, Michael knew, to leave the old man to his night's vigil. He stood up stiffly. His face felt lop-sided, as if, when he smiled again, half of it would slide below his chin.

'You look tired.' McEnroe emptied his glass of tonic and closed his eyes. He waved his hand. 'Go on—you get some sleep while I have me a conversation with the Man who's really God, and try to put all the troubles away from me for the New Year.'

'Good night, then, sir.'

The fierce eyes snapped open. 'I thought I said—'

Michael smiled and shut the door softly. He waited until his eyes readjusted to the dark, then trod back up the cold stairs to bed.

18

Jolting back under ground towards the hospital, her suitcase tucked under her legs in the crush, Rachel considered all she had seen and felt over the past weeks. *No,* she decided. *It's no use going on as before. The New Year has got to be easier.*

She let her eyes go out of focus on the underground cables that hurtled past the train between stations. Nothing could be much worse, she reminded herself, than the three uneasy days she had spent at Michael's house: Kate's rare breaks from formality, Stacey's jealousy, and Ian's alternating joviality and insensitivity. Even in Michael's room, she had not fully been able to believe that he had anything to do with the house. Jack Monaghan was the only one whose kindness—when he was around—reminded her at all that there was any sort of link.

So things at the hospital just have to get better, she told herself. And she began to arm herself for the year ahead.

At least she would know her way around the place this term; for company when she wanted it there were Cecelia, Charlie Christophers, and Crock Basden; and her room—however bleak it was, however grimy the view outside—was at least familiar. She would know better, too, what was expected by the course and the staff.

St Stephen's—or so the Australian had with an air of knowing told her—was unique among all the London teaching hospitals in allowing first-year students a few hours' clinical experience each week of their second and third terms. 'Just what you've always wanted, Rachel,' he'd told her ghoulishly, 'up to your lugs in blood and guts, telling the casualty sister how to sort 'em out.'

She had laughed but was intrigued, looking forward more to that part of her training than to anything else so far. What she had seen with Cecilia on the men's and the maternity wards on Christmas Day had fired her enthusiasm. Her tutor's treacherous question about whether she was on the right career path would fade into the background for her, she felt sure, once she started what she had begun to think of as the real work of her training.

The tube train screeched to a stop, disgorging passengers onto the platform: Rachel among them. She felt lighter now, more able to breathe. A New Year; everything could begin again. Hope sprang up in her.

Her expectations were gradually fulfilled during the early weeks of the term. The head of her tutorial group had turned down her request for a term in the obstetrical ward; she had instead been farmed out to the same men's ward where Cecelia had been working at Christmas.

Along with a dozen others, she trailed Dyer, the senior registrar, and the nurse in charge from bed to bed while they examined patients and held discussions about drugs and other treatment. Disappointment that she was not on the women's ward melted, replaced by admiration and complete fascination. Some of the patients looked up to Dyer with obvious liking and appreciation, while others—often those in the greatest pain or with the most complicated symptoms—vented their complaints as soon as nurses drew the curtains around them.

Sometimes Dyer would turn an urbane eye on her and ask for her opinion—then proceed to demolish her timid judgments. She might have left the ward feeling ignorant and foolish, or carping about the senior registrar behind his back, as some of the others did; instead, she was filled with awe both at the way he reached his conclusions, and at the power of the human body to be healed.

By the third week of term, she felt like a racehorse with the bit between its teeth at the last hurdle. *Yes, yes!* she said to herself as she followed her colleagues around the ward for the third time, *this sure is what I'm here for!*

She realized with some surprise, walking onto the men's ward for the fourth week, that she was *happy*. Deep sleep claimed her every night; the heating in her room was working again; and her cold had subsided. She felt settled now in a way that she knew her mother would applaud; even McEnroe, who had sadly but in no uncertain terms told her he wished she was studying in Massachusetts or New York, would approve this change in her circumstances, this steadiness of conviction.

The first person who caught her eye, always, was Joseph King, the long-term patient whom she had tried—and failed—to comfort on Christmas Day. He still watched as she and the other medical students moved around the ward. His eyes looked curious: irises vivid blue, but as a whole sunken into their sockets and ringed with greyish skin in a white face. They were the only alive and mobile features in a man who might as well have been a living corpse: he was still unable to take any food or drink by mouth, and generally refused to speak or move.

'Just what *is* his problem?' Rachel found herself asking. 'Wasn't the op straightforward?'

The staff nurse shrugged. 'He's not healing cleanly, as I told you. It's as simple as that. And as complicated.'

'Why not?'

'That's the way it often goes with gastric surgery. But there's more to it than meets the eye. Lord, he's been in here since the third week in December!'

'More to it?'

'He's given up, Rachel. Can't you see?'

King lay now with his eyes shut, but the flickering of his eyelids told her he was awake, and possibly listening to them. Recalling his casenotes, she lowered her voice to a whisper. 'He's only fifty-five. Why's he given up?'

As they spoke, two of the nurses went to turn him. He opened his eyes, muttered incoherently, then suffered them to move him.

'Every two or three hours we've got to turn him like that. He hates it. I sometimes think he'd rather let the bedsores take over and the infection kill him. Wife left him just before he came in for surgery. Thinks he's got nothing left.'

Rachel waited until the other students had drifted to a bed further down the ward. 'What's he on?'

The staff nurse looked askance. 'See for yourself in his casenotes. I can't comment on what's been prescribed.' Her voice suddenly turned acid. 'Why? Think you know better? Stand by me when I change the dressings next, and see what a fistula can look like. It's frightening.'

Surprise at the woman's hostility brought colour rushing into Rachel's cheeks. 'No—oh, I didn't mean I knew better, not at all.'

But she was speaking to empty air. The staff nurse vanished into the ward sister's office, and she was left alone in the middle of the ward, the object of curious gazes from the patients.

Later, when she'd attended her last lecture and given herself a few minutes' leisure in the union lounge, she began to think more about King. Flipping idly through a medical journal, her mind half occupied with him, she came across an article on unusual treatments for infected wounds.

She turned back to the head of the article and started rereading. The idea of placing pawpaw on the wounds sounded bizarre, yet the research she had done for her project on alternative medicine had taught her to respect things that on face value sounded outlandish. She read on, now with closer attention.

When she had finished she stood up slowly, sighed, and went straight down the corridor to the journals room of the library. Pulling out *Index Medicus* she began to compile a list of all articles on the use of pawpaw. A few dated back as far as the nineteen seventies, but most were more recent, backed up by research done in hospitals on both sides of the Atlantic. She found the bound journals she wanted and piled them up.

Then she lost all track of time, scribbling furiously on her notepad, and reading with total absorption. *What if King gives up altogether before I can talk to Dr Dyer about him?* A kind of feverish energy overtook her. *I must get back up to the men's ward before next week... but how?*

She had just decided she would go for supper in the canteen when the library lights flickered, and the librarian called across the stacks that he was locking up for the night.

With a quick intake of breath, she glared at the wall clock. Nine o' clock. While she had been reading, the medical school building had emptied, the canteen would long ago have shut, and the whole hospital was winding down for the night. She had sat so motionless in the library that her shoulders ached.

In her room she made herself some cocoa and sat alone in the cramped space thinking about King. She could come up with only one way to get herself back on the men's ward without arousing suspicion or causing trouble: to enlist the support of the hospital chaplain. But she would have to wait until morning, when he came back on duty. And as soon as she could extricate herself from her normal timetable, she would also have to find a source of fresh pawpaw.

When her light was out and the residence hall half hushed to its usual broken night, the whole scheme began to seem preposterous. *'He's given up, Rachel, can't you see?'* The staff nurse's taunts echoed in her head. There would be no help from that quarter. She thought of Dr Dyer's usual scorn for suggestions from his medical student entourage on their weekly rounds; it was impossible to believe that he would listen to a crack-brained idea from her about the application of tropical fruit to the wound. Nor would any amount of exotic fruit heal someone who no longer wanted to live.

Then he has to find the will to live.

She fell asleep praying for him in prayers that lapsed into confused half dreams of what she would do the next day, and of what the chaplain and registrar might say when she approached them. Whatever she did would almost certainly involve her in a breach of hospital protocol.

The risks were obvious; she and the other medics had been told clearly enough at the beginning of the term that any interference or misguided attempts to take over cases would lead to severe censure if not outright exclusion from the course. But she was so convinced of the value of trying pawpaw—when all other treatments had failed—that she would rather be the loser herself than see a patient die unnecessarily.

Long before it was light the next morning, she was awake. As soon as her eyes were open, she remembered what she wanted to do and knew there would be no more sleep. She lay in the lumpy bed and watched dawn break thinly behind the curtains, then dressed quickly in the chill.

First stop Fr Jenks' office. Second stop Dr Dyer. She muttered the words to herself as she dressed—as if she would forget. *I must be crazy.*

After a hurried breakfast, equipped with her book bag and the notes she had taken the night before, she went back across the courtyard to the front of the hospital. The porter nodded as she crossed the reception, and she grinned back. She felt happy, hopeful that she was at last going to make a direct difference in a patient's life.

In the administration wing, the chaplain's office was firmly locked. As she glanced at her watch, she realized she had come too early. But if she had waited any longer she would be late for lectures, and he would be doing his rounds.

I'll have to come at lunchtime, she told herself, disappointed, heavy with anticlimax.

Turning away, she met Fr Jenks himself: his hand outstretched with the key ready to unlock the door. 'Hello . . . Rachel McEnroe, am I right? Well, I haven't seen you for quite a while. You here for me?'

They half knew each other because he had occasionally attended the carol practices she had taken part in before Christmas. She smiled at him. 'Yes—if you can spare a few minutes.' The sense that she was following an insane scheme overtook her again. She hesitated. 'Er—there's someone I want you to visit today, and to pray for.'

'Now? With you?'

She felt flustered. 'Sure—if you've got time. Only I can't go on the ward with you right now. I gotta get to my lecture in a few minutes.'

'I understand.' He stooped for some letters that had been pushed under the door, then held it open. 'Go in, then. I've come in to pick up my messages—that's all. So I'm at your disposal.'

The room was cluttered and reeked of stale cigarette smoke. In the corner, an ashtray overflowed, and traces of ash trailed across the floor. Used coffee cups stood half empty on every shelf.

'Forgive me—I'm not much of a housekeeper, and there was a family in here until quite late.'

She waved her hand in dismissal. 'Please—it doesn't matter. It's just I wanted to talk with you about Joseph King. He's on—'

Fr Jenks' grey eyebrows rose. 'Stop—I know exactly who he is. Long-stay on men's post-op. Am I right?' When she nodded, he went on, 'Funny you should be in here first thing today about him. It was *his* family I had in here last night.' He reached and eased a window open a few centimetres. 'Smokers all. Sorry.'

'It doesn't matter,' she repeated. 'Listen, can I sit down?' Then it dawned on her what he had said. '*His family in here?* But I thought his wife—'

'She did. Left him weeks ago. It was his daughters and their families who came in. All at once. Quite a posse, you might say. Desperate for me to do something. Joseph King may have given up, but the kids haven't.' He sat down, facing her.

Rachel remembered what she had been told before: that no one ever visited Mr King. Plainly, this wasn't true. She began to smile. 'I know it'll sound like pie in the sky,' she said, 'but I'll bet there's a reason they were here last night.' She leaned forward. 'Of course God's concerned about every patient in this hospital. But he's made me aware of this one in particular, and I want your support for an idea I have.'

The chaplain's eyes shuttered; he stiffened visibly in the chair. 'My dear, you're only a medical student. I have little more clout here than you do, in reality.'

'I don't believe that for a moment.'

'And I *certainly* don't influence how a patient is treated.'

Her enthusiasm shrivelled slightly, yet she persisted. 'I know it. But

I'm hoping to talk to the senior registrar, as well. I don't want to get in trouble. Or get you in trouble.' She gave him a fleeting smile to which he didn't respond with any reassurance. 'I'll try to go through the proper channels, truly I will.'

His expression was cautious, measured, and he put the tips of his fingers together, resting his elbows on his knees and staring straight at her. 'All right, then. What's your idea?'

'Prayer, to start with.'

His face creased into a smile. 'I think I can cope with that.'

'Then I want to talk to the senior registrar about pawpaw.'

The chaplain's face reverted to careful impassivity. 'And what about the houseman who's been treating this man? What's he going to say?' He held up his hand. 'No, don't get me wrong! I'm as eager as you are to help Mr King and his family—I've been watching his decline as much as have any of the nursing staff on that ward. See him every day—or try to. But we don't help anyone by rushing in impulsively with half-baked schemes that set the medical staff against each other and against you. You should know already how political St Stephen's is!'

She did not want to hear the voice of reason, saw only in her mind's eye the anguished face of Joseph King; felt only the keen wish to change the look on that face. 'Oh, I'm not worried about what the houseman says. He'll do what the boss tells him, of course.'

'And you'll be popular as can be with him! Am I right? That's naive, my dear. Just think, Rachel, what things'd be like if you ended up on the same firm as that houseman, at each other's throats for the rest of your training. Is that what you want?'

She stared at the smears of white ash on the carpet. Nothing seemed to be going as she'd hoped—not even this first conversation with the chaplain. She took a steadying breath and was just going to answer him when he began again.

'Anyway, I suppose you're talking about using pawpaw on the infected bits. Am I right?'

His repeated use of the phrase 'Am I right?' was beginning to grate on Rachel, so she only nodded in response.

'Even I have heard of that wild idea, Rachel. It would go down like a lead balloon in this place. You're wasting your breath—except in praying, of course—' His voice became gentler. 'You've surely found out how opposed to alternative medicine everyone round here is?'

She smiled faintly and remembered her tutor's guarded reaction to the research she'd done before Christmas. 'Indeed I have!'

Jenks stood up again and plugged in a kettle. With his back still to Rachel, he began to shuffle through the small pile of letters. She heard him tearing envelopes, and she thought he'd almost forgotten her.

'All right, Rachel. I was going up to see Mr King this morning anyway—before his relatives come back and make more attempts to badger him—and fail.' He turned towards her again and leaned against the shelf. 'But I'll be honest—I don't think I've any chance of convincing him that life's worth living, let alone that he should submit to a course of questionable treatment dreamed up by a med student—even if Dr Dyer himself *does* give his blessing.'

Rachel looked at him dumbly.

'But I'm glad you came.'

His sincerity was doubtful. A sense of futility enveloped her, then a fresh realization that time, as well as the traditions of the establishment, was against her. Her chin went up defiantly. 'At least let's pray together for him.'

His face relaxed again. 'Ah—you teach me my own work. Maybe you should be a chaplain, yourself.'

She laughed, but it was an ironic little laugh. *There it is again—everyone doubting what I'm doing here: McEnroe, my tutor, Cecelia, and now the chaplain.* She looked at the carpet again, then shut her eyes and heard Jenks resume his seat.

Over the bubbling of the kettle, he murmured a prayer that restored for her a measure of confidence in him. Then he stood and patted her shoulder. 'You're a good lass,' he said. 'I'll see what I can do. You talk to the senior registrar, then come back and find me in the canteen at lunchtime. If I can grab a break, I'll be there at one.'

She felt patronized, but glad of this small grain of encouragement.

He ruined it again. 'Don't do anything silly meanwhile.'

After that, she couldn't answer him but fled back into the corridor and through the hospital and courtyard to the medical school.

She lost herself in the demands of the morning's lectures. From a distance, Basden hailed her, and she mouthed the words 'Enjoying your obstetrics work?' When he nodded enthusiastically, she smiled back in envy. For a moment she wished she had never heard of Joseph King or been given clinical work on the men's ward. The maternity ward, she told herself hopelessly—knowing all the same that it was a fatuous thought—would be far simpler.

Lunchtime found her rushing out of the front of the hospital to a fruiterer's barrow that stood at hand for hospital visitors. Her heart was thumping with excitement. As soon as she'd bought some pawpaw and spoken again to the chaplain, she could search for Dr Dyer.

The grocer scratched his head when she asked for pawpaw. 'Not 'ere, love. You'll have to git yourself down the Greenwich market of a Saturday and try there.'

Saturday! She repeated to herself in dismay. *There's no way I'm going to wait till the end of the week!*

Any idea of eating lunch or looking for the chaplain or the senior registrar vanished. It was all pointless—*fruitless,* she told herself with a wry smile—unless she managed to buy pawpaw.

Rushing across the courtyard to get more money from her room, she met Charlie Christophers.

'Hey! What's up?'

She explained.

'Wow! You'll cop it if you don't go about it in the right way, Rach.'

'Since when did "the right way" bother you, Dante?' she teased.

'Come on. I'll take you to where we'll get some pawpaw and no trouble. Grab your hat, girl.' And with that he whisked her away through the side gates, down into the underground, and all the way to Knightsbridge and back.

'Haven't you discovered, my dear?' he asked, imitating the chaplain's voice in burlesque that made Rachel howl with laughter in the rattling confines of the Piccadilly Line train, 'that Harrods Food Hall is the only place to go? Am I right, or am I right?'

They returned late for the afternoon lectures, but Charlie was undeterred, and they crept into the back of the lecture hall loaded with a bulging Harrod's bag. All the way through the rest of the afternoon, Rachel smelt the faint tang of the fruit. Whenever it came to her, she prayed for Joseph King.

She posted herself at the canteen doors looking for Fr Jenks at the time when she guessed he might appear for supper. Students and staff swung in and out, passing her, but the chaplain did not appear; he must be stuck somewhere else in the hospital. However, at last she saw Dr Dyer. As usual, he came down the dim corridor with his white coat flapping ostentatiously and a stethoscope dangling unnecessarily from his neck.

'Miss McEnroe.' He nodded in mock deference, and pushed the swingdoors to pass her. Then he looked more closely, and his face changed, frowning. 'You look a little het up. What's on earth's the matter?'

The bag of pawpaw weighed heavily in one hand, and in the other the notes she had taken the night before protruded like a loaded gun from her bookbag. Was this all a mistake? 'Please—I'd like to talk to you.'

His voice was very crisp—'plummy', Basden called it. 'I'm going in for my supper. I imagine you are, too. We'll talk.'

She was surprised that he would give her even five minutes of his time outside their weekly clinical training rounds. But then she thought of the prayers she had uttered on and off all day, and was comforted with the idea that God could move even a senior registrar.

He listened with utter concentration as she broached her ideas to him. Eventually, he stopped eating, pulled off the stethoscope, and laid down his knife and fork.

'I was warned against you, you know.'

For a moment, she felt dizzy. From another table, medical students she knew quite well eyed her with unconcealed curiosity. 'What d'you mean?'

'Your tutor—Dr Tate, as I recall. He saw you were on my clinical list for this term and said I should watch out for a brunette American with one foot firmly in medical unorthodoxy and the other hankering after obstetrics. It was his idea, you know, to put you as far as possible away from your chosen area. "To knock the silly ideas out of her pretty head," he said to me.'

She felt the colour drain from her face. 'If I'd known—'

'Politics, sweetheart.' Dyer seemed to see her properly for the first time. 'Gosh, you have a lot to learn.'

She grinned at him. 'So the chaplain tells me.'

'Oh, he's in on this, too? I might have known!'

She did not know what to say.

He leaned across the table. 'You make a reasonable case. This patient has been a major concern for too long, now. Show me the evidence that there's anything whatsoever sound about this theory of yours, and we'll test it.' He shrugged. 'There's nothing to lose if we do, and everything, possibly, if we don't.'

Relief flooded through her. She bent and pulled out her notes. 'There's this article, and this.'

He thumbed through the sheets. 'Crackpot. Out of date. Won't do, you know.'

'What about these?' She held out more notes, details she had taken from *The Lancet* and *The New England Journal of Medicine* and waited while he scanned them. His face gave nothing away.

At last he laid them down. 'I'm probably a fool. You've a pretty face.'

She flushed uneasily and glanced away from his scrutiny to the other side of the canteen. 'I don't want—'

He smiled. 'Don't worry. I'm a professional, not a ladykiller. You're more than a pretty face, after all, in spite of what Tate says. Get yourself up on the men's ward first thing tomorrow and we'll give it a try. I'll speak to the consultant and the houseman myself.' He shook his head. 'No, don't fret about your lectures ... Lord! What on *earth* is all that?' He bent suddenly and pointed to the Harrods bag.

'Pawpaw.'

He laughed. 'Should've guessed! All right. Get it into Sister's fridge tonight.' He stood up, recovering his stethoscope. 'See you at eight tomorrow.'

He vanished as quickly as if he were Charlie Christophers, moving through the crowded tables with his coat flapping, and leaving behind him only a pile of dirty plates to show that the conversation had ever occurred.

Dazed, Rachel stared at the mess, and breathed a quick 'thankyou'. She hardly slept, waking earlier and even more groggy than the morning before. But, by eight, she was ready. Both Dr Dyer and Fr Jenks—looking exhausted, but pleased to be involved—met her outside the sister's office on the men's ward.

'I twisted the reverend's arm,' the senior registrar told her cheerfully. 'Might as well hedge our bets.'

The chaplain winced, but Dyer winked at her. Cheerfully he led the way to the sluice, where he told her to scrub up and have a mask ready to pull over her face. She felt bewildered by the apparent attention both men were giving her ideas. Suddenly they had become respectable, now that a senior doctor was involved. 'It's the nurses who won't like this deputation, you know,' he said to her as they crossed to King's bed. 'But I'll win 'em round.'

The chaplain shuffled behind them, now visibly uncomfortable as the same staff nurse who had sneered at Rachel came bustling along the ward, starched efficiency emanating from every inch, to block their path.

Her eyes went straight to the senior registrar's face. 'Mr Dyer—we weren't expecting—'

'Oh yes you were. It's all right, you know.'

The staff nurse hovered, barely nodding at the chaplain and openly glowering at Rachel. 'Very well.' Her eyes swerved back to Dyer. 'I suppose you're here for Mr King.'

'You know very well we're here for Mr King.' The senior registrar's voice was smooth and cool; Rachel felt relieved she had no battle to fight herself. 'I discussed the matter with Sister not fifteen minutes ago. I was given to understand she'd brief you right away... Now, you know Father Jenks, I'm sure? And Miss McEnroe—she's in my tutorial group. We're going to try a little magic here.'

Rachel shifted from foot to foot, suddenly panicking. It was all madness. To reduce the healing power that God had put into his creation to 'magic' was more than she could stomach. She caught the chaplain's eyes, but he flicked his eyes away from hers, embarrassed and silent, and she wondered would it have been better had she never approached him.

The registrar blithely ignored the interplay between those around him and instructed Rachel to curtain off King's bed. Drowsy, the patient opened his eyes, then shut them again.

'I want one of the other nurses in here for a few minutes, staff nurse. I'm sure you've got other things to get on with.' He gave the woman a withering glare over his glasses. 'Send in someone with fresh dressings, please... Ah, good morning, Mr King.'

Joseph King's eyelids opened halfway, focused, and opened wider. He muttered something incoherent. Rachel watched to see how Dr Dyer would deal with the man in a visit that was out of the ordinary. Then she quickly realized that King probably neither knew nor cared what day it was, and that to him everything in the hospital must seem rambling and disconnected. The only thing that would be real to him would be the insistent pain, the corrosive work of infection, and the shattering recall, every time he woke, that his wife no longer loved him. It would be a load too much for anyone to bear alone, and perhaps too much for someone to want to share with his children, either.

Pity overcame Rachel. Her impulse was to step forward and try to take his hand again, as she had tried at Christmas; but she made herself hang back, at the foot of the bed.

Dyer was more brusque. 'We're concerned that our efforts on your behalf have brought such slow progress, Mr King. We've tried just about every course of antibiotics in the drug cupboard, and your wound's not responding. Father Jenks has been coming in to see you, as well, I think?'

From behind the curling drip lines, King nodded slowly, grudgingly.

The chaplain went and sat on the edge of a chair on the far side of the bed. 'The doctor wants to start some new treatment.' He put one of his hands on the patient's arm; Rachel saw that it was trembling slightly. 'I'm going to pray with you now, as I've prayed before, but this time with my hands laid on you.'

King's mouth cracked open slightly. From the corner of it, he growled, 'Wasting yer bloody time, mate. Superstitious bloody nonsense.'

Dyer vouchsafed a tiny smile. 'That's the spirit—that's what you need, Mr King. A bit of fight left in the old body yet.'

King's eyes burned with indignation.

The chaplain seemed to have gathered strength. 'We want you to get well, Joseph. It would be better for everyone if you could work with us, not against us.' He shook his arm gently. 'Perhaps nothing I say to you will convince you, but I know you've got more to live for than you think. And I know a God who can work miracles large and small, and who wants you restored to wholeness.'

King sighed and shut his eyes. His expression seemed to say that he had heard it all before.

The chaplain went on, 'Your daughters were in here until nine the other night, talking to me after they'd been to see you. They love you.'

King's lips curled into a sneer.

Father Jenks sought Rachel's eyes for an instant before he turned back to the patient. 'Listen to me, Joseph. It doesn't matter if you have faith or not, if you believe that you can get well again or not— though it would help, as your good doctor here would tell you. We're here to tell you that *we* believe you have every chance of leading a full life again, and of being free from all the anguish you've suffered recently.' Then, resolutely disregarding the patient's indifference, he began to speak to God.

To Rachel's surprise, Dyer pulled off his stethoscope as if it were a hat, and bowed his head. Hastily doing the same, she held her breath.

No magic here, only our longing to see healing.

Afterwards the senior registrar removed the old dressings. For the first time, while King lay grimly passive under their hands, not even stirring when the dressings pulled away, she saw the festering wound. Her gall rose—both the sight and the smell of the pus and putrid mess of the wound sickened her. But she recovered quickly. She would see much worse before her training was complete.

A nurse swished away the curtain beside Rachel and stood near with clean dressings and a bowl of warm water. Quietly, Rachel smiled at her.

'Now you swab him down, will you, Miss McEnroe?'

Glancing at the nurse, she hesitated. It was not her job, and she had done nothing on the ward before except watch; she knew already how much hostility any small suggestion of interference could arouse. But it was Dr Dyer who was instructing her.

She pulled up her mask, swallowed hard, and made herself take the bowl from the nurse. She remembered simple procedures she had observed before on the ward, and tried to match the movements of her uncertain hands with those. Inside the surgical gloves, her palms began to sweat. The iodine solution ran in thin rivulets onto the sheets as she worked, and the man's skin felt so vulnerable that she could almost feel the pain herself.

At last she could see the ugly circular hole of the fistula. The patient had made no sound, and the wound looked as clean as she knew how to make it. With a few deft swipes Dyer finished the job, sliced open a pawpaw, and laid strips of it across the wound. He stepped back. 'Now dress this as usual, nurse.'

The nurse looked at them as if they were all insane. 'What, sir, with all that lot in there?'

The doctor's curt nod and the steel of his eyes over the mask told her not to question. 'Just get on with it, will you? I'll speak to Sister about the next round of dressings I want done.'

Rachel went to her day's lectures feeling light-headed and exhausted. In only half an hour she seemed to have lived a whole day. She went through the motions, pulling her mind back to the lecture whenever it wandered to the men's ward. She could find no legitimate excuse to return to the ward until the following week, at the usual time. She thought of asking Cecelia to find out for her how Joseph King was progressing, then rejected the idea; she had probably caused enough controversy already. *I have to leave it all in God's hands now, anyway.*

The day before the fifth clinical training morning, she found an abrupt note in her pigeonhole from Dr Tate. *Ms McEnroe: See me in my office before your round tomorrow, please.*

In all the excitement of the previous week, she had forgotten the weekly meeting with her tutor. No doubt this was a summons for a quick rebuke; she dismissed it from her mind until she was standing outside his door the next morning.

His face told her, the minute she entered the room and he swung to face her from his swivel chair, that he was angry.

'You went out of the proper channels and spoke directly to Mr Dyer about one of our patients. You shouldn't have done that. No, it doesn't matter if you're in his tutorial group for your clinical training. My students speak with *me* first, Ms McEnroe. You've gone out of court. And that's not all.'

Her fingers knotted together in dread, and she stood still with her heart quickening as he fixed her with a gimlet stare. 'Has Mr King— has he *died*?'

Tate rolled his eyes. 'I've had a complaint from the ward sister. The staff nurse reported that this wasn't the first time you'd interefered with that patient.'

'I have never—'

'Listen to me. Perhaps you did nothing more than comment the first time, but this is an old hospital, Miss McEnroe, and we have traditional ways of doing things. Even new treatments must be approached in the proper manner. You were out of line speaking to the senior registrar. No one can stop you saying anything you like to Father Jenks—he was just doing his job. You weren't. Pawpaw, my foot!' His mouth twisted. 'I'm taking you off the men's post-op ward as from today.'

Two thoughts assailed her at once: that he would take her off clinical training altogether, or that he would redirect her to obstetrics instead, as she had first hoped. But she knew it was courting disaster to offer any question or comment yet, so she remained silent.

'Well, I think you can join that clown Christophers and his other lunatic pals in casualty.' His voice was heavy with sarcasm. 'I know how enamoured you are of young "Dante", and he's as bad news down there as you've been upstairs. The change is effective this morning, Miss McEnroe. The registrar in casualty will be expecting you. I don't want you near the men's post-op ward again until you've finished your MB. Is that understood?'

'Yes, I understand.' Her voice came out clear and steady, stronger than she felt. 'But will you at least tell me about Mr King?'

Her tutor spun away from her on his chair. She waited, reopening the door, trembling.

'On your way, please.'

She knew she was pushing her luck. 'I just want to know—'

He wouldn't even give her the courtesy of turning round again. The voice that came to her across the room was reluctant, dry with irony. 'Well, perhaps it won't surprise you, though it certainly surprised *me*, to know the patient's being discharged at the end of this week.'

That means complete recovery. The unspoken words hung between them, and she knew how much the admission had cost him. 'Thank you for telling me.'

'Now get out.'

Washed with elation, relief, and amazement, she made her way to casualty, stopping only for a quick cup of coffee in the canteen.

In the staff rest area, other medical students were talking loudly, flourishing clipboards and flashing each other knowing smiles. She felt surrounded by an envelope of light and joy. *He's well! He's well!* Perhaps she was grinning foolishly to herself, for a few of them—those she knew only by sight—gave her cursory nods and odd looks. Then

Charlie Christophers came in, and the momentary discomfort vanished.

'Hello chaps! Registrar been in yet? What's on the menu this morning?'

'How should we know?'

'Wait and see what rolls through the door, mate.'

Christophers turned to Rachel. 'What brings you here, little one?'

She warmed to him afresh. 'Remember the pawpaw?'

'How could I forget?'

'It caused me a bit of what you call aggro. So I'll be here every week for now, I guess.'

He rubbed his hands together gleefully. 'Great stuff. Come on, let's get cracking.'

To start with, shadowing the registrar on call in the casualty department seemed similar to shadowing Dyer on the men's ward. All that was different was the speed of response, and she soon got used to the barked instructions of the house officers, and the way the nurses moved so economically to their tasks. Standing beside Charlie, she watched a broken leg reset, glass removed from a woman's hand, and a blistered child being packed in ice for the burns unit.

She was just feeling that she could adjust to the new surroundings when word came in that the air ambulance was bringing in a policeman. The place was galvanized into action.

'Victim of a gunfight,' their tutor explained as staff organized a gurney and began purposefully to set up a feed drip, plasma and blood lines. 'He's arriving with police outriders in estimated twenty minutes. We'll be doing an emergency thoracotomy—the poor man's losing blood internally. One lung's collapsed altogether. The air crew've got him on a ventilator already, but the prognosis isn't too hopeful.' His eyes passed over the row of students to see if they were following him. 'Believe it or not, we can safely leave many bullets in situ. There's a lot of blokes walking round London with all kinds of shrapnel in their bodies. But the air medics radioed in to say this was different. Blood everywhere. We can't leave it.'

He briefed several of them about what they were to be doing, then turned to Christophers. 'You, sir—I want you scrubbed up and following the admissions team when the patient arrives. And you... er, new one... McEnroe, is it? You can sort yourself out as well and go into theatre—see if that's hot enough for you.' His eyes narrowed. 'Not much damage you can do in there. Stay out of the way, and don't make a sound. Watch the video-thorascope, and see if after that you still want to get into obstetrics and gynecology! You'll see miracles done in there, I promise you.'

Tears stung behind Rachel's eyelids as she went in stumbling haste to the women's changing rooms and pulled on the traditional blue gown of theatre staff. In front of the mirror she stopped to check that her mask was ready; she saw herself through swimming eyes. But inside laughter bubbled up, too, *It doesn't matter what they think— Joseph King is well!*

The scrub room seemed fuller than she would have expected. Hospital staff she had never set eyes on helped each other with gown ties and held sterile gloves for each other. There was a strange air both of calm and excitement.

'It's something I often feel guilty about,' one of the junior doctors confided to her, seeing her standing alone on the edge of the group. 'Almost wanting there to be an emergency so that we can do our job.'

Behind her mask, she smiled at him. 'Thriving on adrenalin.'

'That must be it... Look, take that stool to the right of the doorway. You won't be in the way of the runner or any of the theatre staff if you stay there.' He assessed her coolly. 'You been in theatre before?'

'No.'

'Go out, then, if you think you'll faint.'

'I'll be all right.'

'That's what they all say.'

Fascinated, she watched as the unconscious policeman was wheeled into theatre, strapped on his good side to the table, draped and swabbed for the operation. No one hesitated, and few words were exchanged. Staff moved in a leisurely way, but with total concentration.

She watched the theatre sister's quick eyes: observant, missing nothing. She watched one monitor that showed the heart rhythm and marvelled at the other monitor that measured oxygen levels in the blood. Then, once the operation had begun in earnest, she watched the scope as the consultant probed the deflated lung, vacuumed out the extra blood, and located the bullet: an insidious metallic sheen in the light of the scope that shone inside the policeman's body, where no light had ever before shone.

Miracles, indeed!

At last the consultant withdrew the bullet and held it up triumphantly. Relief whispered around the theatre as he went on then to repair the damage, reinflate the lung, and sew up the two 'keyholes' through which he had performed the entire operation.

Renewed wonder overcame Rachel. How could she doubt that she belonged in the medical profession? Perhaps when she went into obstetrics she would never be doing anything as dramatic as removing bullets from women. *But*, she said to herself, *I too will be involved in saving lives—as well as helping new life into the world.*

Absently she watched the theatre runner make notes on the final moments of the operation. Then she heard a stir in the doorway that linked the sluice with the theatre—right beside her.

Everyone except the consultant looked up, and for a moment Rachel thought she must have stepped onto a movie set.

Three doctors standing beside me with pistols cocked.

She blinked and looked again. No, it was no trick of tired eyes. There they were in the blue masks and gowns of the hospital. Nothing to distinguish them except that they held weapons, and under the blue regalia their faces were strained, red, and stubbled with day-old beard growth. Anonymous hitmen, not medics. She could hear their loud breathing—healthy breathing, not like the whisper of the ventilator.

The safety catches went back. She remembered then, *Ah—an operation on a policeman.* Where was hospital security now? She looked frantically to her tutor for a cue, but everyone in the room had frozen. There was now no sound at all except for the hum of the monitors. The consultant raised his eyes and straightened his back. In a surreal and seemingly timeless moment, he just stared. Then Rachel saw him flinch, saw the cool surgical precision she had been witnessing for the past hour dissolve. The man was trembling, his abject terror showing even through the mask.

'What do you want?' His voice was cracked.

'What d'you think we want, doc?'

Silence again, except for the hum of the machines. Absurdly, Rachel thought of the comforting noises of the barn at home when her father was almost finished with the milking. In another world.

The consultant stepped back from the patient and pulled his mask down to his neck. His eyes and voice had steadied again. 'Just tell us what you want.'

One of the men moved the barrel of the gun infinitesimally. 'Back. All of you get back against that wall.'

Rachel found that she couldn't move. Her legs were as dead beneath her as the loose flaps of skin around the neat stitches of the operation. She seemed to see blood everywhere, splattered from her colleagues onto the wall.

'You too.' One of the men raised his gun and pointed it at the scrub nurse, who had hesitated by the table.

'I'm not stirring. This is our patient. You'll have to kill me first.' The nurse's voice was hysterical, falling over the edge of reason, yet far saner than the cold, stabbing voices of the gunmen.

'I don't give a damn about your patient. Get over on that wall. It's the keys to the cupboard out there that I want.'

The scrub nurse broke into sobs and fled to the wall. Still Rachel could not move, was not even sure they had seen her. Without making a sound she turned her head and searched with her eyes for a way through the door, past them, that would let her go through and raise the alarm.

But then something stopped her. She saw the ugly mess of the policeman's lung as she had seen it on the thorascope before the surgeon had done his work. Without the operation, without the speed of the casualty staff's reactions—the man would have died. The thin barriers of ribs and pleural muscles were no walls against bullets. This was no movie set where heroes jumped back from bullet wounds as if they were scratches. The room stank now of death, not hope.

'What keys? What the hell—?' The consultant's face turned white.

'Don't play stupid games. Move, one of you. We want to get in that cupboard now. Push the panic button, shout for help—any stupid tricks like that and we'll blow your brains onto that wall.' An arm suddenly clamped onto Rachel's. 'You! You're coming with us.'

One of the men held her so near that she could smell his stale, hot smell. The smell of anxiety, anger, and even fear.

'Give this woman the keys. Go on, I know one of you's got them.'

No one moved. Rachel felt the cold muzzle of the gun against her head. Everything flooded past her in a tidal tapestry of her life: the fields and trees of the farm, her parents and brothers, the steps of St Stephen's and the last sight of her grandfather, walking away from her, Joseph King and the pawpaw; and, at the end, dimly, Michael.

She closed her eyes and felt herself slumping, losing equilibrium.

Then there was a sudden movement, a jingle as keys were found, thrown across the room, and caught. She opened her eyes again and was wrenched through the door as the three men made a running retreat, dragging her with them.

So it's drugs they want, she told herself numbly. *But what will they do with*—? Even in her own head, she dared not frame the end of the question.

One of them thrust the keys into her hand. 'Here, you know what you're doing. Open up. Go on.'

She looked at the keys, befuddled. Of course she didn't know what she was doing. If the system was the same as on the men's ward, one key would be for controlled drugs—a double or triple locked cabinet; one would be for the main drug cupboard; another would be for the kitchen.

Afterwards she wasn't sure how she stopped her hands from shaking. The picture of the policeman's torn lung appeared and reappeared in her mind, stopping her from obeying any impulse to scream for help.

She rejected the largest key. 'That'll be the kitchen,' she heard herself murmuring, distracted.

'Hurry, goddamn it.' The man who had hold of her shook her arm so violently that she bit her tongue, and when he pulled his mask down his hot breath blazed across her face. His eyes were mad, his cheeks convulsed with blood. It was a face she would never forget.

Tasting her own blood, she tried the other keys, but the main door wouldn't budge. 'I can't—'

'Blow the lock away, you fool!' one of the others hissed over their shoulders.

'No! No shooting unless we have to. We don't want every siren in the place going off. Shift it, little lady.'

She rattled the key into the lock again. She told herself she would need to remember their voices, their faces, even the sickening smell of them. For later ... if there was a later ... when she would be able to help identify them ... if they were caught ... But there would be no later if she couldn't open the door. No later for any of them.

Then she flung the keys on the floor, suddenly, before she had thought further of what she was doing.

I cannot open those doors.

The men grew more impatient and pushed her down, grabbing the keys and trying the outside lock for themselves. She lay against a wall seeing their movements, hearing their laboured breathing and muttered curses through senses half shut down, as if from a great distance.

The first door swung open, then the second. One of them held her at gunpoint, and the others went in. She heard the record book crash to the floor, heard the shriek of metal severed from the wall, and the breaking of glass. Someone had opened the chained trolley as well as the cupboards and was sweeping boxes and bottles into bags in murderous haste.

Only drugs, after all, she thought wildly. *It's not the policeman they want.*

But then it came to her with penetrating clarity that if they took the contents of the cupboards it would be death if not to her, if not to her colleagues, then to someone else. Someone on the streets, who would be sold the drugs cut to something else, diluted, adulterated ... perhaps even poisoned.

That's what McEnroe has staked his life against, she told herself.

'To hell with the codeine,' one voice said. 'Go for the stuff in the controlled cupboard. Opiates, morphine—all the analgesics. Hell, *don't waste time*. Steve'll kill us if we blow a little job like this.'

I will remember it all, she said to herself, concentrating fiercely. *I must remember it all.*

And then McEnroe's weathered old face rose up again, lined with the silver of his thick hair.

She understood, suddenly, why the only hate he had ever felt or shown in his life was directed against men like these.

Part Four

Ring Around the Moon

SPRING 1993

19

Across the farm the crusted snowfalls of February receded, leaving moonscapes of crystalline grit, and ice protruding with accusing, beggarly fingers in the direction of the early March winds. Later they thawed, and Michael looked out onto a world scoured by winter: sere, and colourless, streaked only by mud. But he knew the mud was alive with seeds for the year to come.

Crocuses had burst through the drab earth in Maggie's little garden by the side of the house, and Michael made a point of passing them every day, to marvel at them. Then fresh snow fell: fluffy as egg white, with the temperature hovering around freezing. Thin mist came corkscrewing down the Cattaraugus Valley, and the dead trees dripped, froze, and dripped again. He expected the crocuses to die, but they poked bravely through the flakes: pools of wine purple and egg yolk yellow. Maggie, too, stood for minutes at a time at the side window, as if she were watching them grow, or somehow seeing the sap make its invisible rise in the two maple trees.

She said nothing, but Michael guessed what she was thinking, and what Don thought, also, when he had the leisure to stand beside her. They would be praying for Marianne in Boston, whose sap was not rising; who was now confined to bed, too weak and bewildered to walk, looking out over her own winter landscape where recognizable markers remained no longer, and where faces she did not know passed her like ghosts in a wasteland.

Don and Maggie said little about Marianne or McEnroe when they sat down to eat or went out to work in the barn or the fields, but he knew, all the same, that they thought of them constantly. McEnroe, they told him after returning from a flying visit to Boston, had for now cut back on his work to spend more time with his wife—even though she no longer knew him. Many times Michael remembered the late-night conversation with McEnroe and recalled the anguish in his voice, *She's under the wheels without ever knowing what hit her.*

Guessing what faced them, he did not want to contribute in any way to their stress; they had enough to deal with, he decided. So he made himself broach matters with Don late one March afternoon, walking in from the barn. The day's footsteps and tyretracks across the yard showed trails of frozen mud beneath the snow again, and the farm dogs sniffed eagerly where it had appeared. The season was beginning to turn. Soon he would be back to hosing down the yard again. April, or so Joel and Billy had assured him, usually brought the end of winter and a furious, hot spring before summer rolled in.

He felt his time on the farm was running out, and wanted to say so. 'I'm wondering—would it be better for you if I cleared off soon, now we know Larry's likely to be back by Easter?'

Don stopped abruptly. 'Are you *kidding*?'

'But I was thinking—when you've got so much happening—' One of Don's big hands grasped him by the arm. 'For pete's sake, you crazy man, that's precisely the problem. Don't say you've been headhunted by Grey?'

Michael laughed. At his heels, Wally stood bumping against him with a wagging tail.

'Listen, Larry's doctor says Easter, but how's a guy supposed to know if he'll be up to his usual chores when he gets back? I'll need you to help us make the transition.'

'If you're sure, then.'

'Dead cert. You don't know how great you've been.' Don winked. 'I'll write you a hot reference, Michael—but not till I'm good and ready, you hear?'

'But Joel's leaving school this summer.'

Don shrugged and strode on. 'Come on. There's a load of work between now and next summer. Then Joel'll be off to college. I can't count on him for a while yet. And anyway, there's more to all this than

329

meets the eye. As long as my mother's going downhill, Maggie and I want to be available to my folks if we can. I'm prepared to do what everyone says I never do—fly out there again at a moment's notice. My father can't do everything, and there's no other close family to help, either. I can't leave Tony by himself if Larry's not fit and the kids are still in school.' He trod up the back steps and flung off his boots. 'So you see, friend, I need you around here for as long as you can stay.'

Stepping behind him onto the porch, Michael spread his hands. 'You've talked me right into it.'

'Good. When I'm ready to throw you onto the street, you'll be the first to hear. For now, please don't even think of it.'

His heart lifting with relief, Michael followed Don through the office and into the kitchen. Coffee bubbled on the stove, but the room was otherwise quiet.

Don filled two mugs. 'I reckon Maggie's gone over to the store. Do me a favour and check the mailbox, would you? Tony'll be down in a minute. The Co-op printouts are due this morning.'

He went quickly out again, past the silos, to the end of the driveway. Yelping with excitement, Wally followed him again. Michael tousled the dog's ears and turned into the road.

The snowplow had knocked the mailbox askew. Wondering how the mailman could reach it through his car window, he yanked it back into place and wedged the pole with two large stones from the ditch. Then he opened the flap and pulled out the mail: a local advertiser, circulars from the parish church and the school, and a thick envelope postmarked 'Ithaca'—those would be the printouts Don wanted.

He turned back into the driveway and saw out of the corner of his eye a slender blue envelope flutter into the snow thawing at the edge of the track: a splash of colour along the dull margins of the road.

From Marie. He knew the handwriting immediately, though she had written to him only once—a bright Christmas card just before they'd made their New Year's journey. He stuffed the letter into his pocket and went on, faster now. The dog loped ahead of him, tail in the air.

Tony's boots were in the heap at the top of the steps; he was sitting with Don in the kitchen. Both men set down their coffee and reached up when they saw what he was holding. Michael poured himself a mug and joined them at the table. It was a familiar ritual now, when the computerized sheets arrived each month, about a week after the milk testing supervisor had made his rounds.

'Low somatic cell count on the whole herd,' Don said, turning first to the summaries at the back of the sheaf. 'That's good. No need to call the vet on that score, anyhow.'

Tony chortled. 'No need to call the vet on any score, by the look of those figures.'

Michael leaned across to see what sense he could make of the columns of numbers. 'RHA's up, isn't it?'

Don sounded pleased. 'Yup. Even the butterfat's up—unusual this time of year. Good news all round. The feed balance must be just right for a change.' He scratched his head. 'I'll go and check in a jiffy, but either of you guys remember exactly what concentrate they've been getting this month?' He glanced at Michael. 'Maybe I'm getting forgetful in my old age, but I sure don't.'

Tony shook his head. 'Just regular feednuts, ain't they?'

Michael pictured the maize silage and hay they spread in the double barn every evening, and the feednuts he measured into the hoppers of the automatic parlour feeder every morning. He remembered going to the feedmill on the night of the power cut: checking the labels of the bags in the uncertain light of the manager's torch. But that feed had been consumed long before, and Don himself had made the last few runs for feed. When he opened the bags each morning, he was usually too preoccupied to look closely at them.

'Wait a minute ...' Don was suddenly smiling smugly. 'I just recollected. It's our *own* feed mix we started them on after the last test. Agway bulked it for us—remember?' He pushed the papers away and sauntered out to his desk in the office. 'If I could just find the last report in all this junk ... it's coming back to me now. Yeah—butterfat was down the tubes last time. Four fifty, it says here. Useless for us ... ah ... no wonder the averages are back up.'

Now they knew the encouraging news, all Michael could do was think of escaping for a moment's privacy to read the letter. It troubled him, however, that so rare and thin a sign of Marie's friendship could bring back some of the longing he had felt at the end of December ... a feeling he had dismissed after that small-hours chat with McEnroe.

He got up. 'Excuse me. Be right back.'

The front hallway that ran parallel to the staircase was dim. He crossed it, looked back to make sure the men were well occupied, and slipped into the little-used parlour at the front of the house. He found some newspapers, spread them on the sofa, and sat down on them to open the letter.

She had written to him on college notepaper—perhaps in the middle of a boring lecture when she could think of nothing better to do. He found himself smiling as he unfolded the thin sheet.

Hi Michael!

Thought of you this week. One of my friends just started going with a guy who owns a small dairy herd up near Gloucester. (North Shore, in case you don't know.) She went up last weekend and helped him deliver a calf or two (if that's how you say it). She's hooked! Seems like wherever I turn these days, someone's talking about dairy farms!

He shut his eyes and sighed. Since the calvings had begun as scheduled just after the New Year, he had assisted Don and Tony at more calvings than he could now count. It still made him sweat with dismay, however, to think of the prize calf he had lost in November. And now here was Marie, writing to him about another farm, another farmer, another calf.

As if she cares!

He began to laugh at himself, then. He knew what to expect, after all. Vacuous gossip from the college, perhaps, or from the marina, all liberally sprinkled with exclamation marks.

Sure enough, there was some of both, a whole paragraph given to the delights of her growing friendship with the Galloways, Rita's new customers.

Steve and Julia invited me and a friend onto their launch a few weeks ago. Very mild day, all of a sudden. That can happen up on the shore here, though I don't suppose you poor people in the snowbelt will see much of it until April!

He could imagine her chuckling to herself as she wrote, the teasing curl of her lips as her pen moved across the paper.

We took a weekend and sailed round Cape Cod and over to Martha's Vineyard—it's an island, real pretty. They're fun people to be with! We ate and drank ourselves crazy, and the weather was divine. I could hardly get myself out of bed on Monday to get back to college. I think Steve must have made a killing on the stock market; they have money to burn.

Marie went into more details, then the tone of the letter changed. Michael read faster, finding the more compassionate side of Marie's personality between the lines.

You'll doubtless hear the lowdown from your employers, but the news isn't good from Mama's friends on the other side of town. The senator hasn't been over for weeks, and I heard Ma say Mrs McEnroe is very sick. The worst of it is, she said, Alzheimer's can draw the end out very slowly. Mrs M could go on for years. I feel sorry for them. Meanwhile Ma's been more tense than usual—with spring coming, I guess she's wondering if the investigative work McEnroe was doing, partly on her behalf, has gone onto someone else's caseload or been left hanging. If she knows, she isn't saying; and I don't like to ask, let me tell you!

In spite of this bad news, I can say that I've been real fine and hope you are too. Take care.

Marie

The signature was hastily scrawled. He folded the letter thoughtfully and replaced it in his pocket. Should he say anything to Don and Maggie about the letter? No. They would knew well enough what was going on in Bedford, and it wasn't long anyway since they had returned from an overnight visit to see Marianne.

Reopening the parlour door, he bumped straight into Don.

'Whoa! We were looking for you.' Don gave him a quizzical look.

'Just needed a minute to think about something,' Michael muttered, feeling his face redden slightly.

'Sure. Fine. But let's get outside again. Don't be surprised if there're at least another two calves in the pen by tonight. And I want you to look into something else for me.'

He forgot the letter almost immediately. Outside in the freshening pen Tony was already pulling a healthy calf from its dam, grinning broadly. 'Bull calf, Don.'

'Can't be bad.' Don turned back to Michael. 'We'll manage fine in here. Why don't you take a peek at the hay and oats fields. Take an auger and check the dirt. See how far down the frost's still clinging and how long you reckon before we can do the drilling. If it's clear, bring me down a sample and I'll analyze it properly.'

Michael hesitated. The soil in Kent was familiar; this was not.

Don waved one hand. 'Get on with it. Challenge for you.' He was grinning. 'Wouldn't ask you if I didn't think you could do it.' His mouth twisted. 'Or would you rather stick here and do the clean-up?'

Michael laughed and went back into the March wind. A few snowflakes whirled about in the air, but nothing settled now. He collected what he needed from the toolshed and went on with the wind behind his back.

Up on the hill he chose a spot randomly and began twisting the auger into the soil. The first few sun-warmed inches were easy, then it became harder to turn the handle; the soil was just frost-free, but still cold and heavy. The field was not yet quite ready for planting.

He retraced his way and examined the ground further down. Only in one place—right beside the track, where passing vehicles had exposed the earth to sun and sky—was the soil completely soft. But Don would have expected that, he told himself. No, March was too early to drill in this cold climate.

Don's shoulders shrugged dismissively when he reported his findings. 'That's what I was afraid of,' he said. 'Oh well—let's get on with these calves, now.'

Tony had gone for lunch, so Michael worked in the calf pens with Don. The newborn calves were allowed to suckle for a day, then hand-fed from a bottle of colostrum for two more days before being taught to bucket feed. Michael enjoyed feeding the calves, watching their silky tails wiggle and swish with delight; meeting their huge, liquid eyes over the bottle as they drank. It made him laugh, too, to teach the three-day-olds to drink from a bucket.

He bent now and eased his fingers into one calf's mouth. The calves were used to him, and he felt the strong pull of this one's tongue and ridged pallet on his fingers. 'You're sucking on nothing,' he told the calf. 'Worse than a baby's dummy.'

He edged the bucket forward with his boot until it was directly below the calf's head. Not too fast, or the calf would take fright and kick the milk all over the pen. Talking gently to it, he pulled his hand gradually downwards so that the calf's head came nearer to the bucket. The pressure on his fingers grew stronger as the calf smelled the cream. Then the animal got its first mouthful from the bucket. Michael held his fingers still until he thought it had worked out how to drink the milk, then cautiously withdrew them. The calf regarded him with surprise but went on drinking, seemingly amazed at its own accomplishment.

He chuckled again. Startled, the calf stopped, flung its head up, and sprayed milk all over Michael's overalls.

'Silly moo,' he said, and guided the calf's mouth back to the bucket.

When they had finished with the new calves, their next task was to rearrange the older animals; many of them had outgrown their first pens. Don culled the two-month bull calves and moved them to a large stall near the door of the barn. 'Don't want them to get too cosy. Usually take the first batch to veal auction the last week of March,' he explained.

They then separated the heifers who were ready to be weaned. Michael remembered the way the heifer pens for last year's heifers had been arranged: a few of the oldest by themselves in one pen, a few more in a second pen, and the latest born crowded together in a third—Don had kept them all inside until just after Michael's arrival in the autumn. And now it was time to set up the system for this year's calves: January calves in one pen, and February calves in another. They would stay in, away from late spring winds and summer flies and heat, until autumn came round again ... *fall*.

They closed the stall on the oldest heifers and for a moment stood watching them snuffling in the clean hay of their new, more spacious surroundings.

'Whoever says cats are curious?' Don laughed, resting his elbows on the side of the pen. 'All our cats ever seem to do is eat and sleep and reproduce. But willya look at this lot! Nosier than cats, any day. Curiouser than a bunch of old ladies.'

'Curiouser and curiouser,' Michael agreed.

Joel and Billy strolled in, their faces red from the wind, backpacks full of schoolbooks heavy on their shoulders. The barn was their usual port of call after the school bus had dawdled away.

'Still freezing out there, Dad,' Joel said. Usually the more friendly of the two, he nodded at Michael.

'I know it—quite literally! Michael tested the soil this morning.'

Don glanced at his watch. 'Is it really after three already?'

Billy went straight to the rearranged pens. 'Oh, you've done the spring sort on them, Dad.'

'Michael and I. It was time.'

'Guess it was.' Billy gave Michael a rare grin. 'You can always tell when spring's coming. Never mind the crocuses waking up or what the calendar says. When Dad divides the calves, it's almost spring.'

'Didn't know I was so predictable, Billy,' Don muttered. 'Gosh, I could use some coffee about now.'

Billy doffed his backpack and unzipped his parka. 'Any new ones today?'

'Right down there. Bull calf.' Michael pointed to the freshening pens. 'Lovely little fellow.'

Billy made the appropriate noises of approval, then went further into the barn to where some of the in-calf cows waited. 'Hey—Dad! C'mon over here.'

'Goodbye coffee,' Michael laughed, joining them.

'No, I'll get you all some,' Joel called.

'Good. I can't think where Tony's got to. Nearly milking, and here comes another calf.' Don tugged at the fencing that barricaded the pen. 'Let's get her moved into the freshening pen. No, not you, Billy. Your mother won't appreciate you getting filthy out here. Go change if you want to help.'

While Michael and Don manoeuvred the cow into the freshening pen, Billy raced off to the house. But it was Joel who came back, not Billy.

'Mom says Billy's gotta stay in and finish his homework.' He held out two mugs of coffee.

'What about you, son?'

Joel caught Michael's eye, embarrassed. 'Guess I'd better do the same.'

When they were on their own again, massaging and talking the cow through the calving, Don said, 'What d'you reckon on my boys and the farm?'

It sounded like an innocent enough question, and Don had not even raised his eyes from the cow's rump. But Michael felt he would be stepping onto thin ice if he answered. 'What d'you mean?'

'Well, Joel and Billy ... I think I begin to see why my father used to get so uptight sometimes. He wanted so much at one time for me to follow him into politics or law. Seems impossible now. So ambitious on my account, but it was the wrong kind of ambition for me, or I thought so. Used to tell him he hadn't a hope of understanding me until he came up here a few times and tasted the life we've got. Well, some days I understand *him* better now than I did.'

'You want Joel and Billy to come on after you.'

'It's what Maggie and I've always wanted.'

'And don't you think they will?' Michael recalled what Maggie had said on the subject. *They'll like nothing better than to take this farm when we retire—Billy especially.*

ELIZABETH GIBSON

'Always thought so. Now I'm not so sure. You know what you were saying this morning? Joel's almost through with school. He should be planning for tech now if he wants to take over here, after me. Once I was up to date and the old guys on farms round here—old man Wilkinson, old Grey, all of them—used to say I was ignorant and wet behind the ears. Now I'm one of the old stagers, and there's a new generation. Sometimes I'm as suspicious of the bright young upstart farmers as those old codgers used to be about me. But I don't want to turn into a cantankerous old so-and-so like Elias Grey, who can never learn a thing from the kids.' He flashed Michael a smile. 'You think you're learning a lot here, but I've learned a few things from you already, you know! Well, I'm looking forward to when Joel's a partner. Can't wait till he gets stuck in.' He sighed, adjusting his hands on the calf's ankles and beginning to pull again. 'But sometimes . . . I think he doesn't want to go to tech at all. So what d'you reckon?'

Michael's mouth felt dry. He wondered at how Don could carry on talking as if there were no calf trying to batter its way into the world. He ran his hands over and over the cow's sweating flanks. 'Billy's more interested, I think.'

'That's putting it mildly, and Billy's still got a couple years to go before he picks out a college course—let alone starts work. Joel should be making up his mind now.'

'He will.'

'Look at him just now. Straight back to the books. And it's not science or written work for 4H that he's rushing off to. Literature, French, humanities . . . he takes more after Maggie than me, I often think. Interested in people far more than animals. Sure, he's fine with animals, but you must have noticed how he is with people.'

'You think—'

'I reckon sometimes we've raised us another teacher in that boy, not a dirt farmer. And if you scratch me when I'm feeling *really* pessimistic, I'll tell you I'll end up waving both the boys off somewhere quite different—as my father did with me. And be left with two broken old farm workers and a farm decaying into the same sort of wreck it was when I took it on.' He shuddered.

'I doubt it.'

Don smiled again. 'For goshsakes, here I am pulling another strapping calf out, and talking like that!' He gritted his teeth and pulled again. The cow groaned, and the calf's body appeared. Another push, and the whole calf was out: wet and bewildered, but immediately raising its head and bawling for its mother.

Don stood up; Michael saw that he was shaking slightly. He wiped sweat off his forehead, leaving a smear of blood. 'Boy, am I bushed! Don't listen to me. This farm's thriving—you only have to look at the printouts again to know that. Don't know what I'm complaining about. Billy'll do a great job here, if Joel doesn't beat him to it. C'mon, let's get cleared up here and do the milking. Then I hope Maggie's made a huge pie.' He rubbed his rounded stomach. 'I'm ravenous.'

Michael, too, was hungry. His stomach growled as they did the milking, and his shoulders ached both from the work and from the continuing whiplash of the wind across the yard every time he crossed it. By the time they had eaten supper, he was exhausted; nothing, he thought, would keep him awake.

But sleep was slow in coming. Words from Marie's letter turned and twisted in his mind, strangely interwoven with images of the day. He fell into a kind of half-sleep, dreaming of Don with his forehead smeared by blood, and of Marie dancing with him. Then, in the bizarre way of dreams, Marie metamorphosed into Rachel: not the Rachel he had met in the autumn, but a different Rachel whom he had somehow met at a parish dance. Then a Rachel who moved away from him in the dream until she was smaller and smaller, a mere dot on the horizon of a windy farm landscape, out of reach, and as cold as he was.

He woke to find that he had tumbled the bedclothes onto the floor. He sat up in the dark to retrieve them. The bedroom was bitter. Outside the house he could hear the wind of his dreams blowing through the real world, still tearing at the roof and the trees; there would be more snow in the morning if it died down. Over the wind he heard another sound, fainter, and more familiar: the upstairs telephone ringing. Then silence except for the wind. Someone had answered it, and the digital clock by the bed told him it was only 11.45 anyway.

Burrowing back under the covers, he fell asleep immediately and deeply. No dreams this time... or none he could remember. For the second time, however, he woke to the chill of the bedroom. This time, the door was slowly opening, and the light in the passage beyond showed Don's outline in the doorway: a big man in pyjamas, his hair tangled with tiredness.

'Michael?'

He sat up instantly, his heart crushing inside his chest as the blood rushed upwards. 'What—what's the matter?'

Don hesitated in the doorway, his face hidden by the darkness of the room and the glare of the light outside it. 'Sorry to wake you.'

'No—but what's wrong?' His lips felt dry and cracked. He licked them, trying hard to focus on what Don was saying.

'I don't want to wake the boys unnecessarily. It's you I need.' Don's whisper was strained. 'Something's come up pretty urgent back in Boston, and Maggie and I gotta get over there again, and now.'

Michael shivered, swung his feet to the floor, and pulled a dressing gown round his shoulders. 'Just tell me what you want me to do.'

'That's what I like to hear. First—turn on that light, willya? I haven't a lot of time.'

Michael snapped on the bedside light. Don came and sat on a blanket box at the foot of the bed, his face drained of colour, his greying hair showing signs of silver in the indirect light. Michael expected him to launch into a list of instructions, and mentally prepared himself to absorb as much as possible. 'Shall I get a pencil?'

Don's head came up sharply. 'If you think you need to. Now listen. My mother's dying, Michael. Not the Alzheimer's... no one goes down too fast with that nightmare. No—my father called a half hour ago. Seems my mother's picked up a massive infection in her lungs, and because she hasn't wanted to move around much recently, she's filling up with fluid faster than the antibiotics can get to her. They've put her in the hospital on a ventilator, but it's only a matter of time. That false alarm was nothing; this is the real thing now, I'm afraid.' His head dropped, and Michael saw the big hands twisting in distress in his lap.

'You'll all be flying out to Boston?'

'Just Maggie and I. We're not taking the boys out of school for a wake—that's what it'll be. Not this time of semester, anyhow. I've been on the phone to the airlines for the last half hour. Maggie's throwing a few things into suitcases. We wanna get out of here as fast as we can.'

Michael nodded. 'Of course. Would you like me to take you to the airport?'

'Yes. Not Buffalo, though. No flights out of Buffalo to anywhere this hour of the night. We found a flight out of Toronto, instead. I want you to get us on the flight. Then I want you to come back, talk to Tony over the morning milking, and set up some kind of a rota between yourselves and the boys in their out of school hours. You'll be busy as heck.' He smiled a wan smile. 'Think you'll manage? I reckon you'll do great.'

'Thanks.'

'Tony knows what's what. So do you, matter of fact. Just keep the routine going, and keep an eye on the charts so you know what's coming next. We'll leave you our number so you can phone the house in Bedford if you get desperate—but try not to.'

Don's normal good humour had returned, and Michael found the courage to murmur, 'I'm sad to hear this about your mother. She's such—'

Don held up his hand. 'You don't need to say anything. I'm sad beyond saying, but we've been expecting something like this. It's curious... I've never been close to her the way I am to my father. Maybe that sounds harsh, Michael, to you.'

Thinking of his own parents, Michael shook his head. 'I understand very well.'

Don's voice changed abruptly again, in a way Michael recognized was as typical of him as it was of McEnroe. 'Oh, and that's the other thing I want you to do when you get back from Toronto—phone Rachel. *She's* the one who'll miss my mother.' He sighed. 'Heavens, I wish she were here now, already. She always loved her grandparents in a special way. And, boy, do I miss her sometimes.'

Michael looked directly into the other man's face. 'Don't you think—I mean, wouldn't it be better if you rang Rachel from Boston, yourself? Or if your wife rang her?'

Don's mouth curled at the corners. 'Probably would be, but I've no idea what we'll find by the time we get to Boston. Whether we'll be at the house, or at the hospital, or in some hospice, or something. A lot can happen in six hours. Best if she hears from another person, I think.'

Michael thought of Rachel's soft features, the deep blue eyes and long eyelashes, the way she was watchful, noticing pain and doubt in others. He had almost forgotten her face until now, except in the dream he had dreamed only a few minutes before. He knew she would be very shaken by the news he was being asked to give her. 'I'm not sure—'

'Listen, there's no way I'd call her now. London's five hours ahead, and she'll be fast asleep. The switchboard in the hospital'll send the call all round the building, and Maggie tells me the students don't even have phones in their rooms. It would be scary for her to get a knock on the door in the middle of the night from some janitor or porter. And come to think of it, we haven't heard from Rachel in quite a while... it's not as if I even know what *her* situation is, for pete's sake. Come on, I'll give you the number. All I'm asking is you call her first thing tomorrow—right after the milking, if you like. It'll be late morning by then, and she'll have a choice of flights out. I'm counting on you.'

Michael felt as if he were several paces behind Don, and he suddenly realized where the talk had been leading. 'Oh—you don't just want me to break the news; you want me to get her to fly *home*?'

'I want her in *Boston*. It's where she'd want to be. Not the same with her brothers, you understand. I need them here with you, anyhow.' Don stood up, his face hardening again. 'Now, did you get all that? I trust you completely. I know you and Tony'll manage things the way I would. At the very least you gotta trust *my* judgment in this matter.

And my judgment is that you'll do very nicely, thank you, while we're away. You've known this might happen. Lord, we even talked of it today. So get up, Michael, and get on with it.'

Michael said nothing, and the door closed behind Don. He dressed fast, his hands shaking slightly as he pulled a sweater over his head and pushed his legs into jeans. The digital clock now told him it was 00.35.

He searched for his passport—he would need it to cross the border into Canada then back into America—and pushed it into the back pocket of his jeans. He felt alert now, in spite of the lost sleep, and ready to cope with almost anything.

The highways between Arcade and Buffalo were empty. Don insisted on driving to the airport. 'You'll have your fill of driving on the way back,' he commented laconically. 'And I'm going to feel like a hen in a coop on that plane, so I may's well drive now. You sleep your beauty sleep in the back seat.'

But Michael was too wide awake now.

There were no delays, either, on the wide stretches of the Queen Elizabeth Way in Ontario. He watched the industrial units along the canalside and the roadside flash by. He read the lighted billboards and absently took in the flashing on-again-off-again lights of motels and highrise hotels. Sitting in the front seat of the car, Maggie and Don murmured to each other, while he let his mind float free, pondering the strangeness of being in a North American country that also bore marks of the British Commonwealth. A polyglot place, another place to mark on the map of *visits I have made*; another place to feel he did not quite belong in. Their journey seemed unreal, as if at any moment he would wake and find he had dreamed it.

He thought of Rachel asleep in London. He had passed St Stephen's a few times and could picture well enough its granite entrance steps, its facade of grey stone and grimy Victorian architecture rising half a dozen storeys near the Thames Embankment. She was asleep in some wing of those buildings, nearer to his family than he was, yet perhaps, like himself, belonging more in that strange place than at home.

He thought again of the anguished surprise she would feel when he telephoned in the morning, and of what he could say to her. He thought of his dream of her, and of how important she was to everyone he knew in the country that now seemed to be adopting him; she was important to the McEnroes, and even to the Williams.

Important to God, too, he reminded himself—*as Marianne McEnroe is.* Then he prayed for Marianne, narrowing his eyes against the glare of the artificial lighting.

Before he knew it, they were drawing up in front of the departures terminal of Toronto Airport. For a moment he thought what it would be like to catch a plane to England and arrive on his parents' doorstep without warning.

But he knew he was far more at home in Arcade, and that for all Don's bluffness, he was more welcome on the farm than he would ever be again at home—at least as long as his brother Ian was in the picture. Ian might be the prodigal son, but it was he, the older brother, who had had to go away to find his life.

He waved Don and Maggie through the passport control and went back to the car. On the long loneliness of the road home, he tuned the car radio to a station in Rochester, New York—nearer to him than Rochester, Kent, and less foreign now—and let the music flow over him as he covered the miles back to Arcade.

He would have only an hour-and-a-half to sleep again before he rose to do the morning's milking. But when that was over, he would take the phone number Maggie had given him and ring Rachel.

He dreaded telling her the news about her grandmother. Suddenly, however, he wanted very much to hear her voice.

2 0

Cecelia was already elbow-deep in toast crumbs and smears of marmalade when Rachel found her in the canteen. The skin under her eyes was shadowed violet with lack of sleep. 'Just got up?' She sounded envious.

'Yes.' Rachel set her tray beside the other woman's and moved some empty plates left by earlier medics. 'You just came off the ward, I guess?'

Cecelia took another bite of toast and didn't look up from her plate. 'Worse luck!' She was scowling. 'Quiet enough night, but it always seems to last for ever.'

'Days can seem just as long, you know.'

Cecelia looked over the rim of her coffee, blowing on it. 'You can't forget that raid, can you?'

'I want to.' Rachel smiled then, and stretched. 'But I feel great today.' She stopped to cough. 'Spring's coming. Have you noticed in the ambulatory?'

Cecelia shrugged and wiped the steam off her glasses. 'Can't say I have. Lend me some matches to prop the old eyes open, and maybe I'll have a look on the way to the nurses' home and a few hours' sleep, if I'm lucky.' She frowned. 'And, Rachel, you really ought to see a doctor about that cold.'

Rachel laughed. 'Don't you fret! I know exactly what I have. It's viral, and no prescription's going to shift it. Just give me some time off and some country air, and it'll go.'

'And how do you propose to find that?'

'Soon be Easter.'

Cecelia's face cracked into a broad smile. 'Ah, so it will, and

Shannon here I come! Two whole weeks out of this place! But, wait a minute... where are *you* going, Miss McEnroe?'

'Don't know yet, but somewhere.' She waved her hands in the air. 'I can feel it in my bones. *Somewhere.*'

Cecelia pulled a face. 'I'd love to hear your tutor's comments on the medical accuracy of that observation! Not back to Kent to see the handsome young Monaghan, is it?'

For a moment, Rachel pictured Michael, and her insides somersaulted. 'Oh—you mean Ian?' She laughed. 'No way! But I was thinking this morning I just have to get out somewhere.'

Through a mouthful of toast, Cecelia grinned impishly. 'I heard Crock Basden say he was taking a cheap flight back to Sydney for his brother's wedding on Easter Saturday. If you want sunshine and cuddles with koalas and other good-looking hot-blooded Aussies, maybe you should go with *him*.'

'No thanks. I'll pass. If I want sunshine and countryside badly enough to catch a plane anyplace, I'll catch it straight to Boston or Buffalo.'

'Sunshine in Buffalo?' Cecelia jeered. 'You said even Niagara freezes over some years until March!... So what about Charlie Christophers? I'll bet he's dying to take you home and introduce you to mama and papa and his collection of Dante etchings. Why don't you take a lift in his MG and see what's up the other end of his little country lane?'

'Cecelia, you're disgusting. And Dante's as fickle as the weather this time of year.'

'You're just too choosy for your own good. I thought you said Dante reminded you of Michael Monaghan?'

'No. For the first ten minutes, maybe. I know what I want, that's all.' Rachel listened to her own words. There was an atavistic echo somewhere in them. *I know what I want, that's all.* But she didn't know where it had come from. Perhaps it was what her mother had said all those years ago, when she was waiting (as she had put it) for her father to realize who and where she was, and that she had a love worth giving him, a love that would keep.

She looked away from Cecelia. It was foolish to think of Michael in those terms. She had known him only two days; she had no way of knowing if she would ever see him again; no assurance that she would meet him in England *or* at home again.

'You've gone horribly quiet,' Cecelia teased.

Rachel took a long drink of coffee and shook her head. 'Just thinking you're right. I have to make a plan for the vacation, or it'll be gone like the Christmas break with nothing to show for it.'

'Or else you'll crack your head in the library or the journals room for two weeks, instead of resting.'

'No.'

'Good girl. Well, Rach—I've got to get some sleep. I'll see you soon.' And with that Cecelia was gone.

Basden and Christophers found her still hunched over her coffee, musing about the holiday, a few minutes later. Both men wore ties askew and had not picked up combs before coming downstairs.

'You look full of life,' she told them.

'Well you certainly do, too.'

Rachel's mouth twisted slightly. 'It's the rare pleasure of seeing you over the breakfast table.'

'She's hallucinating. Give her some Largactil, quick.'

'In fact I'm looking forward to the lecture this morning.'

Christophers smacked his lips. 'Me too. Best course here. Women, women, and more women.'

Basden caught Rachel's eye. 'He's definitely in the acute phase, wouldn't you say?'

'Definitely.'

'Seriously, Rach—' Basden's usually deadpan face was for once full of genuine concern. 'You still don't look right this morning. What's up?'

Unconsciously, noticing again his tousled hair, her hand went up to her own, smoothing it down against her neck. 'Don't look right? You mean I'm not sneezing everywhere and looking as if I'm dying of the common cold—for a change?'

'No, no. You look brighter. That's good. But you look as if you're uptight inside, again. Are you?'

Her eyes began to water. Sympathy was sometimes worse than loneliness, and after the raid the Australian had been one of the few medics who had spared her any time to listen. 'Thanks, Crock. I'm OK, really I am. Much better today.'

'I told you when we talked about it before that you can cry on this shoulder any time you want.'

His persistence embarrassed her, especially with Christophers looking on. 'I'm fine. I feel much better, like I said. It's spring, and we've got a vacation.' She wanted to lighten the talk. 'Anyway, you're off to the Antipodes in a few days.'

Christophers leaned over the table and pinched her cheek. 'Leaving *me* to pick up the delicious pieces. Ha!'

She wouldn't meet Christophers' leering eyes and silly smile. She sat back and excluded him by fixing her eyes solely on the Australian. 'You'll be a great shrink one day, Dr B. But you don't need to practise on me any more. As soon as the vacation starts I'm going to sit down and write a long letter to my grandfather and get it all off my chest. That'll be better than talking to a thousand psychiatrists.'

'Your grandfather? Strange girl!'

'You don't know my grandfather. Wise as Solomon.'

Christophers sniggered. 'And old as the hills.'

'Anyway,' Basden's voice was still gentle, 'what would he know about drug Mafia and guns levelled at his head, Rach?'

She stared at the crumbs on the table, her eyebrows curving upwards. 'More than you might expect.'

The men exchanged glances, took a cue from her earnest reply, shrugged, and moved off.

She sat alone a few minutes longer, then gathered up the dirty dishes before returning across the courtyard to the ground floor theatre where the obstetrics and gynecology lectures were given.

The spring light of the courtyard did not follow her into the lecture theatre, which was as usual drafty and cool. She shivered as she sat down in her place, slipped out of her jacket, and pulled filepaper out of her bag. Then she looked around. No one else had arrived—not even Charlie Christophers.

Her throat was tickling again, and she began to cough.

'Hey! That's no good, Rach.' Later than usual for his favourite course, Christophers slid into the seat beside her. 'Listen, I'm sorry if I offended you just now.'

She was so surprised that she had to bite back a sharp reply. She had never seen him so serious.

'You guys have to stop fretting about me.'

Christophers produced an envelope and pushed it over the lecture desk towards her. 'For you.'

Now she was even more startled. 'You don't need to bring on the flowers or the violins or the greetings cards just because I've had a tough few weeks, Dante.'

'No, no. That's nothing to do with me. From one of the porters. He caught me in the lobby just now and asked if I'd cross paths with you this morning. Said there was an urgent message.'

Puzzled, she tore the envelope across. Notes from the porter were always written in misspelled capital letters, and this was no exception.

PHONE MESAGE FROM M MONERHAN, USA.
CALL IMMEDIATLEY.

She felt the blood drain out of her face.

'What is it?' Charlie peered over her shoulder.

'Call from home.' She pushed her notebooks back into her bag and stood up.

Around them, other students were shuffling into their seats. The lecturer came to the podium and cleared her throat.

Christophers seemed to feel that he had to make at least a feeble attempt at a joke. 'RM phone home!' He caught the sleeve of her jacket as she pushed her arm into it. 'D'you want someone with you? You look dreadful.' His face was uneasy, as if he hoped she'd say 'no'.

'No. Just can't figure out why Michael—excuse me.'

She fled out of the courtyard doors, through the back entrance of the main building, and along the now familiar corridors to the reception area at the front of the main building. Visitors were queueing at the desk for information about visiting hours, and the porters look harried, irritated about being disturbed from the tabloid press. The switchboard was lit up, Rachel thought, like the fourth of July.

Breathing quickly, coughing again, she waited her turn.

The porters always called the students 'doctor', whether they had qualified or not, once their faces had become familiar. 'Dr McEnroe?' one of them said at last.

Wordlessly, she waved the notepaper under his nose.

'Right. You got the message.'

'Yes. Was that all?' She pushed the paper back to him.

'That was it.'

'Then I need a phone right away.'

'You know where the payphone is, doctor.' He gave her a sly smile.

'I can't phone the US from a payphone. You'll have to let me use one of the office phones.'

Grumbling, he pointed her to the first office in the administration wing. 'Try your charms in there—if you're lucky. It'll cost you a bomb at this hour.'

Not caring what he thought of her, she bolted straight down the corridor. *Michael called me. What's he want? Why didn't Mom call me?*

Over the soft hiss of satellite or underground cable, the ring of the farmhouse phone sounded alien and far more distant than four thousand miles. She had grown used now to the brighter, quicker ringing tones of British phones; this sounded lazy, sleepy by comparison.

She waited impatiently, trying to picture the circumstances at home. The phone would be ringing downstairs in her father's office; it would be ringing in the barn, too—if her father had remembered to repair the wires; and it would be ringing in her parents' bedroom. But at this time of day—and she checked her watch . . . no one would be up except whoever was to do the milking. The call would wake her mother.

Whatever, it was something important.

At last the ringing ended, and Michael's voice came uncertainly on the line. Had he been asleep, too? 'McEnroes,' he said, after a pause.

She wanted to laugh. In fact he sounded almost as laconic as her father. She felt hysterical, as if anything would tip her over the edge into mad laughter. 'It's me. It's Rachel. I just got your message. I couldn't think—'

He started to answer her, but his words were lost in the cross-Atlantic echo and in the sound of milking machines pumping in the background. '...to call. There's something he thought you should know.'

This time she held her breath, wanting to hear everything, and he went on. 'Your grandfather called around midnight. Your parents've taken a flight to Boston. Rachel, I don't know how to tell you this.'

It was all she could do, hearing his warm voice, and by now completely possessed with anxiety, not to shout passionately at him, *Just tell me!*

'Your grandmother's very ill. Your father wants you to catch a plane if you can.'

Crackling silence followed, except for the ticking and pulsing of the milking units. She shut her eyes and stood in the barn with him. She had never before felt more homesick.

He was waiting for her to say something.

She opened her eyes again and returned to the curious gaze of the administrator whose phone she had commandeered. 'Pa wants me to fly across today? Is it that serious, Michael?' *Of course it's that serious. He wouldn't be phoning me at five a.m. his time if it wasn't serious.*

'Your grandmother's dying.' *Dying. Dying.* The word echoed down the line.

She felt numb. Denial. It was always the first response. 'But—'

'It's a terrible chest infection,' he said. 'They don't know if she'll last more than a couple of days. He was hoping very much you could fly straight over.'

She felt dizzy with the suddenness of it all. 'Of course I'll come. I won't call you back. Just tell them I'll be on the first flight I can find.'

He did not answer her immediately, but when he did his voice was full of unexpected tenderness. 'Be careful, Rachel. You don't sound well, yourself.'

'I'm fine.' She wanted to stop the snapping sound of her voice. How could she react to him in this way? But she was tired of everyone's over-concern. And he would know nothing about what had happened the month before.

He went on as if she hadn't replied. 'It's good to hear your voice.'

She melted then, but could not give herself away. 'Thanks.' Then she snatched at the first thought that whirled through her mind, wanting to make amends for her own abruptness. 'You sound like you're one of the family, Michael.'

He laughed hollowly, and she heard again the note of defensiveness that she understood now must be traceable to his own family. 'Not exactly.'

'But Pa's left you in charge, I guess?'

'With Tony.'

Warmth beat up in her, and she said the words before she could stop herself. 'Well I'm glad he's got you.' Then she was ashamed of herself, ashamed of the rush of longing and hope that flooded into her—now, now, when her grandmother was dying.

'I'll pray for you,' he said.

'Pray for my grandmother.'

'I'm already doing that.'

'Pray for a miracle.' She felt the tears rising, and heard the catch in her own voice, but she tried to choke them back. *This is a transatlantic call.*

'I'll do that.'

'You said you believe in miracles.' It was almost an accusation. She recalled their conversation on his first day at the farm. He had talked easily: *the God who does miracles in drastic circumstances ... miracles ...* The word conjured up as well the registrar's words on the morning of her first day in casualty, on the morning of the raid—*You'll see miracles done in there, I promise you.* Some miracle!

But Michael sounded confident. 'Yes. Well, perhaps there could be a small practical miracle in that you're near Kent. I know my father would be glad to get you to the airport, help with the ticket fare—do anything.'

The sting of her uncomfortable days in Wealdhurst came back for an instant. 'What, at this time of day when he's out at work? Thanks, but I'll get there quicker from here by myself.'

There. She had ruined everything again by her sharpness.

Yet again he seemed undeterred. 'You'll know what's best. I'd better go now.' But he waited again.

There was so much she wanted to say, but she did not know how to say any of it. *I wish I could see you while I'm back home.* No, impossible. *Will you still be there after Easter?* No, it wouldn't matter if he were there or not, because she'd be coming straight back to London to get on with her course. She could take no holiday after the wake... *Or could I?* For a moment the thought of going home to the farm for a few days exerted a magnetic pull. *But if I do, I may never come back here.*

Lamely, she said goodbye to him and replaced the phone in its cradle. With the inquisitive eyes of the clerk still on her face, she felt desolate again.

It wasn't until she was on a plane at last—at about three in the afternoon—that she had time to think properly about what she was doing. The day seemed interminable. As the aircraft lifted through a few lambswool clouds into the pouring honey of higher sunshine, she lay back in her seat, shut her eyes, and relived it all: from the moment of waking, to the desperate conviction that she had to get out of London one way or another, to the crazy bantering with Basden and Christophers... to the phonecall to Michael, and then the frantic calls for flights and the scrambled journey to Heathrow. It was not a day she would forget quickly.

Was it possible, she wondered, that there could be any kind of miracle for her grandmother the way there had been a small miracle for Joseph King?

The flight offered the first real opportunity for prayer, and when she woke later, with a meal being served on a tray in front of her, she realized she must have fallen asleep in the middle of her prayers.

It occurred to her as the plane dipped over Boston Harbor and taxied up the runway of Logan Airport that she had no idea who would be meeting her inside the terminal. For a wild moment, her brain befuddled by exhaustion, she hoped it would be Michael. Then, looking out at the ridges of grey snow pushed aside by the successive ploughings of winter, and realizing with a shock how far behind England's was the American spring, she remembered that he was five hundred miles away on the farm; only her parents had come to Boston. McEnroe himself wouldn't meet her, either, she thought with a pang.

Coming out of the customs hall, her head feeling light, she scanned the crowds for her father's bulky height. She adjusted her suitcase on the baggage carrier and stood still, now searching for her mother.

Neither of them had arrived, so she pushed the cart to one side and waited, head bent, leaning on it.

Someone tapped her on the shoulder. 'Rachel?'

Her heart leaping with both excitement and fear, she whirled round.

'Marie! Marie Williams! What the heck?' The weight of dread rolled off her like a tombstone. It would be so much easier at first to talk with Marie than with Don or Maggie.

'Let me get that cart for you.' Marie grabbed the trolley and began to steer expertly through the crowds. 'You're shattered. Anyone can see that. C'mon, I'll drive you over to Bedford as quick as I can.'

Rachel stumbled after her. The plane had dehydrated her, and she began to cough again. 'I don't understand.'

'Sure you do. Your mother called our house to see if anyone could meet you. Your parents went to the hospital with your grandfather.'

Rachel leaned forward and grasped Marie's sleeve. 'Wait—is GraMar still alive?'

Marie stopped. Her dark eyes showed none of their usual sparkle: only kindness and concern. 'Yes. She was when they called. I think you'll make it in time.' More slowly now, she manoeuvred the trolley through the crowds again, this time keeping abreast of Rachel. 'I was thinking you'd want to go straight to Bedford. But maybe—'

'Thanks, yes. Please let's get to the hospital.'

'But you look terrible.'

'Thanks. Jetlag. I'll get over it.'

'You sure you're not too tired.'

'Marie, I'm tired as a body could be. But I want to see GraMar before she's gone, that's all. If you can get me there, I'll owe you a lot.'

Marie waved a dismissive hand, 'I was glad when your mother called. Least I can do was pick you up and get you wherever you wanted to be.'

Rachel gave herself up to the easy option of letting Marie take charge. She felt bewildered by the loud American voices all around her. Things seemed bigger, brighter, noisier than in England; she had forgotten.

She thought of the last time she had flown into Boston, and of McEnroe and GraMar meeting her off the flight. In only a fall and a winter everything had changed.

On the way past the shipyard and through the tunnel, she closed her eyes and tried to sleep again, but her brain was seething. Although Marie seemed to understand her need for quiet, and said nothing to her for the first ten minutes, there was no hope of rest. Rachel couldn't believe that she was the same woman who had woken peacefully in a London hospital that morning, now driving to a Boston hospital late in the American afternoon, full of anguish.

Resigned to wakefulness, she reopened her eyes with a shock of recognition. Boston in late March looked like London in February: bleak, frozen—even foggy.

'I'd forgotten.'

'Forgotten what?' Marie glanced across the front seat with a faint smile.

'How cold it is in this city in March.'

'Oh, we've still got icicles on our front porch,' Marie assured her airily.

'Not surprised.'

'At least six feet of snow this winter. Started out quite mild, then once it fell in any quantity, it never seemed to let go. As you can see.' She waved her hand over the ugly scars of winter's end: the litter left where snow had melted, the grit that no rain had yet washed away.

Rachel sat up, almost able to smile for a moment. Her face felt frozen, not just with cold but with the tension of wondering what she would find in Marianne's hospital room. 'Worse than London, I have to admit . . . But I can't think why I'm going on about weather. Tell me— what else did Mom say about my grandmother? D'you know anything at all?' She heard the jagged edge of desperation in her own voice.

'I'm sorry, Rachel. I told you all I know. I had to leave right after your mother called, or I would have been late, as it was.'

'Oh, well.'

Marie was biting her lip as she drove. 'Wish I could tell you more. I do know your grandfather's been very upset. My mother told me just this morning he's handed all his work to one of his aides. He's been by your grandmother night and day since they took her in.'

Rachel nodded slowly. 'He would.' She stared out of the window at the traffic. Ahead of them, a pall of fog rose steadily from the Charles River, and car exhaust hovered in an evil grey cloud about a metre off the highway: trapped by the humidity. How much had changed since her grandmother's birthday lunch in June!

Marie seemed anxious to divert her from any more speculation. 'The roads're pretty slick, Rachel. D'you feel the car sliding a little?'

She answered dully, 'I hadn't noticed.'

'I gotta drive slower than you'd like me to. Sorry.'

'You can't help it.'

Marie changed tack again. 'I wrote to Michael just a few days ago. Don't know why, but I got to thinking about him.'

Rachel turned sharply in her seat and searched Marie's face. The other woman wouldn't know how she felt about Michael, and she certainly wouldn't reveal it now, not while her grandmother was dying. She said neutrally, 'Oh, how is he?'

'No idea.' Marie shrugged, and a gleam of her usual amusement with life showed itself.

'Come to think of it,' Rachel said slowly, 'I talked to him, myself, this morning.'

Marie's foot tapped the brake, and the car veered slightly towards the rotary they were approaching. 'Sorry... this morning?'

'Yeah—about a hundred years ago.'

'But why?'

'It was Michael who called me—from home. Said Dad and Mom were on a plane. They asked him to call me.' Her mouth cracked into an unaccustomed smile. 'I'd forgotten that, too.'

'Boy, you *are* tired. Never mind—look, we're nearly there.'

Through the fog Rachel saw the outline of a huge building she had never entered. It might have brought her miles nearer to home, but this hospital was far more forbidding—far less welcoming, even—than St Stephen's in London.

21

The concrete and glass walls of the hospital rose as straight and harsh as a gigantic war memorial through the fog. Rachel stood bareheaded and looked up at it, shivering.

Marie hesitated unhappily beside her. 'Listen, there's a twenty-minute limit here. I can't wait.'

'I know it. There's no reason to.' She forced a smile. 'I guess I'm on my own now.' Jetlag and bewildered grief drew her down; she hovered on the brink of tears. Not knowing exactly what she would find in the hospital made things worse.

'You're not on your own, Rachel,' Marie said gently, grasping her wrist. She gave her a hug. 'All your family's up there, and God knows what's best, whatever we think.'

Rachel stared at her dumbly. *Times are,* she thought, *when I have a very hard time believing that.*

Reopening the car door, Marie put one foot inside but paused again.

'I'll leave your baggage at your grandfather's home. Sure there's nothing you need out of it before I take off?'

'Nothing, thanks.' Rachel felt now as if she were wedged in thick cotton wool; the transatlantic flight had thickened her ears, and everything except the sharp, threatening walls of the hospital and the barb of sadness seemed distant.

Questions buzzed and hammered in her head as she signed for a visitor's pass from the front lobby and rode the elevator to the tenth floor. Outside, the fog actually hung below the top floors of the hospital; she could look out across its wads as she walked the long, straight corridors. Above it, watery March sunlight moving towards evening angled through the tinted windows and made the polished floors gleam under her reluctant feet. She thought of St Stephen's: of the dim, scuffed hallways of the London hospital, and was suddenly stabbed with an unexpected sense of loss. This hospital was newer, cleaner, brighter; but there was something deceitful about it, as if sterile cleanliness could hold death at bay, or make it somehow more palatable.

A few metres from the door that she knew would lead directly to her grandmother's bedside in intensive care, she stopped. Tears pushed out from behind her eyelids and ran, betraying her, down her cheeks. She struck them away. *No. I will not make it worse for her, or for the others.*

Taking a deep breath, she tried to tell herself that she was in St Stephen's, that at any moment Dr Dyer would step out of the room and beckon her in. *There's a patient I'd like you to see, Miss McEnroe. Alzheimer's, but not severe; and it's the pneumonia that's troubling her now, you know.* She could imagine his plummy voice quite clearly. *We've got her ventilated. She must have been a beautiful woman once...* And other words, irrelevant, and stupid, spiralled round her head, which he had spoken to her when they thought Joseph King was dying: *You've a pretty face...*

Cold comfort, all of it, now. And the only way she could persuade herself to walk into that room, even after so long a journey with that very goal in mind, was to tell herself that GraMar was just another patient, and to let the cold in her own head and lungs distance her further from the pain she knew she would feel as a granddaughter. Somehow, she had to be a professional—otherwise she would break down and only magnify the pain for everyone else.

She eased open the white door and paused on the threshold, trying to make sense of the small crowd around the bed. She saw her mother first—Maggie half-rising out of a chair beside her father, next to the glaring window. But Don took hold of her sleeve and was pulling her down again, nodding up at Rachel. 'Hush. Let the doctor finish, first.'

Then Rachel realized that one of the internists was also in the room: a woman with glossy black hair curling over her white coat at the back, bending over the bed and speaking to McEnroe at the same time. 'I'm afraid the respiratory failure is terminal, sir. Her PO2's falling despite 100 per cent oxygen, and her sats are down to 50 per cent.'

Understanding exactly what the woman was saying, Rachel winced. But McEnroe sat transfixed, seemed unable to speak, and certainly unaware yet that she had come into the room.

The ventilator pumped relentlessly. Still, Marianne's breathing was bubbling, full of fluid, and on the monitors the spikes and pulses were slowing down. Looking at the waves on the screens, Rachel felt as if someone had delivered a blow to the pit of her stomach. What use was it now to know how ventilators, EKGs and pulse oxymeters worked? It would be impossible, after all, to keep any semblance of professional detachment. *This is my grandmother, dying*.

'There's really nothing, doctor—?' Don's face was a mask of exhaustion and concern.

The internist shook her head. 'I've already explained, Senator. We've saturated your mother with antibiotics, and she's not responding on the IVs, either. The ventilator—well, you can hardly expect—'

'But will she surface again?'

At the directness of Don's question, McEnroe flinched and bit his lip. Rachel thought she had never seen him so distraught. Hadn't he heard the word 'terminal'?

The internist straightened her back and moved away from the bed. She noticed Rachel and smiled faintly: a kind face, but with a set mouth. 'You must be Rachel, from England. Your mother—'

'*Rachel, from England.' And am I, now?* 'Yes,' she said aloud, then babbled, 'I was worried I wouldn't make it in time. Today seems to have lasted forever.' But the words fell blankly in the heavy room.

Still McEnroe seemed not to have observed her arrival. 'My son asked if she'll surface again—please, please just tell us . . .'

Rachel caught the internist's dark eyes and wondered if she knew about her own training. 'Grandpa McEnroe . . .'

He registered her at last and held out his arms to her. She went into them blindly, not knowing if he was comforting her, or she him.

Brushing away fresh tears, she pulled away a moment later and went onto her knees beside his chair. She took his big, autocratic hands into her own and looked him straight in the eye, though her voice trembled as she spoke. 'The physician has no way of telling us if she'll be conscious again. But I'm sure you know she may be able to hear us. We gotta keep talking to her. We gotta keep talking positively.' She remembered Joseph King again. 'Miracles are real, McEnroe. Just pray—'

Maggie suddenly stood up and came to put her arms around them both.

'Rachel's right. Come on.'

Clumsily, Don reached to the bed and took his mother's hand. 'Mom—we're all here now.' He looked over his shoulder at the doctor. 'If you've finished,' he added gently, 'I think we'd like to be by ourselves now.'

'Of course. Yes.' The internist's eyes swept to the feedline; then she went out.

'I hate those damned machines,' McEnroe growled. His jaw was tight, and his eyes sparked fiercely. 'I'm sure Marianne hates them, too. Why does it have to be this way?'

'No, McEnroe. Without them she would have left us before I got home.'

His face seemed to collapse, and he shrugged wordlessly. He looked as if he had aged twenty years since she had said goodbye to him on the steps of St Stephen's.

Now all the squalling arguments about unplugging life support systems, or keeping them pulsing and pumping, pumping and pulsing remorselessly beside the beds of the dying, came home to roost in Rachel's heart. The impulse was to turn and disconnect the plugs, but she knew—as her grandfather would know also—what the legal penalties would be.

She hated the demand of death, but she hated even more the false demand of life that medicine imposed on her grandmother.

Still holding one of McEnroe's hands, she got off her knees and stooped beside Don to kiss Marianne's cheek. The familiar lemon perfume was gone, replaced by the vaguely antiseptic odour of the hospital bedding, and the heated, plastic smell of the tubes and feedlines.

Marianne lay motionless with eyes closed, only her head, shoulders and hands, palm up and still, showing above the white covers. Her bones seemed to be rising through her skin. She had shrunk into herself, almost unrecognizably, since Rachel had last seen her. Above the scallopped edge of her nightgown, Rachel saw blue hollows and the outline of her collar bones, as clearly as in her textbook diagrams, as clearly as in the St Stephen's morgue. She shut her eyes, then looked again. Only Marianne's face, serene except where it was distorted by the tube in her mouth, was unchanged: the porcelain smoothness of her skin, the delicate lines of laughter and hurt at the corners of her eyes, and the curling mass of her hair. It was the ventilator that made her look otherwise strange and different.

'If only she would wake and say something—anything,' McEnroe moaned.

'She can't, McEnroe—even if she wakes up for a bit.'

'Oh, Rachel, I'm so glad you're here, but I wish you could have seen her before.'

Rachel rallied. 'I have, McEnroe. I have. I won't forget what she looks like. *Looks* like, d'you hear?'

Silently, they sat in a tableau around the bed. Rachel let her mind float. She could not bear to think of what was to come, and what was behind her meant nothing to her now. All her hopes focused on her grandmother. If Joseph King could be healed, why not Marianne?

Later, Marianne's eyes moved suddenly under their translucent lids, and flickered open. They narrowed against the sunset brightness of the room, then adjusted and travelled from face to face around the bed.

'We're all here now,' Don repeated.

Rachel wanted to cry out in triumph. The blue eyes were quite undimmed, just full of surprise.

McEnroe fell on the edge of the bed and clumsily gathered

Marianne into his arms. Exchanging glances, Don and Maggie backed away. Watching, Rachel wanted to weep again.

'Darling, hold on. Please hold on.' The old man's voice was harsh with anguish.

Above the ventilator tube, Marianne's eyes answered him, closing and opening again. They searched the room, looking for someone. She seemed to struggle against McEnroe, raising herself slightly, and pulling at the ventilator.

Rachel hung back, waiting for a sign from McEnroe.

'Rachel's right here, too, honey.'

Marianne found her then, and fixed on her. Her eyes crinkled at the corners. She lifted one hand slightly, and let it drop heavily onto the covers. The effort was enormous. She shut her eyes again.

The room fell completely silent except for the faint noise of the ventilator and the hum of the monitors.

Live, live, live, Rachel intoned inwardly.

Marianne opened her eyes again and turned them on the wall behind them all. Rachel swivelled to glance at the wall, finding nothing but the unmitigating glare of the paint; then she looked back at her grandmother.

The blue eyes remained opened: not staring, but concentrated on a middle distance that Rachel could not see.

Alarms beeped on both monitors. The pulses slowed further now, spiked, then flattened again.

Looking at her mother, Rachel whispered, 'Her blood pressure's dropping to nothing.'

'Oh—don't—I can't stand those alarms!' McEnroe looked frenzied.

Two or three medics rushed in, edged the family aside, and tried to restart Marianne's heart. Rachel watched as if from a long distance again; she felt helpless and angry: understanding what they were doing, but numb with disbelief that they should even think of it. It passed through her mind, irrelevantly, that no such heroics would have gone on in St Stephen's.

Finally the internist switched off the ventilator. A third warning buzzer sounded, then stopped when she pressed another button. She turned to McEnroe with a solemn face. Over the futile beeping of the first two alarms, she began, 'Mr McEnroe—'

'You don't have to say it.' His voice was grey with sadness.

The internist glanced at the clock and noted the time. She spoke softly, barely audibly over the maddening alarms, the murmured grief of Maggie and Don beside the window, and Rachel's own stifled sobs. 'I'm going to take her off the machines now, sir.'

'Good. Thank God for that. You do that. *Switch those alarms off before I—!*' McEnroe's face was contorted.

Rachel slid behind the doctors and put her arms around him, but he broke away from her, refusing to be comforted, and went to the bed again, taking up Marianne's lifeless hands in despair.

The room was growing darker now, and once the alarms had stopped, after the last suspended whisper of breath from Marianne's drowning lungs, it was also quiet.

No one could speak, until the internist had ushered her colleagues out of the door and turned to McEnroe again. 'There's nothing I can say, sir.'

He had collected himself a little. 'No. Of course not.' His sigh was as faint as Marianne's last breath.

'I'll leave you for a while.'

When she had gone, Don pulled away from Maggie and went to his father. Without a word, he took the old man by the shoulders and held him.

Rachel's eyes burned with hot tears. *I can't bear it.*

Then Maggie took Don's place, her arms around her father-in-law, as Don stood back and looked from one to the other of them. He was the first to break the quiet.

'McEnroe, listen to me, now—and Maggie, and Rachel.' He struggled from tears to his normal tones. 'God is in our midst. Let's not forget that.'

Tears pushed out again between Rachel's eyes, and she dropped her head. Hot indignation boiled up in her. *I've prayed for a miracle.*

'We all know he's here,' Don continued. 'We can grieve, and

grieve we will. But she's gone to him now. Maggie—you tell them! Hey, Dad—'

McEnroe's swimming eyes widened. It was years since Don had called him 'Dad'.

'Maggie and I see death every week—somewhere on the farm, it happens. But we also see *life*, and birth.' He shook the old man's shoulders. 'Don't do this to yourself, now! I remember a time when you taught *me* about eternal life, and about the hope of resurrection. Remember? When Ellie had finished her life—we all believed there was nothing else to live for.' He gestured suddenly towards Maggie. 'And look what new life God gave us. Rachel said—' He nodded at her. '—that miracles are real. Well, that's the true miracle, folks. New life.' Don's chin trembled, but his eyes burned with steady conviction.

McEnroe wiped his face. Like Marianne, he seemed to have shrunk. His vulnerability shook Rachel more deeply even than Marianne's death. He went to the window and stood with shoulders bowed, staring out. He would be seeing nothing, Rachel thought, still indignant.

'D'you know what date it is, folks?' Don was shaking, but he threw his hands out and flipped his hair back across his forehead.

Rachel's slow, tired mind leapt to keep up with her father's. She knew what he was trying to do, but she wished he would say nothing, so that they could wrestle with death in their own way, each of them.

In her imagination she saw a calendar, saw the days marching to the end of March . . . and Easter. *Resurrection Sunday*. She looked up, grudgingly conceding to her father's reasoning.

'Yes, it's Holy Week next week.' Don's voice fell to a whisper. 'Perhaps I'm blundering about like a clumsy great bear, as usual, but let's not forget that, either.'

McEnroe nodded slowly. 'Thanks. Dear God, I'll need to hear reminders like that for a long time.'

'I'm going to get us all a cup of tea,' Maggie said. Her eyes were red with crying, her mouth askew as she got the words out.

Don looked up. 'You do that, honey.'

Grateful for a diversion, Rachel took her mother's arm. 'I'll go with you, Mom.'

'It was as if she knew you were coming,' Maggie said as they came back along the corridor a few minutes later carrying white styrofoam cups full of watery tea.

'Perhaps she did.'

'I was scared she wouldn't even know who McEnroe was.'

'Until the end, perhaps.' Rachel swallowed hard. 'I think she knew then.' She felt uneasy that her grandmother had looked for her at the end, not for the others.

'If you're thinking what I think you're thinking,' Maggie said with a shrewd twist to the mouth, 'then don't. Your grandmother loved the whole family like crazy—never stopped. But she'd missed you, too— so McEnroe was saying when we arrived. Ah, he was a rock for her— the way your father's been for me.'

Rachel smiled faintly. 'No, the way *you* are for Dad.'

'You've got it wrong.'

'Not from where I'm standing, but it doesn't matter. I hear what you're saying.'

'She took him for granted. Not in a bad way—I don't mean that. It's the way you take your hands or eyes for granted. They're a part of you. That's how it always was with your grandparents. So don't go wasting a moment's worry about why she looked to you last of all. Like I said, I'm sure she heard us saying you were coming, and was waiting for you before she could let go. And she was in his arms, anyhow. Must have known that.'

Rachel said nothing this time. She thought how like her mother it was that she had to offer comfort, quickly saw the need—though she, too, would be crying inside.

Easter, she reminded herself. *Dad's right.* When the blades of spring grass and the constellations of daisies would be rising again over the new grave in Our Lady of Sorrows cemetery, it would be April, Easter, and a time to recall new life, new hope.

But she felt little hope over the next few days while the preparations for the wake went on. Don and Maggie spent most of the time closeted with McEnroe or on the telephone to relatives. McEnroe hid in his study during the day, and paced the floor of the mezzanine by night, unable to sleep. Unable to sleep herself, she would hear his slippered feet going desolately up and down the long carpets, or sometimes the creak of a stair as he went down to his study for a bourbon. Once she got as far as opening her bedroom door and standing, waiting for him to return past the door from the other end of the big house—then lost courage and softly closed it again, standing in the middle of the familiar room in the shuttered, too-quiet dark, hearing only the sound of her own breathing and not knowing at all what she should do.

She longed to talk to him, listen to him talk to her: to share the sadness that she was sharing anyway, whether he recognized it or not. She ached for her grandfather, felt unable to reach him. And longed for comfort, herself.

At last, the night before the wake, she could bear it no longer. Tiptoeing downstairs, desperate to distract herself with a book, a puzzle—anything—she found McEnroe's study door open and heard him inside, speaking on the telephone. He was obviously at the end of a conversation, for she heard, 'Yes, yes, I know it. Well, I guess that could be mighty good news. Especially now. Yes, I'll sleep on it and call you in the morning when I've decided what I should do ... No, of course I don't mind that you called late, or this week. No, I mean it. Goodnight, now.'

Guiltily, she went on along the passage, past the kitchen, and into the dining room. Her grandmother had always shelved all the novels there: methodically, in tidy rows labelled A to Z by title. This was the room Rachel most associated with her.

McEnroe came and stood on the threshold. His striped pyjamas were crisply pressed, but the robe he wore was frayed at the cuffs; for all his wealth, he cared little about how he looked at home. 'You're up late,' he suggested gruffly. 'And I couldn't get to sleep.'

She turned, feeling the blood mount into her face. 'I'm sorry; I just heard you on the phone.'

'That's OK.' His face was clear, for the moment, but it trembled slightly. 'Can a guy tell you what's happening?'

Other words hung unspoken between them. *No more Marianne to tell, now.*

The blood rushed even faster to her cheeks. 'It's what I've prayed you would do.'

His wrinkled face softened. 'Old folks and young folks—they're the ones who don't sleep too good when things go wrong. Look at your father and mother up there, already. Not a squeak from their room— sleeping the sleep of the righteous, and it's only eleven thirty.' His generous mouth almost curled into a smile. 'God rest 'em.'

'Sleeping like the dead,' she said, unthinking.

He nodded and waved a hand towards her scarlet face. 'Yes, you're right. You didn't mean it, Rachel. It's OK. Come here, sweetheart.'

Weeping again, she went and put her arms round his neck. He was thinner than she remembered. She felt a day's stubble rasp against the soft flesh of her inner arms as she slid them past his ears. *Old,* she thought painfully. *Old, and hurting.*

'Let's sit in here,' he said. He unwound her arms again and pulled two chairs from under the table. 'I'll bring us both a jar of something to warm the insides.'

'Why not in your study? It'll be warmer—'

'That's a work place for me—a retreat from folk. But I don't want to escape now.' His voice slid dangerously downwards, and he coughed.

'No. No, of course you don't.' She felt she was talking to a child. She couldn't bear to see him shed any more tears.

He stomped away, now making no effort to quieten his feet, and banged cupboard doors in the kitchen. Behind him he left the faint aroma of cigar smoke that usually hung about him. He had been smoking while he was on the telephone, then.

Without taking in a word of the print on the first page, she randomly selected a novel and began to scan it. The dining room felt chilly without her grandfather's warmth, and she blew her nose hard. After all the crying, her cold seemed worse than ever.

She thought back to when she had sat in the room with her grandparents, her mother, Marie and Rita Williams for the birthday luncheon the year before. The room had been breezy, sunshiny, and full of light, then. Now it was dim and silent. Voices echoed soundlessly around her, like music half-remembered from childhood. She felt wretched, lost. Where was God's comfort now?

'Hot chocolate!' she said in surprise when he returned.

He said drily, 'So it would seem.'

She got up from the table in a flurry to put out coasters and carry the steaming mugs to the table. She was the one who should have been waiting on them.

He flapped her away impatiently.

'Grandpa McEnroe—?'

'There's a slug of something a bit stronger in there as well. Never did hold with sleeping pills, but this oughtta do the trick.' His face was creased and seamed with lack of sleep.

'At least for two or three hours, maybe.'

He pushed his fingers through the silver mane. 'Yeah, that's about the size of it, right now. Wake up again at four, doze off again for half an hour if I'm lucky, then the light wakes me.'

'It'll get better, truly.'

He nodded slowly and gave her another wry look. 'Speaking with your medic's coat on your back, you mean?'

She felt small and inadequate. 'Yes.'

'Oh, some things will get better. I know that. Seen it with some of the guys at the golfclub. But I hate the emptiness of the bed at night, and the cold, without her.' His voice cracked again. '*That* I will no way get used to, Rachel, honey.'

She blew on the cocoa and watched him over the rim of the mug. After a moment, she prompted, 'You were going to tell me something, I believe.'

This time he did say it. 'I'm glad you all're here for a few days to talk to. GraMar is—was—a light sleeper as well. She was often awake to listen to me hash something out. It didn't even matter, toward the end, if she'd understood very little what I was talking about. She was a good listener.' He narrowed his eyes. 'Trouble is, I can't make out if you're old enough yet for burdens like these on your shoulders.'

'Try me,' she said quickly.

Then he seemed to forget for a while that she was in the room. His voice took on a dreamlike quality, drifting with the ebb and flow of his emotions, and breaking on the sharp rocks of grief. She struggled to follow him, but he repeated himself so much that in the end she did manage to catch at the real meanings, and to understand what was behind the words.

'All the time I was promising I would seize the man who made our lives such hell all those years ago, and I told myself and everyone else that I had to do it before I came to the place where I wasn't competent any more—had to do it for myself—all that time . . . all that time . . . I felt my opportunities running and running away. But then I guess I was also chasing him for your grandmother's sake, and didn't know it. She was closer to Ellie than any of us except your own mother. Understood her better. Ellie's death was a bitter, bitter blow to her. All these years I guess I was trying to compensate for what happened by hounding the state's pushers and traffickers and addicts and kidding myself that it was politically smart, as well as personally necessary. But it was more than that, I see now. I wanted to catch Garshowitz—Garcia—whoever—*for what he did to your grandmother*, as well as to Eleanor and me, and your parents. It went way beyond politics, whatever I've said to the press in the twenty some years since.'

He stopped, and his teeth ground together. 'But now I can't catch him in time for your grandmother to know, and it makes me madder than I can tell you.' His eyes sparked again. Some of the grey despair had left his face. 'I just got a tip-off from a guy in town.' His lips curled. 'My own "Deep Throat", you might call him. We know where Garcia's holed up at the moment, and there's every reason to think he'll break cover within the next few days. Not drugs, this time, if my informer is to be credited. He's far too smooth and clever to touch the stuff directly himself, these days, anyhow. And things have gotten tougher since the state legislature took my cue and cracked down on those guys. So his lackeys've gotten more desperate. Taking chances. Grabbing for almost anything except crack—too smart for that. Oh, I pray I nail the whole pack of them.'

He gave her a swift, appraising look. 'Why, I found out from the FBI some weeks ago that they've even traced his network to your new home town, and a series of raids there. He's been working with the Triad gangs there, would you believe.'

'London?' Rachel's throat clotted, and the word came out in a squawk. She opened her mouth to tell him what had happened that day in the operating theatre, then shut it again. *He* needed to talk. Her own discomfort was nothing, and the raid was surely an isolated incident that could not be repeated again in St Stephen's now that security was tighter. And he was talking to her now because he needed to explain the complexities of his own grief, not listen to the details of hers.

His voice rumbled on. 'They've been after amphetamines across in Britain. Dexamphetamine sulfate, and all its derivatives—to be precise. "Dexies", they call them. Or "daisies". Innocuous sounding names for vicious drugs.' His clouded face suddenly cleared for a brief interval. 'Ah, but I suppose you know more about those things than I do, these days.'

'Not a lot,' she squeaked, feeling a liar. *Dexamphetamine sulphate. That's some of what went missing from St Stephen's.* Now that he was going into details, her cover-up would be even harder.

'Twenty years of wickedness, and still they're not satisfied at the lives they've ruined. Keith Garcia killed Ellie, and I blame him for killing your grandmother, too. Years of it, Rachel—not knowing about Ellie's last minutes. The fact that we never saw her settled and with kids like your parents—that's what dragged your grandmother down, in the end. Alzheimer's hits people worst who have carried too much grief in their lives, as the doctors told me when she was first admitted.'

Rachel longed to interrupt. 'But, but—' she stammered. 'It wasn't just that.' She thought of Marianne's infectious, almost girlish gaiety the previous summer—of the laughter and the radiance. But the sadness had never been far below the surface. Perhaps it was understandable, after all, that McEnroe should so long have wanted redress.

He seemed to have read her thoughts. 'It's not revenge that's driven me on, or that's driving me now,' he continued. 'I hope you know that.'

She looked away, embarrassed.

'It's that I want justice where there's injustice. Remember what the scriptures say, Rachel? God wants nothing more from us than for us to "do" justice and walk humbly with him.'

Indignant with love for him, she threw up her head. 'But that's exactly what you've done, McEnroe! You've always been like that.'

He smiled sadly. 'No. You didn't know me in the old days. Lately, perhaps. But I was a hard fighter in the old days. In the State House, or in the courtroom, if I punched, they went down with a smack, and I would crow.'

'Not any more.'

'Not any more. Life's too short, sweetheart. Love is always stronger than hate—that's what I've had to learn, usually the hard way.'

It suddenly struck Rachel afresh what would happen in the morning—only a few hours away, on the other side of the darkness. Tomorrow there would be a packed wake at Our Lady of Sorrows, and Marianne would be buried in the church cemetery on the edge of Bedford.

She set her mug down, empty, on the coaster. 'I love you, McEnroe,' she said simply.

'I love you too. So now you know what was keeping the old man awake.'

'It really wasn't anything to do with the drug ring,' she said, feeling that she was pushing her luck.

'Maybe not, young Dr McEnroe. But everything's connected. For years I haven't been able to keep work apart from things at home. That's as true now as it ever was. And tomorrow—' He let out a groan. 'Tomorrow, God help us, I might have another chance to get Garcia. If I decide it's right, I'll have to go for him right after the wake.'

She was horrified. 'But how can you?'

'If have to, I will. That's what I was on the phone about.'

She stared at him wordlessly. The sense of his being in danger reasserted itself—something she had been able to push away during the past few months. And wasn't he suffering enough without going out after more trouble? But it was no use saying what she was thinking. He was an old man, and he would do what he wanted to, what he thought best.

After the wake, when some of the guests had said their goodbyes and driven away from the cemetery, Rachel saw that McEnroe's resolve had hardened. His face looked as bleak as a winter storm, and his tie was askew. She watched her parents struggling to find words for him, but it was hard to talk either to or about her grandfather. The indignation of the days before had gone. Numb: that was how she felt in the sea of emotion that surged around her now.

But anger vibrated from McEnroe throughout the reception that followed the wake. When the front door had closed behind the last guest, the family went as if pulled there to the dining room. He stood in his black suit like a thundercloud among the wreckage of superfluous food the housekeeper had prepared and looked from one to the other.

His steely, hot eyes rested on Rachel first. His voice was low, and menacing; she had never heard him like this. 'And now, by God, I'm going to do what I said I would last night. Get the man who brought so much of this sorrow on us.'

In spite of his warning the night before, she was dumbstruck.

Maggie had slumped into a chair beside the table. She was composed now, her face dry of tears and her hair, for once, tidy. She too must have heard the rage resonating in his voice, for she reached a restraining hand to his sleeve. 'What do you mean?'

A white thread of spittle formed at the corner of his mouth as he spat the name out. 'Garcia, that's what I mean. His number's up. The drug enforcement people have run that fox to earth at last. He's down in Newport under close surveillance. Putting his precious boats to water, they said. I've arranged to go with the DEA and see him arrested. *Now*. He'll be busted before the night's out.' He waved his arms. 'Wakes—I can't cope with all this. I want to forget.' His face crumpled again. 'God knows, I want to do something *useful*. And if we can nail him today—sure we will—it'll be the best day's work I've done in years. It'll make all the other days worthwhile to me, and it'll save other lives, before he and his people can do even one more day of damage on the East Coast.'

Don stood up and faced McEnroe squarely. 'Wait. This is insane. Mom's hardly in the ground. You need to be here and rest a while.' McEnroe elbowed him aside. His voice was terrible. 'That's the counsel of cowardice and procrastination. I will not—'

From across the hallway, the telephone in his study pealed.

Maggie leapt up. 'I'll get it.'

'No.' McEnroe's voice was barely more than a whisper. 'No, I know who it is, and I'll get it, thanks a lot, Maggie. That's my ride to Newport—courtesy of the DEA. So I'll be going.'

He stepped through the dining room door, then returned a few minutes later wearing his tie reknotted and a clean jacket—one of the ones Rachel had seen him wearing as he went out to work in the city.

'By the way,' he said, reaching into one of the pockets. 'I almost forgot this. It was on Marianne's finger before they shut the casket.' His stormy eyes found Rachel's again. 'I know she wanted you to have it. Here.' He threw it, and the bright metal looped across the room to her, clinking against a vase of lilies and rolling on the table for a moment amid the neat triangular sandwiches and platters of half-eaten smoked salmon, half-drained glasses of wine.

It was the daisy ring.

22

The dining room windows had been wound open. Through the screens came the lazy buzzing of early insects and the smell of soil and green things starting to grow. McEnroe's gardener had uncovered and cleaned the pool, beyond which a light breeze lifted the cedars' great, scented boughs. Sunshine poured into the room: bars of honeyed light. Today spring in Boston was ahead of spring in London—or spring in Arcade, Rachel guessed.

She left the spoon in her half-full bowl and leaned back against the ladderback chair. Breakfast was as tasteless as all food at the moment: bland as cotton wool, and equally unappealing. *How can the sun go on shining so merrily when GraMar isn't in here to share it with me?* She closed her eyes and let the light and warmth fall on her, comforting. Then she thought, *Ah, but GraMar's standing in a different sort of sunshine now, on another shore.*

Opening her eyes again, she twisted the daisy ring on her finger. It glinted and winked at her. She was still turning and turning it, her eyes misting and out of focus, when McEnroe's gaunt frame filled the doorway.

'All alone?' he asked.

'They're putting the last things in their bags. Still upstairs.'

'Oh—I guess.' He hesitated, for a moment seeming to lose direction. Then at the polished mahogany sideboard he poured himself a bowl of cornflakes. He sat down heavily beside her, but he ate nothing. 'Don't know why I did that. Never could stand this crap.' He pushed the bowl away and turned his face towards the window. 'Your father was right,' he said softly, 'at least it's almost Easter.' He inhaled appreciatively.

'Ye-es,' she agreed slowly, 'but you can't live on spring air.'

'No, doctor.'

She placed her hand on his sleeve and realized that he was wearing neither his casual clothes for weekends and home, nor his city suit for the office or State House. Instead he wore a loose blue wool cardigan over a cream poloneck shirt and moss-green trousers. *His golf clothes*. She looked at him in wonder, but said nothing about them. 'Er—at least have some orange juice.'

He seemed unconscious of her curiosity. 'You sound just like your mother.'

She smiled, then. 'Thanks. Taken as a compliment.'

Absently, he leant to kiss her cheek. '*Intended* as a sort of compliment.'

She saw what his drained face betrayed—the concave half-moons under his eyes, the slackness of his mouth, and the lifelessness of his skin—that he had missed yet another night of sleep. But this time she herself *had* been able to sleep. She was afraid he would catch her staring with unwearied eyes, and she looked away, pained. *Could you not watch with me one hour?* She thought of the previous night, and how glad McEnroe had been to have her company for a while in the late hours. But, for her, things had changed now that Marianne was buried. She missed her, and she missed her *now*, but the beginnings of acceptance were already glimmering like the tiny light given out by the ring.

McEnroe recollected himself. 'You're right, of course, Rachel.' With a quirk at the corner of his mouth he poured himself half a glass of juice. 'Anyhow, what time's your flight this afternoon?' He heaved a deep sigh. 'I forget.'

How empty the great house would be when they were all gone! Rachel again felt tears prickle behind her eyes. She knew how dear the family was—all of them—to her grandfather. And what purpose would there be for him, now even Marianne was gone? Would he let Rachel stay for a few days more if she were to ask? Or would he pack her off and say he wanted time alone to lick his wounds and grieve in private? Or perhaps there was a side to her grandfather she did not yet know—an independent, tough streak that had seen him through bitter courtroom battles and political in-fightings: the will of a survivor to go on strongly, whatever happened.

Then she remembered with a rush of adrenaline that since the wake she had not actually seen him at all. He had been away with DEA officers. This was, in fact, the first time she had seen him since his unexpected announcement that he was leaving to have one more attempt at hunting down Garcia.

Did his haggard face mean that the drug dealer had once again eluded him?

He was trying to get her attention. 'Your flight, I said?'

She knew she must have looked blank with the shock of realization. 'Oh, oh—' she stammered. 'You'll have to ask Mom. Two-thirty. Something like that.'

He nodded. 'So I should be back in plenty of time to drive you to the airport.'

Her fingers closed on the scratchy wool of his cardigan again. She felt chilled. 'Back from what, Grandpa McEnroe?'

His face broadened into a smile—the widest and most natural she had seen since last autumn. 'A couple rounds of golf, of course.'

'But you—'

His hands closed warmly around hers. 'Listen, long goodbyes aren't my scene any more than they're your father's. I'm sure you understand that. We've laid—oh, we've laid—your grandmother to rest, and what they all keep telling me is how important it is that I try to get on with my life, not keep hashing over the past. I am going to try, Rachel. I'm going to try, God knows.' His mouth quivered, then thinned into a determined line; his voice wavered, then steadied again. 'I've also laid that villain to rest, in a manner of speaking, I suppose. He's incarcerated—denied bail.' He eyeballed her as she drew a quick breath. 'Now tell me why when you aren't leaving till this afternoon an old guy can't go and smack a few balls up the fairway and breathe in more of this spring air I need to live on for the time being, eh?'

'You got him then?'

'We got him all right.'

She slid her hands from between his, turned in her chair and gripped his shoulders. 'You sure you got him? You don't look like you got him!' She heard the mounting excitement in her own voice. If it was true—

He hugged her. 'You loon—sure it's true!'

'Then why on earth do you look so wasted? You should be singing.' She came back so fast at him that he recoiled from her.

'Easy to say. I wasn't home till three-thirty.'

She hung her head. 'I'm—I'm sorry.'

'If it had been a month ago, or better still at Christmas, then I would have been singing and dancing as well. When your grandmother would have understand what I'd done. Now—well, it's not that simple.' He stood up, glancing at his watch. 'I'm teeing off in forty-five minutes—so that I can be back in time for you guys.'

She leapt up. 'I'm all packed.' She felt suddenly shy. 'Couldn't I go with you—caddy for you?'

He chuckled. 'It never even crossed my mind. I have a buggy these days.'

'The heck with the buggy—then you could tell me what happened yesterday.'

'Your parents'll want to hear, too.' He frowned. 'Guess I shouldn't have planned this game after all. It's not as if they'll want to drag round eighteen holes like their keen-as-mustard daughter.' He rubbed his fingers through his hair and went on, 'I may not have Alzheimer's yet, but things aren't as straight up here as they used to be. I'll have to get a new secretary so I don't doublebook myself.'

She wanted to sweep all the petty obstacles aside and insist that he let her go with him. *This* was the moment to be alive, and thankful to be alive. *This* was the moment to be together. 'Well, McEnroe—could I?'

He shrugged amiably, almost like his old self. 'Why not? Get moving, then. Go find a jacket. I'll go tell your parents I've got a date with my granddaughter—' He winked. 'Then I'll dig you up some golf shoes, and we'll hit the road. Sound like a deal?'

Fifteen minutes later they were speeding along the highway towards the club where he had played golf for almost fifty years.

'I needed this. You maybe can't see it, but there's a lot of bitterness in my soul, still, that your grandmother didn't live to see the day we caught that guy.' His expression hardened. 'Especially when I realized that I could have caught him before. Right under our noses he was, at New Year's. Arrogant—oh, unbelievable. I feel hot with rage every time I think of what he had the gall to do.' He shuddered.

'And I go cold when I hear you talk that way. You said love is always stronger than hate.'

He sighed again, nodding. 'Yeah, so it is. But I'm only human. And sometimes hate gets the upper hand for a while.'

'New Year's—what did you mean about him being right under your noses?'

'You were there yourself. You saw him.' She gawped at him, and he turned his eyes from the highway. He shook his head in consternation. 'No! What the heck am I talking about? It was young Monaghan—that was the name, I think. You know—Marie's friend, the Englishman. *He* was there.'

Marie's friend. Her mouth quirked into an ironic smile, but she kept her eyes on the cars ahead.

'Garcia played a twisted little game that night, I'll tellya.'

She felt suspended, cut adrift from the moorings of her own comprehension. *Michael... New Year's... Garcia... a twisted little game...* 'Tell me, then,' she urged.

He reached and ignited the cigar lighter. 'There was a party. Sure your mother must've written you about it. A regular New Year's session. Your mother'd brought Monaghan over for the vacation, and she persuaded him to keep us company. Williams were with us, as well.' He stopped. The memory was vivid and painful for him. 'Hey, undo me a cigar there, wouldya?' He pulled one out of the top pocket of his shirt and passed it to her. While she rustled the seal off it, rolled it between her fingers as she had seen him do, and cut the end off it, he continued, 'It was one of the last times I remember your grandmother being more or less lucid. Rita Williams introduced them to us. GraMar was 'charmed.' He took the cigar between his teeth. 'Er, thanks. Now hand me that lighter.'

She was losing the thread. 'Introduced who?'

'A man and a woman Rita said were new customers at the marina.' He removed the lighter from the end of the cigar and drew three times on it until the end glowed; then he exhaled a ring of fragrant blue smoke in a long sigh. 'Yeah, they were new customers OK. It was Garcia himself, and his common-law wife, Julia. Lord, she was a beauty—how a woman as classy as that ever got mixed up—like Ellie did. He always did have a taste for gorgeous women. But I didn't know the half of it until yesterday. *Yesterday*—if you can credit it! They must have laughed themselves sick all the way home after that party. "Sitting with the McEnroes," they would've jeered. What a laugh for them—with the very guy who's been after his tail for twenty years! *But I didn't know him*, for pity's sake! Steve Galloway—that's his alias right now. And she called herself Julia Galloway. British, she is. A very slick little madam in her own right, as we already found out—last night, in the wee hours. Gave Garcia his entree into the British drug scene, I'm almost certain.'

Rachel remembered the hospital raid again, and in dismay hunched further into her seat.

'Last night when we got 'em, the woman had herself a sharp as nails lawyer up there within twenty minutes. They tried plea-bargaining right away—they know we've got enough evidence against them now to send them down for several lifetimes. But she's willing to squeal on her boyfriend—husband, whatever—in return for some immunity. Once her hot-shot lawyer got there and we gave them a little time for a pow-wow, she started singing like a canary. Enough tip-offs to keep the DEA frantic for six months! And I did get a few surprises, I'll tell you. Like the direction they were launching off into next, according to her—'

Rachel felt punchdrunk with amazement, but also anxiety. 'Do you feel easier now? Now you've got the lynchpin, I mean?'

He nodded, and the thin disc of ash on the end of the cigar brightened to orange as he did so. 'You bet I feel easier. Especially when she began spilling the beans the way she did. Seems like—oh gosh! You don't need to hear all this! Ah well—' His eyebrows lifted. 'The DEA will have its work cut out!'

'So,' she began slowly, 'you're telling me this couple showed up at a party, in your *own* country club, and that you sat with Garcia all evening without realizing who he was?'

'Right.'

'But how—?'

'I never met the guy twenty years ago, when Ellie was with him. Sure I've seen shots of him, but he's been pretty smart at staying out of the limelight; and the district attorney's files may've been thick with paper, but they weren't exactly brimming over with glossy photographs. Camera-shy, our man was. A couple blurred ones, if we were lucky. I had no way of knowing exactly what he looked like. Pushes his lackeys up the front and into the line of fire; keeps the heat off himself very cleverly.' He signalled for the gateway entrance to the golfclub and waited for a gap in the traffic. 'Of course this is all strictly off the record. I must be getting worse in my old age; like I said the other night, I can't keep home and work apart in this case. A man's innocent until proven guilty, but—' His mouth curled bitterly. '—I'll see him in for as many life sentences as the courts can hand out, if I have my way. My last and biggest inditement. The district attorney'll enjoy it too. A pair of nasty conniving old men, we are.'

'That's hardly a fair description for two lawmakers who've been trying to bust a criminal for two decades.'

'Ho-ho! And you aren't too prejudiced, I guess! Don't butter me up. I just hope this car ain't bugged, that's all.' He guffawed. 'And now I want to forget Garcia-Galloway-Garschowitz and crack that ball for all I'm worth. Just make sure you keep up with me, OK? Or I won't bring you again. It'll cause enough of an upset that we won't be riding in the buggy, let me tell you!'

In the clubhouse as the men chose partners and opponents for their four-ball, there was a lot of good-natured ribbing about Rachel. Their heartiness seemed thin to her, as if they wanted to avoid the pain of anything more than a few perfunctory words of respect and condolence, before getting down to the real business—something they understood and could cope with: hitting a ball.

'Sorry to hear of your loss, Senator... What a lovely woman she was, McEnroe... Your granddaughter's along to show you how to hold the club? Why, that's dandy, ain't it!'

Under their wind-burned skins she saw the discomfort in their eyes as they shook hands or passed by, heard the whispered asides—which she hoped he would miss—of anxiety. 'Whatever the heck can you say to a guy who's out on the course the day after he buries his wife?'

If only they knew! she thought, trailing the four players, pushing his clubs to the first tee.

Walsh and Burrows, McEnroe's opponents for the day, were ill at ease at first. Only his partner seemed natural and straightforward with him—one of her cousins, a city magazine editor called Pete, who obviously knew and understood McEnroe well.

'Good to see you, Rachel.' He gave her a civil nod of the head, then turned to McEnroe. 'I'm glad you decided to get out here today. Do you the world of good.'

'Surprised to see you here, Pete.'

'Not my day, usually. But I'm happy to take you on. Heard on the news this morning that the DEA nabbed Garcia last night, and I had a hunch I might find you here today.'

McEnroe held up one hand and with the other drew his driver out of the bag. Rachel steadied the clubs. She saw him pale. 'Peter McEnroe!—you're not seriously going to quiz me about that, I hope?'

Pete backpedalled fast and shook his head. 'No—listen. Forgive me. I know you think I'm a typical press hound, but I hope—thanks to Bobbie-Ann at least—I've got a little more tact and generosity of spirit than that.'

McEnroe's eyes wandered to the line of trees along the edge of the first fairway; only a few aspens showed any sign of life: yellow-green leaves newly minted among the other dead branches. 'Tact? I believe you have... sometimes.' His voice was droll. Then he gripped his driver and whacked the ball in a perfect arc towards the first green. Following the ball with his eyes until it dropped out of sight on the other side of a rise, he gave Rachel another wide smile. 'This is just what I need, honey, like I said.'

'Thought you only played nine these days.' Pete paused, then swung the club down with such a powerful stroke that the shaft cracked like a whip through the air. His ball disappeared after McEnroe's. 'Or is that just a rumour put about by other old guys who wish they were as fit as you?'

The banter continued as the four men moved from hole to hole. Rachel heard outrageous, apocryphal stories, and felt healed by the laughter—saw her grandfather beginning to unfreeze at last.

Mc Enroe was lining up a putt on the fifth green. 'What about that day—?'

'Uh-oh! Not that fable about a *fox*.'

'You saw it yourself!'

Pete's low voice cut across McEnroe's. 'A tale about a fox from one of these old foxes? This I have to hear.'

Rachel felt the sun on her shoulders and saw a genuine smile in her grandfather's eyes for the first time since she had arrived in Boston. 'Go on,' she pleaded.

'If you insist. But I gotta sink this putt first. Cut the chit-chat, folks, for a moment.'

The air around them fell so quiet that Rachel heard the screech of a bluejay from the trees, and the sound of men ahead of them on the sixth fairway calling to each other, searching for a lost ball.

As he prepared to putt, McEnroe's bristling brows contracted fiercely. The other players froze, and the ball dropped with a satisfying clunk into the hole. Stooping with a groan, he retrieved it, then all five moved to the next tee.

'We were right near here, Rachel,' McEnroe began. 'Seventh fairway, I think it was. It's a four-hundred-yard par four—long fairway, straight, but with a dip in it that fools almost everyone. You'll see for yourself in a while, anyhow. Walsh here could tell this tale, only he's too embarrassed.'

The other man let out a guffaw. 'Embarrassed, heck! You're the one should be embarrassed making up that stuff.'

McEnroe gave Walsh a withering glare, then noticed that Rachel was struggling to get the cart up the hill. 'Here, you're useless with that thing. Worse than a trainee driver. Give it me.'

She began to protest. 'But I came specially to caddy for you!'

'It doesn't matter, honey. Anyway, like I was saying—Walsh hit his ball nice and straight—I'll give him his due—clear down the fairway. Only trouble, it went into the infamous dip and rolled there, pretty as a picture to my eyes, right in the middle, where it's open. We came down after the balls, when what should run outta the woods but a sleek young dog fox, cocking his snoot at poor Walshie. Picked up the ball in his mouth as gentle as any spaniel with an egg, and trotted away back into the woods.'

Walsh's face reddened as they all began to laugh. 'It never did, you son of a gun! It was *your* ball the fox ran off with!'

'I don't believe any of it,' Pete put in. 'You guys should start a "tall tales" golfers' weekly. I'll bet you could keep a rag like that going for weeks on your own legends, for a start. I'll publish it as a supplement to *Citizen* if you like. Probably boost the sales no end. We'd make a bomb.'

Rachel pushed her arm through McEnroe's free one. 'I'll bet it *was* your ball, not Mr Walsh's.'

McEnroe winked. 'If it was, I'm not telling, and the fox isn't telling either. Pete, if it's still sitting down there on the edge of the woods, you can interview it and see what it says.' He winked again.

A short while later they stood on the seventh tee. The air was warmer now, swirling in light breaths around the small plateau of the tee. From where they stood, Rachel could not see the flag fluttering a quarter of a mile away on the green, but she could see the deceptive dip half way along the fairway. She looked at McEnroe for confirmation of where the fox had run out of the woods, but his eyes were fixed eagle-like on Pete as he swung his club, then on the ball as it sailed away and seemed to vanish into the sky.

'Where'd it go?' she asked.

'Right where it's supposed to. Other side of the dip.'

She looked up in wonder. 'You've got such clear vision. I can't see it at all.'

Burrows played next; then it was McEnroe's turn again. A smooth swing, and the crack of the club on the ball had the other men groaning. The ball lifted, but not as high as Pete's shot; low and true it flew straight down the fairway and landed where Rachel could just see it, two hundred metres away: a minute white dot on the mown spring grass.

'You can see that, I trust?' McEnroe's voice was dry.

'Sure can.'

'Well played, McEnroe,' the others all congratulated him.

Walsh and Burrows grumbled, 'No contest when he's around. Just too damn good for an old man.'

'Hush your mouth, Walshie. Save your strength for finding that ball of yours.'

'Maybe the fox got it,' Rachel laughed, starting again to push the clubs along the path at the edge of the fairway.

They crunched their way, five of them, over the woodchips of the path. For the first time since the previous summer at home, Rachel smelt the warm smell of resin-soaked bark chips. *Sap,* she thought. *New life in what looks like old bits of wood.* And then she remembered the maples at home. Maggie would have hung buckets six weeks ago for the sap, and they'd still be boiling off the water in the shed to make syrup for the family. *Ah, Lord, I can't wait to go home!*

She stole a glance at McEnroe, walking abreast of her. His head was down, and she saw the shadow of grief spreading again over his face. The laughter of golfing partners only carried him so far; then he would be recalling things Marianne had said and done, dreams they had dreamt together...

'Don't be sad,' she whispered so that only he would hear.

His right arm came round her shoulders in a strong squeeze. 'Thanks. Sure you can manage those clubs?'

'No problem.'

He released her and turned his head, suddenly, so that she saw the sheen of silver on his hair. He stopped. 'Wait up! You hear that?'

'What?' She waited beside him, while the others trudged on ahead, widening the distance between them, eager to play their second shots.

He was shaking his head now. 'Thought I heard geese—but if I did they must be real high up. Can't see them.'

She strained against the glare of late morning to see the familiar, arrowed outline on the sky. The blue was limitless, arching over them like a great, translucent dome. Then she heard it, too: the wild crying of webbed geese, tracking their way across the vastness.

'Yes! I hear them.'

A distinct whirring sound beyond the trees grew in strength; then came again the mournful honking of the geese. A skein appeared, flying powerfully north over the course: she heard the singing rhythm of their wings and the corresponding clamour of their voices. The downbeat of their feathers brought a light breath of air across their faces, soft as if some great, invisible creature had brooded and brushed over them.

McEnroe's voice shook with emotion. 'I'm glad, I'm glad I saw them.'

She wanted to ask if geese meant something important to him, but could not. His haggard face spoke enough words for them both; it would be a long time, she thought, before he could do something as ordinary even as playing golf without thinking of times with Marianne.

He gathered himself slowly and tried an uncertain smile. 'Sorry.' He pulled out a striped handkerchief and wiped his face. 'It's gonna get to me sometimes.'

'I know. Oh, McEnroe, won't you let me stay longer here with you—till it gets easier?'

He shook his head sadly. 'Not a great idea for you, honey. I know you wanna get back. There's so much going on here. I'm better off on my own for a while ... I was just thinking, you know, how your grandmother used to play a few holes now and then, in the old days ...'

There might have been more reminiscences, but Pete was hailing them from farther along the fairway. 'Come on, you guys! Walshie's found his ball. It's your shot, McEnroe.'

They quickened their pace, her grandfather now a few steps ahead of her on the path.

Out of the corner of her eyes, among a thick stand of aspens, Rachel thought she saw something bright gleaming: silver as the light on McEnroe's hair. She squinted to see what it was, but the air grew still again, the trees motionless, and whatever had moved had now stopped.

She had the odd sensation that they were being watched, and the hair rose on the back of her neck.

'McEnroe—' She leaned forward to make herself heard, panting with the weight of his clubs in the bag.

He turned to wait again, smiling at her. Then a great rose blossomed on the front of his cream poloneck shirt. Blood spurted scarlet from his chest.

He's been hit! Hit. Hit by what? A golf ball? No. No!

Simultaneously she heard the faint *poff* of impact, then the wailing scream of her own voice, '*No! No!*'—as if from far away and belonging to someone else. With helpless, uncomprehending eyes she saw McEnroe collapse right in front of her.

Abandoning the bag she ran forward, no thought of any danger to herself.

McEnroe, it's your shot—The words re-echoed in mockery in her head. She could not believe what she had seen—that a ball hit from somewhere behind them would strike him in the chest and fell him like that.

Something in her training clicked into motion. Her first attempt at a cry for help was soundless, as in a nightmare.

But then Pete came at a loping run, back along the path, his feet falling with a crunch, crunch, on the woodchips.

'Don't!' she screamed, her voice high as a seagull's. 'You'll be killed.' She knew now it was no golf ball.

Someone had shot McEnroe with a silenced gun. Someone invisible, in the woods.

To their left came the crashing of men clumsily retreating through the trees. She saw again the flash of something metallic, heard a shout in some foreign language that meant nothing to her. She wanted to chase after them. She wanted to save McEnroe's life. But she could do neither.

When Pete reached her, McEnroe's blood had drenched the front of her clothes and she was on her knees by him, keening, rocking herself, frenziedly trying to revive him and staunch the blood. McEnroe's open-eyed face still smiled at her, but the smile was fixed and terrible now, hardly his own. Had he seen those men, too, or felt their presence, before the shot cracked silently into his chest?

'My God! He's bleeding to death!'

Pete flung himself on the path beside her. Rachel's mind had gone blank. She could suddenly remember nothing about resuscitation.

Checking McEnroe's airways, Pete barked orders. 'Tear your jacket off. No, do what I say. That's it. Now make a—yes, tear it.'

Blindly, dumbly, she obeyed, pressing a pad of the torn jacket over the hideously small, neat hole. She was blank with shock, unable to feel anything, only aware of one thing at a time: Pete's voice, the cracking of branches in the wood, or the bullet wound itself, dark and terrible.

Trembling, she moved her hand, and the blood spurted up again, fountaining onto her hair and over Pete's cashmere sweater.

'You *gotta* keep still and keep that there. I gotta roll him—he's choking on his own blood.'

Rachel started to sob. *It's no use. We can't do anything when he's shot like that.*

The nightmare returned. Only a week ago she had watched the doctors trying with idiotic insistence to start Marianne's heart. And now, full of grief, but full of life as well, just minutes before, here was McEnroe in a pool of blood.

The two older golfers came breathlessly back along the path to them, open-mouthed in surprise and horror.

Pete's face was dark. 'Burrows—for heaven's sake call the rescue guys—go on. There's a phone right by the seventh green!'

Walsh knelt beside them. 'Rachel—let me. Then you can take over again in a minute.'

She slumped exhausted next to Pete. His face was white with effort. Between clenched teeth, he said to her, 'At least we know now who did this.'

'Do we?' She felt as if someone had cut through her body with one of the old-fashioned scythes her father kept hanging in the toolshed at home. 'Garcia's lackeys, of course. His accursed *mob*.' He swore under his breath. 'Your grandfather should have known, for heaven's sake! They'd be watching him like never before after what he and the DEA did yesterday.'

Rachel stared at him. It made no difference to her who had done this thing.

Some part of her mind instructed her insistently that McEnroe's chest was shattered, and that he was dying, but she could not take it in—what the blood meant, what her own tears meant. Looking away from him, she let her eyes drift away to the trees and felt horror mass over her like a landslide.

The deluge would have to turn aside if she—if any of them—were to survive.

23

A thin drizzle began on the windscreen of the truck they had borrowed from the Wilkinsons. Michael switched on the wipers to clear it, then realized as the blades spread a semi-circular coating of mud across the glass that it was fruitless exercise; the truck was just too dirty.

'I'll throw a pail or two of water over it when we get to market,' Joel volunteered.

Joel and Billy said little on the short journey from Arcade to Springville. The bellowing of the calves from the trailer was loud enough to drown conversation; and since the call from Massachusetts announcing McEnroe's death, both boys had been subdued anyway. Wedged together in the tight front cab of the truck, all three of them stared ahead through the murky early morning sky at the ribbon of route 39. Over the drab landscape, grey and drained by winter's end, the road twisted and bumped along the Cattaraugus Valley to Springville— where the veal auctions were held.

The round of farm work had comforted them all, especially now that school was out for Easter. Even with Don away, they would have found time hanging heavily on their hands without the daily round of milking, feeding, checking for mastitis, stock-keeping, telephone and paperwork. They could have waited for Don's delayed return, but Michael insisted that they take the first batch of calves to market on Easter Saturday, as Don's farm diary showed he always did. It would be one less thing for Don to catch up with on his return; and it was something else to occupy the boys' thoughts.

Glancing away from the road, he gave them both a swift appraisal. He felt closer to them now than before. When the first sad news had come, then more, he had tried to share their shock, grief and confusion; listened as they discussed whether they should fly out to Boston on their own initiative, then decided they were more help to their father at home. It was almost as if he had watched them grow up during the past two weeks.

They passed the white board that indicated the town boundaries of Springville.

'I thought it would be a bigger place,' Michael commented, noticing modest white clapboard houses like those in Arcade.

Joel scoffed. 'Oh, Springville's not much. But wait till you see the market.'

'Humungous,' Billy added helpfully.

Michael eased his foot off the accelerator. 'You've both been over here often?' He knew quite well from things they'd said when they planned the day that they must have been many times, but he'd found it best to keep them talking.

'Yeah—almost every time.'

Three weeks before, Michael would have felt intimidated by the task at hand—choosing the best stock, earmarking them with Don's number, loading them in a trailer-truck, discussing reserve prices with the McEnroe boys, and finally making the actual journey to the auction. But the landscape had changed in the last two weeks—and not just because the snow had at last melted.

'Tell Don for me I'll be in touch when he gets back,' a stranger's voice had said over the telephone—it was Larry, calling to say that he had been advised not to return to work for the McEnroes. 'I hear good things about you, kid. I'm glad McEnroe and Tony've got you around. Stick at it—you never know.'

That phonecall had signalled the first and most startling change in Michael's attitude: the conviction that there might after all be some permanence for him on the farm. A chance to belong, at last.

But more subtle changes were afoot. Often in the last few days he had thought back to the middle-of-the-night awakening, just before Marianne had died, and to Don's list of instructions. Though he had at the time tried to conceal his uncertainty from the family and from Tony, he had begun his work in Don's absence without any confidence; sleepless with anxiety about what would happen if—or how he would handle things if—

But this trip to the auction was now just another day's work. With good-natured supervision from Tony, and occasional help from Joel and Billy, he had managed the farm quite adequately in Don's absence. His confidence had grown—something he knew Don would identify with and applaud.

Open iron gates marked the entrance to the market. There a man in faded dungarees with a torn black golf umbrella flagged them down, issued them with identity tags, and directed them to the pens that had been reserved for them.

Acres of wet and muddy concrete spread before them, mostly divided by movable pens, and mostly open to the raw air. Everywhere calves milled, butted, and pushed each other, lifting their noses over the rails as other loaded trucks passed them.

Farmers, wholesalers, and other buyers were already circulating through the alleyways between pens. Joel and Billy waved at those they knew, telling Michael each time whom they'd seen.

'There's Dad's best pal, Old Man Grey,' Joel jeered, pointing.

'Wish Tony wasn't having a day off, don't you?' Billy teased.

'Yeah—Grey's right next to Dad's pen, as usual.'

With a frisson of the old anxiety, Michael glanced at the bent, wiry figure of the old man. Elias Grey stood with his arms resting on the top bar of his pen, watching the calves, and unaware of any scrutiny from behind. His sparse hair was plastered to his skull by the rain. Seeing him from twenty yards away, Michael was struck by how thin he looked, how wasted by age and viciously hard work. He felt something he had not expected to feel for him, carrying as he did some of Don's own animosity for the man—a stab of compassion. Bareheaded in the wet, the man was a pathetic sight.

Michael parked the truck, and they all leapt out of the cab. 'D'we have any spare caps or anoraks?' he asked Joel.

'Not in the back. Under the seat maybe. I guess Wilkinson would be the kinda guy to keep extra clothes in the cab. Why?' Joel eyed him. 'You too cold with that thick jacket on?'

'No, no.' Michael pointed. 'I was thinking of Grey over there. He looks so vulnerable.'

'Don't you believe it,' Billy chipped in. 'Tough as a coon hound, and far more bad-natured. Take my word for it, if he wanted a cap, he'd be wearing two or three of them.'

Joel laughed, but Michael climbed back into the cab. 'Why don't you open up the side of the pens and bring the ramp down,' he called over his shoulder. 'I'll be right with you.'

The boys shrugged and went to work. In the cab Michael opened two compartments, then found what he was looking for: a down-filled blue jacket and battered winter hat. Both were splattered with mud, but both were serviceable.

'You'll get small thanks for them,' Joel warned as Michael crossed the alleyway towards Grey.

His throat felt thick, and his heart beat high in his chest as he thought about his last stinging encounter with Grey, in the feedmill. But he made himself keep walking, telling himself, *If I'm going to stay here even for only a few more months, I'd like to be at peace with my neighbours*. There was a risk, certainly, that the old farmer would curse him away. But at least he would have tried.

Grey turned rheumy eyes on him as he reached the railings over which he was leaning. His eyes flickered over the clothes in Michael's arms. 'Oh, it's you.'

Michael decided there was no need for any preamble, any niceties. 'You look cold and wet. Here—take these.'

Grey narrowed his eyes. 'What're you up to, son?'

Michael thrust the clothes at him and turned away. Whatever he replied, the old man would find a way of twisting it; he said nothing at all and returned to the truck.

Joel and Billy had released the ramp at the sides, ready to lower it. Then Michael noticed that there was no straw in the allocated pens. He looked around hastily and found that few of the farmers bothered to put straw down.

'Wait,' he instructed. 'I'm not happy with this. Don't we have any straw?'

'Couple of bales just inside the ramp, remember?' Billy said. 'I shoved 'em in at the last moment—Dad usually does.'

'Right. Joel and I'll get the ramp down and hold the calves back. You open the bales in the pen; then we'll let 'em out.'

Soon they were funnelling the calves into the auction pens. Michael examined them with a critical eye as they jostled for space, nosily pushing against the rails to see calves in other pens. Disturbed by their journey, they were no longer as bright and sleek as when they had left the farm, but they were still handsome animals and, judging by the Holstein calves he could see in other pens, they should fetch the agreed price.

He set out buckets of clean water for them. Around them, all the other pens were now full. Several times Michael caught Grey—now wearing the clothes he had offered—eyeing Don's calves from a few metres away. But the old man made no move to thank him or to speak, and Michael tried to disregard him.

The auction was now in progress, the auctioneer moving from lot to lot taking bids for each farmer's calves, when a middle-aged man with a leathery skin and round-framed spectacles suddenly approached Michael.

He stuck his arm out straight, offering a dry hand. 'The name's Grey. Elias Grey's son, Jed. You're Monaghan, ain'tcha? For McEnroes?' His eyes shone blue and fierce behind the glasses.

Michael was taken aback. He murmured a confused response and shook the proffered hand.

Grey was like his father, apparently: a man of few words. He came immediately to the point. 'We've been looking over Mr McEnroe's stock. Fine job you've done rearing 'em, I'd say.'

'Thank you.'

'Ain'tcha surprised I'm tellin' you this?' The man's face was crooked with amusement.

'A little, I must confess.' Michael felt stiff and unnatural, thrown off balance.

'Well, no big deal. It's just my father would never tell you himself. Not like that. Dad ain't gonna change in a hurry—too old now. But... he was surprised when you brought them clothes across. Since he'd never say thanks himself, even so, I came to see you m'self, and say thank you.'

Michael smiled at him. 'To use one of your own phrases, you're welcome. It's nothing.'

'I'll see you get the clothes back, anyhow.' Grey rested his hand across the muzzle of one of Don's calves. 'Gee, these look healthy as can be—we gotta hand it to you.'

Michael couldn't resist testing his sincerity. 'Oh, you want to buy them off Don—or are you just conciliating?'

The leathery face cracked into an appreciative smile. 'The hell with it, son! My father'll always be the way he is, but I'd rather just get on with farming. I came to admire your stock, is all.' He threw his hands up, pantomiming acute dismay. 'Blast the agri-politics, and blast the local feuds.'

'I was thinking along the same lines a moment ago.'

Grey offered his hand again. 'Well, then, we may be seeing more of each other in the future. Meantime you and Mr McEnroe might like to know what Dad said—all things considering with the soil we got, and all, McEnroes've done damn well.' He grinned. 'And that's about the best thing he's ever got around to saying about your folks. You better take even grudging praise while it's on offer.'

Michael laughed. 'We'll take it.' In a measured voice, he added, 'Why don't you talk to Don when he comes back? He might be glad after all these years to speak peace to your family—if you know what I mean. I can't really speak for him.'

Grey picked up the cue. 'Sure you can't. Hey, I gotta go.' He wiped the rain off his glasses. 'Looks like the auctioneer's got us next on the list. Be seein' you.' Then he was gone amid the throng that had suddenly gathered around his father's pens.

Joel and Billy came pushing through the crowd to him. Together they watched the bidding on the Greys' calves. The sale was made within minutes, the words falling so fast from the auctioneer's lips that Michael could scarcely follow them. He was bewildered by the system of bidding by cards, as well.

'You'll have to keep me straight,' he told Joel, 'when it's our turn.'

Both the Greys caught his eye when the sale of their own animals had been completed and the auction entourage was making its way towards the McEnroe pens. His confidence wavered again, and he felt sweat break out under his heavy clothes. If he didn't return to Arcade with high enough price for the calves, Don would be disappointed.

Jed Grey gave him the thumbs up sign but did not rejoin him. Trembling slightly with the sense of responsibility, Michael handed the auctioneer and his secretary the reserve price envelopes, waited while they slit them open, then listened with awed interest as the auctioneer opened the bidding.

'Remember not to touch your card during the auction,' Joel had cautioned with a nudge, at the last moment. 'You might end up buying the beasts back from yourself!'

Wholesalers and slaughterhouse owners lifted numbered cards so fast to place their bids that he could not follow the bidding. Within minutes, however, the calves had been sold to a fat man who nodded cheerfully in their direction when the bidding closed. All Michael had to do was collect Don's cheque from the office by the gate.

He met the younger Mr Grey along the way, returned the thumbs up sign, and went back to Joel and Billy feeling ridiculously pleased with the morning's work. As if in affirmation of more changes to come, the rain at last dwindled. A light westerly wind swept across the market.

Back in Arcade, Michael let the cows into the home pasture for the first time that season. He left the huge double doors at the back of the barn open so that they could wander back to their mangers if they wanted to, but he felt it was warm enough, at last, for them to be outside for a few hours. Milky sunlight fell between fleeced ivory clouds, and a thin mist rose from the Cattaraugus. For the first time since he had been with Marie in Boston all those months ago, he felt the stirrings of warm weather to come.

Joel and Billy drifted away until the afternoon milking. Michael stood in the double doorway and watched the cows flicking their tails in delight, snuffling the thawed ground, and lowing to each other in the happy freedom of the field. He felt as they did: that he did not want to be inside on the first warm day of the year.

Coming to a sudden resolve, he took a rake and barrow from the toolshed and trundled them round to the front yard—a wide patch of tough grass just under the parlour windows. It was time to rake away the brown remains of winter so that the shoots of spring grass could come up.

He smiled to himself as he worked, opening his jacket, feeling the sweat begin to gather on his neck, arms, and back. Guilt niggled at him for being happy when the McEnroes were enduring so much turmoil, but he was happy.

At four-thirty the watery sun dropped like a plumbline behind the hills. One minute he was hot, and the next minute the breeze had chilled, and it was harder to see the ground. He raked a few last wisps of dead grass into a barrow, then pushed it back to the farmyard. He would find the boys and do the milking.

As he rounded the corner of the house, he heard the faint ringing of the house telephone. Abandoning the barrow, he ran up the porch steps and through the screen door into Don's office. The door crashed behind him, and Wally barked. But just as he reached for the phone, it stopped ringing.

Slightly out of breath, he waited for a minute in case it rang again. He wondered why the boys hadn't answered it—so often they were the first to dive shouting for it when it rang, arguing over whose friends would be at the other end of the line.

But the phone remained silent. He pulled off his boots, shoved them out onto the porch, and shouted up the stairs for the two brothers. No answer.

A little puzzled, he shouted again. This time, when they didn't reply, he put on his boots again, went quickly outside, and called a third time. Still no answer, but there was another sound, now, that would drown his voice and perhaps the telephone as well: the milking units were pumping.

Surprised, he crossed the yard to the barn. Grinning widely, pleased to be managing by themselves, Joel and Billy were milking the first batch of cows and had the others penned and waiting in the holding yard by the double doors.

Over the noise of the machines and the blaring beat of music from WGR55 Radio, he called to them. They waved, grinned again, and went on working.

When the milking was finished, the units turned off, the cows back in the barn for the night, and all the equipment flushed out again for the next day, Michael had an idea. 'Let's not scratch around for our supper tonight,' he said. 'I'll buy us all a pizza in Arcade. How about that? We've all earned it today, I reckon.'

Half an hour later they were back on route 39, retracing the first part of their morning trip to Springville. His hands resting easily on the wheel of the family pickup, Michael reflected on the differences between spring evenings in Kent and in America. He was used now to the sudden darkness that fell on the Allegheny foothills; it was hard to imagine the protracted twilit nights of England any more.

Behind the trees that lined one side of the road, a silvery half-moon was already rising into a clear cobalt sky. Here the road ran straight, dipping and rising, familiar now; and every few seconds Michael took his eyes off it to look at the moon. Sometimes when the weather was clear enough for him to see it, he would think of his family in England, marvelling that they would have seen the same moon, if from a different angle, five hours earlier. In Kent now, the moon might soon be setting... And in Boston?

'I wish Pa and Mom would be home for Easter.' Billy's subdued voice, whispered into the darkness like a prayer, cut across his thoughts.

'Don't you think they will?' Joel asked.

'Mom would hate to be away on Easter Day, I know that.'

Michael said soberly, 'But it's not that simple, is it?'

'Michael's right, Billy. So much to do after GraMar died—never mind after—after we don't know what all else's happened.'

Michael kept silent. He knew they still found it much harder than he did to accept that McEnroe and Marianne had died within a week of each other.

Joel went on, comforting, 'Listen up, if they could find any way of coming home for Easter, they would. I just know it. They'll call, and they'll come.'

Michael took a quick breath. Uneasily, he said, 'The phone did go—when you were in the barn this afternoon.'

'I didn't hear it.'

'Me neither.'

'That barn phone's useless. Only working half the time.'

'We mightn't've heard it, anyhow, with all the racket we made.'

'I tried to get into the house and take it. Sorry—didn't get there fast enough.'

Beside him, Joel shrugged. 'They'll call again if they can make it. Or we can give them a call when we get back. Don't sweat it, Billy.' In the moonlight, he turned his face towards Michael. 'Sorry if it sounds like we're not happy with you.'

'Of course not!'

'You did real well these last two weeks.'

He smiled; he knew the older boy didn't intend to sound patronizing. 'Thank you.'

'But I can't help missing Mom, that's all.' Billy was tired, tremulous now. He might be able to do a man's work on the farm, Michael thought, but he was still only a boy.

'And *you* did well, too, Billy,' Joel added, reassuring.

'Gee, thanks!' Billy began to whistle tunelessly through his teeth, in embarrassment.

Listening to the way they talked, Michael felt a pang of envy. What made the difference, he wondered, between the way he had grown up with Ian, and the way the McEnroe boys had grown up together? Both sets of parents were still alive and at home; that wasn't it. *All four of us,* he thought, *know we're loved—however haphazard, limited, and unevenly shown that love might be.* Still, he knew there was a fundamental difference between the way Joel and Billy got on with each other, and the way he and Ian barely tolerated each other.

Wait! I'm too adult, he decided, suddenly, *to go on blaming my mother's favouritism for some of the conflict we've had.* He sighed quietly to himself, keeping his eyes on the pale beams of the truck lights as they picked out scrubby bushes, ditches, and small stones in the road. *It's time I took complete responsibility for how I feel, make my own decisions, and get on with life.* Then another internal voice answered the first. *Listen, mate, that's what you are doing! You've chosen your career; you've chosen your place to belong, God willing, and you're getting on with it.*

The thought was electrifying. It brought another smile to his mouth, quickened his breathing, and made him join in with Billy's whistling. Within seconds, all three of them were singing loudly the only Easter hymn they all knew the words to—'Jesus Christ is risen today, Alleluia!'—while Don's old pickup truck bucked and bounced along the road and the lights of Arcade spilled over the night sky, blanking out the moon.

Returning a couple of hours later, Michael wished the boys goodnight and took a flashlight round the outhouses to check everything was secure for the night. In the darkened barn the only sound was the thin mewing of a new litter of kittens and the rustle and steady chewing of the few cows who were still awake. Behind the house the farmyard lay peacefully in the dimness of the cowebbed porch light. The hens were roosting in their arks; he shut them in for the night.

Something prompted him to check the front of the house too, and to sniff the new-grass smell of the front yard where he had been working only a few hours before. Softly he stepped along the now-familiar path. Dew was rising underfoot. Something brushed against his leg; he jumped, but it was only Wally, pleased to have found him, shadowing him again.

On impulse he switched off the flashlight and lifted his face. White diamond-chips of stars winked like daisies on the black field of the night sky. The half moon had risen higher now. Away from the lights of the town, it was no longer obscured.

Paschal moon, he whispered to himself. The blue-white beauty of it awed him.

Then he noticed that a strange crystalline light surrounded the moon. Unlike anything he had seen before, it formed a perfect shimmering circle around the crescent.

Moon dog, he murmured. Maggie had spoken of them when he'd first arrived, saying that September or October was usually the best time to see them. 'But they sometimes show up in the early spring, as well,' she'd added, almost as an afterthought. He had forgotten until now.

Around him the air breathed lightly, growing frostier again, but he stood still in the wet grass and watched the moon. He could pick out the part of the Sea of Tranquillity that was not obscured by the Earth's shadow—a silver-blue indentation on the moon's surface, strangely illuminated by the illusory light of the moon dog. The crescent seemed to wax even as he watched, and for a crazy moment he imagined he could feel the earth spinning beneath his feet, the sky racing overhead, turning and turning towards Easter morning.

He went inside and slept deeply, oblivious of everything.

The alarm woke him early. It was Joel's turn to help him in the milking parlour, so he made coffee for them both and woke him. The morning was chilly and grey, the night's clarity vanished behind low veils of wet cloud. Rain had fallen late in the night, but there was no rain now, only dripping mist. While Billy slept, they milked the herd without speaking. Michael's mind moved ahead to the Easter Mass they would attend later in the morning; he was full of sorrow now for the McEnroes, but full of hope, still, for his own future.

During the service, the skies cleared again. When the three came out of the flower-filled church, even more vivid banks of colour blazed at them: the clouds had melted away in the warmth; in the front yards adjoining the church, daffodils trumpeted yellow and full of bees, and borders of vermilion tulips stood budded, ready to open.

Joel and Billy blinked in the brightness, coming down the path right beside him.

'Let's go home,' he said to them. *Home.*

Billy sighed deeply. 'If only Mom—'

'They'll be home soon, Billy.'

Once again, the telephone was ringing when they stepped onto the back porch to unlock the door. Joel fumbled with the keys, muttering in irritation, dropping them, then eventually opened the door as—yet again—the phone stopped ringing.

'Blast it, that's twice.'

'They'll call again.'

'No, let's call "McEnroevia" and see what's happening.' Billy's face was determined. 'It's no good wondering all the time. I want to *know*.'

Michael waited in the office with them as they placed the call, but there was no answer. He felt strangely responsible, almost as if the thanksgiving he had just offered God for his opportunity to be in charge of the farm meant that the time would be extended even further. It was a nonsensical, irrational feeling; and he too wished now that he knew when they would return. A worm of anxiety twisted in his mind. It was unlike Don not to have kept them informed. Thinking about McEnroe's murder, he began to be afraid. He looked at the boys' faces and saw that the same fears had visited them, as well.

Resolutely he cajoled them into making themselves busy. He and Billy would let the cows out again, he said, and Joel could make them all some sandwiches. 'You'll find some chocolate eggs in the dresser, as well, by the way,' he added, remembering where he had hidden them, smiling, and feeling like an older brother.

Lunch was a spartan affair, and for the brief time that they sat together around the wooden table Michael was conscious that in spite of all his efforts the brothers could think of nothing else but their parents. He knew Maggie well enough himself, now, to know that she would have laid on a lavish Easter meal for them, and that they would have been eating and drinking until late in the afternoon. But it wasn't just the meal they were missing, he knew. The farm was empty without Don and Maggie.

He waved a hand towards the window. 'Why don't you go cycling this afternoon?'

Billy brightened. His mouth full, he turned to Joel. 'Great idea, or what?'

'Why not? But you should come, Michael.'

He shook his head.

'You're not going to *work*, are you?'

'Not exactly work. Something I want to do, that's all.'

When they'd cycled away, saying they would make for the waterfalls in Letchworth Park, he went round to the front yard again to continue what he had begun the night before. Compared with work in the barns and fields, raking was effortless: something he did for his own satisfaction.

This time followed by both dogs, he paced the grass he had raked the day before and saw that the rain and sun were already working their miracle on the ground. Between the remaining dead brown blades of last year and the thin green arrowheads of this year's growth opened the blue eyes of speedwell and even a few wild violets. They were so small that he would not have noticed them had he not bent as he moved, intent on looking.

He began to rake again, more slowly than last night, searching for every sign of spring, and singing loudly. Small insects wove their way among the grass and smudges of purple-blue flowers. A few daisies seemed to have appeared from nowhere. Feeling a little foolish, he stooped and picked one. Deceptively simple, it was in fact a complex flower with ranks of white petals and already a dusting of pollen in the middle that left a faint yellow smear across his cupped palm.

He went to pull it through one of the buttonholes of his shirt, then thought of what Joel and Billy might say; laughed, and dropped it. He began to sing again.

The farm dogs suddenly woofed sharply, growled low in their throats and came half off their haunches with their hackles rising. He rested on the rake and listened, but heard only the noise of an occasional passing car or truck on the highway.

Then the dogs raced away, barking furiously, hurtling across the front yard to the driveway. A Dodge truck he did not recognize right away was turning into the broken gateposts, jolting along the rutted driveway. It disappeared behind the silos; then he heard it pulling into the farmyard at the back.

A moment's fear returned to him, but curiosity was stronger. He left the rake and took the shorter path round the north side of the house, now running, himself.

Their neighbour and friend Joel Wilkinson leapt out of the truck first. His face was sober, his clothes unusually clean. He lifted his hand in greeting.

'Hello.' Michael went forward, puzzled, but the dogs—especially Wally—went on barking and growling.

'Look who I just brought from the airport.'

Don was climbing out of the truck on the other side. Then down the step, jumping awkwardly, came Maggie.

He wanted to run and hug them both. 'Oh, they'll be so glad you're back. What—?' He looked to Wilkinson for an explanation, but it was Maggie who spoke first.

'We tried a couple times to reach you, see if you could meet us at the airport.' She laughed gently. 'Finally we gave up, called Joel here, and took the plane. No problem.'

'You're a surprise!' Michael felt as unbalanced as he had felt the night before, gazing at the half-moon. At the same time, he realized he had to let go of the proprietary sense of pride and ownership that had overtaken him in the past few days. This was the McEnroes' farm, not his—as welcome as they had made him feel on it.

Another movement on the far side of the Dodge made him look away from Don and Maggie. Someone else was climbing from the truck.

Her brown hair blown across her face, it was Rachel who now walked towards them.

He had remembered her, after all. In a way, however, he had forgotten her, too.

She was smiling at him, her cheeks pink with an emotion he couldn't fathom. 'Hello, Michael Monaghan.'

Her accent had shifted slightly, the vowels more clipped than those of the rest of her family, more like his own.

'You're even more of a surprise,' he said, collecting himself a little. 'I thought you'd be back in London by now.'

The others might as well not have been there. All his senses were suddenly attuned to Rachel, as if he were seeing her for the first time. He saw, though, that her interest in him had outdistanced by far his own thoughts of her. On the other hand, she did not appear struck in the same way by meeting him again. She was acting as if they had seen each other only days before, as if he had been present to her throughout the time she had been away, as if there were really no novelty in her being at home again, when he also was there.

With a meaningful glance in Maggie and Don's direction, she said at last, 'Back in London? Well, it's a long story.'

Already Don was ambling off to look in the barns.

'Oh, not in your good clothes, please, honey,' Maggie wailed. 'Go get changed, for pete's sake.'

Don grinned. 'For your sake, you mean. Come on, Wilkinson. Come and have coffee, if the kitchen's still standing. I'll get Michael here to take me round the place later.'

Michael took his eyes off Rachel feeling as if he had been flattened by a gale. Perplexed, he helped the other men move the luggage to the foot of the stairs. Immediately at home, Maggie tut-tutted over the disorder in the kitchen, but he saw the warm looks of delight at being back that passed between her and Don as she brewed coffee for everyone.

Then Michael felt almost as he had on the first day in the farm kitchen: a watcher, detached, not part of things any more. Joel Wilkinson and the McEnroes were rehearsing all that had happened in Boston—no doubt at least for the second time—and catching up on local news as well.

He set down his half-full mug of coffee and left them to it. With a quick look back at Rachel, whose face was now hidden again behind her hair, he returned quietly outside. Soon it would be time to do the afternoon's milking.

After that the rhythm of the farm would go on as before. He had been raking for another quarter of an hour when he heard the screen door at the back slam, followed by the roar of the Dodge engine and the crunch of its wheels in the driveway.

He turned to find Rachel had come to the corner of the house and was hesitating there. Her hands were thrust into the pockets of what he recognized as an English jacket.

'I'm not going back,' she said simply.

24

In the darkness, Rachel woke abruptly. Outside her closed door she heard the creak of the old floorboards. They creaked in exactly the same places as they had creaked ever since she was a child in the same room, when she lay still sometimes and heard her father moving around before he went down to do the morning milking.

She held her breath and listened, her heart hammering with the suddenness of the awakening. Her father's feet were heavy on the boards. She knew them well, but those were not his movements. Her brothers had looked exhausted the night before, when they had finally all given up for the night and decided to go to bed; the footfalls did not sound like theirs, either.

No, it was Michael who was treading along the corridor to the head of the stairs; Michael who was awake to do the milking.

She had not slept deeply, long, or well. Until almost midnight they had all sat hunched over a parade of coffeemugs, then tea and cocoa, in the kitchen. Michael had banked up the wood-burning stove, and the cluttered room had grown hot with the press of six bodies, the rhythm of talk and tears about both funerals; the more matter-of-fact exchange of information about the farm that went on between the menfolk; and the sporadic questions that her mother would suddenly fire at her, in undertones, about her studies in London.

She couldn't tell them, yet, what she had decided. For nearly two weeks she had sidestepped the issue, saying that English Easter holidays went on longer than the American vacation, and that she needn't return, anyway, for another week. Which was true, but it was only half the truth.

She was surprised at how she had blurted it out to Michael like that: at a loss for something, anything, to say in the first minute she had found him alone. *I'm not going back.*

Had she even made up her mind until that moment? Or had she been putting off the decision, afraid of what it would mean?

Restlessly she turned on the bed to face the wall, wrapping the pillow around her ears so that she might after all go back to sleep. But the drowsiness that had been slow in coming to her the night before was more laggardly still now.

The screen door crashed, and she smiled. Even if she were in the deepest of sleeps, she would know if she heard that sound that she was at home.

Home, and Michael is here.

After all the months of waiting without expectations to see Michael again, she longed for some sort of sign from him that there might come to be more than friendship between them. It was a hope she did not have the courage to put into words to anyone, or frame fully even to herself. Maggie might guess, but neither of them would say anything.

She raised her hand and lifted the edge of the curtain. The movement unexpectedly brought back to her the poignant hours when she had slept in Michael's bed over New Year's Eve, waking to January in much the same way—a long time before full daylight: to a room that felt strange, a room where she could not help thinking of him.

But it was different this time. *This time* he was at home with her, just out of reach, outside, going to feed and milk her father's animals, perhaps talk to the Co-operative driver who would hook up his truck in the farmyard for the milk, this day, as on any other day.

For the driver and for Michael, perhaps, it was an ordinary morning. For her, everything was new.

Her head ached, though not now with the chronic cold; that had at last gone for good. Instead, it felt swollen from the tears she had cried over the past fortnight, her throat scratchy and her eyes dry. Yet all that sadness was from something past: nothing to sentimentalize, nothing that need permantly cloud the *now*, the peace of finding herself here, at home, in a moment of quiet grace.

She sat up. *I want no more of grief for a while,* she thought.

So as not to wake the family, she moved about softly. The floorboards seemed to shout out as she went to the stairs and trod down them, but she relied on the familiarity of the noise not to wake anyone.

The smells of farmyard and barn brought sharply back to her a flood of memories: of growing up, and of the last day before she left, when she had stood in the barn doorway and told Michael, *I'll miss it all like crazy*. Words that had been truer than she could ever have predicted.

Still, crisp air. A faint smell of mud and dung from the concrete yard under her boots—pervasive, despite the daily ritual of hosing and scrubbing that it underwent. And in the barn and milking parlour, straw, dry and clean; the rich scent of the cows themselves, and the sweetness of fresh milk.

After the darkness outside, she squinted against the brightness of the naked bulbs within. A shadow detached itself from the wall under her father's barn desk and slunk towards her. Wally. She lowered one hand gingerly and waited, not sure if he would remember her. The dog paused a few metres away, sniffing and baring his teeth; then sidled off, apparently content.

She watched the dog's muscled shoulders stride out to where Michael was working. She knew he hadn't heard her over the noise of the machines, and not wanting to startle him, she waited until he had released the current batch of cows into the home pasture.

Opening the doors for the next batch, he noticed her at last and came towards her. He smiled, but his face was still half-folded with sleep. 'You're very early.'

'I know it. Couldn't sleep.' She pushed her hands into her jacket pocket again, feeling as awkward now as she had felt the afternoon before. She had to raise her voice to make herself heard over the noise. 'D'you mind company?'

'No. It'd be good.' His eyes ran over her old clothes in swift appraisal. 'Dressed like that, you could even give me a hand.'

She laughed. 'Not sure I have the first idea, now—'

'It'll come back to you.'

She let him speak to her like a newcomer, demonstrating then directing her how to let the measured feed into the troughs so that the cows could eat as they were milked. When he had finished the milking and driven the last cows outside; when they had finished running the automatic cleaner, brushing away the last slurry that the machine had missed and hosing down the channels—by that time Rachel was tired out.

'Don't know how you do this for a living,' she said, wiping her hand across her hot face.

'It's what I've always wanted to do.' He climbed up to check the bulk tanks, noted some figures on the chart above her father's desk, then turned back to her. His eyes seemed to fix on her mouth.

She felt her heart quicken as he came to stand opposite her, lifting one hand to pull away a strand of hair that had caught in the corner of her mouth. It was a small but intimate gesture. The blood rushed to her cheeks, and her insides turned to water.

'There,' he said, simply.

She stepped back, away from him, afraid that the desire would show on her face, and walked away in confusion. Mindlessly she repeated his words back to her, gabbling as she spoke. 'Oh, it's what you've always wanted to do...' Her sudden movement seemed to unsteady him.

'Yes,' he said softly, and the word lost itself in the dead acoustics of wood, aluminium and straw, '—just as you've always wanted to be a medic.'

Now she felt on more certain ground. 'Ah, well, there's been a change of plan there, I'm afraid.'

He propped himself on the edge of Don's desk. 'You said you're not going back. Is that it? Do you want to talk?'

She understood now how Joel and Billy had overcome their initial apprehension to respect and accept Michael so well. It was this kind of directness and even tenderness that would have won them over. 'Sure. Wish I could.' Her voice sounded small, anything but sure. All the same, for some reason it seemed quite natural to be in the barn with him, at home again, at six thirty in the morning.

'Come on then, and we'll walk a bit if you like.'

'Don't you have to—?'

'There's nothing I need do at the moment. Your parents'll be up soon. Your father's giving me a few days off after this.' He grinned. 'I'm ready for them, let me tell you.'

Standing side by side at the sink, they scrubbed away the remaining dirt of their work. The water splashed and splattered both of them, and when they went outside, Rachel felt how chilly the dawn was, after all.

'Remember the day you left?'

They were walking now along the track below the hayfield. The land still lay in deep shadow; twilight had not yet merged into daylight, and there was only a wash of half light. But already the hay was several centimetres tall, the new growth pushing relentlessly through the old. Though the oats weren't up, Rachel could see their blue-green stalks in her imagination, germinating silently but powerfully where Don would have sowed the seed, just before the wakes.

'Of course I remember.' *And better than you think.*

'We went for a tour of inspection and found Wally in that trap.'

'Yes. It's all very clear in my mind.' She could still see now the gentleness of his hands on the body of the terrified animal.

His voice dropped. 'I wished later I'd had more time to get to know you.'

'Well I'm not going anywhere in a hurry now. There's plenty—' She stopped, aghast, wanting to conceal the intensity. 'But what about you? Larry'll be back, and you—'

'There's been no time yet to tell your father some news that will change a lot of things around here. And I shouldn't tell you yet, either.'

She had to be content with his cryptic answer, but there was something in the curve of his mouth that told her the news was good, that he might be staying longer than he had expected.

'But if you want to, you can maybe tell me what *you're* going to do, Rachel.'

Already she was warmed by his concern. 'I don't think I can go through with all the training I thought I wanted.'

His forehead creased. 'Should you decide something as momentous as that when your grandparents have just died, and you're four thousand miles from St Stephen's?'

'That's just it. I was deciding weeks ago, in a way. This trip was the jolt I needed to make me see things clearer.' She began to tell him about the raid, about the homesickness, then about her disappointment with the medical world. 'I suspect I'd find it the same if I trained here, after all. All I know is that I can't go blindly into years of training just to sit in a doctor's office—surgery... whatever you want to call it—and fob off people with dumb little prescriptions on nice tidy little bits of white paper. I want more than that.'

He said nothing. She wasn't sure she had managed at all to communicate the swirling complexities of her decision.

'Didn't you like the people you worked with?' He sounded surprised.

'Not the politics in the hospital. The patients, yes, when I could get to them. Not so easy in the first year, the way St Stephen's operates.'

'Then—?'

'I was thinking about it over the last couple weeks when I couldn't sleep.' She found she couldn't look directly at him as she spoke, and her eyes went ahead along the track to where it bent to a battered gate at the side of the empty cornfield. The sky was paling now towards dawn. 'There's never been any doubt that I should do something in the medical world. Never. I even thought for a while about veterinary medicine. Useful here...' She began to stammer. 'But that's not what I'm meant to do, either.'

'What then, Rachel?' His hand came suddenly and took hold of her elbow. She felt his warmth even through the fabric of her sleeve. 'You needn't suppose anyone thinks the worse of you for "giving up" on your training, you know.' He let her go again and made rabbits ears in the air to signify that he was making fun of the words 'giving up'.

411

She wished he would touch her again. More hesitantly, she went on, 'No. I will get round to telling them in the end. I'm chicken just now.' She allowed herself to smile. 'It's somehow easier to tell you, even though we hardly—'

'That's OK.' He reached to open the gate, held it for her as it swung erratically on delapidated hinges, then shut it again behind them. Their steps were slower now, without any purpose or hurry. 'Say on. You've another idea, have you?'

She remembered Christmas and the hour with Cecelia on the maternity ward. Reminded herself how she had pressed her tutors at the hospital to let her do part of her first-year training on the obstetrics ward, and how frustrated she had been when they had refused. 'It's not such a sudden whim, nor such a big jump from what I always wanted to do,' she said, plucking up the courage. 'Midwifery.'

He grinned. 'What can I say?'

She laughed too. 'You don't have to say a thing! All I know is I'm not going back to England for it, that's all.'

He was silent again.

She blundered on. 'It may have taken me a while, but I know I don't belong there.'

She saw his face illuminated with the sunlight that suddenly burst from behind the farm buildings, two fields away, on the right. His mouth curled into a cheeky grin, and his eyes sparked at her. 'I know that feeling well, believe me.'

'I'll break it to Mom and Pa soon enough. I'm home again. That's all I want just now.' She saw him nodding in recognition and understanding, and they walked on again.

When they reached the end of the track, where the creek divided McEnroes' land from Wilkinsons', Michael stopped beside her. 'It was right over there,' he said.

'What?'

'Where we went in the woods that day and the dog got caught.'

Unconsciously she looked around as if Wally was somehow summoned by the memory. For once, however, there was no sign of him. 'I remember clearly,' she said, 'as I told you.'

'A lot's happened since then. For both of us.'

She watched his face, wondering if he still wanted Marie. If he did, she was only making heartbreak for herself. She had wrapped herself in a little cocoon of joy since she had come home and was near him again, but it could break open at any time and spill her into the cold world again.

After they had passed back through the gate, he replied to her thoughts, quite unexpectedly, by catching at her fingers with his own. He chafed them, smiling at her. 'You're cold,' he said.

Her teeth were chattering. 'No, I'm not.' She could hardly get the words out, felt as if she was lost in the flood of feeling that ran over her when she looked into his face.

'Breakfast,' he said. 'That's what you need.'

She had never cared less about breakfast.

Then he said, 'I'm learning that life is full of risks and surprises. Miracles we talked about before, they're real enough … but risks … even more frightening.'

She couldn't answer, recalled her bitterness in the hospital when Marianne had died. And she was afraid to wonder why he had started to talk about risks.

'God moves us on, and half the time he takes us up turnings we didn't know were there. Miracles and risks—things out of *our* control; things we can't engineer for ourselves.'

'You said that to me before, when you first got here.'

'Did I?' He did not look at her.

'What sort of turnings?'

'Like you, here, now. Home after all that grief. Like me, here, now, living here after looking a long time for where I wanted to be.'

'And is this where you want to be?'

The sun rose higher in the eastern sky.

'I have felt I belong here.' He took her hand more closely in his, stopping and turning it over, examining it. Then he lifted it to his mouth and touched it lightly, moving her so that she faced him.

She saw in a moment of unbelieving panic and joy that he wanted to kiss her. The happiness she felt being held in his arms was like a bright shaft of light going through her body. She felt as if she were going blind to everything else except him. She had to look at the farm, at the crackling, empty maples—at anything except Michael. The rapture on her face would give everything away. 'To get here, to where we are now, has been a long road for us both,' she said.

'This is only the start, though, isn't it.' But he bent towards her, his eyes fixed on hers, a little anxious.

Her lips parted in wonder and longing, and then he drew her nearer. She buried her face in the rough material of his overalls. He said her name once, and laid one hand on her cheek. His mouth bent closer.

Then suddenly the sky was filled with the wild cries of geese. A wave of horror went over her. She relived the moment on the golfcourse when she and McEnroe had watched the skein fly north over the fairway.

Michael misinterpreted her sudden movement and stepped away.

She was dumb with shock and confusion, wanting the kiss so much.

Tentatively he put his arm around her shoulder. 'What's wrong. Whatever's wrong?' He followed her gaze, a frown of dismay matching her own.

She shivered violently. 'Geese, that's all.'

He grinned, but she couldn't grin back. 'Of course they're geese.'

'No, You don't understand. *Geese.*' She shuddered to a stop, waiting until the rush of fear dwindled. 'We saw geese ... right before they shot him.'

'Ah—dear—I'm sorry. Come here.' He eased her against his body again and held her close. She shut her eyes and listened to his heartbeat, steady and even, while the terror subsided. For a long, aching moment they did not speak.

At last he said into her hair, 'There's something you could try to remember—if you see geese.'

'If!'

He stroked her hair. 'I mean it.'

'What then?'

'Where my father comes from in Ireland, some people think of the Holy Spirit when they think of geese.'

For a childish, irreverent moment she wanted to laugh at him. 'When they hear that hideous racket?'

He gave her a little shake. 'No, when they see the way geese travel in the circle of the seasons. Coming in winter, going in spring. Messengers of hope.'

Tears began to gather in her eyes again. She lifted her face and pushed them away, embarrassed. In a low voice, she said. 'Thank you. I'll remember.'

'That's better.' Now he began to tug at her hand. 'Come on, Rachel. Let's run in. You need to get warm. You won't forget what happened, but, look, love, at the sun coming up—come on.' He pulled her along, and they ran breakneck down the track. Rachel was laughing and crying at once, hearing the geese strike away into the white north, and seeing the eastern sky bloom with the colour of what was to come.

They stopped breathless in the home pasture. She watched in puzzlement as he moved aside some dead plants near the back of the toolshed and bent down, releasing her hand. She saw a flicker of colour where something moved, and he stood up again, turning to her. In his hand were four or five opening daisies.

'A bunch of flowers for the lady,' he said solemnly. 'Nothing special, mind.'

She reached for them. 'Oh, but they *are*.'

He whisked them away. 'If my fingers weren't so awkward, I could make you a daisy chain.'

She laughed.

Then he leaned forward again and dropped the daisies one by one onto her hair. She felt the petals brush her, light as air.

Without thinking where they were walking or why, or who would see them from the side windows of the house, and wonder at what they saw, they went across the farmyard to stand by the pond. In the smooth surface was reflected the now-orange glow of daylight. The ducks still slept with heads curled under wings by the water's edge.

Nothing moved except the busybody yellow disk of the sun, making its steep climb to morning, unbuttoning the spring day.

Under the long filigree of its light, he kissed her for the first of many times. The sky over their heads splintered into great pale petals around the sun's heat.

They had come to the place where they belonged: he to the wheel of the seasons on the farm, and she to the circle of home.